"Whitehead's New York of the '70s is a fully realized universe. . . . [*Crook Manifesto* is] a reminder, as if we still needed one, that crime fiction can be great literature."
—*Los Angeles Times*

"Through brilliantly constructed twists and turns, set in a vibrantly detailed 1970s New York City, Whitehead once again demonstrates his prowess as an author whose work can stand out in any genre."
—*Time*

"*Crook Manifesto* continues the brilliantly realized sequence that began with *Harlem Shuffle*, intricately depicting cultural history and family drama with the compelling energy of a crime thriller and the sharp wit of social satire."
—*The Guardian*

"In this stylish social novel for the twenty-first century, Whitehead soars to new heights."
—*Esquire*

"Remarkable. . . . Bigger and better, together [with *Harlem Shuffle*], than anything Whitehead has written before." —*The Washington Post*

COLSON WHITEHEAD

# CROOK MANIFESTO

Colson Whitehead is the #1 *New York Times* bestselling author of eleven works of fiction and nonfiction, and he is a two-time winner of the Pulitzer Prize for Fiction, for *The Nickel Boys* and *The Underground Railroad,* which also won the National Book Award. A recipient of MacArthur and Guggenheim fellowships, he lives in New York City.

colsonwhitehead.com

OTHER BOOKS BY COLSON WHITEHEAD

*The Intuitionist*
*John Henry Days*
*The Colossus of New York*
*Apex Hides the Hurt*
*Sag Harbor*
*Zone One*
*The Noble Hustle*
*The Underground Railroad*
*The Nickel Boys*
*Harlem Shuffle*

# CROOK MANIFESTO

*A NOVEL*

COLSON
WHITEHEAD

VINTAGE BOOKS
A DIVISION OF PENGUIN RANDOM HOUSE LLC
NEW YORK

FIRST VINTAGE BOOKS EDITION 2024

The Library of Congress has cataloged the Doubleday edition as
follows:
Names: Whitehead, Colson, [date] author.
Title: Crook manifesto / Colson Whitehead.
Description: First edition. | New York: Doubleday, 2023.
Identifiers: LCCN 2022026702 (print) | LCCN 2022026703 (ebook)
Subjects: LCGFT: Novels.
Classification: LCC PS3573.H4768 C76 2023 (print) |
LCC PS3573.H4768 (ebook) | DDC 813/.54—dc23/eng/20220616
LC record available at https://lccn.loc.gov/2022026702
LC ebook record available at https://lccn.loc.gov/2022026703

**Vintage Books Trade Paperback ISBN: 978-0-525-56728-8**
**eBook ISBN: 978-0-385-54516-7**

*Book design by Pei Loi Koay*

vintagebooks.com

Printed in the United States of America
10  9  8  7  6  5  4  3  2  1

*To Clarke*

# CONTENTS

# RINGOLEVIO

## 1971

"Crooked stays crooked
and bent hates straight."

# ONE

From then on whenever he heard the song he thought of the death of Munson. It was the Jackson 5 after all who put Ray Carney back in the game following four years on the straight and narrow. *The straight and narrow*—it described a philosophy and a territory, a neighborhood with borders and local customs. Sometimes when he crossed Seventh Avenue on the way to work he mumbled the words to himself like a rummy trying not to weave across the sidewalk on the way home from the bars.

Four years of honest and rewarding work in home furnishings. Carney outfitted newlyweds for their expedition and upgraded living rooms to suit improved circumstances, coached retirees through the array of modern recliner options. It was a grave responsibility. Just last week one of his customers told him that her father had passed away in his sleep "with a smile on his face" while cradled in a Sterling Dreamer purchased at Carney's Furniture. The man had been a plumber with the city for thirty-five years, she said. His final earthly feeling had been the luxurious caress of that polyurethane core. Carney was glad the man went out satisfied—how tragic for your last thought to be "I should have gone with the Naugahyde." He dealt in accessories. Accent pieces for lifeless spaces. It sounded boring. It was. It was also fortifying, the way that under-seasoned food and watered-down drinks still provide nourishment, if not pleasure.

There was no retirement party when he stepped down. No one gave him a gold watch for his years of service, but he'd never lacked for gold watches since becoming a fence. The day Carney retired he had a box of them in his office safe, engraved with the names of strangers, as it had been a while since he made the trip to his watch guy out in Mott Haven. His farewell to the stolen-goods biz mostly consisted of rebuffing former clients and telling them to spread the word in their criminal circle: Carney is out.

"What do you mean, out?"

"I quit. Done."

The door onto Morningside, carved out of the building to facilitate the night trade, became the innocent route for afternoon deliveries. Two weeks after the Fortuna robbery, Tommy Shush knocked on the Morningside door with a black leather briefcase tucked under his arm. Carney took a look at the diamonds to test his resolve—and bid the thief good luck. The next day Cubby the Worm, one of his white regulars, showed up after hours with "some real hot stuff." Cubby specialized in unlikely hijackings that took years to off-load—the man was up to his eyeballs in Chinese pogo sticks and pantyhose encased in plastic eggs. Carney turned him away before he could describe this week's misbegotten haul, nothing personal.

They stopped coming by, the thieves, bit by bit, only momentarily glum, for there was always another hand, another conduit, another deal to be made in an enterprise as vast, complicated, and crooked as New York City.

\* \* \*

"Touch it—it won't bite. It's like grabbing a cloud of heaven."

Across the showroom Larry reeled in a customer, a wizened specimen who flipped a red beret around and around in his hands. Stoop-shouldered and wilting. Carney leaned against his office doorway and crossed his arms. A reliable subset of his clientele consisted of old men splurging on simple things they had long denied themselves. Then the creaky chair's springs poked through too many trouser seats, or the doctor offered remedies for poor circulation and obscure pains, and they came here. Carney pictured them, counting his blessings, the old men who lived alone in slant-floor railroad apartments or dim-lit efficiencies: bus drivers looking for new armchairs to eat soup on while they pored over racing forms, cashiers at one-hour dry-cleaning joints who hankered for something to prop their tired feet on. The abandoned. They never haggled about prices, ticked off to break into the savings but proud to have the money on tap.

The article in question was a 1971 Egon club chair in tweed Scotchgard upholstery. A tank of comfort, aprowl on Pro-Slide brass casters. "Heaven," Larry repeated.

When the customer entered the store he'd shaken Larry's hand and introduced himself as Charlie Foster. Now he danced his fingertips across the green-brown fabric and chuckled in delight like a toddler.

Larry winked at Carney. When Rusty, Carney's longtime floor man, threw out his back and was laid up for three and a half months, Carney needed a fill-in. Larry showed up on the second day of interviews and stayed.

Larry was a study in controlled ease, a slow unfurling of pure style. Greet him when he punched in and he'd raise two fingers in a hold-on gesture as if in the middle of a transatlantic call with foreign powers, then respond after he changed out of his striped vest, flare trousers, and suede bucket hat or whatever groovy plumage he'd chosen that day. Once in his salesman costume, he'd finally offer a velvety "What's up, baby?"

He belonged to that tribe of black player so nimble in his skin that all others were *baby*—old man, young mother, red-faced beat cop. Your average square would use the word *slick* to describe him, on account of that jaunty smile and stream of hectic patter, which Larry would take as a compliment. Slick was an asset in the sales game. He was only twenty-one but had lived many lives, even if Carney suspected he had emerged full grown from a vat of Harlem Cool five minutes before he first laid eyes on him. Line cook at a Madison Avenue hotel; topiary wrangler at two cemeteries; chauffeur for the wife of a Connecticut marble magnate; "gassing doggies at Gotham Veterinarian," which Carney assumed required some sort of specialized training or licensing, but no matter. And now Deputy Sales Associate at Carney's Furniture on 125th Street, "Fine Furniture for the Community for Over 15 Years."

"Never stays late, always has a date," Carney's secretary Marie liked to sing, stealing the tune from *The Patty Duke Show*. Like Carney's late cousin Freddie, Larry claimed as his hunting grounds uptown, downtown, and every meridian of pleasure in between. Hearing Larry's chronicles of New York at night, and its multifarious cast, was like getting a morning-after report from Freddie in the good old days. It lifted Carney's spirits.

Carney kept Larry on after Rusty got back on his feet. There was more than enough work and it allowed Carney more time off from the floor. It was as if the store had always been the four of them. Even when withered and hungover, Larry never let a customer see the misery. *Keep your secrets in your pocket*—an unspoken job requirement at Carney's Furniture. Marie sometimes wore sunglasses to cover a black eye but never ratted out her husband Rodney. Carney of course was well practiced in hiding his crooked aspects. Only Rusty was what he appeared to be, a genial Georgia transplant still befuddled by the city after all these years. As far as Carney knew. Perhaps Rusty was the most accomplished performer of them all, and come quitting time ran around performing brain surgery or routing SPECTRE.

Another siren passed up Morningside Ave.

"Is it sturdy?" Charlie Foster asked. "I like a sturdy chair." He poked the left armrest as if nudging a water bug with his shoe to make sure it was dead.

"Like the USS *Missouri*, baby," Larry said. "You buy cheap, you get cheap, right? Egon prices these babies nice because if they do that, they make it up in loyalty. That's how we do business, too. Sit, my brother, sit."

Charlie Foster sat. He appeared to merge with the club chair. Shedding years of worry, from his expression.

*That's a sale.* Carney returned to his office. He'd bought the new executive chair in April and repainted last Christmas but his office had changed little over the years. His business-school diploma dangled from the same nail, his signed picture of Lena Horne remained in its holy perch. Business was good. The fencing sideline had allowed him and Elizabeth to buy the place on Strivers' Row and sprung them from their cramped first apartment before that. Made possible the expansion of the store into the bakery next door and helped them to ride out numerous rough patches. But buying 381 and 383 West 125th Street? That was all Carney's Furniture. He bought the two buildings from Giulio Bongiovanni the first week of January 1970. A new decade, full of promise.

If you'd said when he signed the lease that one day he'd own the joint, he would've told you to get lost. *Carmen Jones* was holding its movie premiere down the street at the Hotel Theresa and as he held the keys in his hand for the first time it was like all that light and noise were for him. The property wasn't much to look at, but it might make a man his fortune. For the first two years he dropped off the rent by hand at the Fifth Avenue offices of Salerno Properties, Inc., not trusting the U.S. Postal Service, as if at 12:01 A.M. on the second of the month the marshals were going to bust down the door and throw his shit out in the street. He felt the 12:01 A.M. thing had happened to someone he knew, or his father had known, but now that he was settled and middle-aged recognized it as a tall tale. Most likely.

Carney met the landlord for the first time when he called Salerno about expanding into the bakery. One of the baker's regulars had been alarmed to find the store still closed at five past seven, then noticed the legs sticking out from behind the counter. Out of respect for the dead, Carney waited forty-five minutes before inquiring about the lease.

Giulio Bongiovanni let his staff handle the tenants, but he'd been curious about Carney for a long time. 383 West 125th had been a cursed retail spot since before Bongiovanni took over the real estate side from his father. Two furniture stores, a men's haberdashery, two shoe stores, and more had come to swift ruin after signing the lease, and the bad luck had followed the owners even after vacating the space. Cancers you'd never heard of that afflicted body parts you'd never heard of, divorces to be studied in family law courses for generations, a variety of prison time. Crushed by a large object in front of a nunnery. "It got so I was afraid to rent it," Bongiovanni told Carney.

"I'm doing okay," Carney said. The man subjected him to a never-seen-a-Negro-like-you-before look, not a novel experience for Carney. He reckoned it occurred more frequently these days, all over. Lunch counters, the voting booth, next thing you know they're running successful furniture businesses in Harlem.

"More than okay," Bongiovanni said, and he gave Carney permission to break through the wall into the bakery.

Giulio Bongiovanni's roots on 110th Street went way back, to when East Harlem was the biggest Little Italy this side of the Atlantic. He talked like a guy from around, but distinguished himself with his tight polyester polos and Muscle Beach physique. When asked about his regimen he attributed it to positive thinking and Jack LaLanne, whose show he watched daily and vitamin shipments he awaited monthly. "Don't knock the Glamour Stretcher," he said, posing in a forty-five-degree twist. "It's not just for the ladies, as you can see for yourself."

His grandfather had operated two grocery stores on Madison, and his father had bought 381 and 383 West 125th Street as investments when the Jews split the changing neighborhood. The family groceries still thrived, although the Bongiovannis no longer lived upstairs. They had decamped themselves for Astoria after World War II and now Bongiovanni was leaving the area for good. "The city is going to hell," he told Carney when he proposed the business deal. "The drugs, the filth. I'll take Florida."

Carney was flattered that the Italian thought he had the scratch to buy the two buildings, that the white side of town recognized his successes, then quickly assumed something was wrong and Bongiovanni was dumping bum properties on him. The city itching to condemn, some expensive disaster in the sewer below, or the final version of the Curse of 125th and Morningside finally come due. None of that turned out to be true, although Mrs. Hernandez in apartment 3R of 381 had a mysterious stain in her bathroom wall that returned each time it was patched and repainted and which bore an eerie resemblance to Dwight Eisenhower, a curse if ever he heard one. "He stares at me," she said.

Bongiovanni asked Carney if he was ready to be a landlord. "People calling you all hours, the water's too cold, the heat's too cold, my wife hates me?"

Carney meant to feast upon their complaints and grievances like they were a big bloody steak and potatoes. "Yes."

"Good man." They did a deal for the two buildings and three months later in Miami Bongiovanni keeled over while doing his sunrise calisthenics—aneurysm. The family brought him home and buried him with his ancestors in Calvary Cemetery in Woodside, plum view of the expressway.

*Churn.* Carney's word for the circulation of goods in his illicit sphere, the dance of TVs and diadems and toasters from one owner to the next, floating in and out of people's lives on breezes and gusts of cash and criminal industry. But of course churn determined the straight world too, memorialized the lives of neighborhoods, businesses. The movement of shop owners in and out of 383 West 125th Street, the changing entities on the deeds downtown in the hall of records, the minuet of brands on the showroom floor.

Carney's legit trade had transformed during the four years of his criminal retirement. Argent, his biggest client, the name he built the store on, was bought by Sterling in '68, who phased out their lines two years later. Sears swallowed up Bella Fontaine and assumed exclusive dealership. Collins-Hathaway overextended themselves in their Canadian expansion and got wiped out in last year's recession. Carney kept their Authorized Dealer plaque up above his desk as a souvenir.

To replace the hole in his inventory, Carney signed up with DeMarco, the American arm of the big Norwegian concern Knut-Bjellen, currently specializing in low-slung, boxy "lifestyle components." Palette: earth tones. Market research warned that the U.S. consumer was suspicious of "foreign"-sounding household products, so DeMarco renamed their lines for the American market, rechristening their modular couch system the Homesteader, their recliner the Mitt. The product moved so Carney didn't care what they called it.

His only complaint concerned the photo shoots in the DeMarco brochures and literature, which unfolded in far-off ski lodges and mountaintop aeries. Prodigious fire in the hearth, rust- and mustard-colored lifestyle components arranged around it, and white ladies with furry hand muffs and white guys in wool turtleneck sweaters adrift in dopey bliss on the shag. Carney didn't want to put people in a box, but he wondered how many of his customers saw themselves reflected there. The shag.

"Welcome to my chalet," Carney said whenever their latest catalog arrived.

*Hope y'all niggers like fondue,* Freddie chimed in from beyond.

Another siren. Business, orderly business, unfolded inside the walls of Carney's Furniture, but out on the street it was Harlem rules: rowdy, unpredictable, more trifling than a loser uncle. The sirens zipped up and down the aves as regularly as subway trains, all hours, per calamity's timetable. If not the cops on a mayhem mission, then an ambulance racing to unwind fate. A fire engine speeding to a vacant tenement before the blaze ate the whole block, or en route to a six-story building kerosened for the insurance, a dozen families inside.

Carney's father had torched a building or two in his day. It paid the rent.

This was a radio car's siren. Carney joined Larry and Charlie

Foster at the window. On the other side of 125th, two white officers hassled a young man in a dark denim jacket and red flare
trousers, their vehicle beached on the sidewalk. The cops pushed
him up against the window of Hutchins Tobacco, known for cigarettes without tax stamps and for its vermin problem. The flypa-
per was booked all year round, no vacancies, the chocolate bars
in the candy counter thoroughly weeviled. Hutchins locked his
front door and glared from behind the glass with his hands on
his hips.

The 125th Street foot traffic bent around this obstruction in
the stream. Most did not stop; nothing special about a roust. If
not here, somewhere else. But the manhunt had people edgy and
off their routines. They lingered and muttered to one another,
sassing and heckling the policemen even as they remained at a
distance that testified to their fear.

The taller cop swept the man's feet apart and patted the inside
of his legs. An onlooker howled, "Touching his junk?"

"What'd he do?" Carney said.

"They pulled up, tackled him like he robbed a bank," Larry said.

"Acting crazy," Charlie Foster said. "Looking for those Black
Panthers."

"Black Liberation Army," Larry said.

"Same thing."

Carney didn't want to interrupt when there was a fish on the
line, but the disagreement between the Panthers and the offshoot
Black Liberation Army was about more than names. The philosophical dispute encompassed the temperament of the street,
law enforcement's current posture vis-à-vis Harlem, and all the
sirens. Step back and maybe it contained everything.

\* \* \*

"Reform versus revolution," Carney explained to John. Two and
a half weeks earlier, May 12th. The verdict in the Panther 21 trial
had come down and his son had questions.

"It's like in my store," Carney said. "Reform is changing what's already there to make it better, like stain-proof upholstery, or wheeled feet, and then wheeled feet with brakes. Revolution is when you throw out everything and start new. You know the Castro Convertible?"

John nodded. The TV commercials were inescapable.

"The convertible sofa is revolution," Carney said. "Takes every idea we have about sleeping, about space, and flips them upside down. Living room? Boom—it's another bedroom." He paused. "Bet you didn't know the inventor of the convertible bed was a black man."

John shook his head.

"Leonard C. Bailey, businessman and tinkerer. Filed a patent in 1899 that the U.S. military put into mass production. You can look it up. Revolution."

He had entered that stage of a black man's life when some days the only thing that got him out of bed was the prospect of sharing stories of Black Firsts and neglected visionaries of their race.

John nodded vaguely. Carney picked up the pace. "The Panthers are opening food pantries, they have that free-breakfast program, legal aid—reform. The BLA wants to overthrow the whole system."

"If they're for reform, then why did those Panthers try to blow up the subway?"

"Just because the cops said it, doesn't make it so."

That afternoon the longest and most expensive trial in New York City history had wrapped up in a surprising acquittal. The Panther 21 had been arrested two years ago, fingered by undercover cops who'd infiltrated the organization. They faced one hundred and fifty-six counts of attempted murder and arson and etc. in a conspiracy to blow up the Bronx Botanical Garden, various police precincts, a few subway lines, as well as Alexander's, Korvettes, Macy's, and other department stores for good measure. The retail targets were an anti-capitalism thing, presumably, but it was unclear what they had against flowers.

John asked if they wanted to blow up Carney's store, too. Carney told him there were probably a lot of white stores to blow up before they got to his.

It took the jury ninety minutes to deliberate and twenty minutes to read out the one hundred and fifty-six Not Guiltys. "The undercover agents made up their stories out of whole cloth." A humiliating turn for Frank Hogan, the Manhattan DA. What's the world coming to when you can't railroad a bunch of Negroes?

"Why would the cops lie?" John said.

"Why does anyone lie?" Some things a boy has to figure out for himself.

Carney tried to picture himself as a kid, asking his father about political action. Inconceivable. Big Mike Carney pegged the civil rights movement—"these so-called righteous brothers"—as fellow hustlers. How much were they skimming when they put their hand out for soup kitchen donations, pocketing from the overhead when they cut the ribbon for a new rec center? Work rackets for a living and you see them everywhere, the possibilities, the little crack where an enterprising soul might sneak in a crowbar.

For a black boy growing up in Manhattan, John had an inspiringly naïve outlook. Fighting for survival made you think quick; John took the time to consider the world from every angle, claiming as his right the luxury of thoughtfulness. Sometimes Carney saw him as a version of the boy he might have been if he'd grown up in a different apartment, where there was food in the cupboard when he got home from school, with a mother to greet him, one who had not died young. A father who was not crooked. Carney liked that there was a version of that boy somewhere, even if it couldn't be him.

May took after her mother. Strident and assured, a flinty fifteen years old. A week after the Panther 21 trial, Carney and the kids were eating breakfast in the dining room. To exercise a paternal muscle Carney skipped his Chock Full o'Nuts ritual to spend time with John and May before school.

May tapped the newspaper. "These are some heavy dudes," she said.

Carney took the *Times*. Someone had claimed responsibility for the police shooting Wednesday night. Two cops guarding DA Frank Hogan's apartment were in critical condition, machine-gunned by "two young black males" in a car. Hogan had been under guard since last summer, when the house of John Murtagh was firebombed. Who was John Murtagh? The judge in the Panther 21 case.

Last night, the shooters had dropped off packages at the New York Times Building and at the offices of WLIB in the Theresa, down the street from his store. The packages contained a .45-caliber bullet, license plates from the car identified in the attack, and a note:

*May 19, 1971*

*All Power to the People,*

*Here are the license plates sought after by the fascist state pig police. We send them in order to exhibit the potential power of oppressed peoples to acquire revolutionary justice.*

*The armed goons of this racist government will again meet the guns of oppressed third world peoples as long as they occupy our community and murder our brothers and sisters in the name of American law and order. Just as the fascist marines and army occupy Vietnam in the name of democracy and murder Vietnamese people in the name of American imperialism, and are confronted with the guns of the Vietnamese liberation army, the domestic armed forces of racism and oppression will be confronted with the guns of the black liberation army, who will mete out in the tradition of Malcolm and all true revolutionaries real justice. We are revolutionary justice.*

*All Power to the People*
*Justice*

The syntax dizzied but he got the gist. "Militant," Carney said.

"Somebody has to say it," May said. "Vietnam. The ghetto. It's the same."

"The Man sure keeps busy."

"It's not funny." She snatched the paper back.

"I'm not laughing."

"Did you get the tickets?"

Carney winced. "I told you they're sold out, honey."

"You said you'd get them."

John dragged a pencil through a maze on the back of the box of Honeycomb cereal.

The next night there was another attack, successful this time. Saturday morning Carney was going over the accounts with 1010 WINS on for company. *All News. All the Time.* The newscaster mentioned the Colonial Park Houses on 159th. Carney had customers who lived there, he had arranged deliveries. A little after ten on Friday night, Officers Waverly Jones and Joseph Piagentini had been returning to their patrol car when they were ambushed from behind. Jones was black; he was shot twice. Piagentini, the white cop, was shot eight times. Aunt Millie was on duty at Harlem Hospital when they wheeled them in. "It was a damned mess." Mayor Lindsay attended their funerals, all choked up on the telecasts.

The NYPD described their response as a *show of force.* "A motherfucking siege" is how a man in line at Chock Full o'Nuts described it, paying for his bag of doughnuts ahead of Carney. "I was in the war." Patrolmen staked out corners, a new magnitude of prowl cars hit the streets, with unmarked units shadowing them for extra protection. Midnight raids on suspects. Activists and movement figures on downtown lists were rounded up. It reminded Carney of the '64 riots, or '68 after they shot King. There was a special hotline to call if you knew anything.

At 240 Centre Street they downplayed the BLA link at first. Now they embraced it, Carney noticed. Three more attacks on policemen followed in the coming days, nonlethal—the same party, or copycats? Edward Kiernan, the head of the Patrolmen's Benevolent Association, held up Piagentini's bullet-perforated shirt on TV and implored every cop on duty to carry a shotgun. "With a pistol, the odds are one in five that you will miss," he said, "but with a shotgun the odds are ninety-nine to one of a hit."

That was lynching talk. Percy Sutton told him to quit it. Sutton—Tuskegee Airman, lawyer to Malcolm X, and currently Manhattan borough president—would have set Big Mike's eyes rolling. "This is New York City, not Alabama," he said. "We don't do 'shotgun justice.'"

The days passed. The manhunt continued. The sirens continued.

\* \* \*

First week of June. Start of another wilting New York summer. The air-conditioning unit over the front door wheezed and coughed like a crosstown bus, but it got the job done.

It was cool beneath the machine. Carney, Larry, and Mr. Foster huddled there. Carney supposed the crowd across the street contained various uptown factions: movement sympathizers, young people drunk on the counterculture, revolution-minded folks who frowned on shooting cops in the back, and those who just wanted to go about their business without getting fucking involved. Like Mr. Charlie Foster, whose expression soured at the display.

A dark brown Plymouth rounded Morningside and honked, sending bystanders scrambling. It pulled up on the curb and disgorged two white plainclothes. The detained man shook his head as they hollered at him.

"Pigs," Larry said.

"When I was coming up, they hear you say that, make you a cripple," Foster said.

"*Constables*," Larry amended.

The patrolmen handcuffed the man. One of the plainclothes

gripped his neck with one hand and steered him forward with the other. When Carney was little, his father worked at Miracle Garage in between jobs. The owner, Pat Dodds, had this gray mutt out back and when the dog made a mess somewhere, he grabbed the dog's neck and rammed its face into it. That's how the cop grabbed this young brother's neck.

For a moment it appeared that the young man stared into Carney's eyes, but with the sun where it was the man would only see his own face reflected in the store window. Such was the character of light on 125th Street at that time of day, making everything into a mirror. The plainclothes shoved him into the backseat. The sedan lurched and retreated from the sidewalk. The radio car followed suit.

This tall brother in a floppy suede hat started a "Power to the People" chant, but it didn't catch. With the cops' departure, there was nothing to bind them. They moved their feet, as if the WALK/DONT WALK sign had switched. Carney thought: GAWK/DONT GAWK.

Charlie Foster cleared his throat and donned his beret. Something had put him off the sale, it was written in his posture. "I'll have to think about it," he said.

Larry protested. Carney slunk back to his office. It was a bust.

Mr. Foster hit the street a minute later. Sometimes Carney wanted to say, "Buy it, for Chrissakes. Do something for yourself!" Some black men of that generation trained themselves to not have permission, all those Charlie Fosters denying themselves since before Carney was born. He conjured the lonely scene awaiting Foster at home—then checked himself. Maybe the man was happy and satisfied, hoisting squealing grandchildren all day like barbells. He didn't know anything about these men, their choices and consequences. Just that they were looking for a comfortable chair. Occasionally Carney wove a private dread into a universal condition.

He took the stack of MEMORIAL DAY SALE signs off his desk and dropped them in the trash can. The sale had gone gangbusters, he'd make it an annual thing. When Carney heard they were renaming Decoration Day and moving it from May 30th to the last Monday in May, he hadn't seen the point. He sure did like the receipts, though. Three-day weekend, time on your hands, sometimes the mind starts thinking about home goods. It was the first time since he could remember that he approved of something the government had done.

Above Carney's desk, left of the window onto the showroom, hung the Polaroid that Rusty had taken of him and Elizabeth and the kids in front of the store in 1961. May was four, John maybe two. No matter when a picture was taken, Elizabeth looked the same: lovely and imperturbable. It had been a nice Saturday, the four of them enjoying one another and the weather. May's mouth curved the way it did when she suppressed a smile.

He didn't want to disappoint her, but he'd run out of leads. He called Larry over.

"What's up, baby?"

Carney told him the Jackson 5 were playing Madison Square Garden next month.

"That's a hot one," Larry said, in a weary, insider tone. He had "friends in the industry" from a former incarnation and occasionally doled out improbable gossip to him and Rusty and Marie during slumps. A tidbit about the harmonica player on War's third album, or scout's-honor intelligence from Aretha Franklin's dentist.

"May's been asking."

Larry shook his head. "If I had that in, I'd be going myself."

Carney'd made the rounds. The Dumas Club was a bust. Inside dope on pending legislation, who to bribe downtown, when influence was the currency and when it was cash—these things the Dumas members excelled in. They were not so savvy when it came to Jackson 5 tickets. Lamar Talbot, whom people called "the Black Clarence Darrow" for no reason Carney could discern, had represented the Garden in a wrongful death suit. Construction worker killed while laying the foundation, Afro American lawyer at the table might smooth it out. No dice. "I save their bacon, and look how they do me."

He specifically remembered Kermit Wells bragging that Berry Gordy, the father of Motown Records, was his first cousin. He cornered him after a scotch tasting. Wells claimed that Carney had misheard; his wife's friend was related to Berry Gordy, but she and his wife had had a falling-out. Plus, Kermit added, if he had an in, he'd grab those tickets for himself.

Carney's father-in-law, Leland Jones, cooked the books for sundry entertainment lawyers and managers who'd kept him in orchestra seats for decades. It shriveled his pride, but Carney hit him up. For May's sake. Whenever he heard Leland's voice nowadays, the trembling delivery announced how much the years had diminished the man. Had Carney despised him once? Strong emotions were wasted at this point. He asked after his showbiz contacts.

"I haven't talked to Albert in quite some time," Leland said. "And Lance Hollis passed away years ago."

Lately Carney was afraid to turn on the radio, lest one of their goddamn songs remind him of his failure. Who had he forgotten?

Munson. It had been a while.

Carney usually left a message when he called the 28th Precinct. The man was a rambler. Today someone picked up on the third ring. "Anyone seen Munson? Who's this?"

Another siren. He said his name.

Munson got on the phone. "Carney," he repeated, as if trying to place him. The detective's voice scraped: "Why didn't I think of it before?"

And like that, in the time WALK turns to DONT WALK, Carney was out of retirement.

# TWO

Carney caught the 1 train at 125th Street and grabbed a seat on the east side of the car. The Manhattan viaduct lifted the train tracks one hundred and sixty-eight feet above Broadway and 125th, and if you didn't have your nose in a book or the daily paper or a tattered ledger of regrets, the view was a pleasant reprieve from the gloomy tunnel. It held no charm for Carney. If he sat on the opposite side he was liable to see his old place, catty-corner to the tracks, which for many years had made him a captive audience to the viaduct's longest-running show. It was the same performance repeated without variation, the curtain rising multiple times an hour, relentlessly exploring through choreography and noise a single theme of the human condition: You Can't Afford a Better Apartment.

Rumble rumble. He didn't take the 1 train as often as he used to, since they'd moved to Strivers' Row, off Seventh. Enough time had passed that he now associated the line above 125th with that crooked period in his life and its steady complexities. One day it was an elaborate handoff with a thief too afraid to show his face on the street, the next a transaction with a paranoid diamond dealer who drew his rendezvous tactics from spy thrillers. It was a relief to be done with those men, that secret world and its dumb rituals.

He refused the implication that moving to Strivers' Row had made him quit. That he was so shallow of character that a little respectability made him renounce his ways, made him think he had risen above the unruly elements that had formed him. It would take more than a dignified facade of yellow brick and lime-stone to hide his premises.

Elizabeth never complained about their first apartment. When a train screeched into the station across the way, she paused and allowed it to pass before she resumed speaking, a portrait of regal poise. "Like Queen Elizabeth waiting for a fart to clear," Carney teased one time, and from then on she arched an eyebrow for effect, a hint of disdain that made her twice as elegant. Look—the place was a dump. A rat slinked out of the toilet one time, whiskers dripping. Murderous arguments between men and women resounded above and below. The sub-way vibrations made the building's nails hop in their holes. She showed miraculous restraint. Now that the apartment was years behind them, Elizabeth allowed that it "definitely had character."

Celebrity architects had designed Strivers' Row's four lines of townhouses in the 1890s. 237 West 138th was part of a Federal Renaissance strip conceived by Bruce Price and Clarence Luce; Carney pretended to have heard of them. He came across the list-ing in the paper. He never looked at the real estate pages but that day he did. When they saw number 237 that first time, emptied of furniture, dusty halos where pictures and paintings had hung, silent save for the odd insolent floorboard, Elizabeth said "I could get lost in here" with an exquisite mix of longing and belonging. It could be hers and had already been hers: She'd grown up across the alley on the 139th Street line, five houses down in a townhouse with an identical layout. Same floor plan, different arrangement altogether. She'd left this lofty stretch of Harlem to be with him. To return here was—what? A homecoming and also a reward for her love and patience. Of course they were going to buy it. What else was an ongoing criminal enterprise complicated by periodic violence for, but to make your wife happy?

One night soon after they moved in, Carney got home late from a meetup with Church Wiley, a smash-and-grab operator who hunted in Baltimore and came up to New York to off the goods.

High-quality stuff that always came with a lot of heat. Baroque arrangements ensued when Carney had to pay him off: knock two times on the door at the end of the fifth-floor hallway of an abandoned tenement on 167th; split out the back room of Blue Eyes on St. Nicholas and 156th, throw a rose into the dented garbage can and count to a hundred, etc.

This time Church was two hours late and Carney had to wait in what he decided was a shooting gallery that had recently been vacated after a raid by the cops or a triple murder. There was no one inside the dilapidated brownstone, but it was well populated with evidence of miserable doings. Cold March night. Wind whistled. He set one buttock on the arm of a 1940s Collins-Hathaway sofa that looked diseased. It had never occurred to him that furniture could be sick, but from that day on he knew it when he saw it, the way human beings infected everything. Church finally arrived. He looked around and said, "This place has really gone downhill."

When Carney got home that night, Elizabeth had fallen asleep in the parlor in front of *The Tonight Show*. Roscoe Pope doing a bit about encyclopedia salesmen. Carney turned out the lights, put the house to bed. He checked on May and John on the third floor in their respective bedrooms. The kids were sprawled out in sleep, pinwheels on the sheets. He touched the back of his hand to their foreheads to check their temperature.

Downstairs he tucked a blanket around Elizabeth, rather than wake her. She didn't care for the latest craze for low sofas— or much of the current offerings in Carney's showroom, to be honest—so they'd held on to the three-year-old Argent, birch with champagne finish. He turned off the lamp. The shadow of his wife emerged from the darkness as his eyes adjusted. She trusted his excuses for his ridiculous hours. Any sane woman would accuse him of an affair. The real reason for his sneaking around would get him twenty-five years in Sing Sing. What was worse?

The streetlight penetrated the parlor window in a sheer purifying beam. The silence and calm put him in a renouncing frame of mind. He was done.

Dropping the thieves and heisters was no problem. Chink Montague and Munson were another matter. Carney rendered unto Chink an envelope every week for permission to operate. Mobsters by and large did not respect conventions like two weeks' notice. Carney informed Delroy, Chink's bagman, that he no longer dealt in previously owned merchandise but would continue his weekly contribution to express gratitude for all their good work together. The envelope was recategorized as *protection,* like Carney was just another schlubby shopkeeper getting leaned on. Which, to be sure, he was and ever had been.

Carney invited the detective to Nightbirds and Munson toasted his retirement: "To the most famous nobody in Harlem." He came by for his handout the next week, and the one after that, but trailed off. After a time Munson only showed up at Carney's office at Easter and Christmas to collect for the "Widows and Orphans Fund." He hadn't visited in three years.

Apart from tending to his extensive shakedown network, cultivating criminal alliances, and occasional forays into police work, Detective Munson was an accomplished fixer. Sometimes that meant ushering a state senator out the back fire stairs of a Lexington Avenue whorehouse during a bust, or handing some mope's blabbermouth mistress a one-way ticket to Miami on the Silver Meteor. Doubtless he had dumped a body or two in Mount Morris Park when it was all the rage.

Sometimes a fix entailed snagging that week's hot ticket for someone—the Frazier–Ellis fight at the Garden, or whatever big act was in town. Carney remembered Munson gloating over taking his wife to see Sinatra, taking his ex-partner's ex-wife backstage to meet Vic Damone, and taking one of his young girlfriends to see the Dave Clark Five at Carnegie Hall. Carney had no idea what the detective was into these days, the nature of his schemes and scams, but if Munson had half as much juice as in the old days, there were Jackson 5 tickets coming his way.

At what price, he didn't know.

* * *

As instructed, Carney waited by the phone booth across from the 157th Street subway station, northwest exit. The tiny triangular park contained six decrepit pigeons and three benches. COMIDAS, FARMACIA. From the signs and stores, this stretch of Broadway had grown more Puerto Rican and Dominican since his last visit. On 125th, it was Jews and Italians out, blacks in, and up here the Spanish replaced the Germans and Irish when they split. Churn, baby, churn.

Carney had time to kill. He called home and told John that he'd be back late. "There are Swansons in the freezer," he said. "Your mom is back tomorrow and she'll probably make you something good. If she's not too tired." The train from Chicago got in around noon—it could go either way. May cackled in the background. "Tell May she's in charge." He hung up.

When May was younger, there was a face she'd put on when she got intemperately excited, this mask of joy. The face drew from Elizabeth's features, but Carney was proud to have contributed. He didn't realize how much he missed it until the Jackson 5 came along. Half her conversation these days came from 125th Street flyers: "It all goes back to the miseducation of the Negro, Daddy." Black Power guys and their pamphlets were worse than Jehovah's Witnesses. Stopping him on the street: "Where do you stand on Mozambique?" What did he know about Mozambique? But when Carney hollered across the house that the Jackson 5 were on *Flip Wilson*, or the jaunty opening chords of "ABC" capered from the living room Panasonic, it conjured that face from bygone days. He was going to get her tickets.

Busy boys, the Jackson 5. He didn't know if they were sexually active, but they were certainly promiscuous, with sponsorship deals with no less than three breakfast cereals. May and John crooned their Alpha-Bits commercial all the time, in constant harassment: "Grab your Alpha-Bits and come with me, we'll eat through the Alpha-Bits from A to Z!" The lyrics made sense, Carney allowed, but they were dumb. Fold-out posters from Super Sugar Crisp boxes covered May's room, joining those from *Flip* and *Tiger Beat.* Her bedroom was a glossy temple to the Boys from Gary, Indiana. Jumping, dancing, lounging in the park, solo and in group shots, bounding onstage in funky harlequin outfits and silvered space-age jumpsuits, every image equipped with their otherworldly smiles.

May entered a *Teen Beat* contest to "Win a Banana Split Date with Michael!" in March, and *Tiger Beat*'s "Win a Roller Skating Date with Michael!" in April. She was passed over, despite her impressive essay on why she deserved the honor: "Michael is for the people, like me." To one-up Super Sugar Crisp, Alpha-Bits started including flexi 45s of "ABC" and "I Want You Back" in their boxes, which in turn drafted Honeycomb into the novelty collectibles arms race. Honeycomb's secret weapon: balloons in the shape of the Jackson 5's heads and imprinted with their likenesses. Macabre tokens all, but May would not be complete until she got the Michael.

The quest continued for weeks. Supermarkets were declared "lucky" or "dead," corner grocers struck off the list or patronized with feverish dedication. Word among the junior set held that a bodega on 132nd had cracked the code. Carney received orders to check it out.

He ripped the top off the cereal box and rummaged. "The Michael!"

"It's Marlon."

"It looks like Michael." The latest Marlon joined the sagging menagerie (four Jermaines, three Jackies, sundry Titos and Marlons) on her windowsill. It took fourteen purchases. Like everything in life, the Jackson 5 promo was rigged. Carney approved: Teach 'em early.

The pay phone rang. "Smile for the birdie."

Carney searched around. Across the street was a restaurant called El Viejo Gallo. He squinted. Perhaps there was a phone in the vestibule as you walked in. He looked up—Munson could be in any of the buildings surrounding the park.

"Behind you," Munson said.

The nine-story building sat at the southern tip of a wedge-shaped block. The eastern side was a street he'd never heard of—Edward M. Morgan Place, which ran for a block and a half before it turned into Riverside Drive. A block and a half, shit. Morgan should have killed more Indians or stolen more money, everybody knows that's how you get the long streets. Munson buzzed Carney in.

The detective was holding the apartment door ajar when the elevator doors opened, posture indicating a gun held out of view. He motioned Carney over with a jerk of his head and made sure no one else stepped out of the car.

The one-bedroom apartment had been cut out of a larger unit, the decorative moldings terminating at the new walls. Munson told him to make himself at home and returned the .38 to his duty holster.

The place was a mess—if Carney lived there, his kids would be pushing a broom to earn their goddamn allowance. Last he knew, Munson lived downtown somewhere with his wife. This joint was a hideout, with just enough furniture to make it habitable. Bring a girl here, maybe, if you straightened up. Nothing personal in sight, save for a three-foot-tall ceramic imp, red-and-black in a Chinese style, which had the markings of a souvenir you'd swipe at the last stop of an all-day bender. It was set at a forty-five-degree angle to the wall, as if sneaking away from something unsavory.

Munson walked past Carney and shut the bedroom door before he could get a look inside.

"Dead body?"

"Some of those *Laugh-In* girls sleeping it off."

They sat on the couch, a sad, shoddy piece you'd carry out same day from a discount store. Munson sunk in with a sigh. He looked terrible. Pale, unshaved, blond hair spiking around the new bald spot on his scalp. When they first met, Munson had been stout and solidly built, one of those cops you think twice about starting with. The detective had softened over the years as he availed himself of the myriad perks of his job, the steaks on the house and the free rounds. Lumpy, like an army bag full of soiled laundry that had sprouted legs. Now he'd shed some of that bulk and looked harrowed, slimmed down in a way that you'd mistake for an exercise regimen if you didn't know it was from running from something that was gaining on him.

Munson took a big swig from his can of National Bohemian.

"Taking a break from the manhunt?" Carney said.

Munson tossed him a beer can, which Carney set on the table.

"Matter of time. Those scumbags took their service revolvers, did you know that?" Munson burped. "That's like someone taking your dick."

"One imagines."

"Everybody's working the streets, trying to get those poor guys' pieces back, find those assholes. The same way you hope they'd do it for you."

"Don't you have people on the inside? Like with the Panthers?"

Munson looked disgusted. "You saw how that trial went. Should have made that case, but they yanked it too soon."

Back during the '64 protests, Munson had told Carney about the young officers he'd sent to infiltrate CORE and SNCC, to strangle the protests. The white detective didn't take Carney into his confidence out of trust but because the furniture salesman was no threat. What was he going to do, write a letter to the *Amsterdam News*? White cops did as they pleased. Crooked white cops? Untouchable.

Munson had emerged one day like a wart, self-generating. Before the Theresa job in '59, Carney's fencing business had been small-time in every way—appliances, the odd emerald pendant off an old widow's bureau. For a small cut, he acted as the middleman between uptown crooks and a gem guy on Canal. Then Chink Montague put out the word that he wanted to recover a Theresa item—a necklace he'd given his girlfriend Lucinda Cole. The uptown fences were put on notice, and Carney got added to the criminal Yellow Pages.

Munson showed up for weekly tribute soon after, half to put the bite on Carney and half to hit on his secretary Marie, before she got married. The detective came in handy years ago during Carney's revenge campaign against Wilfred Duke, the crooked Harlem banker, but they hadn't been up to anything nefarious in a while.

"Got something for you to see," Munson said. He disappeared into the bedroom, pulling the door behind him.

By now, Carney was sure there was at least one dead body in there. The things you do for your kids.

He walked to the snub nose of the room, where the building tapered to a wedge. Eight stories up, the windows had a spectacular view down Broadway, the Hudson peeked out here and there to the west, and over the tops of the shorter tenements St. Nicholas Park huddled in gorgeous green. A good sentry spot, with its survey of the subway entrances and the little triangle park. The lookout came with a director's chair and a milk crate to hold an ashtray and empty beer cans.

"To see who's coming," Munson said, returning. He held a brown paper bag.

"You hiding out?" Carney had reached Munson at the station house, but the man acted like he was lamming it.

"I have to take care of some things." The detective swept the pile of newspapers and balled-up sandwich wrappers from the coffee table. Inside the paper bag was another scrunched paper bag, out of which Munson scooped handfuls of long diamond loops. High karat, set in glimmering gold and platinum. He coughed and scratched his stubble.

Carney kneeled by the mound of jewelry. Disentangled the pieces, shaking his head at the disrespect. He was rusty, but the majority appeared to be 1940s pieces by Marjorie Baxter in Boston, some swanky cocktail and bib necklaces. The smaller pieces were the same vintage, American designers, like the two Raymond Yard ruby-and-diamond bracelets and the Louis Long chokers. The kind of assortment you'd get if you knocked over a collector who specialized, or smashed a glass display case and grabbed what you could while the alarm blared. "This what you're up to these days?" Carney said.

Munson took a big swallow. He was hunched over in the director's chair like a rooftop gargoyle, not taking his eyes from the jewelry. "This is a one-off. What do you think?"

"Somebody had a nice score." In the old days, Carney would have been up on the latest robberies and known their origin.

Munson asked how nice.

"Rough guess—a couple of hundred thousand. Depending on who takes them."

Munson slapped his hands together. "Great. I need it tonight."

Some shylock putting the squeeze on him, or a bookie. Munson had the same look in his eyes that time years ago when he hit up his route for their envelopes a few days early. A shit bet at Garden State Park, bum tip. It was rare to see that look on the detective's face—just another civilian, subject to higher, more powerful forces. Carney stood. "I'm out, Munson."

"Think of it as a one-off."

Carney's posture said no. "I have to head to the office."

"You don't want to do that."

Carney didn't like the tone. "You don't need me."

"Things are a little hot these days, tell you the truth. You read in the papers about the Knapp Commission? Looking into cops?"

"You?"

"Who, me?" The grin was mischievous. "I got to find some work-arounds for a while. But you—you've been out. Nobody's looking your way."

"Nobody looking my way because there's nothing to see."

"Jackson 5," Munson said.

"For my kid."

"You have a kid?"

"You fucking know that."

"I get tickets. I get tickets to everything," Munson said. "I tell you I went backstage at Vic Damone? He's from Brooklyn, he didn't put on airs. Some of these cocksuckers . . ."

Brown paper bags. It was undignified. Took away the romance. Because Carney was smitten with those beautiful stones. "Good tickets," he said. "Up close."

"I know everybody and everybody owes me." Munson smiled. "How long will it take?"

They did a deal for the concert tickets. Carney departed with the paper bags, supporting the bottom like they held leaky coffee cups.

# THREE

You knew the city was going to hell if the Upper East Side was starting to look like crap, too. Things were in decline here and there at the edges of Carney's vision: half-finished graffiti on the metal grate of a closed-down drugstore; a crop of overflowing garbage cans past due for pickup; the aftermath of a smashed windshield, glass squares on the asphalt like knocked-out teeth. It was carved into the faces of the Upper East Siders, where something more downcast had replaced the smirks, and behind the eyes one discovered a vague and unformed hopelessness instead of the standard entitled cheer. Things were definitely in decline all over, across zip codes. Strike threats and work stoppages, the yellow stain of pollution above and dangerous fractures in the infrastructure below. It was creeping on everyone, like a gloom blowing over the East River and into the vast grid, the apprehension that things were not as they had been and it would be a long time before they were right again.

Commerce proceeded.

Carney still had the business card: Martin Green, Antiques. Why hadn't he thrown it out? Because he knew or wished a day like this might come. Crooked stays crooked.

Green lived near the corner of Eighty-second and York, in a white-brick number notched with cramped terraces and equipped with a lobby that was recessed from the street. To overcompensate for the building's newness, they decked out the doorman in an old-fashioned getup of red and gold, like the leader of a marching band that had deserted him. The doorman called up to the apartment.

Martin Green was the only fine-gem guy Carney could think of. The men he trusted had fallen hard since his retirement. Boris the Monk got caught holding the Fox-Worthington haul, which had been heisted from the heiress's Fifth Avenue penthouse. Ellen Fox-Worthington's usual domain was deep in the gossip columns; the robbery elevated her to the front page. The cops had been on the lookout. Now Boris was doing eight to twelve in Dannemora, where Carney's original connection Buxbaum had died last spring, gut cancer. Ed Brody's place on Amsterdam got knocked over so many times he enrolled in night classes to get his real estate license. Now he sold marsh-adjacent lots in Florida to a variety of suckers. Brody sent a Christmas card every year: "I'm making more than I ever did hustling stones."

There were new players, but no time to make a proper inquiry. Martin Green was his only lead. A phone call confirmed he was still in the trade, and after a stop at the office to upgrade the paper bags to his black leather briefcase, Carney caught a taxi downtown.

Green had dropped by the store in the fall of '69 to introduce himself. Carney had white customers—neighborhood lifers, college kids, and intrepid young couples after cheap rent and undeterred by Harlem's current decrepitude. The moment he saw Green, he knew the young white man was not one of them. He was in the showroom observing an Esme Currier wall feature, a brass-and-steel lattice overlaid with a series of blue-and-green enamel crescents. He scrutinized it with the tip of his eyeglasses stuck in his mouth, as if he stood on the cool marble of a museum. "I love it," Green said, before Carney could speak. "Can I take it home with me?"

He wore a white linen suit and a shiny yellow shirt, the top three buttons open to reveal pale, freckled skin and a turquoise

Indian pendant. Green was lucky he didn't get beat up, walking around uptown like that. The man was oblivious.

In the office he shared the real reason for his visit: to present his services as a dealer. Harvey Moskowitz, Carney's old contact, was a friend and had informed him that Ray Carney was the man to talk to if you were looking to do business uptown. "He said you're an honest apple," Green told him. "And that you catered to an underserved community."

*Underserved community* was an amusing way to say *Black thieves refused service by white fences downtown*. He asked Green if Moskowitz had explained why they'd stopped working together.

"He mentioned an incident, and that the blame was entirely his." Green spotted the Hermann Bros. safe. "Wow, that's a beauty."

The secret fraternity of Hermann Bros. safe aficionados. Green gave his pitch. Like Moskowitz, he was the American point man for a European network. Anything put in his hands would be out of the country in seventy-two hours. He was careful, he said, and discreet. No one had anything on him—criminal, cop, or Fed— and he meant to keep it that way.

"Which is all to say," Green concluded, "if you need a venue one day, I'm your man." He hooked his thumb toward the showroom. "Now about that Currier piece—it really is exquisite." He peeled off some bills.

Carney liked him—despite his association with Moskowitz, who'd sold him down the river during their last encounter. Nonetheless: Carney was retired, and sometimes whole hours passed where he didn't have a crooked thought.

He kept his card.

He didn't know Green's rates, but this was Munson's deal and the cop had a timetable so Carney wasn't going to sweat it. It was coming on seven-thirty. Whether or not this went down tonight depended on how Green rolled. Maybe he kept this kind of money on tap and maybe he didn't. The detective might have to wait until tomorrow—unless Carney fronted some cash tonight as an advance. Became more than a go-between. If this remained an exchange for concert tickets, Carney could tell himself he was still retired. To get more involved—

"Apartment 19J," the doorman said. "You can go right up."

* * *

The foyer gave way to a spacious, modern living room exposed to the north and east. A conversation pit dominated the center, the sunken green vinyl banquettes surrounding a low coffee table of dark walnut. The other pieces—the dining-room set, the lounger, twin arc lamps—were amalgamations of chrome, leather, fur, and plastic. Closeout sale at Barbarella's. There was a time in the fall of '67 when Carney tried to move some of that cold European stuff in the store: zip. His customers looked at him like he was practicing witchcraft. Despite its lower price point, the wall sculpture Green bought from Carney hung in seamless complement.

"So glad you came by," Green said. His smile was at once practiced and sincere. He was dressed in a white Nehru jacket and a purple-and-pink paisley shirt. Psychedelic noodling, heavy on the sitar, emerged from the hi-fi.

Carney checked out the view while Green got him a cola. A few months ago the apartment would have had an unimpeded view of Randalls Island and Astoria, but new residential high-rises rose in every direction, construction lights burning bright in skeletal, half-completed floors. That slow-motion race.

"Queens, Bronx," Green said. "Know what you can't see? Brooklyn. My back is to it." He got a hold of himself. "Let's see what you have for me."

They set up at the dining-room table. When Green got a look inside the briefcase, he said, "Where are my manners?" and retrieved a large black felt mat from the chrome sideboard. "May I?" He laid the pieces out with religious care. Gloves had materialized on his hands.

Carney returned to the window to let the man work. He had the items cataloged in his head, nothing was going to disappear while his back was turned. The high-rises—it was like they were stacking floors to escape the madness on the street. As if the distance would make them safe. Last week the city had released its new crime study and the papers gave it a good gnaw: CRIME INC, MURDER SHOCK, ROTTEN APPLE. In the last ten years, the homicide rate had quadrupled, rapes and car thefts and burglaries were at historic highs, and you couldn't walk a block without packs of knife-wielding muggers descending on you, and so on. The statistics were set in bullet-pointed lists, in cheap ink that stained your hands like blood.

125th Street didn't need the papers to deliver that news but maybe now it was sinking in below Ninety-sixth. Some white flight ditched out to Long Island, the suburb constellations, and some was *up,* floor after floor. You can run out of land but not sky.

"You're out of retirement?" Green said. His verdict: It was wonderful stuff.

"A one-off," Carney said.

"It's gorgeous, like I said. Marjorie Baxter? But it's only been a week and there's so much heat on it, I have to pass." He took off his gloves. "Anything else comes your way—anything else—I'd love first crack at it."

"A week of what?"

Green arched his eyebrows. It was odd that Carney didn't know their provenance, or that he pretended not to. Green opened the dry bar's cabinet—a black Maison Jansen rip-off with chrome fixtures—and unlocked the compartment at its base. He withdrew a folder.

They'd updated the format for police bulletins since Carney stepped away. It was easier on the eyes these days. The inventory from last week's armed robbery of J. M. Benson Fine Jewelry on Third Avenue matched Carney's mental inventory of Munson's goods. The suspects were four Negro men, ages twenty to thirty, average height. Taking into account inflation for the insurance, Carney had nailed his estimate of the stones' value.

Green reiterated that Carney should call him the next time he was looking to partner, but the Benson haul was impossible. "Word is, it's the Black Liberation Army," he said. "They've been knocking over banks the last few months. Doing robberies. Between that and the policemen shootings, they're too hot."

Of course. Black hoods didn't take down East Side jewelry stores in the middle of the day. Only crazy radicals and nutjob revolutionaries pulled shit like that. Green had put his back to his home borough, but the way he said "knocking over banks" struck a Brooklyn spark.

Green said, "Moskowitz said you severed your business relationship over what he called 'high visibility merchandise.' I apologize that we find ourselves in similar circumstances."

"He gave me up."

"Not very collegial," he said, with evident disgust. "I asked him who was the most honest man he worked with, and he said you."

"Right."

"He died last year. Fell over in his living room like that."

"Sounds quick." Moskowitz had sold him out to the men who killed his cousin. Occasionally Carney had imagined the shape of his revenge, but let it go once he retired. Step away entirely or you haven't stepped away at all.

Carney packed up the stones.

* * *

Out on the street, Carney decided to walk some blocks before looking for a cab. Sweet June nights like this, before the summer crashed down, were rare in the city, like honest mayors and playgrounds free of nodding junkies and broken bottles.

If Munson had to pay off his bookie tonight, it wasn't going to be with the Benson haul. The BLA—no wonder the detective was strung out. Did Munson contract them to pull the job? Carney wouldn't put it past him to work with cop killers, if there was money in it. But with every cop in the five boroughs looking for them? More likely he'd ripped them off. Perhaps killed them as well. There was no telling what the white man was into these days.

What Carney already knew about this mess was dangerous enough. This was his stop, time to get out. Return to 157th, give Munson back his diamonds, and call it a day. He took Eighty-third west, stopping at a phone booth to tell the kids he'd be back by ten.

Tomorrow Elizabeth was home and this brief foray into his former occupation would be behind him. She'd been gone twelve days. One night in April they were lying on the couch watching the news and she said, "Isn't it odd I send people places I've never been?"

Elizabeth dispatched her clients all over the globe yet rarely strayed beyond the city limits. The family had vacationed in San Juan and Montego Bay, but that was it. The agency was practically hers now, since the founder, Dale Baker, had stepped away from the day-to-day. She had changed the company's name from Black Star, figuring that the nationalist ring might put off their more conservative customers. As Seneca Travel & Tour prospered and her responsibilities increased, Elizabeth continued to skip the junkets and conventions, and had never set foot in their satellite offices in Atlanta, Los Angeles, and Chicago. When Carney urged her to reconsider some invitation, she shook her head. "You know me," she said.

Part of it was traveling alone as a woman, a black woman. She arranged safe and hospitable itineraries for her clients despite her distaste for some of the destinations. "You won't find my ass in Birmingham for a million dollars, those redneck motherfuckers." Part of it was not wanting to leave May and John, especially when they were younger.

Then her mother Alma died. Elizabeth missed her. Carney did not. Alma had been underfoot for most of their marriage, carping about his unworthiness, insulting the store, his speech, the colorful Carney family history. Alma embodied the traditional

Strivers' Row qualities of propriety, rectitude, and gentility. Her son-in-law did not. Alexander Oakes, the fine young man who grew up with Elizabeth and now worked at city hall—now there was a worthy match for her daughter.

Carney had read an article in a magazine about the average human lifespan and figured he could endure his in-laws' disapproval. Then Elizabeth's parents had been forced to sell their townhouse, the home that Elizabeth had grown up in, due to a financial reversal. Carney moved into the Row a few years later. It was plain to Alma: Not content just to steal her daughter, her street nigger son-in-law had moved on to grand larceny and stolen her whole neighborhood.

Each time she came over she relived the trauma of this robbery. "It's changed so much," she'd grumble as she hung up her aging fur coat, with its worn hem and loose pelt. The four rows of townhouses had been a dignified oasis, protected from Harlem's shifts in fortune. Now the local deterioration had finally jumped the ave. The younger generation divided the houses they'd grown up in into three or four apartments, hungry landlords chopped up grand residences into single-room occupancies for winos and bums. Cross Seventh Ave and there were "druggie houses," as Alma called them, between torched tenements, and heroin dealers staked out the corners. One Christmas Eve a purse snatcher had knocked her to the pavement and broken her hip. "I barely recognize it these days."

After Alma's heart attack, Elizabeth tucked herself snug into her mourning. Carney didn't know how to comfort her. He tried. Carney's own mother had died when he was young and he had lacked the equipment to properly say goodbye. When his father passed it was a blessing; he experienced a new freedom, an alleviation of symptoms. He could only make observations on the alien process of his wife's grief.

Elizabeth threw herself into work, returned spent, then installed herself on the parlor sofa in quiet misery until she drifted off. She had become an accomplished cusser as she entered middle age, but no longer had the energy for invective. In other ways she was not diminished at all. May and John knew her as firm and patient; Elizabeth's new, short fuse startled them. Mother and daughter butted heads constantly, especially when one of them recognized something of themselves in the other and felt compelled to squash it.

Elizabeth proposed the work trip that spring. The itinerary: a survey of the new hotels opening in Miami, then quick stops in Houston and Chicago to spend time with ST&T staff, capped by a ride home on the Lake Shore Limited, or whatever Amtrak was calling it now. She had booked tens of thousands of people on those long train rides but had never taken one herself. "It will be an adventure," she said.

He wondered if the trip would transport her past this sad patch. Twelve days away from home. He was no traveler, either—five days was the longest he'd ever been out of New York City. Even the corner of Eighty-third and Third was a foreign land, now that he stopped to look. The window displays were less cramped, humbly arranged, as if to spare genteel sensibilities. The lettering on the signs for the florist, the stationery store, the dry cleaner's was classy and confident. You walk in, you're not in for some shabby treatment. It was like the sign makers had segregated the nice letters. His own sign was due for an update. He took notes.

It was early enough in the summer that the concrete and asphalt hadn't begun to radiate stored-up heat all night. The breeze carried a pleasant smell that was not that of garbage or gutter water. A more learned man would have been able to identify the species of plant, but the best Carney could offer was that it smelled "like trees"—those intermittent sidewalk plantings hanging in there, making a go. Carney hadn't walked this stretch of the East Side in years. If he hadn't been carrying a briefcase full of stolen jewelry, he would've walked home. No: There were too many fucked-up stretches between here and home. Still, it was a nice thought, that the city had once been safe enough to walk where one pleased.

Uptown, Carney played a game, Is My Stuff in There?, where he tested various models of how far his furniture had dispersed in Harlem. X many pieces sold to X many customers over X many years, adding complicating variables as time passed—dilution by new apartment construction, ebb and flow of uptown population, frequency of redecorating. He had a mental map, like on a cop show, full of red pins demarcating clusters, thin spots, dead spots. Where was the southernmost red pin, the edge of his enterprise? Ninety-fourth Street? How far east? Where did it start, the invisible barrier that separated his city from the white city.

The first blow to his skull sent him buckling. The next one to his kidneys drove Carney forward into the side of a parked van. SULLIVAN FURNITURE REPAIR AND REUPHOLSTERY. The wheel well was rusted—in his quick zoom in, it was like a mouse had nibbled a cracker. The man lifted up Carney and shoved him against the blue van. Carney looked for help—no one in either direction on Eighty-third—and then into the face of his attacker. He couldn't place him until he spoke. "Thought I lost you."

From what Carney recalled, Munson started working with Buck Webb when he transferred uptown from vice. Munson's affability undercut the power inequities between white cops and those they were paid to serve. Buck Webb didn't see the advantage in ceding ground. He was an old-school Harlem cop, bull-necked and burly. A black boy grows uptown, over the years he creates a composite of a white cop. Buck Webb was faithful to the loathsome image formed by a generation of black boys. Times changed. Men like Buck Webb did not.

Carney had occasionally seen the partners together—hassling some brother across the street, looming over a hood—but got his proper introduction inside Nightbirds one night. The cops had just braced some hustler at the back of the bar, left the man humiliated with a busted snout. Webb's natural tint was a fish-belly white that turned completely scarlet when he got angry, like a lizard on *Mutual of Omaha's Wild Kingdom.* He was scarlet as the partners made their way to the door, flushed with violence.

CROOK MANIFESTO | 39

Munson stopped to say hello and introduced Carney to his partner. Hello as in "See you tomorrow," it being Envelope Day Eve.

"Carney?" Buck Webb said. "Son of Michael Carney?"

Carney blinked.

Webb laughed. "Munson, I busted that nigger so many times I
needed a turnstile. What's his story?"

Munson placed a hand on Carney's shoulder to cool it down. In
the history of time itself, no black man had ever struck a white
cop in Nightbirds, but the gesture signified. "He's an upstanding
citizen," Munson said. "We should be going." He gave Carney a
neutral look, which in this situation served as sympathy.

"Called him Big Mike, I think," Webb said. He turned to the
door. "He wasn't so big."

That was that. Carney rarely saw Webb. If Munson was with his
partner, it meant he was on the job, doing actual police work or a
higher-level grift, so it had nothing to do with Carney. Munson
tapping him on the shoulder, on his own, is when he had to watch
his wallet. Webb was so scarce that Carney used to joke, "Where's
Webb?" Making fun of Munson's shakedowns, but also not wanting Webb anywhere near him with that white cowboy shit.

Now here he was, a nightmare on Eighty-third. Buck Webb
picked up the briefcase. "You have my shit?" The case's weight
told him all he needed to know. "You got out of that cab and went
straight into the building—I thought I was screwed." He shook it
again.

At the corner an old white lady paused her shopping cart to
take in the tableau. Webb gave her the thumbs-up. He turned
to Carney. "You've got that 'Munson screwed me' face. No mis-
taking." He socked Carney in the stomach. "You tell Munson he
knows where to reach me. We can straighten it all out quickly.
Straighten it out like two white men."

# FOUR

When the furniture salesman returned, Munson was
at the window in a sweat-soaked undershirt, left fore-
arm swaddled in bandages. Bloody fingerprints dot-
ted the white gauze like rose petals. He crunched a
can of National Bohemian, tossed it in the direction
of the kitchen, and gingerly stuck his wounded arm
into his oxford shirt. "I had to collect from somebody," Munson told his visitor. "We tussled. You?"

The detective watched Carney walk stiffly to the
cheap couch, hand on his stomach. Carney caught
him up while he tenderly probed the back of his head.

"That's a setback," Munson announced. He lit a
cigarette. The furniture salesman told the truth—he
bore the earmarks of a Buck Webb Special, heavy on
the gut work.

The director's chair creaked when Munson sat
down. The view brought him back to ringolevio
again. Twice in two days—he hadn't thought about
the game since he was a kid. The Memorial Day holiday reminded Munson first, the warm afternoons
and slow pace conjuring the old pastime, those
long-ago days playing ringolevio through the endless blocks and shadows of Hell's Kitchen. Hide-and-
seek and cops and robbers, with a twist. Munson
made himself slim behind mailboxes, tried not to get
creamed by buses as he darted into traffic, hunched
in the darkness of piss-soaked stoops while they
searched for him. On the run, like a rehearsal.

Munson chuckled, remembering how the grown-
ups shook their fists at him and his crew, this tribe
of juvenile delinquents cutting them off on the side-

walk and skidding about. Those outside the game couldn't see it, even as it unfolded around them with anarchic purpose. Then one of the brats collared someone on the other team and shouted *Ringolevio, one-two-three, one-two-three, one-two-three!* and the game broke through to the civilian world in a burst of noise. Old biddies dropped their grocery bags in surprise, deliverymen swerved their hand trucks and cursed.

The only non-players hip to what was happening were those watching from above—the shut-ins, weirdos, and geezers who spent their lives at the window, chests and arms perched on dingy pillows that rested on the sill. Every block had them, these silent judges. Their stories circulated: got beaned his first at-bat with the Brooklyn Robins and now his brains were scrambled; drank a bottle of nerve tonic after she got left at the altar and ever since she got out of the booby hatch she watches and waits for her man to come for her. They saw the whole thing from up there, the feints and reversals, the gambits and misbegotten sprints. When young Munson crouched behind a milk truck, he'd look up and see the former shortstop gaze down at him, face empty.

Now Munson was one of them, watching from his 157th hide-out, ejected from the game. Once you're out, you can see the system in its entirety, make out where gears bite gears, how the mechanism works, and scheme accordingly.

Munson rolled his arm and flexed to test the injury. Usable, if painful, his thumbs and fingers. The caveman: opposable thumb on one hand to hold a club, middle finger on the other hand to flip 'em the bird. He stretched and winced. Turned to Carney. "You're married, right?"

"You fucking know that."

"I ain't trying to jump to conclusions," Munson said. "The family unit is complex in the ghetto, I know that. You got a wife, you know no matter how much you love her, no matter how great she is, she's going to drive you batshit sometimes. With how she walks and talks, how she chews her fucking food, fucking breathes. Sometimes. All the time, if you're unlucky." A beer can materialized in his hand. "That's what it's like having a partner. Sitting in the car, babysitting some scumbag, it's cold, he's telling the same story you heard a hundred fucking times, you're telling a joke you told a hundred fucking times, smelling each other's farts, staring in the darkness—it's a marriage. Same shit."

Munson's guest frowned. He glanced at the front door, as if for reassurance it still existed. "Did you get divorced or something?"

"Divorce," Munson said. "That's what I'm saying, you have to ride out the bumps. Step back. Cool off. Otherwise, you're going to tear each other's eyes out." He stubbed out his cigarette. "You know what a pad is?"

"The Serpico thing," Carney said. "It's how a precinct divvies up bribes."

Everybody knew about Frank fucking Serpico. Last year, *The New York Times* ran a whole series on police corruption, starring Serpico as "the Whistleblower." Serpico was straight, everyone else in his precinct was bent. The little things that made the job bearable—meals on the arm, cooping, pocketing twenty bucks to rip up a speeding ticket—Saint Frank found distasteful. Which made big things, like the pad—a marvel of grifting ingenuity— morally unacceptable. Serpico tattled to his superiors, who did nothing (no surprise), went all the way up to the mayor's office, who did nothing (ditto), until they got wind the *Times* was about to publish. Then Mayor Lindsay got the Knapp Commission together to study "the problem."

Among the freebie meals and shakedowns of bar owners, working girls, and any unlucky fool who believed they could operate for free, the pad underwent particular scrutiny. "Everybody pays money to operate," Munson explained to Carney, "since time immemorial. Even if they called it something different, shekels or whatever. A couple of years ago a wise man said, Why don't we organize this? In the station house. That's the pad—everybody's envelopes made nice and orderly. On collection day, two bagmen make the rounds for the whole division. They hit up the local sports book, the numbers joint, the man behind the big dice game. Then that big stack of money that gets divided up according to who you are, your rank and seniority. Patrolman, let's say he's getting six hundred extra a week, a sergeant makes eight hundred, up to the captain, who gets a share and a half."

In Harlem, anyway, Munson added to himself. That's why they called it the Gold Coast. It's why Munson transferred up from vice, no-brainer. Patrol the streets, making twelve grand a year if you're lucky, the Gold Coast brings a nice bonus. In the good old days when Munson was the bagman for his division he ran a scam where he inflated the number of plainclothes. The bookies forked it over. Since Munson was the one who divvied up the pad, he pocketed the made-up shares. Wasn't a bad racket.

"Guys like me," Munson said, "I get my nut, but I also work nights, you might say. I extract additional tribute from certain parties for my own private contracts. Like you. Chink Montague. Notch Walker now. He pays the station house to operate, and gives to me to keep it running smooth. One's gasoline in the tank, the other is the oil."

"It runs smooth until it breaks down," Carney said. "Serpico got shot in the face. They said it was cops."

"Bent hates straight, Carney. Putting on airs—*You think you're better than me*?" The detective shrugged. "Only a matter of time before someone tried to clip him."

Carney got up to open the window more. It didn't budge.

"You want to know why Webb jumped you," Munson said. He lit a cigarette. "Two weeks ago, the BLA shot those two men on patrol and declared open season on cops. The whole force is mobilized to put them down—what'd Malcolm X say?—by any means necessary. It's a holy mission. Webb and I are running all over the city. Get a tip about some militant assholes who use a soup kitchen for a front. We go in, bust some heads—"

"Soup kitchen?"

"You ever read that Panther paper? Soup kitchens are how they get a foothold in a neighborhood. Giving people what they need. A lot of these people are from out of state, out-of-state agitators.

California, Oakland. And they come in with their talk and try to turn our own blacks against us."

"Yours?" From Carney, the tone qualified as incensed.

Munson put up his hands: People were so touchy these days. "Point is, we're all over town following leads. Last Friday, I get a tip from a guy I know—breaks kneecaps for Notch Walker. Sometimes feeds me stuff, I don't know his game yet. I meet him in the back of Baby's Best and he asks me if I'm still looking for those cop killers. What do you think? He gives me the address of this place one of their girlfriend's at."

Munson and Buck sat on the apartment, a five-story tenement on 146th between Amsterdam and Convent. The third-floor window didn't have a curtain. The apartment was lit, shadows play on the walls. The detectives waited in the car.

Two colored guys came rolling up the street. They carried themselves differently than the local talent, a different species entirely. Munson and Webb looked at each other: Okay. The men didn't buzz up or produce keys—the front door was busted. They went upstairs to join the party.

Munson sighed. "I should point out that me and Buck, our relationship is showing signs of strain. We've ridden together for many years, have kicked down doors and collared every brand of knucklehead on God's green earth, but like I said, a partner is eventually going to get on your nerves. Buck's on my case. 'You're really putting away the booze, maybe you should lay off the bennies, stop burning the candle at both ends.' I go, who are you to talk—"

"I get the gist," Carney said.

"Point is, you know how when your wife starts yelling at you about ABC, it's never A, B, or C that's actually pissed her off, it's really Z, the last thing on her list? But she can't say it until she goes through the whole alphabet?"

"Grab your Alpha-Bits and come with me, we'll eat through the Alpha-Bits A to Z."

"What?"

Carney shrugged.

"Buck's going through the whole alphabet," Munson said, "and finally he gets to Y, which is how much money I'm making. Why didn't you cut me in on this, why didn't you cut me in on that, naming shit I haven't thought of in a long time. People been dead for years, old deals from way back. What does he expect? I'm enterprising.

"Finally he drops Z. Z is what he's really pissed about. Z is, he says he got a subpoena from the Knapp Commission and why him and not me?"

Why Buck and not him? It was not something Munson wanted to ponder overlong. Before the City Council granted Knapp and his crew subpoena power, nobody was sweating them. Another phony commission for public relations. Running stings on low-level patrolmen putting the bite on bar owners and tow-truck drivers, penny-ante bullshit. But in March they got that subpoena power. And people are getting served. And people who should definitely be getting served are not talking about getting served.

Munson first heard of Knapp back in the '50s, when the assistant DA busted up the waterfront rackets. A serious man. It was public knowledge that the commission's budget ran out July 1—Munson had figured on waiting them out. But if it was Memorial Day and they're calling the guy who sits next to him, how much longer until they came knocking? Sometimes Munson thought he should've gone into the corruption beat, back in the day. Steady work, and you can probably come up with some higher-level grifting from the inside.

Munson lit a cigarette. That was two he had going. He commenced to alternate. "I've been with Buck for ten years," Munson said. "Seen men wet their pants when we roll up. He's got that 'mean fuel' from his childhood. But he got shot two years ago and he is not the same man. Buck's wife's got this divorce lawyer, she knows where he gets his cash from, wants to use that to juice him. In his prime, he was something else. Now he's scared money.

"I have to wonder," the detective said, "they bring him in, can they break him? In the old days, forget about it. But these are not the old days. The city has changed. It's crumbling around us and we have to outrun all the shit raining down." Munson stopped to consider his guest. Did Carney understand what he was saying? One of those inscrutable colored guys who never let you know what they're thinking. Most of the time it was fine. Tonight Munson had to know if Carney had what it took to keep up his end.

We'll see.

"Can they break him?" Munson said. "That's the question I am mulling when the lights go out in the apartment and those cocksuckers we've been sitting on come out of the building."

Munson and his partner had a choice: Follow the three suspects or go on up and toss the place. Were they ducking out for cigarettes or are they up to something worth tailing them for? He put it to Buck and Buck voted to go upstairs. His partner smelled it, too, it was floating on the breeze: They were about to make a score.

Five stories, two apartments per floor. Some mamacita was cooking up some Spanish shit and it filled the halls and made Munson hungry. The stairwells were empty, no junkies nodding off on the landing or baby in an overflowing diaper crawling down the black-and-white tile. Never knew what you were going to find. TVs blaring, gunshots ringing out on the same cop show everybody's watching floor after floor. Munson's hands shook these days but Buck, for all his recent lack of vim and vigor, still had his knack with locks. They're inside like that.

Apartment 3F was one bedroom and a living room, with a tight fit in the hallway from the bags and boxes piled up. The apartment belonged to a religious type, Jesus bleeding out on the wall and what have you, but the place had been overrun. One of the BLA guys picks her up in the park—You love Christ our lord? I love him, too, he's the fucking bee's knees—and next week his whole crew has moved in. It was mattress to mattress on the floor, no sheets, army bags of clothes. Munson figured there were five or six people staying there now.

Buck took the bedroom, Munson handled the front room. A big, ratty red rug covered most of the floor. Boxes of revolutionary newspapers and pamphlets made it cramped. "The usual scholarly articles on the cover," Munson said. "Kill Whitey, Stand Up for Our Yellow Brothers in Vietnam." He removed a pillow that had been stuffed into a milk crate. Under the pillow were four revolvers and a couple of boxes of ammo. Two automatic rifles beneath the couch like kicked-off sandals.

"Buck called from the other room," Munson said. "Upbeat, like his old self, and I know he's found the score we smelled down on the street. Go back there and he's holding a duffel bag of cash, and there's another bag inside of that—what turns out to be the haul from the J. M. Benson rip-off a couple of days before. We toss the room looking for more, but that's the plum. We nod. Nothing more is needed. We're taking the whole thing."

No sign of Jones's and Piagentini's service revolvers. Munson took one of the milk-crate revolvers. It'd come in handy sooner or later. That was a reliable quality in revolvers.

He hadn't seen Buck that happy in months. Grinning like a big Irish ape, skipping down the stairs. At the top of the stoop, though, he gave a signal: The BLA were coming up west on 146th. The same three guys.

"Our car is in the wrong direction," Munson said, "so we know we're going to beat it, call in the location, and return later. The priority is to tuck the score away safe and sound." Maybe even join the fun later. It was fun to rob some shitheads, split, and then show up with the responding officers. *What have we here?* Ten bucks if you can make your partner laugh.

There was one black radical that the others deferred to, the top dog. He was a tall man with a big Afro and goatee, striding forth in combat boots and an army field jacket with leopard-skin epaulets. When they exited the apartment, he had scanned the street like a pro while his lieutenants jived and joked. Later, Munson double-checked the militant casebook at the station house. The man was Malik Jamal, born Robert Taylor from Chattanooga. Wanted for armed robbery and assault, former member of the Black Panthers and currently a big honcho in the Black Liberation Army. Since the cop killings, brass had kept everyone up to speed on black radical activity. The BLA had been pulling jobs here and in California the last few months to build up a war chest. "Expropriations," they called it. Knocking over after-hours clubs, bank jobs botched and successful, and more brazen daylight capers like J. M. Benson.

"Jamal meets my eyes as we turn up the sidewalk and he's made us. Buck is cradling the bag so it's mostly out of view, but two beefy middle-aged white men who walk like cops? On that block, coming out of that building? He makes us in a second. He shouts, we're running, and then one of them starts firing. We give some of that back, but main priority is to get the stuff out, not pull out a badge and make this official."

Ducking between vehicles for cover like he was playing ringolevio. Is that when it all started, the link between him now and who he used to be? Munson said, "Friday was warm if you remember so on Amsterdam there's a lot of civilians out, playing loud music and dominoes. The BLA breaks off—they know with the stepped-up patrols, there'll be cars in a flash. Buck's wheezing, out of shape. I'm pretty winded, too, to be honest. We grab a Checker cab when we get over to Broadway. It's like the old days, me and him pulling off a number like that. Like I had just transferred to Harlem and there was money all over, coming out of the sidewalk like crude."

For the last five years Munson and his partner maintained a pad on Fifty-fourth off Lexington. "You know in movies when they show a really nice building, they have rich broads coming out walking poodles? I swear whenever I walk up, this rich cunt with a poodle comes out, it's crazy." The detectives entertained girls there, stored sundry items from time to time. The fourteenth-floor view provided a sweep of the unconquered city night and the illusion of invincibility. The impassive skyline betrayed no indication of its opinion on the matter. Everybody got a kick out of the wet bar, which had a Western theme. Squeeze the horn next to the ice bucket and it mooed.

At their pad the detectives got a proper look at the Benson take. It was magnificent, the culmination of their illicit careers, all those small scores over the years and the hard-won experience and dedication to craft. Buck took a handful of cash, Munson grabbed another and they counted it up: a hundred and twenty-five grand. It was a good haul, what Buck and Munson brought home that night.

"We are indebted to the rebels in Algeria and North Vietnam and whatever the fuck for inspiring the Black Liberation Army," Munson told Carney. He jabbed out his cigarette and lit another. "It helps calm Buck about the subpoena. We've always made money because we're smart and ride it out while the other guys flame out. We can handle Knapp and his commission because we always do." The stash was safe on Fifty-fourth until the coast was clear.

The holiday bestowed various gifts upon Munson. Like when you sit down to play cards and catch a rush: Gimme, gimme, gimme, I can't lose. Fred Stevenson threw a barbecue at his new split-level in Union City. Sausages and peppers writhing on the grill in a succulent brown funk, and a truncated view of Manhattan across the river, tinted by the smog so that it looked like a picture of the Old West. Nightfall he drove out to Bay Ridge to pick up Pam and they went to the pictures, *Support Your Local Gunfighter* at the Loews. It wasn't as good as the first one, but when they walked out Pam said he reminded her of James Garner. How so? "Because you're funny but also strong." Compliment accepted. She worked at the Young Miss Shop at Korvettes and said she could hook him up if he wanted something for a niece. He said, "I'm on permanent discount." He crept out of her pad at dawn when the pigeons woke him up with their morning bullshit.

Sunday was a blank canvas. He doodled. Somehow he ended up at the old place on Forty-sixth. All new faces, even the watchers in the windows had turned over, with their sooty pillows and silent judgments. The city had a quiet feel, like it was sighing.

\* \* \*

After Green's cosmopolitan bachelor module, Munson's 157th Street hideout resembled a sparsely propped film set. Push too hard on the walls and they'd topple.

Carney was relieved Munson was unperturbed that Buck Webb had ripped off his score. He looked doped up, which bode well for Carney's exit from this escapade. It was between the two white men. Munson believed his story, that was the main thing. He could endure the monologue and then go home and take some aspirin.

"This morning," Munson said, "I'm about to enter the station house and I hear my name. It's in my hands before I can do anything—I've been served. Fucking process server dropped that shit on me and made like Jesse Owens. Out on the street in front of the whole 28th to send a message. Knapp's calling me in."

Munson wasn't trying to pay off a bookie. He was splitting town. "I see why your partner is mad," Carney said.

"I was going to send Buck his share," Munson said. "Who does he think I am? I liquidate the stones, collect some debts around town, and cool it somewhere quiet. But he wouldn't have let me go to a fence, given the other complication."

"What's that?"

Munson lit a cigarette. "I could have pulled it off. Calmed down Buck, I know how. The Black Liberation Army—thirty thousand cops in the city looking for them—it's just a matter of time before they get picked up. Shooting cops for kicks, but their main thing is funding their operation. Robberies, bringing in weed from California for Notch Walker to sell on the street. Notch has been helping them out with weapons and logistics. Other stuff, too, it turns out."

Carney said, "That's not good."

"It's not good, Carney, you're right. They're partners, like on the J. M. Benson job. Half the stuff I gave you today—it belongs to Notch."

"Notch Walker."

"Yup. One of my guys works behind the bar at the Emerald Inn, last night he tells me that those guys on 146th Street have fingered me and Buck, and Notch has put the word out. Uptown fences ain't going to open the door, I come knocking. But someone like you, off the beaten path . . ."

Munson finished his beer and rose. "Probably got a bounty on my head. Thought I had some time before Buck noticed the score was gone. But maybe he heard Notch was looking for us and assumed I was going to split, or he meant to pull his own disappearing act." It was Buck who handed Munson the phone when Carney called the station house. Buck must have remembered Carney's fencing days and put it together, Munson said. The detective popped two pills and fastened his chest holster. He slipped a .38 into the one above his ankle. "You ready?"

"I'm heading home."

"I need you to drive." He raised the injured arm. "Division of labor."

"I can't."

"I wasn't asking."

Carney stood.

The moment passed. Munson grinned. He put on his sports coat, a thin blue number that was tighter than it used to be, and patted after his wallet and keys. "Give me a lift and you're off the hook. You'll get your tickets, we'll wrap this up, and you can be on your way."

Carney had worked with the detective long enough to know he was lying, and lying about the tickets as well. It was his own fault. He had been on the straight and narrow for four years, but slip once and everybody is glad to help you slip hard. Crooked stays crooked and bent hates straight. The rest is survival.

# FIVE

535 Edgecombe Ave. An address from the invoice pile on his desk, one of his customers. Puerto Rican lady, two kids, curly red hair tucked under a green-and-white gingham wrap. New convertible sofa and his apologies for not carrying bunk beds. Her name escaped but the musicality of her delivery had imprinted itself. *Five three five*: a delicate filament; a fragment of a TV jingle; the voice of an ambitious starlet stealing the scene, flirty and determined.

In better times. The place had been torched. Plywood sealed the first-floor windows and those above were dark and haloed in soot. Carney hoped they made it out okay.

"Insurance play," Munson said. "Landlord buys it for cheap, it's got a big mortgage and tax liens. Load up on insurance and *boom*—burn that sucker down." He stepped out of the car to piss. "Up here, Brooklyn and the Bronx. I'd like to get in on that, boy."

A racket predating Carney's birth, he didn't need the lesson. His father came home reeking of kerosene on occasion. Some of Carney's fencing clientele dabbled. "You light some rags and get out of there," Skip Lauderdale told him once. They were waiting for his coin guy to call back. "You hear people arguing down the hallway, kids laughing it up, and hope the guy who's supposed to call the fire department will do his job. Usually the fire's out before anyone gets hurt." *Usually* meant sometimes it went another way.

The arson game was more brazen nowadays. State inspector's in your pocket, who's going to flag suspicious payouts? Another sign of the city's advancing deterioration. Driving on the expressway, Carney'd look over to find a plain of rubble instead of a neighborhood, a scatter of bricks that used to be tenements containing the hopes and miseries of tens of thousands of newcomers, strivers, and the humbly plodding on. A man lights a match and a building goes up in smoke. A landlord stops paying taxes and surrenders the building to junkies, who move in and drive out the families, and then the city razes it all. Crater by crater. An organized shamelessness that verged on conspiracy. Simpler than conspiracy was Carney's take: In general, people were terrible.

In April, the papers covered a delegation of mayors who came to town for a conference, with a field trip to Brownsville. Elizabeth read out quotes, using her Caucasian voice for the outraged visitors:

*Kevin White of Boston said the twenty-block area "may be the first tangible sign of the collapse of our civilization."*

*"God, it looks like Dresden," said Wesley C. Uhlman of Seattle.*

*. . . and most of them said it reminded them of home.*

Ha ha. That last quote became a punch line when she and Carney were out for a stroll and encountered tokens of neighborhood decrepitude. A pervert squatting on a park bench, ladling goo out of an iron bucket; an alley cat with its head smashed flat; a baby's grimy doll missing half a face: *It reminds me of home!*

The east side of Edgecombe was Coogan's Bluff, and the top of the stairs to the old Polo Grounds. Bums camped in the park beyond the stone wall, in shanties nestled against the rocks. Sheet-metal walls held up by pipe. One of the residents had taken a pet: a mutt with matted fur, tethered to a concrete block by a long, curly telephone cord. A few blocks over from Munson's hideout and he'd crossed the border into a different city.

Munson whistled at the dog and received an indifferent response. He got back in the car.

"This is a stakeout?" Carney said.

"In that we're waiting. Not similar in that there's no mystery."

No mystery because they waited for his partner. Munson had

reached out to Webb from a pay phone three blocks down from the 157th Street apartment. When he turned to dial, Carney weighed the pros and cons of running. Elizabeth was safe out of town, scoop up the kids and split before this night got worse. Because it was getting worse minute by minute, like he was a nail being pounded deeper and snugger and stuck. Two white cops being pursued by the Justice Department, black radicals with submachine guns, Notch Walker. This was unsustainable. His assessment: It was Tuesday night, a warm pleasant night in Washington Heights with people around, witnesses, and Munson couldn't stop him if he ran.

"Carney." Munson cupped his hand over the transmitter. "Don't even think about it."

He got off the phone and informed Carney they were headed to Highbridge Park to square things with Buck. "Maybe even get him to apologize for belting you. What'd he, hit you in the kidney?"

"I don't know what you call it."

Munson shrugged and told him his car was around the corner.

Carney drove the Cadillac over to 158th and Edgecombe, one block south of the meet. Fifty-fourth and Lex, 157th. "How many hideouts you have?" he asked.

"They're like women—you got to have a few spares."

Carney only had the one. He'd been deliberating, but now there was no question he was taking tomorrow off to meet Elizabeth. The kids wouldn't be home until after four. He'd have to explain the knot on his head and the bruises blooming on his stomach. Last time he got a black eye on extralegal business, he told Elizabeth that a druggie had socked him and run off. "It's crazy out there!" This time around, he was going with *mugged,* given the state of the city these days. If Alma were still alive, he'd have picked a mugging location to irritate her—in front of her church, broad daylight, or outside Broken Wing, that orphan charity she was on the board of. For the first time, he felt her loss.

"I know Chink," Carney said, "but haven't met Notch Walker. He started in Sugar Hill?"

"Until it got too small for him," Munson said.

Carney had been out for four years, but Notch Walker's name came up plenty among the old crooked bunch at Nightbirds or the Blossom. Hookers, heroin, numbers. Like Elizabeth, Notch was a kind of travel agent, trafficking in escapes: sex, intoxication, the dream of a jackpot. The products sold themselves, so he directed his promotional campaigns at competitors: chaining lieutenants of rival crews to benches in Riverside Park and setting them aflame; a shootout at an after-hours club that clipped a bunch of civilians and made the national news. A running gunfight with Chink's crew up Lenox one blustery Christmas Eve forever ruined caroling for more than one bystander. It was an aggressive rollout.

The *Amsterdam News* ran a picture of Notch strutting out of Sylvia's, imperial grin on his mug. He was tall and broad-shouldered, dressed that day in tight brown-and-white houndstooth slacks and a double-breasted leather trench that made him look like a Negro pirate. Bumpy Johnson in his natty Harry Olivier pinstripe suit and Homburg hat were relics of a bygone Harlem. Notch was the type of gangster the streets stamped out these days: flashy, lethal, and remorseless.

Munson lit a cigarette. Every couple of years a new player came on the scene and tried to make his name, he said. "The old guard smothers him in the crib, or doesn't. The new guard becomes the status quo, and then they're the ones the young guys are gunning for." He clocked a Cadillac DeVille that coasted up Edgecombe. The driver was a long-haired Spanish guy with healthy muttonchops. Munson said, "Notch is the crab that got to the top of the barrel."

In his retirement, Carney had joined the good and decent folk, pulling the drapes tight when shots rang out down the street and tsking at the turf battles and bloody rumbles in the morning paper. Just another square. He liked standing with his back to the window, ignorant of whatever dumb drama occupied the warring clans that week. Why then did he drop by Nightbirds, not so often but often enough, and Donegal's, too, and the Blossom, where a face from crooked days never failed to appear? It didn't take much for them to spill the latest, and a free drink did the trick with reluctant correspondents. Why did he go there, and why did he keep Green's card when he was happily, resolutely retired?

Silence in the Cadillac. Both men traveling the rut of their thoughts. Munson rushed in: "Did you guys play ringolevio uptown?"

"It's not a foreign country, Munson." There was stickball, there was handball, and there was ringolevio. Carney had loved the game. It was like tag, but bigger and more monstrous. One team hunted and the other was pursued. "Jail" was a front stoop, or the trunk of a car owned by somebody who wouldn't beat you for touching their ride. To capture an opponent, you had to hold on for the time it took to scream *Ringolevio, one-two-three, one-two-three, one-two-three.* Necks were hooked, shirts ripped as the enemy tried to wriggle free. If the stoop started filling up, a jailbreak was in order. Those first heists, where you dashed in to spring your pals—*All free, all free, one-two-three, one-two-three*—without getting nabbed. This last part involved pulling your best Fred Astaire shit, leaping and twisting.

Most of the time Carney and his buddies played outside Freddie's house on 129th Street. Depending on appetite and enthusiasm, the boundary was a couple of blocks or the playing field encompassed the entire city, wherever your feet took you. Once everyone was imprisoned, you switched roles and started again. There were legends of games that went on for days, pausing at dinnertime when everyone was called home to their grim tenements—the drunken fathers or indifferent mothers or whatever miserable arrangement had claimed them—until the next morning, when the game resumed.

Carney said, "It was always kids with older brothers that told stories about the all-day games. An older-kid thing."

"No, it was true," Munson said, "we played for days on end." He lit a cigarette. "They should have called it cops and robbers. Collaring the other team, or running around trying to stay out of jail: cops and robbers."

Carney said, "We called it jail because it was a place you didn't want to go." If his father heard him say he was playing cops and robbers, he would have taken off his belt. Shit, take Carney's belt, too, and whup him double.

"You were a cop and then a robber and a cop again. It didn't matter how you saw yourself, you were both at the same time," Munson said. "We'd run all over Hell's Kitchen. All over the city. All day. Take a break and buy a soda and then one of the guys snatched you and went, *Ringolevio!* I was, Wait—we're still playing? Of course you were playing, the game never ended." He grunted. "Next day, start all over."

Buck Webb floated past in a dark green DeVille. Webb and Munson shared a nod that Carney took as silent cop signal. Webb pulled over up the block.

The partners drove the same make. Munson's was red. "You buy them together?" Carney said.

"I know a guy." Munson picked up the vinyl bag at his feet. He flexed his injured arm. "Going to apologize to the man, explain, and give him his half." He tapped the vinyl bag. "Then we'll do that errand I mentioned."

"I thought *this* was the errand."

"This? This is just Buck." Munson exited and walked up to the DeVille. He bent to speak through the window and got inside.

Carney had ridden with Munson once before, years back. While the cop hit his envelope route, he performed a slow-burn interrogation of Carney over his cousin Freddie. Took Carney a few blocks to catch on. He patted the upholstery. This wasn't the same car but he was sure it had seen its share of trouble. Racked up the violence like miles. You kept track of miles because it's important—beatdowns of black men, they didn't bother with those records.

He wondered if any of the guys he grew up with had been worked over in the backseat. Brad Wiley! Bradford Wiley, most definitely, after he knocked over a luncheonette or snatched an old lady's welfare check. He was "always bad," as Aunt Millie put it. Lie in your face, plain as day, like when they played ringolevio and he'd deny going out of bounds when he couldn't have snuck around without a transporter.

Carney and his buddies didn't hold all-day ringolevio tournaments like the ones Munson went on about, but they'd spend hours hiding and chasing, lurking in vestibules, screaming down the street like one mad, pell-mell creature. You nabbed someone and were nabbed in turn. Delivered the incantation before the enemy squirmed away.

Hoarse at the end of the day from all the screeching. He and Freddie were always on the same team, good luck trying to separate them. Carney was living with him and Aunt Millie then, Pedro when he was around. Freddie was the recruiter. He kept tabs on everyone who was down to play, the kids from upstairs, up and down the block, the next block. The Jones twins, Jesus, Roger Roger, Timmy the Crip. Vouching for some runny-nosed chump you'd never seen before: "Oh that's Sammy from Jamaica, he's cool." You never saw them around, they only existed on this earthly plane when Freddie called a game.

There had been historic ones over the years. The drizzly afternoon Roger Roger knocked over Mr. Conner's fruit cart and had to work it off all summer. That time Carney and Freddie hid out on the roof and saw the naked lady across the street do a little dance with her garters. Freddie almost fell over the side trying to get a view. And that final game, whose grisly majesty outlived childhood mythology and remained a clutch anecdote.

It was the spring of 1942. Freddie and Carney were on the hiding team and laying low in Morningside Park. The park was out of bounds that game, but his cousin had proposed that they sneak out, kick back for a while, then return to free their incarcerated brethren. "It's not the same if you don't cheat a little," Freddie used to say. Carney was a slow learner. It didn't take much to enlist him in one of Freddie's schemes. Playing hooky to catch a double matinee or blowing up trash cans with a bunch of Chinatown cherry bombs, Carney was in.

Ten minutes into their Morningside vacation, they were bored by the transgression. Freddie leapt from bench to bench, pretending the cracked Parks Department concrete was lava. Carney kicked cans off the walkway into the grass, cleaning up after someone's party.

"Hey, look," Freddie said.

Carney came over. A man in a dark brown suit was lying on the grass, turned away from them. Legs entwined, arms outstretched—the posture was too tortured for him to be sleeping one off.

There was no one else around. Carney shrugged. Freddie nudged the body with his shoe. Nothing. No rising and falling to signal breathing. They crept around to see his face. Half of it was gone, a gory mess. What had appeared to be mud on the small of his back and on the seat of his trousers were bullet wounds.

"They shot him in the butt!" Freddie yelped. They tore out of there.

When Carney got home he told his father what they'd found. He was back living with him at the 127th Street apartment at that point.

His father said, "He a high yellow nigger with a mustache? That was probably Clive." He cackled.

Carney asked if they should tell the police.

"Who do you think dumped his ass there?"

Would he have laughed more or less if he knew that one day the cops would cut him down, too? More.

The usual New York City childhood: stickball, ringolevio, and bullet-ridden corpses. When John and his pals played ringolevio—the kids still played the old game, the chants echoing in the alley behind the townhouses—Carney ordered them to maintain a Strivers' Row boundary. The Row wasn't what it used to be, but it ran low on surprises.

The muzzle flash lit up the inside of the Cadillac DeVille for an instant, silhouetting the front seat, the back of Buck's head, Munson in profile. Munson shot his partner twice—another flash—and walked back to his car. The gunfire roused no movement in shanties in the park or buildings opposite. The mutt gnawed at its hindquarters.

Munson got in and placed the vinyl bag and Carney's briefcase at his feet. "That didn't go as well as I hoped."

Carney pulled on the door handle and Munson grabbed him with one hand, jabbed a pistol in his gut with the other. The detective gritted his teeth at his injury but held Carney fast. "You should drive," he said.

Carney couldn't stop himself from looking over at Buck Webb's ruined face as they drove past. His stomach flopped. When he turned west, people reappeared on the sidewalks, there were lights in the windows. The Cadillac had punched through, back into the world again.

"Where are we going?" Carney said. He was vibrating.

"It's more than one stop, I got to confess."

"Yeah?"

"Yeah," Munson said. "You're my partner now, Carney."

# SIX

They called him Corky because his older brother tried to drown him in the creek when he was five, but he "kept floating up." His longevity in hazardous trades reaffirmed the nickname. He made his money as a bookmaker in the '50s, covering the big fights, back when the dagos had it all fixed, from the boxers to the ringside judges to the sanitation trucks that hauled away the trash from the floor of the Garden the next day. When Bumpy Johnson muscled him out, loan-sharking covered the bills. Black dentists and black undertakers catered to a steady client pool; black shylocks more so.

In 1957, Corky Bell opened his private games to any comer who could handle the action and began a new career as a poker impresario. The first—and last—Memorial Day weekend game at the Aloha Room was arranged at the request of one of his longtime players.

Until recently the Aloha had been a dependable if unremarkable after-hours joint on Mount Morris Park West, its tiki decor a novelty uptown. Now that the fad had crested, the Aloha wore its age in the flaking Polynesian sea scenes on the walls and the smiley-face graffiti defacing the wooden totems. The red bulbs of the electronic tiki torches had burned out years ago and were no longer manufactured. Tendrils of fabric resembling long blades of grass skirted the small tables; most had fallen off or been plucked. Customers cottoned on to management's indifference—the surly and incompetent bartenders galled—and a new neighbor upstairs, a lawyer, liked to lodge noise complaints. Currently the Aloha Room was reserved for private engagements.

Corky Bell got it for free. The owner owed him six grand, couldn't scrape up the vig, thus this arrangement. For the game, Corky Bell brought in a generously sized poker table with dignified green felt and sturdy oak legs, so incongruous with the Aloha's South Pacific theme that it might have been a meteorite from a secret corner of space.

"They're going to remember where they were that first Memorial Day weekend because they spent it with Corky Bell," he told Lonnie. It was Thursday, May 20th, one week before the game. Lonnie was a dealer, on the up-and-up, and one of Corky Bell's first calls when he pulled something together. Regulars on the circuit knew him from Mo Mo's games at the Sable Club, or Mike Yella's Morningside game, where T-Bone Givens was gunned down by the Ryan brothers in the summer of '67 and went facedown in a bowl of potato salad. Lonnie didn't talk much. His sympathetic eyes took the sting from bad beats, and when complimented on his magic touch after a monster hand, he did not reject the notion.

Lonnie was in. It was almost like old times. In their heyday, Corky Bell productions were a holy enterprise. His game the weekend after New Year's was the hottest ticket in town, his July Fourth smoker a certified hoot, and his one-offs unforgettable if not always remunerative. His tables attracted politicians and bone breakers and narcotics peddlers, doctors, bankers, and preachers. White players took taxis up Park Avenue and commuted from the new suburbs to test themselves against authentic criminals. The grub was top notch, sandwich miracles from the storied Jewish delicatessens and sometimes prime rib under a heat-lamp gizmo, and the bartenders kept the players topped off, on loan from whatever cocktail lounge or nightclub was the rage that year.

Celebrities popped in. Not just his cousin Sylvester King, not just local musicians, but Hollywood types. New Year's '63, Peter

Lawford took a seat, in town "doing research for a part." Said he'd play a round and stayed for two days, cycling through a greatest hits of anecdotes when it got quiet or he felt unappreciated. "I look her over—she's got legs—and say, 'Any more like you at home?'" Sonny Liston sat in after he got laid out by Leotis Martin. Leroi Banks, the ventriloquist, was on hand with his dummy Mr. Charles flapping on his lap, just like on TV. The dummy talked shit all night, working blue material that wouldn't make it past the censors. "You went to the free clinic, baby? They say you got *splinters*? I wouldn't know anything about that." Liston had a reputation as an animal but giggled like a little girl at every dumb joke out of Mr. Charles's painted mouth. Big tipper, too.

Corky Bell didn't put on as many games as he used to. External forces: His girlfriend Stacey asserted New Year's rights and July Fourths they now spent in Sag Harbor, where she kept a bungalow. Internal forces: The rush, the pleasure of harnessing the energies of good luck and bad luck, of being a momentary conduit of fate, had been replaced by cold dread ever since Chickie James shot Skippy Damon in the face over a full house and the geyser of blood soiled the felt surface and cursed the chips, both of which had to be replaced.

Another bad omen. Too many to count. Harlem wasn't the same. Crooks these days had no code and less class. A cathouse set up next to his favorite fried-fish joint, and he had to see these young girls whored up outside when he got a craving for whiting on white bread. As a grandfather, it upset him. Slumming it in Harlem was more dangerous than exotic these days and white men with a taste for seven-card stud or hi-lo now hit the goulash houses in the Garment District. Corky Bell checked out the goulies once. Lasted twenty minutes before this cracker with a toupee and busted yellow teeth complained to management about sitting next to colored players. *Colored* was not the word he used. It was long enough to get the picture: fixed decks, colluding partners, bowls of steaming goulash if you got hungry, and unventilated rooms if lung cancer happened to be a side hobby.

When he got the call from Cameron Purvis about setting up a one-off Memorial Day game, he didn't realize how much he missed cards. Cameron Purvis grew up on Arthur Avenue in the Bronx and had been a mainstay of the holiday games, driving up from D.C., where he worked for the government. Corky Bell couldn't tell the white players apart, but Purvis stuck out because of his fucked-up job. "I'm out there introducing America to the wonders of 'Our Friend the Atom,'" he told him that first New Year's game, "one of the best friends we have these days." With new innovations in demolition, medicine, and agriculture, nuclear energy was more than a bomb, it was the future, today. "Let me tell you a thing about radioisotopes . . ."

By '63, the Cold War proved an impossible headwind. "I'm in shelters, now, buddy," he explained. Hawking backyard bunkers for the American Fallout Shelter Company. "It pays to be nimble." He was delighted to see Corky Bell arranging the seats when he arrived at the Aloha Room early Friday evening. Corky Bell was not the only one grateful for a reminder of the good old days; Purvis's work was not as fulfilling as it used to be. "I got sick of feeling like an errand boy for the RAND Corporation, you know what I mean?" The table stared silently. Currently he consulted for the U.S. military, doing image rehab on tactical-use herbicides like Agent Orange. "The average American hears the word *chemical*," he told the table, "and gets all sorts of negative associations. It's my job to rearrange the brain." The players nodded.

The first hand was at 8:06 P.M. on Friday, May 28th. Eight players opened up the action and the game sustained a vigorous ebb and flow of new blood, chumps, showboats, and colorful protagonists for the next few days. They rotated through five-card stud, draw, razz, ace-to-five lowball, deuce-to-seven, and hi-lo, with an all-day seven-card stud marathon on Sunday in honor of Purvis's dad, who served in two world wars and had been an aficionado. Memorial Day—a time to remember those who served. When the energy flagged, Purvis started up a round of "From the Halls of Montezuma" and revived the proceedings.

Diehards napped in the back room and returned after an audit of their botched hands and miscalculations, men skipped Saturday and returned for a forty-eight-hour stretch on Sunday. When Corky Bell needed shut-eye, his nephew George presided. Old-timers reminisced over previous menus, like the Reuben sandwiches from Levi's and the time Corky Bell ordered trays of fried chicken from Lady Betsy's and had to pause the game until "motherfuckers learn how to use a goddamn napkin." Was there enough food? Booze? The table mix of personalities lively and invigorating? A fistfight almost broke out over who fried the better bird, Lady Betsy's or New Country Kitchen. The scramble made Corky Bell feel ten years younger.

Holiday weekend games—July Fourth, Labor Day—usually petered out Monday afternoon, submitting to the real world and its imperatives. One can inhabit a dream for only so long. This Memorial Day seemed as if it was going to follow suit, but Cameron Purvis needed to keep going, and he made converts. He canceled his flight to Los Angeles—"meeting some idea guys from DuPont"—and informed his secretary of a death in the family. Players crawled home, showered and shaved, returned. Word got out and guys who couldn't make it Monday appeared Tuesday for another round. Corky Bell arranged for another day of the Aloha Room's shabby hospitality, rang Blackeye P's about a platter of roast beef sandwiches, and told his man at the station house that they'd be dropping off another envelope. Perhaps it was this call that drew the detective's attention to the game.

Lonnie switched off with two other longtime Corky Bell dealers until he punched out Sunday night, weary but content. Corky felt bad calling him up Tuesday morning. Lonnie said the tips alone were a month of shifts at the Whistle Stop, the bar he worked at off 125th. The dealer hosed himself off and was back at the Aloha by dinner.

At 10:35 P.M. on Tuesday, June 1st, they were down to four players. Only Purvis and Nelson Wright remained from the original table four days before. They were making too much money to leave: Purvis was up sixty K, Wright twenty-five. Wright operated a cathouse on Broadway that catered to visiting businessmen. Before the Hotel Theresa was converted into office space, the concierge used to slip guests cards with the name of the place—BILOXI—in neat type. Wright was the only Harlem crook at the table. Times had changed.

The other white man besides Purvis was a self-described talent manager, whom Corky Bell pegged as a degenerate gambler type. Over the course of play it became apparent that no one had heard of his clients or the "big rooms" he claimed to book them in, but he leaked money, a sopping failure, so went unchallenged.

The final player was a soft-spoken Negro architect from Newark. He told them what he did for a living, to uncomprehending stares.

"Black architect?" Wright said. "I didn't know they let us do that."

"They don't *let me* do shit," he said. "I take it." He had designed two hospitals and a nursing school. That was his angle, medical facilities.

Wright nodded, considering. "Solid."

Four players, plus Corky Bell, and Lonnie, and the security guard at the door, when the gunmen appeared.

In the old days, Corky Bell retained bruisers of the old school, stone-cold killers with specialties: stranglers, mincers, men with strong opinions on quicklime versus sulfuric acid. They barely moved or breathed, fading before the flamboyant antics of the table until suddenly called into action to manhandle a drunk, snap a bodyguard's femur, headbutt a white kibitzer who'd forgotten where he was.

Men misbehaved at Corky Bell games. No one had dared to rob one. To do so was to disrespect the uptown order and suffer the consequences. Doubtless the robbers were aware of this fact when they targeted the game.

Over the weekend, a two-man team had protected the Aloha Room, one on the door and the other at the bar. Finding replacements for Tuesday took longer than Corky Bell had anticipated. With the game winding down he decided to save a few bucks on the muscle and on the bartender, as he was happy to fix whatever the boys wanted—two lapses in protocol he wouldn't have permitted himself in the old days.

Tuesday's guard was Arnie Polk, a third-rater who'd been bounced from Chink Montague's organization for being "kind of spacey" and having "his head up his ass," per his performance reviews. Arnie would be the first to admit that violence was not his first passion.

From the brief, Arnie expected a docile crowd. His attention drifted. He made frequent forays to the sandwich platter and had the temerity to complain about the quality of the mayonnaise. When the robber pistol-whipped him, Arnie had been daydreaming about the Newport 30, the snazzy-looking keelboat on the cover of the May issue of *Top Boating*; he subscribed. Because of his bleak outlook, he'd furnished his daydream with misfortune: After a wrong turn, the sailboat wobbled on the mad heave of the Hudson in the wake of a cruise liner. He assumed the man had come to play—whoever heard of a white man knocking over a card game in Harlem? The robber slugged him and Arnie buckled to the parquet floor, where he played possum for the duration of the robbery. His deception went undetected. Didn't even flinch when the white robber took his gun, though it tickled.

The white one did the talking. He was sweating and disheveled and he wore a harried expression, but his bark made the players jump. The black robber's tentative air—"a startled quality" as Purvis put it later—made more than one player think he was on drugs, and thus a dangerous, unpredictable variable. His partner told him to hold up his gun. The black man did as instructed, but his arm slowly sank, capitulating to an invisible burden. This occurred multiple times during the robbery, as if he had a wrestling match inside him. "He was obviously a ruthless killer," the talent manager told his accountant later, "fighting hard not to murder us all."

Corky Bell stood. "Detective Munson?" he said, squinting.

The white man said, "Yes, yes."

"We paid your man at the station," Corky Bell said. "What the fuck are you doing? Also, you look like shit, motherfucker."

"I'm working," Munson said.

"Munson," Wright said. As the longtime proprietor of a neighborhood whoring concern, Wright made regular contributions to the 28th Precinct's pad. This man, his division, was in his pocket. But who was that nigger with him? He looked like a spaced-out druggie. Should be knocking over pharmacies for cough syrup, not card games.

"A policeman," Purvis said, trying to wrap his head around it.

Corky Bell turned to the black intruder. "You a goddamn cop, too?"

The gunman's hand dropped and he gave a slight but unmistakably guilty shrug, as if caught biting into the last cupcake.

The Aloha Room presented a tableau of tension and confusion, against an absurd tiki backdrop. The violation of a Corky Bell game, the interracial composition of the robbers, the revelation that the white man was a cop—it confounded. Corky Bell was right: None of them would forget this Memorial weekend game.

While the greater robbery unfolded, parties considered private capers. The architect made a quick assessment of the table; if the opportunity presented itself, he'd pocket some chips. At the same time, the talent manager surveyed Purvis's formidable, many columned empire of red and green chips. An outer settlement appeared undefended.

From the minute changes in their posture, Corky Bell gathered that the architect from Newark and the so-called talent manager were planning to swipe chips when no one was looking. Didn't matter how many chips these dummies stole if these thieves grabbed the bank.

To wit: Munson asked after the cash. When Corky Bell reiterated that he had paid the precinct and that the detective had no right, Munson shot a round into the ceiling.

The talent agent shrieked.

Corky Bell pointed to the bar. Munson told his partner to cover him and reminded him, with evident impatience, to hold his gun up "properly." As if scolding a kid over untied shoes. Half a minute later, the black man's gun pointed at the floor once more.

By now Lonnie and Nelson Wright were certain they recognized the second gunman. Lonnie thought he was that stick-up guy who liked to drink himself into a smudge at the Blossom, back when he worked there. Later that night, Wright decided he knew him from church, alto in the choir. Both men had purchased items at Carney's Furniture in the past, Lonnie an Egon dresser and Wright a Sterling Dreamer recliner.

Purvis said, "Oh, my lands."

Munson kept his gun on his captives. He chomped a roast beef sandwich from the spread, then reached down for the big metal box and set it on top of the bar. He gestured at Lonnie with his .38 and ordered him to get the key from Corky Bell.

Between dealing cards and tending bar, Lonnie had been embroiled in three stickups and three proper robberies in his life, on top of untold tantrums abetted by lethal props. He had dealt at tables where a bad beat or a suspicious flush had sent men reaching for their pistols, watched in muted wonder when Blackjack Martin pulled a .22 on the Accountant for flipping two pair. Each time he was certain he was going to die. His father, a button man for Caesar Mills back in the '40s, had been rubbed out and dumped in Mount Morris Park, over by the seesaws. Lonnie avoided the park and its reminders, and had been unsettled the entire weekend due to the proximity. He was sure, looking at the detective's gun, that Mount Morris was about to claim the latest member of his unfortunate bloodline.

Corky Bell opened his waistcoat and glared at the wall opposite. Lonnie reached into the man's pocket and extracted the key.

"We paid off the cops." Corky Bell sulked. "We paid you off."

"Lodge a complaint at the precinct." Food tumbled from Munson's mouth as he spoke. He ordered Lonnie to unlock the metal box. Munson had him covered if his hand emerged with a piece. It did not. Who wouldn't smile at all that cash? Players had cashed out, come and gone, but from the chips on the table there was more than a hundred grand. His estimate was correct. Four days of dinks, dummies, and whales splashing money around? A hundred grand easy.

Munson said he might as well take the box. "Beats wrapping it in my jacket." He closed the lid and commenced his retreat to the exit. His wounded arm—the weight of the box made him squint in pain. The players didn't move, and neither did Lonnie or Corky Bell and especially not Arnie the guard, who was making his bid for being the Laurence Olivier of playing possum.

Munson reminded his companion to hold up his gun. He did so. By the time they reached the door, the black man's arm was limp again.

Corky Bell said, "This is a Corky Bell game, goddamn it."

Munson cursed and charged back to the poker table to smack Corky Bell across the face with the butt of his gun. Corky Bell shrank to the floor and covered his head against the next three blows.

It was 10:49 P.M. on Tuesday, June 1st. The black robber had departed. Munson told the players to go back to their cards and wished them good luck. As the front door closed, they heard him shout after his partner, "Where do you think you're going?"

# SEVEN

Munson was cashing out. Ditching the force, his shakedown network, the city of his birth, and presumably his wife to start over far away. Carney assumed far away—you didn't split across the river to the Jersey suburbs after a burn like this. "I've had big scores, sure," Munson explained. "Plenty. But a real jackpot? Tonight I have to carve it out of the rock." He rat-a-tatted on Carney's briefcase, which was half full of stones and cash. Room for more.

Carney had stopped hearing the sirens when Webb slugged him. After Edgecombe, they filled the night again, each one a warning.

At the corner WALK turned into DONT WALK. Do it—drive the Cadillac into that diner, crash through the plate glass. That was one way to kill this evening in the crib.

Munson had murdered his partner minutes before. He dry-swallowed a pill. A species of upper, from his behavior. "How long have you been planning this?" Carney said.

"Thought I had a few more weeks. Mulling shit over. Then I got the subpoena, and it had been such a lovely weekend, like I told you, that I thought maybe it was a good New York weekend to go out on." He worked his jaw. "There's nothing here now."

Buck Webb said he wanted to "straighten it out like two white men." He got his wish. Was bumping him part of the plan or an improvisation? At some point, when Munson got in his partner's car or earlier, he'd considered whether or not the Knapp Commission could break his friend. Decided in the affirmative.

Munson allowed Carney to breathe as long as he was useful. Carney had an idea to call Calvin Pierce to ask the lawyer about his legal options. Such as: Was he now an accessory to a murder? He'd been a murder accessory before, once or twice—he'd lost count, frankly—but not to rubbing out a cop. Call Pierce—like Munson would let him pull over at a phone booth. Like he'd survive the night.

He intended to. His wife was coming back from a trip tomorrow and he missed her. "That—" Carney began.

"I don't want to talk about that," Munson said. "I have a list of errands. Some final collections. Then you drive me down to the Philly airport and I wave goodbye."

"Sure," Carney said. No point in asking where he was flying to. Bimini or Buenos Aires. Knowing which airport was too much information, given what Carney had just witnessed.

No, Munson was not going to let him go at the end of this. Like father, like son—the cops shot Big Mike Carney to death during a drugstore robbery.

The detective directed him downtown, to an address off Mount Morris, a wide Italianate brownstone. The Aloha Room? He'd heard of it. On the parlor floor, top of the stairs, bright light squeezed out of cracks in the thick curtains.

Munson held out a .38.

Carney stared.

"It's not loaded. It's not a trick."

Carney took it. "I'm not."

"You hold it. The more convincing you look, the less likely they are to fuck with you. Like most things in life."

"No."

"I already lost one partner tonight."

Carney's mouth flattened to a line.

"Joking," Munson said. "We go in, you just stand there."

"If they start shooting?"

"Avoid the bullets."

*Conscientious objector.* That was the term Carney was looking

for. *Because of my moral constitution, I must decline to serve.*
This was Munson's war, not his. He took the revolver.

First stop was the Aloha Room. His arm was so heavy it sank,
he couldn't help it.

Second stop was the pimp. A crime of opportunity, as they
put it.

They were on 126th and Lenox. Munson's last order after he
locked the poker haul in the trunk: "Drive." Carney took them
north, toward the 157th hideout. Perhaps they were done.

Munson said, "Pull over there." Pointed to two men on the
corner.

The flamboyant quotient in Harlem was at a record high these
days, thanks to manufacturing innovations in the synthetic-
material sector, new liberal opinions vis-à-vis the hues question, and the courageousness of the younger generation. The line
between the stylish and pimpified was unstable, ill-defined, but
everybody was having too much fun to complain. The men on
the corner were pimps, no doubt, given the warm night and the
superfluous layers. The taller one wore a purple suit with silver
piping, and a white, spangled broad-brimmed hat. His companion's long black leather trench coat draped on his shoulders like
a cape. The tiger-fur pattern on his shirt and red, white, and blue
cowboy hat created a macabre circus effect.

Munson directed Carney to park across the street. He asked for
the keys before setting out across the avenue.

"Detective Munson!" the taller man yelled. "Making the
rounds!"

Carney couldn't make out Munson's reply; its physical expression was plain. Munson grabbed the man by the coat and beat
him repeatedly across the face. The man staggered and sank, and
Munson battered him to the pavement.

The one in the black trench said, "Oh, my man, my man," and
split west, clacking in his crocodile-skin Cuban heels.

Munson kicked the man in the purple suit in the stomach
twice. He was out of breath. He walked to the corner and dragged

an aluminum trash can over with his good hand. He dragged it onto the man's body, and started kicking him through the can.

It might have been a terrible dream but for the old bat who threw open a window on the second floor and screamed at Munson to knock it off, she was trying to get some goddamn sleep. That's how Carney knew he was in the real New York City and not the nightmare one. Perhaps there was no difference anymore.

Munson returned to the Cadillac. He didn't rob the pimp; the beating was the point. The man moaned and squirmed on the sidewalk, so Carney knew he was not dead. Munson gave Carney the keys and waved his hand northward.

"I always hated that fucker. Everybody's bad, but some are worse, Carney." He popped a pill. "He's worse."

At the third and fourth stops, he told Carney to stay in the car but didn't ask for the keys. He thinks I'm trained now, Carney thought. Letting out a little more leash.

The bottle club was on 145th, a few doors in from Amsterdam. The front window was painted black and a line of red bulbs above it served as a sign. It was a weeknight, sneaking on midnight, but men and women milled around the entrance, refreshing themselves from the steamy interior. Smoking cigarettes and reefer and sipping booze out of disposable cups. Carney didn't believe Munson would start shooting up the joint but he'd certainly hurt someone if they stepped to him. Others came to the same conclusion, as evidenced by the stampede that boiled forth after he went inside. They followed Harlem Safety Rules, withdrawing far enough so as not to be the first cut down when the action spilled outside, but close enough for a good look at whatever craziness went down next. Tomorrow they'd shame friends who went home early.

Carney sank down in the front seat of the DeVille. Two men at the poker game were customers. (He confessed to a twinge of pride.) There was no telling how many of those carousers across the street were fans of quality, affordable home furniture. He'd advertised his holiday weekend sale in the *Amsterdam News* and two Caribbean papers; it was perfectly reasonable that some of these souls had come by for bargains. He started the car and waited.

Munson charged out of the club, cradling a dark blue bank pouch like a football. He whooped, stood disoriented in the middle of Amsterdam, then found Carney and the Cadillac. "Let's go, let's go!" The detective jumped in. Best he could, Carney hid his face from the crowd as they pulled away.

The fourth stop was quieter. The bodega was the only thing open on 132nd and Eighth. Munson checked the street, uptown and downtown, walked inside, and was out two minutes later. No person, no sound—gunshots, say, or agonized cries—exited the premises during his visit. The bodega money was in a rolled-up paper bag. "I'm like Robin Hood," Munson said, "except it's all for me!"

Carney didn't ask.

Munson added the cash to the briefcase and assured Carney he'd return it to him at the end of the night.

The fifth stop was Clyde's.

You didn't go to Clyde's Classic for a cut. The barber—there was only one—would fuck it up so bad, turn you into such a walking humiliation that you'd never return. Which was the point. Nonetheless, there was steady traffic in and out, and odd hours kept. The barber punched out at six P.M., and a very large man commenced his shift on a wooden chair outside the door to the back room. At all times the radio was tuned to 1600 AM—"The Big RL!"—at excruciating volume. From time to time the man in the chair tapped his foot to one of the new Motown numbers, or one of the increasingly slick sounds emerging from Philadelphia, but for the most part he kept his arms crossed, his chin sloped, and his lizard gaze level. His name was Earl.

Clyde's was a long-running front for Chink Montague's policy racket, confirmation of the longevity of his Harlem operation and his arrangement with the police. There had been two previous attempts to rob this numbers bank, in 1960 during Chink's war with Bumpy Johnson, and two years ago. The day after the 1960 attempt had been Earl's first shift at Clyde's; in addition to replacing his dead predecessor, he had helped sweep up the glass. The more recent raid was put down quickly. The would-be thief had been a neighborhood lowlife named Dizzy Huntley, immediately recognized despite the fake mustache and dark-rimmed glasses. It had been a slow night so Earl steered him into the back room, where he and the boys taunted and belittled Dizzy over his shoddy robbery skills and generally lackluster criminal sense until they got bored and punched his ticket.

Chink had assumed control of the location from Smiling Rick in a 1958 territorial expansion. As a souvenir, he kept the man's picture on the wall, where Rick posed star-crossed and Zoot-suited in front of the Cotton Club. Chink's runners dispersed over southeast Harlem, collecting slips from housewives and war vets, plumbers' assistants and bail bondsmen, working men of every stripe, the doomed and the blessed alike, as they bet the three-digit combination that might unlock the Vault of Happiness. The money and slips traveled from the network into the back room. After the day's races posted, determining which numbers had hit, the runners paid the winners their portion of that day's take. The majority remained in Clyde's back room until Thursday, when couriers picked it up to take to another of the gangster's headquarters.

"If I could wait two days," Munson said, "I'd really be in the money." He lit a cigarette. "But I ain't waiting around that long."

Carney and Munson had been parked twenty yards down from the barbershop for half an hour. Clyde's occupied the ground floor of a townhouse on Lenox off 121st. A residential block with a smattering of first-floor businesses. It got livelier up Lenox, as you approached 125th Street. Here it was quiet.

Carney asked what they were waiting for.

"You asked, what's a stakeout? Sometimes it's sitting and watching. Sometimes it's the wait for one last confirmation of what you've already decided to do. A man appears. Someone leaves. And the switch is pulled and it's time to go."

The dark green M102—OUT OF SERVICE—chugged up Lenox, as bright as it was empty. May and John took the 102 sometimes to New Lincoln, in the more honest hours. Were they worried he wasn't home yet, or glad for a night without parents? Who'd pay their tuition if Carney bought it tonight? He heard a whisper sometimes when he thought about Elizabeth's trip, that goblin voice. How did Munson put it, about partners and spouses? *They will drive each other batshit.* Was she sick of him, was that why she split town? A work trip. Or a man from the old days who lived in Miami or Chicago now, maybe a colleague from a satellite office she dreamed of meeting in person. He didn't detect anything when they talked on the phone. Still: the whisper. May and John's dad turns up dead in the gutter, their mother has started a new life in Chicago with some slick motherfucker. No, she had sounded fine when she called from the hotel and sincere that she missed them. If he ended up dead tonight, she'd be home tomorrow to take care of the kids. An image of Buck Webb's demolished face brought him back to 121st Street.

Munson probed his wound through his jacket. His finger came back dark and wet. "Whatever happened to that girl you used to have around the office?" he said. "Marie."

"She got married. Had a kid. Left, came back." A Munson envelope pickup, in the old days, was preceded by a short flirt with Marie. She feigned shock at the detective's banter but wore her "nice earrings" and her special lipstick on collection days. When it came to her attitude toward Munson, you had to infer from details. She kept her mouth shut about various aspects of Carney's store, and it was the same with her own business. It was clear her husband, Rodney, was bad news; whether she was capable of changing her life was less so.

"Husband's no good, huh?"

"I didn't say that."

"It's how you said it."

Carney had never met the cop's missus. Taught art in an elementary school, if he remembered correctly. Brassy Irish broad in Munson's characterization over the years, recognizing flaws, forgiving some, occasionally drawing a line. If she was out of the picture, it helped explain Munson's behavior, the dishevelment and the cornered-animal aspect on display.

"Angela coming along with you on this trip?" The moment Carney said it, the thought popped up: *He's killed his wife.*

Munson checked his gun. "My blushing bride has decided to visit her sister in Pittsburgh. Perhaps she will join me at a later date. You can't force people into things."

"But a gun helps," Carney said.

Munson ignored him. "Even if I didn't have a rain of shit coming down on me, who wants to live in this dump?" Munson said. His voice an exhausted growl. "Used to be the ghetto was the ghetto—now the whole city is the ghetto. Shitheels dumping newborn babies down garbage chutes. Thirteen-year-olds carrying their daddies' babies. Woman gets put through the wall so many times she blows out her old man's brains, then eats the gun herself. Old ladies chained to radiators while their grandchildren steal their welfare checks."

"Cycle of life."

They laughed.

"Asking about my wife," Munson said. "Pissing me off like we've been riding around for years."

"The gun. With Webb—it's the one you took from the Liberation Army."

"Yeah?"

"So you can plant it somewhere."

"Here I was, doubting you."

With that, they shut up for a time.

Once again he'd been swept up in someone else's scheme. True, Carney had called Munson first, but the detective had taken advantage of his salesman's personality, out to please. Seven years ago, Freddie spent his final days trying to undo a cata-strophic robbery. Carney hadn't gotten his cousin killed, but he'd been along for the ride. Like he was now, on Munson's kamikaze run through Harlem, riding shotgun to his rampage. Hurt who you want, take what you want. Kill who you want. When Munson talked about ringolevio, he was talking about the thrill of impu-nity, of bending the city to his will, then and now. What were civilian rules to white cops like Munson and his ilk? The last two hours had proved it plenty times over: Nothing.

Ringolevio—everybody played for different reasons. Carney cherished those days because no matter what happened, Freddie was there to bust him out. When he got nabbed, it was only a mat-ter of time before his cousin sprung him. And vice versa—if Fred-die went down, Carney started drawing up plans for the jailbreak. Half the time they got caught, it was for breaking the other one out of jail. The sun throbbed on windows and chrome and broken glass and then came Freddie's head popping out from behind the moving van, scoping out the territory, gauging his chances. Car-ney hopped on the stoop like a base runner, arm outstretched: I'm here, get me outta here.

Freddie wasn't around to spring him anymore. He'd have to do it himself.

* * *

The movement drew Earl's attention from yesterday's *New York Post*. He sat in his chair outside the back room, from which he had not stirred for hours. The sentry frowned. Carney was aware that his own expression curdled whenever Munson showed up for his envelope; he hadn't been aware it was a universal response. Earl rose and unlocked the door.

The radio was playing "I'll Be There" by the Jackson 5. Carney shivered. If Munson recognized the song, he made no sign.

Earl said, "Detective Munson." His affect reminded Carney of a rascal installed outside the saloon in a Western, slow-talking and too long unchallenged.

"Let's head back there," Munson said to Carney.

Earl took a step back. He appraised Munson, then Carney. The gun in the detective's hand made his intentions obvious, but the mind resisted. "So it's like that?" Earl said, with distaste.

Munson waved his gun, indicating for Earl to walk ahead of them to the count room. He patted him down. He stuck Earl's pistol in his waistband and tossed the blackjack onto a barber's chair. Munson noticed Carney. He'd told Carney to skip the gun this time and merely do as directed, but had not anticipated that the furniture peddler would raise his hands, don't-shoot style, once business started.

Munson shook his head. "Open the door, will you," he said.

The public face of Clyde's was dingy and yellow, the signs on the walls speckled with greasy clots of dust, the labels on the canisters and jars peeling and faded. The count room in back was the opposite, chipper and inviting. If you were going to spend long shifts tending the wheels and levers of a proper numbers operation, you might as well be comfortable. The oak paneling was a vestige of the building's life as a luxury townhouse on a once well-to-do stretch of Harlem, the icebox and stove were new-model avocado-green Frigidaire jobs. A chandelier full of bright glass hung over a '68 Collins-Hathaway dining table, upon which were the vestiges of a late supper of ham and potatoes. Carney hadn't eaten since noon.

The counting station—a cedar table with a neat array of automatic bill counters, task lamps, and organizers—was shut down for the night. A big Eureka Co. safe squatted next to the table, and on top of it a Panasonic portable TV showed a Christopher Lee Dracula picture with the sound off. Probably Channel 9, and John staying up past his bedtime to watch it. Carney wished he was home to scold his boy and then join him on the sofa to watch Drac do his thing.

The two back-room operators were Carney's age. Same make, different mileage. The short, sour-faced man was named Driscoll, Carney found out later. His dark trousers were held up by wide-band suspenders over a shirt of stiff white cloth. He had the probing gaze of a mechanic as he tries to figure out how much he can soak you. The cigarette stuck to his bottom lip whipped up and down when he spoke.

The taller man was Popeye. A lattice of small slashes marked Popeye's face, from close combat or a protracted torture session. His lifeless eye was a white teaspoon of milk. Popeye's spare, skeletal build and the tufts circling his bald head gave him a meek air, like he was a broken old man they kept around to sweep up. As the episode proceeded, Carney understood the man was completely feral.

Carney didn't recognize them. He'd tangled with Chink's drivers and muscle before, but there had been churn over the years. Hazards of the profession. Carney knew their boss, of course, and before he opened the door, was cursed with a brief vision of Chink Montague himself behind the door, glaring from his throne. Notch Walker was in ascendance, but Chink still owned a good share of uptown. Carney was relieved to find only these two men back there.

Munson directed the three men over to the icebox. Carney frisked Driscoll and Popeye, a procedure he conducted gingerly, to glares and half-muttered malice. He apologized.

"Watch those knives," Munson said. There was a knife block on the yellow Formica counter, next to a line of ceramic jars. Carney moved it out of reach.

"What's the joke, Munson?" Driscoll said. He looked at Carney and tried to place him.

"The joke is, give me the fucking money. The joke is, you think I won't shoot you."

Next up, the DJ put on "Maybe Tomorrow." Evidently they had stumbled into a Jackson 5 block. *No one else can make me cry the way you do, baby.* The song saddened Carney when May sang it at the top of her lungs, cavorting on her pink-and-yellow blanket in her room. What did she know of heartbreak and disaster? She didn't understand the truth of the words yet; she would. All the sorrows he met on the road remained at their stations, waiting for his children to come along. You sing the sad songs first, then you act them out.

If he was doing anything right as a father, however, his children would be spared kidnapped-by-homicidal-policeman. Few songwriters took this up as a subject.

Driscoll said, "You don't want to fuck with Chink."

"Chink will take it out of your hide," Earl added.

"Chink," Munson said. "They call him Chink because he's got eyes like a Chinaman. You think he likes that? It's disrespectful."

Driscoll frowned. He possessed the ability to articulate perfect sentences with a cigarette embedded in his mouth. It was stuck to his lip by saliva or a special epoxy, Shakespeare monologues couldn't budge it. To Carney: "Who are you?"

Carney resumed his don't-shoot gesture, as if pushing away something hot or sharp. "I'm just here," he said.

"What's your name?" Driscoll said.

"He's going to need something to put it in," Munson said. "The money." He pointed to the sample cases next to the counting table. Not the first time they had been stuffed with the lifeblood cash of Harlem. He ordered Driscoll to tend to the safe. Carney handled cases.

Driscoll glanced at Popeye: What to do? If someone was going to rob Chink Montague on your watch, might as well have it be a cop. You were protected in a way, like when a bank got hit and the teller handed over the goods—it's insured. Nothing you could do. Popeye's sour expression did not change. Driscoll kneeled before the Eureka safe and began his supplications.

Popeye spoke for the first time: "You touch that money and see." He had a high voice, womanish. Carney sized him up like a customer. Popeye appreciated that you didn't come back from a transgression like this. Chink paid good money to operate. If Munson let this crew live, Chink would be hunting for him inside an hour. Him and Munson's cop buddies, too, for fucking with the pad. Depending on Corky Bell's mood after the Aloha robbery, maybe the cops were already after him.

Next up the radio in the other room played the Jackson boys' "Ready or Not." Carney was certain that the night had driven him mad, and now he heard Jackson 5 songs all the time between sirens. He was thankful May didn't want Archies tickets. *Ready or not, here I come, you can't hide.* DJs sometimes played tapes to take a break, to have a cigarette on the roof or eat a sandwich in peace, let a girlfriend sit on their lap. It occurred to him that the DJ had stepped away from his booth, stepped away like God, and left them to interpret and endure his choices, like God. Set it up, roll the spools, let it happen.

"You guys don't know Detective Munson, like I do," Popeye said. "We know each other from his vice days, right, Munson? How long ago was that?"

Driscoll paused when Popeye spoke, turning from the dial to figure out his role in what was about to happen. Just as the barbershop was a front for the numbers operation, Driscoll's agreeability covered Popeye's vicious character. Something was going to happen; after riding with Munson all night, Carney was attuned.

"Keep going," Munson told Driscoll. The detective concentrated: Popeye and Earl by the icebox, the other one by the safe. Interpreting muscle twitches and tiny movements of the eye.

"What was that lady's name?" Popeye said. Outraged, not over the story but because his place of work had been defiled. He sneered a line of gold teeth. "Pimp name of Prince Mike had this sweet piece, worked those midtown hotels. What was her name, Munson? I know you remember. What you did. If you forgot, the Devil will tell you—it'll be on his list."

From the opposite side of the room, the low flame beneath the pot was undetectable. Popeye grabbed the handle and launched the contents of the pot—greens in oily, boiling water—across the room. It scalded Munson's face and hands and he screamed. He recoiled and fired, first at Popeye, and then at Earl, who had taken advantage of the distraction to grab a chair from the dining table and toss it at the detective. The chair hit Munson's chest, throwing off his aim. His shot missed Earl, but it stopped his insurrection; the man shrank back to the stove. Popeye fell and grabbed his leg, leaning against the icebox. The bullet had hit him below the knee.

Driscoll hadn't made a move. His face remained blank and bovine.

Munson said, "People in this fucking city. They will test you." He looked over his red hands. His skin ran scarlet, but he had not been badly burned. "Hurry the fuck up," he said. He shot a hole into the avocado icebox in revenge.

The safe unlocked with a sprightly click. Munson told Driscoll to join his companions on the other side of the room. He nodded at Carney. "Go ahead, brother."

Carney hadn't seen this much cash in one place since his extracurricular days. His own Hermann Bros. safe released a cold, metallic scent when opened, one that Carney associated with money. He had expected that scent here. Rubber bands tied the bricks of cash. He started transferring them to the first case.

"You got Stepin Fetchit here doing your business," Popeye said. He regarded the blood on his hands. "Notch put you up to this? You his nigger now?"

Munson shot Popeye three times, hitting him once in the chest and twice in the head. Three more holes in the Frigidaire; they were going to have to replace it. Everybody hit the ground, noses to linoleum. Only Munson stood, gun drawn, immobile. Carney peeked through his fingers. He thought the cop looked like a statue. A bronze figure off in the corner of a tiny city park, commemorating a man of power and influence, covered in pigeon shit. A name on a street sign. You pass it every day and never stop to see who it was you were supposed to remember.

# EIGHT

Ask the hungry dreamers to define *jackpot* and you'll get a thousand different answers. The waitress at the hash joint playing her same three numbers every day, the safecracker squinting through sparks, the hijacker kicking the driver from the cab and steering the truck to the drop—what's a jackpot? One says, hitting the jackpot means escape, the exit from miserable circumstances. Another offers that a jackpot is enough money that you never have to worry about money again, logic so circular as to be impregnable. Others might interpret *jackpot* in light of a different sort of fortune—good fortune, like a comfortable life, or a loving family, or a surfeit of luck in a terrible world. As he helped Munson bring the haul up to the 157th Street pad, Carney arrived at a more practical definition: If you need two men to carry it, it's a jackpot.

Heavy money. Carney held his briefcase. It contained the jewelry-store goods and the bodega cash. Munson carried the two black sample cases from the barbershop, into which the bottle-club money had been added. It had started raining, a tentative drizzle, foretold by cool winds around corners since the Aloha Room.

The front door of the building on Edward M. Morgan Place didn't lock. As Carney waited in the vestibule for Munson to open the second door, he checked out the ceiling. A new habit of his since he visited Aunt Millie one day and stumbled on a guy shooting up in the entrance. To flush the syringe of blood, junkies aimed upward and pushed the plunger. Over time the ceilings of certain vestibules and bathroom stalls and elevators—whatever removed you from the eyes of the world for a minute—became mottled with crimson spots. They lurked above everybody's heads, unseen, these sordid constellations.

Carney and Munson crossed the black-and-white tile of the lobby to wait for the elevator. It was a loud one, rattling in the shaft like a coffee can full of nails. "Don't apologize when you frisk someone," Munson said, "it's poor form. Hold a gun or don't. Frisk a man or don't."

"I sell home furniture."

The detective tested the weight of the cases, pleased. "The point is, choose—you're in or you're out."

"When did you choose to take out Buck?"

Munson shut up the whole elevator ride. When they got to the apartment, he said, "He wasn't the same man. They would have broken him."

The detective lit a cigarette. The briefcase and the sample cases perched on the coffee table like primitive totems. "Anyway, it's after midnight," Munson said, "so that's a yesterday thing. Today is about waiting for the man who's bringing me a new name and a new ID. We hit the airport and I'm out of your hair. Can you handle that?"

Carney said yes.

Munson made like he was going to open one of the cases and count the money. He looked at Carney and stopped himself. "There's a twenty-four-hour joint up the block on Broadway— why don't you pick up some sandwiches?"

"I won't run?"

"We both know that. And some beer—more beer."

Carney was the only person on the street. The streetlight changed with a foreboding thunk, and a handful of cars surged forward. Out this late, he was usually more aware of what was going on around him, per his father's lessons. In Mike Carney's world, the city was overrun with nasty characters out to "knock you upside your head." Vigilance was paramount. After a few hours of being Munson's partner, he'd take getting knocked upside the head.

Two men killed tonight. Munson had stopped his rampage after dropping Popeye—no one, including Munson, had known which way it was going to go. Carney emptied the barbershop safe and they were out on the street a minute later. No curses or oaths from the remaining men followed them, just the chipper harmonies of the Jackson 5 singing "Stand!"

A few hours earlier, Munson didn't permit Carney to be alone in the car with the keys. At the bottle club and the bodega, he let Carney keep them. Now Carney was solo, headed up Broadway to the only establishment open on this stretch, a corner bodega with a red-and-yellow awning and blinking lights: El Charrito Grocery Deli.

Maybe he and Munson were partners now, after all Carney had seen. Certainly Carney was sick of him, one of Munson's signs. He recalled that first ride with the cop in '64, when Munson bragged about infiltrating activist groups. Who would Carney tell? Family man like him, with vulnerabilities. Who would listen? Munson was invincible.

He gestured to the clerk through the bulletproof glass and waited for the two ham and cheese and the two six-packs of Rheingold. El Charrito was the terminus of the leash, the boundary of the game. The rain snuck under his collar.

How did Freddie put it? "It's not the same if you don't cheat a little."

\* \* \*

They gobbled up the sandwiches, Carney on the couch and Munson slouching in the director's chair. "The guy's a genius," Munson said. "Forge anything—I've seen it. From the Ukraine, now he lives out by Coney Island. He's always going on about Nathan's. His granddaddy used to make sausage, and he says the Nathan's hot dog is a perfect forgery of what he used to get back home. He aspires to the art of Nathan's." He dislodged a nugget of gristle from his teeth. "Anything in the world, you can find in this city. Or that used to be true."

Munson pointed at the red-and-black ceramic imp and claimed to have a funny story about how it came into his possession. Carney had been correct—it was a souvenir of a big night out, in this case when Munson and Webb put the squeeze on a massage parlor in Chinatown. He tuned out the story, distracted by what awaited as morning approached.

"You want it?" Munson said. "Maybe sell it in your store as a decorative piece."

Carney declined.

"I'd have to get my cut."

"You take your cut, Munson."

"You're looking at me like, why all this tonight?" Given the night's adventures, his face remained untroubled. "The money comes in, the money goes out. I have a boat. It is a very nice boat, keep it in Bay Shore and I can't take it on the plane. You know how it is. You bought those two buildings?"

"Yes."

"Heard about that. I had a piece of a building once." Munson lit a cigarette. "They have a saying at the DA's office: Detectives are poor in their twenties, rich in their thirties, and in jail in their forties. Which is a fucking insult, because I made plenty of money in my twenties."

"There's still the jail part."

"We're here to head that off at the pass."

The bedroom door had been closed since Carney returned from El Charrito. The money was no longer on the table, so he assumed that's where it went. How much did Munson take in tonight? Enough to find a hidey-hole and fix it up nice, and off the jewelry when he got settled. He noticed one of Munson's guns on the rickety coffee table, next to two empty beer cans. Was the other one in the ankle holster? He couldn't tell.

Munson rose to get a better view of the street. "That him now?" It wasn't. "The view from our place—my place—on Fifty-fourth is something out of a postcard, but I'm starting to like this one better." He yawned. "It's not so lit up this late, so it's like a person: getting shut-eye, looking peaceful after a long day."

The snub nose of the building reminded Carney of the prow of a ship. The director's chair wasn't the helm but the crow's nest, allowing a survey of the dark blue motion of the city night. Munson's head dipped drowsily. Carney saw him fight it off. For all his bravado, the vicious front tonight, the detective was spent. The days when the streets were his streets and he swaggered through with rude and rowdy charisma were over. He wasn't the same man he'd been ten years before. It was 1971 and the man and his city were versions of themselves, embers burying themselves in layers of their own ash.

"Here he is," Munson announced. "Charging me an arm and a leg for the rush job and the schlep." The Ukrainian rang the buzzer half a minute later.

Munson returned to the crow's nest to stub out his cigarette. He lit another. "What I don't get is, where's the apostrophe?"

Carney gathered he was supposed to join him at the window.

"The DONT WALK sign," Munson said. "It goes WALK, then DONT WALK comes on and they forgot to put in the apostrophe."

"I assume it was on purpose," Carney said. "To save space."

"All this time I thought it was a mistake and everyone pretended not to see it."

The Ukrainian knocked on the door and Munson padded over to let him in. It happened quickly: Notch Walker and two of his men thundered out of the hallway and into the living room. One of Notch's men wrestled with Munson, the duo banging against the walls until they crashed into the center of the room.

Notch sidestepped the mayhem when they got close to his feet, mouth wilted in disdain. "This cracker thinks he's Bruno Sammartino." Notch's other goon kicked Munson in the stomach until he capitulated.

One man covered Munson with a small pistol while the other frisked him. Frisked him with conviction and purpose—Munson would approve—and directed him over to the wall. The detective squatted next to the statue of the imp, arms crossed, sadness and fury in his eyes like a beaten junkyard dog.

Two young men joined the party, leading a gaunt, middle-aged white man into the living room. The Ukrainian. He didn't look scared; more curious. His red wool hat had gone askew. He straightened it. Carney gathered that they'd put his face in the peephole for Munson to approve, and rushed in once the door opened a crack, Notch's men collaring the detective.

From their mirthless features and military attire, the two young men herding the Ukrainian were not Harlem hoods, who usually perked up at a burst of violence. Berets were a neon sign these days: We are throwing off our chains. Not Panthers, cool and slick in black turtlenecks and black leather jackets. These guys were BLA, training for the coming war. Race war, class war—they weren't picky, long as it got going toot sweet.

The next time Carney saw the leader was in the newspaper months later: Malik Jamal of the Black Liberation Army. The accompanying photograph came from a bank's security camera. In person, he was tall and lithe, with a soapbox voice strong enough to drown out passing trucks and heckling drunks on 125th.

"It's me again, pig," Malik said, confirming that the detectives had robbed him last Friday. The second BLA soldier had the build of a heavyweight boxer and wore a tight black T-shirt and camouflage pants. The lenses of his sunglasses were very, very dark, but he found his way around okay.

Munson looked at Carney, as if he wanted him to grab the detective's gun from the coffee table and toss it over. Or start shooting. Carney kept his face as blank as cement.

Notch Walker grimaced as he appraised the messy apartment. Between his imperial poise and large frame, he seemed too big for the room. A long, burgundy leather trench hung on his shoulders like a tyrant's cape. His shirt was untucked; he'd thrown some clothes on hastily.

"Detective Munson!" Notch said. "Look at you, with the exploits. Been hearing about you all night."

Munson cussed, his voice regressing to a rascally Hell's Kitchen accent. Notch's men slapped him around to quiet him.

"You the furniture guy?" Notch asked Carney.

"Carney's Furniture on 125th."

The gangster frowned. "Got me out of bed," he said. "Where's the shit?"

Carney nodded toward the closed bedroom. He exhaled: sprung from jail.

Carney had asked the bodega clerk to break a dollar bill. The man claimed to be low on change. That left Carney with three dimes and little time before Munson got wise. No one answered the phone behind the bar at Nightbirds, which was unfortunate and exasperating.

The operator put him through to Donegal's and the receiver lifted for a moment—raucous music and laughter—and then cut off again. He checked over his shoulder to see if Munson had come downstairs. Buford answered the second call.

Donegal's remained the preferred watering hole and refuge from family for an older generation of uptown crooks. Carney's father had been a regular, and on more than one occasion had left young Ray on a barstool for a few hours while he went out on "business." The clientele was older, but Carney felt at home among these retirees and fellow dropouts from the game. They traded gossip about the big scores, the latest capers, and dispensed wise and rueful jokes about raw deals, bonehead crooks, and the nefarious workings of the metropolitan law enforcement apparatus.

Buford tended bar Tuesdays, but sometimes he didn't. Carney finally drew a good card after a day of busted hands. Buford was an answering service for criminal associates, his yellow reporter's pad by the cash register an almanac of crooked enterprise. If the cops had been able to break his code—which was not really a code but a species of atrocious penmanship—they'd close a thousand cold cases, decades worth of confidence games, executions, and hijackings big and small.

In this case, Carney asked him to deliver a message instead of taking one, and the bartender was glad to oblige, seeing as he owed Carney for a sweet deal on a dinette set last December. Buford had reconciled with his long-lost daughter and wanted to host a proper Christmas dinner for the first time since that "fateful winter of '46."

Carney had never seen the man outside Donegal's. The barkeep shuffled sheepishly through the furniture store, ashamed to be caught in a square activity like browsing. Buford said, "I want classy, but not stuck-up."

Carney said, "Gossamer by Egon."

Buford's ability to get in touch with Notch Walker's people was self-evident. He'd suggested they hit Nicky Boots first, who'd settled up half an hour before and should've been home by then. "We'll wake his ass up." Nicky Boots was out of the game, unless some trifling penny-ante shit came up, which he found irresistible. He lived off his military pension. His sister's boy was roguish and sold dope for Notch Walker. Nicky Boots thought his ten years in Sing Sing might deter his nephew but it proved unpersuasive. He'll get the word through, Buford told Carney.

"Make sure they enter where they can't be seen from the top floors," Carney said. "He'll be watching." He propped open the interior door of the vestibule with an A&P flyer. Four minutes later he and Munson were eating ham and cheese.

Munson's mouth worked silently as he reconstructed Carney's betrayal. He shrunk. "I would have let you go," he said. "I just needed a hand."

Carney looked away, to the statue. Of Munson's several errors this night, informing his captive that there was "probably a bounty" on the cop was particularly ill-advised.

Malik Jamal's lieutenant covered the detective while Notch's men looked for the money. They emerged with the briefcase and the sample cases and opened them up on the couch. Notch Walker whistled. "Anyone you didn't fucking rob today, nigger?" He nodded to his men, which they interpreted as an order to toss the place. They started with the bedroom.

"They said you beat up Long James," Notch said. Carney took this as a reference to the pimp on Lenox.

Munson glared at Notch and Carney in turn, unable to decide which man he hated more.

"What for?" Notch said. "He never hurt anyone."

"Of course he did," Munson said.

"As far as pimps go . . ." Notch shrugged. No point in nit-picking. He noticed Carney. "My mom bought a living room set offa you. Way back. Still has it."

"I like to think people come back because it reminds them of home."

"Nicky Boots says you're a fence."

"Formerly."

"Because I have some stuff I'm trying to off—nice stuff."

"I'd be happy to find it a nice home. For your mother."

The Ukrainian had been sitting quietly in the director's chair by the window, where he'd been assigned after they frisked him. The forger squinted at the rest of the cast; he had joined an improbable ensemble of cops, furniture salesmen, gangsters, and black revolutionaries. Dangerous theater. It couldn't be said he did not meet interesting people in his line of work. The Ukrainian knit his fingers and held them between his thighs, like a dunce who'd been sent to the corner. "Life's rich pageant," he mumbled.

Malik approached him, stopping to kick Munson on his way over. "Who are you?"

"I'm what they used to call a scratcher," the Ukrainian said. "Dupes, counterfeits, identification. Turn wrong names right. I was making a delivery." He reached into his windbreaker pocket—slow—and gave Malik a folded manila envelope.

Malik examined the driver's license inside and asked if the

man had a card. "Never know when you might have to run to Cuba." The Ukrainian wrote his information on one of the blank business cards he kept in his wallet and gave it to him.

Munson asked for a cigarette. Malik said they cause cancer and smacked him.

Notch's men banged about, punching holes in the bathroom's drop ceiling, pulling drawers to the floor, cutting up the mattress and the living room couch. They didn't uncover any treasure beyond the steamer trunk of firearms in the bedroom closet—pistols, shotguns, a submachine gun. They dragged it into the living room. Malik Jamal smiled.

"We'll split that," Notch said.

"Of course," Malik said.

"Right."

Notch nodded at Carney and said he'd be in touch about the bounty and the merchandise he wanted to get rid of. Malik looked over and opened his mouth to speak, but thought better of it. A request? A warning? Carney never found out.

*Did you play ringolevio uptown?* Everybody played, but maybe the rules were different place to place. Munson had been straightening things out like a white man all night. He was about to learn how Harlem sorted things out.

The detective had stopped muttering and cursing and now fixated on a spot between his shoes. One of Notch's men hoisted him up, Munson groaning at his manhandled arm. The pistol jabbed between vertebrae kept him docile. The gangster took the briefcase and the revolutionaries carried the sample cases. Notch's other man tugged the crate of guns behind him, scoring the parquet floor in grooves. Carney hated to see a nice old wood floor get nicked up.

Munson didn't look at Carney as they led him out. The Ukrainian brought up the rear. He doffed his cap. The door clicked shut.

That left Carney and the statue. Two witnesses who would never testify.

The odds of recovering his briefcase from the mobster were poor. Best to think of it as part of the price of escape.

There was the matter of why Munson had been so protective of the bedroom. It wasn't the guns. Apartment 8B had been slovenly, but the current shambles was absolute. Notch's men had tossed the bedroom with dedication and ardor, jumbling the dresser drawers in a pile, flinging Munson's few clothes—a spare tan suit and some undershirts—on top of the ripped-open mattress. The white envelope caught Carney's eye. Inside were two tickets to the July 16th Jackson 5 concert, fifth row Rotunda at Madison Square Garden.

The rain splashed off the sill so he closed the windows. He hoped the kids had shut the windows at home before they went to bed. He'd be there soon either way. As Carney closed the crow's nest windows, he spotted two fires in lower Harlem, the big blazes roiling and scheming in the dark. Burning ships on black water. Fire trucks were on the way, from the sirens.

# NINE

He asked May why they went by the Jackson 5 when there were six of them.

"Johnny Jackson's on drums. They say he's a cousin but he's a friend they grew up with."

The Jackson boys were up front, three of them dancing and singing center stage, flanked by the guitarist and bassist.

"Who's that on guitar?" Carney asked. "Marlon?"

"Tito! Shh!"

The opening act was some combo Carney had never heard of, the Commodores. They were fine. He knew all the Jackson 5's songs from May's endless replays—the speakers in that portable record player of hers infiltrated every corner of the house—and now that they were onstage he was really enjoying himself. It was his first time in the new Madison Square Garden. The bowl was huge, a massive arrangement of tiered bleachers and boxes. The payoffs, kickbacks, and overall construction grifts must have been a magical thing.

Carney was a last-minute substitution for Elizabeth. Once he got the tickets—after all that struggle and blood—the concert was swiftly classified as a Girls' Night Out deal between mother and daughter. Their squabbling ceased on Elizabeth's return, and now she and May were in a new romance. Six weeks later, however, the big Alabama floods forced Elizabeth to the office to rebook travel. Catfish were swimming in the lobby of the Birmingham Grand, they said. Carney was delighted to escort May after paying for the tickets in various currencies.

The crowd was mixed, mostly under twenty-one. Carney and the other dads exchanged nods and pretended to enjoy the proceedings less than they did. The young girls screamed at every flirty remark from the stage and smacked their hands together at the choreography. The music was loud, the clothes louder. The Jackson boys capered and twirled in tight costumes with multicolored zigzag patterns. Rainbow vests with layered spangles swished and snapped, and the guitarist's red satin applejack cap was big enough to smuggle in a Christmas ham. Carney's upbringing was such that he couldn't help but opine that flare trousers were well suited for quick access to an ankle holster.

Munson's Garden connection had come through with primo tickets. There had been two hours between Carney leaving with the Benson haul and his return. Munson must have gotten the tickets then, and got stabbed or shot in the arm while doing it. Unless he'd robbed someone else on his way back—he'd crammed a lot into that final night.

So had Carney. He was lying on the parlor sofa, sore and exhausted, when Elizabeth got home that Wednesday. She wore a smile, partially because of her mood, which had improved, and partially because she wanted to see his reaction to her hair. She had cut it off and now wore a natural, inch-high. She posed, showing off her profile, the exquisite curve of her skull. The Afro suited her. "I got the name of a woman on the South Side."

He groaned when he stood to embrace her and explained he'd been preyed upon by two young men. One of them had a gun. The other one socked him in the stomach. Luckily he didn't have any money on him. "Oh, you poor thing. This city is something else." He said he'd bruised up. She said, let me see. One thing led to another. She was back.

That was the day after Munson's jackpot. Once the kids left for school, he'd hit Three Brothers for an egg sandwich and picked up a stack of papers at the corner. Webb's murder had made the morning edition. Martin Diaz Jr. of Edgecombe Avenue was out walking his terrier when he discovered the dead cop in the Cadillac. Around midnight—was Munson robbing the bodega at that point? Carney's recollections of that night were disintegrating. The bruises on his chest provided physical proof. A week later they were gone.

The first reports pegged Webb's death as another cop killing by radicals. Carney searched for more, but the newspapers dropped the story after Thursday's update that Munson had disappeared—ditched town, or dead. With the Knapp Commission probing the two partners, downtown must've been going nuts. If there was an investigation underway, it happened away from public scrutiny. Carney no longer had a source in the police department, and it would be years before he got another one. By then, Munson's and Webb's activities were dwarfed by the abuses of the Special Investigations Unit. Times change and you have to keep up. Shaking down a poker game was a failure of imagination compared to stealing millions of dollars of dope out of the evidence room and selling it back to the peddlers you'd confiscated it from.

The Jackson 5 shook off the last song and readied for another sortie. The smallest Jackson movement, every tremble, elicited a wave of squeals from the Garden.

"I'd like to talk to y'all tonight," Michael said, "about the blues."

Carney chuckled—the kid was ten.

"The blues?" Marlon or maybe Jermaine asked.

"Yeah, the blues. Don't nobody have the blues like me. I may be young, but I know what it's all about."

The boys bit into "Who's Lovin' You" and the building rattled. The girls screamed. There were rumors about guys the mob had rubbed out and buried in the concrete foundation below. The noise would've woken them up. Carney shouldn't have laughed. What ten-year-old black child didn't know the blues?

Friday night, three days after Munson's uptown tour, the police apprehended suspects in the Jones and Piagentini murders and the attacks on the two policemen who'd been protecting DA

Hogan's residence. Social-club stickup on Park and 171st in the Bronx, one of the victims sneaks away and rings the cops. Two of the robbers, Richard Moore and Edward Josephs, had been Panther 21 defendants, but jumped bail and fled to Algeria for a while.

Reading the *Times,* Carney couldn't tell if they were Panthers or ex-Panthers who'd joined the Liberation Army. One resembled Malik Jamal's sidekick, the guy who'd dragged out Munson's crate of weapons. Carney followed the story but never came across a better picture of him. When Malik Jamal knocked over that bank in Secaucus, New Jersey, did he have Munson's shotgun in his hands? Munson had ripped them off and ended up underwriting the revolution.

The other half of the jackpot went to Notch Walker. Notch stopped in Carney's store that autumn with a satchel containing six Panerai Radiomir watches from the 1940s. Miraculous devices. Carney's go-to watch man couldn't handle that kind of weight, but Green had mentioned a contact who specialized, an old Polish guy. Green was turning out to be a good connection. It was nice to tuck away bricks of cash into the old safe again.

Munson was right: You're in or you're out.

Notch could have sent one of his men. He came in person. In the daytime, he dressed more conservatively, and might have been any young man on his way to an office job downtown— charcoal flannel suit, white shirt, and bland necktie. His bodyguard waited in the showroom and appeared to be in the market for a new floor lamp. Larry descended upon him.

Notch and Carney did a deal for the watches and shook hands. There was no mention of a bounty. Perhaps it had slipped Notch's mind, and on subsequent occasions as well. The gangster took his leave. He stopped in the office doorway and gestured at the display models.

"You pay Chink to operate?"

"Yes."

"For now."

The next week when they firebombed the Satin Room, one of Chink Montague's after-hours joints, Carney assumed the mobsters were embroiled in another war. *Eyewitness News* on Channel 7 ran footage of the firemen "bravely battling the blaze," which had overtaken the surrounding tenements. The dispossessed formed a crescent at the edge of the twirling lights, haggard in their pajamas, clutching whatever they could rescue.

Local signs of an ongoing collapse. Sometimes when Carney got wind of the latest outrage—a bloody slaughter in a Vietnamese hamlet, a rash of lethal ODs from a bad batch, an unarmed teenager cut down by cops—he suspected the revolution had already happened, only nobody could see it and no one had come along to replace what had been overthrown. The old order was rubble, bulldozed into a pile with the long-held assumptions and rickety premises, and now they waited for someone to tell them what was next. No such person appeared.

"Good night, New York City! We love you!"

The boys from Gary, Indiana, were a soft touch for an encore. The Jackson 5 started up "Never Can Say Goodbye" and Carney thought of the death of Munson. The bassist and the guitarist—Tito, whoever—tumbled into the wistful melody as their brothers swayed and sang between them, three bodies expressing a single lament. May looked up to the stage and crooned with Michael, preserving every pause and intonation from the vinyl; she had summoned them to her city through her devotions. She grabbed Carney's hand. It had been years since she'd taken his hand in hers. Carney found himself mouthing the words, though the song was a lie. It wasn't hard to say goodbye at all. As the days smeared into each other it only got easier.

# NEFERTITI
## T.N.T.
1973

"City like this, it behooves
you to embrace the fucking
contradictions."

# ONE

The furniture was not to Zippo's taste—it was perfect. The sleek silhouette that had been omnipresent a few years before, all those jet-age lines and tapers, was yesterday's news. Overflowing sofas, chubby ottomans, and plush, bulging armchairs surrounded him in the showroom. Country in a recession, everybody feeling the pinch, but you can enjoy your comfy throne at home. Couches like that orange-and-brown behemoth along the wall were what real people sat on, the great unwashed audience. Zippo had walked past Carney's Furniture all the time when he lived uptown but had never been inside. Look at this stuff. His hunch had been correct: The store was perfect.

This slick young brother popped out from a back office and zeroed in on him. Downtown, Zippo's ensemble would have repelled the staff of most stores. Who's this hippie-ass Negro in snakeskin pants and megawatt yellow blouse? Uptown, he was not so novel. Downright square in some circles. He asked the salesman if the owner was around.

Zippo plopped down on a big mustard-colored sofa while he waited. Black-and-white-striped leather boots on the zebrawood coffee table, crossed at the ankle. As a rule, he only dug uncomfortable, minimal designs from Europe—leather pinned by chrome, densities of curvilinear plastic—but he had to admit this sofa made an eloquent case for owning comfortable furniture.

"Zippo," Carney said. He looked the same. Humble merchant, upstanding muckety-muck in the community. Having worked for the man back in the day, Zippo knew otherwise. "What can I do for you today?" As if it hadn't been years. Like he'd sold Zippo a rug the day before.

"I have a business offer," Zippo said.

"I'm not in the market for photos," Carney said.

He frowned. "I don't do that anymore. I'm a director now. Movies."

Zippo watched the man cook up distasteful scenarios. "Not that kind," Zippo said. "Hollywood movies." He cranked up his work smile. "I'm going to put you in pictures."

\* \* \*

Nine years ago the *Harlem Gazette* ran the best pics from Zippo's Miss Laura–Wilfred Duke series, with prominent play on the cover and in the spread inside, credited to "Anonymous." What was the point of getting his work out there if no one knew it was his? Usually people called pics like that blackmail stuff, "compromising photographs," but Zippo considered them just the opposite: uncompromising. They didn't flinch from the primitive mechanics of desire, the hardwired yearnings. The black bars across his subjects' faces turned them into vessels for the viewer's erotic truth. When the cheap newspaper ink smudged on your fingers you understood you were implicated. Yes: A precise and uncompromising art.

Zippo restrained himself from badgering the newsstand guy: "I did this." He thrilled to see his work in the world, in the hands of a faceless but approving public. Out in the open—unlike his boudoir work, stashed under the mattress or hidden in the sock drawer and occasionally pulled out for dreamy appreciations or masturbation fuel. He owed Carney for this realization, for hiring him in his scheme to ruin the banker Wilfred Duke.

After the Duke job, Zippo continued the boudoir work, posing shy wives and compliant girlfriends and budding exhibitionists, and laid off—more or less—check kiting and other illicit activities. He added pet portraits to his services. The pet sideline was lucrative and generated strong word of mouth, as opposed to the risqué stuff. In a few months he'd gone legit.

It took Uncle Heshie's death for him to make a change. Zippo had always been the old man's favorite. "You see things cock-eyed, like me," he told the boy as he shared his latest tinkerings, the sketches and doohickeys that populated his workshop. Herschel Lefkowitz was an inventor, a father of patents. He was born in Odessa and settled on Ludlow Street on the Lower East Side in 1906; his family's house had been burned down the previous October. Pogroms, massacres. America was in the massacre racket, too, Heshie observed, but they concentrated on Negroes and Indians for the most part. He figured they'd come for him once they ran out, but that might take years.

According to Heshie, there were two types of inventors: those who identified deficiencies and provided remedies and improvements; and those who could see the invisible, discover what was lacking, and will it into existence—"fill the hole in the world." Uncle Heshie belonged to that latter tribe. "I'm an artist, the way I look at it. I have it in my head and then I bring it into being." Of all his inventions, among the reversible zippers and spring-loaded can openers, the most lucrative and enduring was the ceramic toothbrush mount, that sensation found above bathroom sinks the world over. When his niece Dorothy married Henry Flood, a Negro schoolteacher from Harlem, he hosted the ceremony in the garden of his Riverdale mansion. Toothbrush money, the whole shebang.

Heshie was the only member of the Lefkowitz family in attendance that day. They'd made the trip over within months of one another, a staggered heap of battered briefcases and bad teeth, but had since diverged. Where his relatives saw in Henry a colored brute, book learning or no book learning, Heshie recognized a fellow refugee. He'd fled Europe's genocidal rehearsals and Henry the murderous designs of Alabama. Now they were New Yorkers.

When Zippo was seven, his father had a heart attack on the

A train. They were returning home from the Children's Zoo in Central Park. As his father slumped at his feet, the other riders noted the boy's detached affect, as if the tragedy was happening to someone else. As if he were a passenger on another train altogether and rushing through a separate darkness. Zippo's balloons bumped against the ceiling of the car and made a sound like a distant heartbeat. Heshie looked after the boy from then on, paying for his summer camp and underwriting his hospitalizations when "the fire thing" manifested itself.

Everybody called him Zippo after the fire thing, even his mother. Not Uncle Heshie. "No one got hurt," he said. "Except some buildings."

Heshie left Zippo a monstrous sum in his will, contingent on his nephew finishing his education; after high school Zippo had pursued an autodidact curriculum of photography and petty larceny. Zippo's next incarnation was Heshie Lefkowitz's final invention: He enrolled in art school, Pratt Institute in Brooklyn, and stepped into himself.

A fire will catch on its own, given the proper conditions; an accelerant multiplies its power, velocity, and hunger. Pratt was kerosene and the changing culture a bellows. Zippo made his mark on campus with his first group show. He was a couple of years older than his fellow students; his experience on the crooked side enriched his work. *Blue Movies* reframed twelve photographs from his boudoir days, with a row of six close-ups of faces over another row of six clients' bodies. Frames in a film strip. None of the faces—expressions in a spectrum of coy, downcast, aggressive—belonged to the fragmented bodies. Feather boa, strap of a nightie. Elbow crevices and somehow maudlin nipples.

"I chose the ones with the maximum erotic charge," Zippo told the class.

"A brittle sensuality," answered the professor. Zippo's photography professor lacked black acquaintances and it had never occurred to him to consider black people as sexual beings. He gave Zippo an A.

Like many artists Zippo had been starved of attention in his younger days, and like many artists he channeled a modicum of praise into a contempt-of-audience phase: Invincible! He took to dressing like a Negro Salvador Dalí and penciled in a handlebar mustache. Shambling in velour, he pushed a watermelon in a baby carriage down DeKalb Avenue and harassed strangers, demanding to know if they "liked his baby chile." Everybody assumed he was high most of the time. He wasn't.

The jazz loft scene was taking off downtown. Greene Street was holy, Mercer Street was almost holy, Wooster Street was on the way to holy but the train was delayed—Manhattan in pockets was a refuge of sacred hip. Two dollars got you keg beer and discordant reveries that harassed the bones. One night Zippo and Ornette Coleman stood before the open windows of a second-story loft owned by some music-industry guru. Gulping the night air. He asked Ornette Coleman how much his own loft cost, a few blocks away.

"What?" Zippo said. The music was loud.

Ornette repeated the sum.

Zippo could swing that. Toothbrush money. He bought a two-thousand-square-foot loft on Greene Street for twelve grand. A Pratt buddy studying architecture made sketches; he got an A when he turned them in for his final. The Greene Street space, aka the Grotto, was outfitted with a projection room whose six seats had been rescued from the Pussy-Cat Playhouse after it was closed down by the Health Department. Another room was referred to as the Lot. Zippo painted it to resemble a lunar surface—deep-space black over deathless gray—and spent a week making papier-mâché boulders. It was the backdrop for dozens of shorts over the years, wherein a succession of acting students performed the world's great monologues on the moon while Zippo prowled with his 16mm Bolex. "It was like walking on the bottom of the sea. As if I had died long ago." There was even a room for his mannequins, cooled by a window unit.

The money liberated Zippo from normal-people worries, the ascendancy of the hippie-weirdo complex expanded his notion of possibility, and the downers took care of the rest. In the summer of 1972, he rented a bungalow in Venice Beach. He had chased a casting agent named Doris across the country. He met her downstairs at Max's and immediately mistook her universal agreeability for a specific affection. He lingered on the West Coast even though it was clear even to him that nothing was happening between them. It was in California that he suffered (his word) the first part of a two-part epiphany while watching *Blacula*. The country was entering a recession after all; self-realization on the installment plan was a prudent move.

Blaxploitation movies had left Zippo cold up to that point. He had witnessed his father keel over on the A train; forgive his hankering for heroes. *Sweetback, Shaft,* and *Super Fly,* that first wave, gave him cartoons instead. Then Blacula flew in through the window. The plot: When the African prince Mamuwalde (William Marshall) pitches European power brokers on the antislavery movement, Count Dracula of Transylvania punishes his uppity ass by inducting him into the ranks of the undead. Centuries pass. In contemporary Los Angeles, Blacula stumbles upon the reincarnation of his dead wife and vows to make her his. (Movie mummies and vampires were always stumbling upon replicas of women they'd loved hundreds of years before. Zippo couldn't stretch a relationship past a month.) In the "bloody finale," she accidentally gets shot while Blacula is busy slaughtering the LAPD. What's the point of a lonesome eternity? He kills himself by walking into the sunlight—purified and destroyed by fire.

Even in the vampire world the races led segregated lives. You never saw a white vampire walking into the sun. If Blacula had waited another couple of centuries, he probably would have run into his dead wife again. Nonetheless, the film remained a fine testament to love undying and supernatural blackness.

Months later a Christmas matinee of *The Poseidon Adventure* furnished Epiphany Part Two. Zippo liked seeing white people get got as much as the next guy, so disaster movies were right up his alley. He wanted to see what made the blockbuster tick, as research. He emerged from the theater profoundly moved.

The church has rebuked hip Reverend Scott (Gene Hackman) for his unorthodox views. "Angry, rebellious, critical, a renegade," he says. "Stripped of my so-called clerical powers, but I'm still in business." The luxury liner *Poseidon* ferries him to his demotion: "Banished to some new country in Africa. Hell, I had to look it up on the map to find out where I was going." A tsunami overturns the boat and Scott leads a ragtag group from danger, deck by deck. Almost to safety, only a suicide mission will save his dwindling flock. "What more do you want?" he demands of God. "You want another life? Then take me!" He saves his crew and disappears into a burning oil slick.

Christmas in LA was a disorienting affair: the Santas wore shorts and the workshop elves were past-prime centerfolds and future Waitress #2s. The city was like an Antonioni film. The first time you see it, it sucks, and then you see it a second time and it's incredible. It was like that, except the second time it still sucks. The end of the year found Zippo in a philosophical frame. What did it mean that Blacula came from Africa and Reverend Scott journeyed to it? The motherland, the source. Both men longing for meaning and finding it in sacrifice.

Both of them burning.

Zippo had outgrown the Warholian experiments of his Grotto. Enough with the gesture—what about committing the act itself, without irony? A full embrace of low culture in all its gorgeous vulgarity.

What kind of hero to put on that big white screen? Dealers, pimps, private dicks—it had been done. He wanted to combine his recent preoccupations, the vampire and the preacher. Blacula embodied an occult power from Africa, the cradle of humanity. At the end of the movie he's brought LA to its knees, tearing it all down like a bloodthirsty revolutionary. The maverick Reverend Scott served the system while trying to reform it, within and without at the same time. Like the Negro—of America and yet not American, as Du Bois put it. Like Zippo, who walked among the normals as one of their tribe while all sorts of wicked ruin flickered in his mind.

A secret agent, then. James Bond—but a sister. In one of those more-secret-than-the-CIA operations, working for the Man, but really working for the Black Nation from the inside.

Nefertiti T.N.T.

Los Angeles was a hex, New York the hexbreaker. Back on Greene Street he wrote the first draft in longhand on a legal pad, working from one of the Pussy-Cat Playhouse seats, the empty screen taunting him with what he might put there. He played *Nuggets* at full volume. At the end of each side he flipped the record over with the solemn focus of a monk. *I can't get your love, I can't get a fraction / Uh-oh, little girl, psychotic reaction.* Four days in he had the hi-fi system ripped out and put in the latest model, one more aggressive across multiple sectors. He didn't tell anyone he was back in the city. He wrote and wrote. When it got dark, he dog-paddled up West Broadway and then picked a new direction once he hit Houston, any direction he hadn't hit last time.

On these walks, half in a stupor, he tried to reconcile *idea* with *object.* Uncle Heshie said his inventions came from seeing something in his mind's eye and then delivering it to the world. That was art—manifesting your idea in the world. If it were enough to have the idea, all those white boys Zippo went to art school with—who talked and talked but never got off their asses— would be celebrated geniuses. The idea had to be executed, find its worth in its passage into existence.

It was different with fires. Zippo's doctors had told him that it was perfectly fine, perfectly normal to have dark fantasies if he didn't act on them. It was okay to imagine the flames gnawing a set of drapes, the whistling gases escaping, the heat on his skin, as long as it stayed in his head. Same with erotic photography. There was nothing shameful about a naughty thought or series of escalating scenarios provoked by a nude photograph. If it was in your head and not out there with other people, it was okay.

It was a quandary. Best to concentrate on the screenplay.

He met Samuel Z. Arkoff at a bar mitzvah in Flushing, Queens. Samuel Z. Arkoff, famous producer of *Blacula* and *The Incredible 2-Headed Transplant*—among other classics—was a family friend of the Lehmanns, and Zippo and Josh Lehmann were school pals. Josh's brother was the one getting the big-boy treatment. Zippo cornered Arkoff at the reception and told him he was making a blaxploitation picture.

"Marvelous," Arkoff said. He had a small plate of hors d'oeuvres in his hand and dots of soft cheese in the corners of his mouth. The king had one piece of advice: Never use your own money. Zippo had enough toothbrush reserves to shoot that winter in New York City, if everything came together. "Not your own money," Arkoff repeated. "That's what people are for." Arkoff's father had been a Russian immigrant like Uncle Heshie, placing a bet on America. America, inventions, moviemaking—Zippo detected a common mix of dreaming and pragmatism. Arkoff gave him his card: Look me up when you're done. American International Pictures had cashed in with *Blacula* and *Slaughter*, and just released *Coffy*. Blaxploitation = box-office cash money. For now. Juvenile-delinquent movies, beach-party romps, biker flicks—the fads come and go and you have to stuff your pockets while you can. "Sooner the better, my young friend."

Zippo converted the Grotto into production headquarters. Entities from his Pratt days returned from the stint in the real world ready to collaborate, just as they'd promised each other years before. They didn't have much going on. The production designer took "a leave" from her job in the framing store; the soundman hopped a Greyhound from his parents' house in St. Louis; and Toby Fairchild, a tremble-handed painter who had yet to face that his skills lay elsewhere, got roped into business

affairs. Zippo pulled out his money and courted Harlem investors. Offering points—he had a whole pitch. Checkbooks loosened as the cast came together.

Doris, the woman he'd flown across the country for, had a
hunch about Lucinda Cole and Roscoe Pope and was correct.
Roscoe Pope signed the contract a few days before his concert
record *Memo from Dr. Goodpussy* hit the charts. Good timing.
His manager wouldn't have taken Doris's calls if it had come out a
week earlier. Pope grudgingly agreed to fulfill his obligations for
a week of shooting in NYC.

Lucinda Cole tracked an opposite trajectory. Zippo remembered her sashaying to the VIP tables at Harlem night spots, back
when she dated local hoods. Next thing he knew she'd hit the big
time as the outspoken nun in *Miss Pretty's Promise*. Critics compared her confident turn to Dorothy Dandridge's splashy performance in *Carmen Jones* and the movie's theme song, "My Heart
Is a Pasture," made the Top 30, which put Lucinda's face on the
movie mags for a few weeks, even though the studio had dubbed
in another, better singer for the movie.

Zippo was young enough to think that if you got a break like
that, you were set. Not black women. He caught Lucinda on TV,
on *Dragnet* playing the distraught mother of a teenage junkie
(they looked the same age), as the principal of a community
school on *The Mod Squad*. He was glad to see her and sad to see
what Hollywood had to offer her. How did "My Heart Is a Pasture"
put it? *Sometimes I think I was planted upside down / And that
I've grown away from the sun.*

Lucinda Cole hadn't occurred to him until Doris suggested
her; from that moment on Nefertiti could be played by no other.
They held their casting sessions in an eighth-floor room at the
Sandbar Hotel in Santa Monica. Lucinda Cole floated in and
said, "I think I stayed in this very room the first time I came to
LA." Diaphanous muumuu, white leather boots, sunglasses the
size of dinner plates—Zippo didn't know which persona she
was squeezing herself into. But who did these days?

She liked the script. "It's better than a lot of the blaxploitation garbage they're stuffing down people's throats these days," she said. Was she saying that she didn't consider it blaxploitation, or that it was of a higher quality? In any case Lucinda Cole was in. Her downstairs neighbor was a disciple of Bong Soo Han, the father of hapkido, and had already agreed to teach her martial arts.

Zippo and Doris high-fived each other in the elevator. It took three attempts. The film was coming together. Doris was perfect at her job, perfect overall toenail to tooth, but Zippo accepted that they'd never be together. Perhaps they'd loved each other four hundred years ago when they were different people, or maybe four hundred years in the future they found each other once again for the first time. The thought lifted his spirits when he was feeling rotten.

*Super Fly T.N.T.* came out that summer and wrecked him. He was disconsolate to find out that Ron O'Neal had ripped off his title. Zippo remembered telling him about it at a party at Robert Guillaume's pad and Ron smiling strangely. Now he knew why. He cheered himself up with the knowledge that the film was a flop. And so *Nefertiti Jones* was born. Needless to say, Zippo suffered a relapse when he walked out of the Broadway–Lafayette subway station a few weeks later and saw the gigantic poster for *Cleopatra Jones.* He talked too much, that much was clear, and never should have spilled his guts to Max Julien that night at Fargas's.

Enter *Secret Agent: Nefertiti.*

Zippo reserved location scouting for himself. He saw the words up there on the screen, the last thing the audience takes in before the lights came up: FILMED ENTIRELY ON LOCATION IN HARLEM U.S.A. He zigzagged through the uptown grid as if led by a dowsing rod, pursuing the buildings he saw in his mind. Back in the motherland. He found Nefertiti's limestone townhouse—it overlooked the school playground and that younger generation that reminds her of who she's fighting for. Picked out the bar where the stoolies, hustlers, and other turkeys deliver the word on the street. The stoop where the neighborhood flasher messes with the wrong lady (comic interlude). He cast the showroom and office of Carney's Furniture in a small role.

Sometimes at street corners or next to a vacant lot that had once been a cherished place, he was Aaron Flood again, before Zippo came along. He toured his spots: the playground on 131st, whose gravel or broken glass was still embedded below his knee like war shrapnel; outside Jimmy's Tap on 135th, where according to family lore his mother first kissed his father. Dewey's, the soda shop she took Zippo to after his father's funeral, was a record store now. He'd ordered Rum Raisin in his dad's honor and forced down every wretched bite. He hated Rum Raisin. None of those places made it into the movie. Everyone maintains a private reel.

Location scouting was no excuse that final night, as the next day was the start of shooting. The pretext served to get him uptown again, wandering his old neighborhood, and then past it. He finally found the place he'd been looking for all along: the perfect location. He was over by the East River, on avenues beyond the map of his experience. The entire block had been bulldozed except for one three-story townhouse. Corner to corner the rubble rose and fell in red waves, flotsam of wood slats and iron pipes breaking the surface. Exposed masonry on the lone holdout's exterior indicated where the adjacent buildings had been. Zippo imagined they'd been swept away by a river of bricks.

The plywood across the front door proved to be unattached. Others had preceded him. No one was inside now; Zippo searched the building from the basement to the top floor. He chose a former bedroom, third floor, rear. Four blocks away he'd come across a tweed overcoat dangling out of a junker and sensed it might come in handy. It did. He kicked some newspapers on the floor into a pile and added the balled-up overcoat. He withdrew the can of kerosene from his bag. Took a whiff. Naughty-pantie.

It brought him back. He heard the sound of the match against the box before he struck it—his audio track was off. As it prospered and fed itself, the fire put him back in sync.

Zippo watched the flames. It had been years. Good luck heat, good luck smoke. The flames tickling the ceiling snapped him out of that old, comfortable delirium and he beat it to the street while he was still able.

Tomorrow when he called *Action,* the idea in his mind would begin its passage into this world. With art, it wasn't enough to conceive of it; you had to make it. It was like that with fires, too, sometimes. Sometimes you need it right there in front of you, crackling, dancing, devouring: more alive than you will ever be.

# TWO

It all went south after that night in Carney's Furniture. Pepper had been working security for a week, since Day 4 of shooting. Two tungsten lights—rented—vanished while being loaded onto a production van, disappeared by fleet-footed scavengers. Word had it the criminals swooped down with the speed and ferocity of a seagull snatching french fries from the Coney Island boardwalk.

"That's fast."

"Coney Island seagulls? Fuck it."

Zippo hired Pepper. The thieving stopped.

Pepper sat and watched. Before the production moved to Carney's that afternoon, they put in a few hours outside Nicky Tavern on Amsterdam, an episode where Nefertiti beats up a snitch. He had hoodwinked her, Pepper gathered, and now she had to beat the truth out of him. Once they got to the furniture store, Pepper set up a stool on the corner of 125th and Morningside, radiating menace. Would-be robbers considered easier prey. The job reminded Pepper of Newark, of the old days working the door at those Barbary Coast spots. His technique: glaring with his arms loosely crossed; lifting a skeptical eyebrow when civilians got too close to the perimeter; the occasional grunt to warn someone off. He was a six-foot frown molded by black magic into human form. It sufficed.

"You're getting paid to be yourself," Carney said. "Not bad." That sarcastic smile of his appeared for a moment. He handed Pepper a 7UP.

Pepper grunted.

Carney stopped smiling once the crew arrived and started fucking with the joint. After an establishing shot of the showroom—Zippo wanted the store as is, save for mirrors that cast reflections—the invasion began in earnest. The white men of the *Secret Agent: Nefertiti* production team were long-haired hippies with gnarled beards; ransacking, malnourished Vikings, from Carney's reaction. They relocated a bank of sofas to the other side of the room, rolled up rugs into dusty tubes, cast a dark network of electrical cable across the floor. Carney recoiled. "Watch the floors!" "The chandelier!" Over the years, Pepper had seen the man patrol the showroom, making imperceptible adjustments, arranging his merch in harmony with his secret order. This was a disaster movie. "The mentality that sets a Sterling ottoman next to an Egon club chair," Carney muttered. Pepper didn't know what he was talking about.

Pepper hunched in the front door, clocking the street while taking in the shooting prep. The effort required to get something up on the screen. Nagra, f-stop—it was a different language. This white girl named Lola ran around doing things like "continuity"—making sure the actor's scar was in the same place scene to scene. In Pepper's experience your scars stayed put.

Zippo had vamoosed to meet a potential investor. Over by the far wall of the store, the gaffer plugged a gigantic lamp into a socket that had been obscured by a long, low, burnt umber sectional. Carney said he didn't know the socket existed. *Pop*—the store lights flared and the juice cut out. When Carney and the gaffer returned from the basement, Rusty told his boss to go for a walk. "I'll handle it," Rusty said. "The furniture, it's too close. Too close to your heart."

Pepper had first met Rusty twelve years before, when he started using the store as an answering service. He walked in and there was Rusty, slender-armed and potbellied, hair conked in frozen waves, chasing a fat fly with a swatter. Time and the city had elevated the hayseed into an upstanding member of the Harlem community. Fatherhood played its part—no encounter was complete without an inspection of his wallet photos of wife, Beatrice, and their three boys. Plus he was churchy, which conferred an air of legitimacy on all comers. Deacon, serving the congregation and such. One time he invited Pepper to check out their services, Church of the Holy Whatnot over on Convent. "It doesn't matter how long you've been outside," Rusty said. "There are no locks on His door, no buzzer, and you're always welcome." Pepper's expression ensured that it was a onetime invitation.

As promised, Rusty took care of the store. The salesman directed the young white men to keep the Sterlings with the Sterlings and the DeMarcos with the DeMarcos and herded the floor lamps into a flock of silver and bronze. It wouldn't be difficult to restore everything to Carney's liking. He seized on the boom operator's accent—they hailed from different parts of Georgia but had tuned in to the same radio preacher every Sunday. Now the two of them were up in New York City working on a movie about a black lady secret agent in the cracker-killing business. Secret agent or kung fu lady—Pepper hadn't read the script. Did black movies get into theaters down there? The KKK probably kept a roadblock to keep them out of the county.

Rusty's competence and amiability made him a de facto production assistant; Larry's easy charisma got him a cameo and a line of dialogue. Most days Larry was too slick for Pepper's taste, but he was less annoying compared to the rest of his generation, with their eye-melting clothing and tiresome, uplifting slogans. When Pepper showed up that morning, Larry was pacing figure eights on the sidewalk and mumbling to himself. Rehearsing, he said.

He told Pepper how it went down. The day after Carney agreed to let them use his store, Zippo made a special trip to see Larry. He slid his dark sunglasses down his nose. "Do you act?"

"No more than the next guy," Larry said.

"You have a quality," Zippo announced.

Larry's character worked for Charles & Co. Furniture, the name of the store in the movie. He holds the door for Nefertiti and makes a flirtatious remark when she comes to see Mr. Dudley, the owner. "I've been working on the line for days," Larry said. "It's stressing me." No matter what he did, it always sounded the same as the first time he said it.

Pepper asked him what it was.

*"Look at you, foxy."*

The problem was obvious. There was no way to improve the delivery. Larry said it like that when the cameras rolled hours later: One take.

\* \* \*

Frankly the racial-harmony shit put Pepper on edge. The majority of the film crew were hippie freaks, but Zippo and the director of photography and Angela, the lady who did wardrobe and makeup, were black. The white people did what they were told.

This was America, melting pot and powder keg. Surely something was about to pop off. It kept not happening.

Pepper had never worked jobs with white people before. Pulling shit in Newark, then uptown in those days, that was the reality. It was not done. Occasionally he'd get asked to join a crew with a white wheelman or a bankroll and that was a sign to wait for the next gig. His current refusals were simple common sense. Pepper barely trusted Negro crooks—why extend the courtesy to some cracker motherfucker who'd fuck you over first chance? Sometimes black people fell over themselves trying to vouch for a white man who hadn't wronged them yet. Yet.

His work on *Nefertiti* didn't break his rule, he decided—as freelance muscle, he was on the outside. No reason not to take the opportunity to learn a thing or two. His second day with *Secret Agent: Nefertiti,* they were shooting a dice-game scene behind a bodega. The bodega was real—Tiny's Extra on 132nd, where Skitter Lou had severed Bull Moreland's windpipe by the ice-cream freezer back in '67—but the craps were pure Hollywood, from the too-nice threads on the players to the soft faces of the players. A proper dice game featured at least six kinds of plaid—slacks, shirt, jacket—and one dude with a buck-fifty scar. Pepper had read in one of the militant papers that twenty-five percent of cowboys in the Old West were black, and whenever *Secret Agent: Nefertiti* strayed too far from True Harlem, he liked to share that fact as commentary. Meaning, Hollywood always got it wrong. The movie guys nodded, changed nothing.

Between bodega takes, Pepper summoned Pete the Grip. "Let me see that," he said.

"Here you go, Mr. Pepper," Pete the Grip said. Pepper's voice never failed to startle the young white boy and he almost dropped the walkie-talkie on the pavement. Pete had yet to find his Harlem sea legs, heading uptown when he wanted to go south and losing track of subway entrances as if they shifted moment to moment, three-card monte style. It didn't help that Pepper gave incorrect directions when asked.

Pete's Windsor walkie-talkie was a new model, sturdy. Pepper tested its weight, how it hung in the pocket of his windbreaker. Volume knob wide enough for purchase if you wore gloves. The old Windsors cracked like eggs when they slipped out of your hand onto concrete. He returned the device to the kid. It was entirely possible that Pepper hadn't kept abreast of advances in portable short-range communication. Next free day, he'd check out the hobby magazines for the latest.

The hippie Vikings covered the front windows of Carney's Furniture with black sheeting and the constant barking of instructions and epithets migrated to the back of the store for the office shoots. Chip the Soundman sank into one of the mushy couches, reading a *Doctor Strange* comic and reeking of reefer. One of those Greenwich Village types you only saw uptown when they were handing out leaflets about Vietnam or Cambodia and lecturing folks about getting more involved. Getting in black people's business.

"We're almost ready," Lola said, then five minutes later she said, "They need more time." *We* when it was good news, *they* when it was bad. Pepper was accustomed to the pace by now, the rickety subway of a film set. Workers tended to failures in the dark and things lurched forward again until the next breakdown.

Lola appeared to have taken over Marie's office, darting in and out like a rat. Pepper hadn't seen Marie all day. They had closed the store to customers when the movie people arrived. Perhaps she'd already left by the time he got there.

Pepper relocated his roost to the Morningside door, where they'd trained lights and filters on the interior of Carney's office. In time to catch Carney when he returned from cooling off. He was more relaxed and gave Rusty a thumbs-up for maintaining order. Carney told Pepper that May's basketball team had a game in Brooklyn but that John was coming by to watch.

"Done with school?" Pepper said.

"It's seven o'clock at night," Carney said.

So it was. Pepper hadn't seen the boy since the summer, when he ran into Carney on 125th outside Chock Full o' Nuts and walked away with a dinner invitation.

"What are you having?"

"Chicken?"

Nothing else going on. En route to the Carney household that evening he passed a cart on Eighth Avenue and picked the least-shabby bouquet, a challenge. Pepper hadn't bought flowers since he was with Hazel.

He rang the doorbell. Boys tossed a football in the street and hollered at one another. He still wasn't used to coming in the front door on Strivers' Row. He'd snuck through the back way plenty, looting, those rear alleys practically begging.

Elizabeth opened the door and her face livened at the flowers. She thanked him and went for a vase. Mrs. Carney had figured out he was crooked years ago. Pepper knew this because she had stopped asking questions about his life and because of her general bemused attitude toward him. She didn't hold it against him. He wondered what she knew about Carney's various sidelines.

May was playing loud music upstairs—that funk stuff, from the bass. John read a book on the sofa in the front room. "Hello, Uncle Pepper," he said.

"Pepper," he corrected, as he always did.

"Sure, Uncle Pepper," John said, grinning. Years before, Pepper had promised himself he would not manhandle them for sassing him. He had remained true to his word.

Pepper asked to see the book's cover: *Planet of the Apes.* He recommended seeing the movie, it was faster. John said he'd already seen it five times. The boy wanted to see what they'd changed from the book.

Pepper nodded. Sometimes when Carney talked a certain way, and the words had an edge, he saw Big Mike before him, the old crook returned to Harlem for a moment. Now there were times when John opened his mouth and Pepper recognized young Carney in the intonations and attendant gestures. A glimpse of Carney before he stepped into himself.

A couple of years ago, Carney had asked Pepper when they had first met. Carney had this idea that he'd been a little kid when Pepper used to hang around their old apartment on 127th Street. He corrected him—Carney was in high school when Pepper started pulling jobs with his old man. Carney's mother was dead, and it was just him and Big Mike. Teenage Carney would greet his father and his crew, eyes to the floor, and then hide out in his room until the men left for that night's caper, an armored car rip-off, a payday-eve raid on a department store. Scared of the crooks or embarrassed by his father or merely wanting to be left alone.

Carney got home from the store soon after Pepper arrived and they had a nice meal, a chicken thing Elizabeth had clipped from the *Times.* He didn't see Carney again until November. The furniture salesman visited the bar every so often to catch up. At first it was business—Carney had to put the squeeze on a dealer who'd pulled a Houdini without paying, or needed a bodyguard at a meet with some trifling bitches. On occasion something more complicated. Then Carney retired the fencing sideline and he visited the bar to shoot the shit. Next thing Pepper knew, Easter with the Carneys was an annual affair and the kids called him Uncle.

\* \* \*

That November night when Carney showed up, Donegal's was half empty and the TV was cranked up with some Ray Milland picture. It wasn't clear what Milland's character had done; he was a weasel type who sweated a lot, embezzler or guilty hit-and-runner. They watched the movie for a while, not talking. Pepper didn't discuss business as a rule—you were in on the job or you weren't. But the Gillette commercial came on and Pepper mentioned that he'd spent his last score and that it was time to rustle up another. Carney said if he wanted something easy, he knew a man who needed muscle. "He's scruffy but professional," Carney said, and explained how he'd come to get involved in the movie business.

Carney had known the director since he was a teenager, when the kid hung around with his cousin Freddie. He hustled small-time for a while—kiting paper, selling blue movies—and now he was a director, making one of those black movies. As it happened, John and May loved those ghetto flicks, silly and violent as they were, and Carney had come into some money.

"Money what?" Pepper said.

"Watches."

"Sure."

Carney fell for Zippo's spiel, like one of those people who entered his furniture store to ask for directions and got sweet-talked into a new credenza. Zippo had grown up to be a good salesman—maybe that was part of being a good director, steering people into the roles you want them to play. Carney went in for points. That's how they financed movies these days, Carney said—points. A bunch of dentists make a consortium, or it's a businessman looking for a place to put money. The movie takes off, you make a bundle.

Like: The big story at the Dumas Club last year concerned Don

Newberry, fine-scotch enthusiast and chairman of the Admissions Committee. Newberry was a lackluster estate lawyer but his father had been one of Tammany Hall's Negro liaisons, helping to deliver the Harlem vote, and Newberry coasted his whole life on that association. He also happened to live upstairs from the actor Ron O'Neal and agreed to help out the makers of *Super Fly* with some contracts, no sweat. Got ten percent of the movie and a year later—boom. A million dollars and counting.

"Give a black man a gun and let him mow down some white people—it's not art, but it puts the butts in the seats," Zippo said. He'd come to Carney's store to finalize the office shoot and leaned into his pitch when the moment was right. *Secret Agent: Nefertiti* was art, he insisted, but also contained plenty for those of coarse sensibility. His work derived from a list of aesthetic principles called the ZIPPO Method. "It's kind of a personal credo." ZIPPO was an eponymous acronym, an admitted rip-off of Samuel Z. Arkoff and his ARKOFF Formula. He elaborated on the key ZIPPO concepts and qualities:

**Z**eitgeist (From the German, *the spirit of the times.* Tap into the culture.)

**I**ntelligent (Elevate our idea of the world.)

**P**rovocative (Knock the audience out of their bourgeois complacency.)

**P**rofane (Profanity, violence, and sex, artfully employed. See *P,* above.)

**O**ratory (Notable dialogue and speeches.)

"That's ZIPPO," Zippo said. Carney related the gist to Pepper, but had trouble remembering what *zeitgeist* meant, "maybe because of the war." The main thing was that Carney needed to wash some cash and his kids got excited when he told them about it: He was in.

The filmmaker had one more request. He'd been eyeing the Hermann Bros. the entire meeting. "Can we use the safe?" Zippo asked.

"No."

"For the scene."

"No."

"He asked to use your safe?" Pepper said.

"For the scene, he said."

Pepper took a drink. You don't touch a man's safe.

Buford the bartender set down another two beers. According to Carney, he and Zippo did a deal for the location fee and shares in the film. Zippo had called that morning and mentioned that some of the neighborhood kids had been boosting their gear. The next day Pepper headed over and signed on.

Pepper needed some scratch for operating expenses, sure, but more than anything he was bored. It had been a long time since he had beat a man senseless. The film work might provide access to those in need of a beating. A contusion or, what do you call it, detached retina. As for the job itself, a lifelong crook doing part-time security work wasn't so strange. Half the cops in New York were thieving bitches first and cops second. City like this, it behooves you to embrace the fucking contradictions.

\* \* \*

Lola's promises meant nothing. The surest indicator that they were about to shoot was a manifestation by the director. He walked in the front door, scanned the preparations, and offered a heartfelt "It's totally ZIPPO in here, baby." Today he was dressed in red jeans and a black cable sweater riddled with moth holes or acid burns. His trademark silver bracelets jangled with his every movement, so much so that when the camera rolled he froze into a mannequin, in a series of what had to be rehearsed poses. One got accustomed to the sight.

The crew jumped to it. Pepper didn't think much of Zippo during their first meeting—in general he regarded the younger set with a mixture of pity and stupefaction. But the man had a way with the crew, who did what they were told and with efficiency. It was odd—they seemed to believe in him.

Word around the set was that the British brother playing

Mr. Dudley, the shady furniture salesman, was a big honcho in Shakespeare circles. They were mystified by and grateful for his presence. "It's a shame he only has one scene," Lola said. Johnson Gibbs was stout, dignified, exquisitely muttonchopped, and carried himself with the self-satisfaction of a bank manager or reverend. It was odd to see someone besides Carney at that old desk, but the actor looked at home. Mr. Shakespeare stared through the window onto the showroom and silently mouthed his lines, gripping his lapels as if overlooking Gettysburg.

Then Lucinda Cole appeared. She'd been next door at Skinny's for hours—the production had hired out the bar for wardrobe and makeup and "holding." (As far as Pepper could tell, *holding* was person storage until they were needed, like when you sit on some dummy you've ransomed.) Pepper was unfamiliar with her work. In their initial meeting, Zippo had listed some projects. He shrugged. Zippo hummed a song from one of her movies. It didn't ring a bell. Pepper asked about her character's name. "Nefertiti—that's some Afrocentric shit?"

Zippo said, "It means, *the beautiful woman has come.*"

Pepper didn't care for fanciness, whether it was Strivers' Row fanciness or Park Avenue or Hollywood, but once he met Lucinda, he conceded the justice of the name. She had an hourglass figure, not in its shape but in the melancholy reminder that time is running short and there are things on this Earth you'll never experience. Although they'd only spoken once, his first day, her brief smile every morning was an unexpected comfort, like a nod from the clerk at the corner bodega or the waitress at the greasy spoon, the newsstand guy. A quick neighbor, even though her costumes declared her from outer space.

For the furniture store scene, they'd put Lucinda in white leather pants and a shimmering midnight blue blouse under a black leather cape. Lucinda's round face was framed by her large Afro wig, set like a brown jewel. The wig itself was an audacious number that opposed the laws of physics and was pinned by a headband embroidered with odd symbols, hieroglyphics that represented Zippo's "myth system." Pepper nodded off whenever the director explained them. On anyone else the ensemble was a Halloween getup. She pulled it off.

The actress tottered into the office. Lucinda was tall, and the ruby red platform boots made her more impressive, even if they provided a technical challenge to kicking chumps in the throat; the myriad chump-kicking and -stomping had required multiple takes in previous days. She perched on Carney's desk and leaned over to inspect his signed picture of Lena Horne. She approved.

Lola chased everybody off the set so Zippo could break down the scene with his actors. Carney and John joined Pepper at his Morningside post, where a patch of sidewalk gave the boy a partial view of the office. Carney's hand rested on his son's shoulder. Pepper realized that John was about the same age Carney had been when he met him. Twenty-five years ago? The boy was helping out in the store some afternoons, Pepper knew, but he looked bored whenever the subject came up. He wasn't a crook and he wasn't a salesman—so far.

Whoever he might be one day, tonight he was a boy on a film set. Carney asked him what he thought of the whole operation and John hopped like a damn puppy.

In the office, Zippo explained his grand design. As usual, Lucinda was soft-voiced and retiring between takes; she turned into a mean dervish once they started rolling. Mr. Shakespeare listened and nodded soberly. He asked a question. Zippo ran down the backstory of the store owner, Mr. Dudley.

Carney stiffened. "Did he say the man has a furniture store that's a front for his fencing operation?"

"Sounded like," Pepper said.

Carney walked into his office and ordered everybody out except for Zippo. Troy, the director of photography, scowled and took a seat on a showroom Sterling. Pepper extended a don't-worry-about-it shrug to John. The set was clear, but the electrical cables propping the doors allowed those nearby to hear the tirade.

Zippo called everyone back in. "So he's a bookie," he explained to Mr. Shakespeare. "More ZIPPO."

They shot the scene where Larry lets her in and set up for Nefertiti's confrontation with the bookie. Still quiet on Morningside at this hour. Once the night orchestra struck up with gusto, they'd have to contend with a full menu of racket from outside. Pepper shooed away a wino and the man hooked a U-turn toward 126th, crooning mangled Motown. Most passersby crossed the street to avoid their setup, uninterested. The movie lamps pushed out a cold and unsettling light, an eerie bubble onto the street. 125th was its standard hurly-burly but up Morningside the streetlights were busted, the lights in the church across the street were out, the abandoned tenements down the block dark, and no one was home in the house on the corner. Like the street was a darkened theater, and the rectangle of the office door the glowing movie screen. Soon they'd be done shooting and on to the next location and then finished altogether and where would Pepper be then? In the dark seats again, between shows.

Zippo called for one last take and it was a wrap.

Carney took John home after the boy wrangled autographs for him and his sister. Pete the Grip and his fellows loaded the van and it chugged around the corner. The wind had come up. Pepper split for the subway. *How was the take? Let's go for one more take.* Like they were ripping off a bank. Filmmaking was a heist, same animal. To knock over a warehouse or hijack a truck or shoot a scene you had to wrangle all the variables, the landscape, the players, and bend them to your will. Setup and execution broken down into pieces. What's the quality of light at that time of day, the access points, the pedestrian and vehicle traffic. Everybody's got their special role, following the script. One guy to punch out the safe, another at the wheel. Wardrobe, lighting, boom mike. The obsession with the clock—after money, time was the favored currency, in a bank vault and on location. Do you have enough time to pull it off? And if you pull it off, is it the jackpot you thought it was?

All the work they put in. On a film if you fucked it up, you got to do it over. They weren't going to shoot you in the face.

And like a heist, just when you think it's going according to plan, everything goes to shit. The day after Carney's they set up outside one of the CCNY gates. Nefertiti enters campus, and then there's a bit in an empty classroom where she consults with Dr. Beryl Boyle, a professor of nuclear physics, about sinister diagrams on microfilm. The crew was anxious, it was in the way they moved and spoke to each other. Pepper registered the trembling web like a spider. No Zippo. He asked Pete the Grip what was up. "It's Miss Cole," he said. "She's missing."

# THREE

Pepper took the film job because he was low on cash and he was low on cash because the Anson job crapped out. Church Wiley's prep work had been top-notch. It usually was. Church couldn't remember the names of his own kids, but ask him the average speed of Anson Freight's driver on the Jersey Turnpike and he'd mumble, "Fifty-seven miles per hour, sixty if it's cloudy." He only had two kids.

The Thursday driver was named Phil Burgher and he drove the Alexandria-to-Newark run every week to ensure that the Magnavox warehouse made its Friday deliveries. Phil was steady, steady as in predictable, the best kind. He permitted himself one stop on his route, at the Pedricktown service area just over the border from Delaware. "It's a real 'Welcome to Jersey' place," Church said. Two diesel pumps, a big pile of gravel, and a greasy spoon called Teddy's Place. The name of the joint winked in and out in a hum of busted red neon. Burgher had a thing for the waitress. She was a beehive hairdo with a bent cigarette sticking out of it. The trucker typically lingered after his meal in luckless flirtation and hit the head before the final push to Newark. There were two stretches on the turnpike that suited their purposes before you reached population centers.

West Side Garage had been raided by the larceny squad a few times, but Pepper preferred Tom Gerald over any other shady outfit. He'd never heard of one of Gerald's cars getting traced back and it was almost twenty years now Pepper'd been buying wheels from him. Pepper headed over to 165th off Broadway. Tom was getting on; his last bid upstate had turned his hair white and his bones creaky. He came out of his office to greet Pepper but quickly retreated to let his son take over. Billy took after his mother, with his oval face and long lashes. From his accent they spoke Spanish around the house.

Billy vouched for the two cars, the Dodge Dart and the El Camino, both '67. He rapped the hood of the Dart and said it was a little monster that could handle any curves and action that might come up. Pepper said, yeah. More interested in the Camino: "Got that cover for the bed?" Billy was about to make a joke about it being extra, but thought better of it once he looked at Pepper's face. He threw in the cover for free. They didn't use it in the end. A cut-up square of brown carpet did the job just fine.

Thursday night was soft and sugary, one of those perfect objects that summer doled out once in a while to torture you with how it could be all the time, if it cared. Pepper had known women like that, women stingy with the better parts of themselves, and perhaps there were those who'd say the same of him. He shrugged and sipped the sweet night air. Church and Pepper were in the El Camino, parked a few yards over from the concrete cube housing the public toilets. Across the lot, the truck driver Burgher hunched in the diner window, clocking the waitress as she bused the next table.

Gus Burnett and Burt Miller waited in the Dodge, next to the dumpster behind the restaurant. Pepper didn't know them; they were Church's guys, from Alabama. Twenty, twenty-one, greyhound lean and not too talkative. This time tomorrow they were supposed to be back down South, sucking crawdads or plucking homemade banjos or whatever they did down there. They appeared to follow simple instructions fine and gave correct answers when Pepper quizzed them on the setup. Solid enough.

Pepper had worked with Church a bunch and held no doubts about his abilities. Before the action, Church always chatted like a lonely aunt. Pool sharks and card hustlers talked a lot when they worked, probing for weaknesses and weaving distractions.

Church's talk was the opposite—he was testing himself to get the kinks out.

He was behind the wheel of the El Camino tonight. "Pedricktown," he said, drawing out the syllables in boredom. He pointed at the gravel pile and said, "That's the mayor."

Pepper exhaled and checked the service area in the rearview.

"You're good at, uh, 'nonverbal communication,'" Church said.

The side of Pepper's mouth curled. A tumbleweed cloud skidded above.

"Here we go," Church said. He tapped his door to signal the men in the Dodge.

When did Burgher get hip something untoward was underway? When the El Camino in front of his truck slowed down for no reason? Or when he looked over to pass the car and saw the Dodge keeping pace with his cab and the black man in the passenger seat aiming the pistol up at him? The semitruck was a twelve-ton monster and if its driver had a mind for violence it could have smushed or swatted away either car. According to Church, Burgher had two assault beefs on his sheet, barroom shit gone awry. That's why they painted a message for him, in big letters so he couldn't miss it: DIANA CORY LINDA. They'd made sure it was visible from various truck cab angles but not from a passing car, and that headlights picked it up at night. Man sees the names of his wife and kids in the bed of an El Camino, he's liable to interpret it as an implicit threat. If not, the gun provided a subtitle.

"Should I put a skull and crossbones?" Church had asked, paintbrush dangling, and Pepper answered in a nonverbal fashion.

Burgher pulled over. There was a discussion. Gus Burnett, the Alabaman with the revolver, clambered into the rig and drove the truckload of new TVs to Newark, to a disused icehouse west of the train yards. Burt Miller drove the Dart, tailing the El Camino on the toll road and until they got off and made for an overpass on the raggedy edge of New Brunswick. They parked. To the east the woods had been cleared for a construction site. Work shut down every day by seven, Church said. Crisp white light described a silhouette of dirt mounds and earth-moving equipment. Church and Pepper looked at each other—a quarter mile back they'd passed an old man, plodding along, pushing an empty, wobbly fruit cart. Did it need to be addressed? They got out of the car: Forget it.

Church walked over to the Dart and addressed the trunk. "What's up, slick?"

Burgher's response could only be described as muffled.

"Count to a hundred," Church said.

"Five hundred," Pepper said. He unrolled the mangy carpet to cover the message in the Camino's bed.

"Count until you lose count," Church said, "then you open that trunk and go about your day."

Burt Miller hopped in the back of the El Camino and they headed for the icehouse. Pepper looked back at the overpass. How many times had he abandoned cars or vans in New Brunswick after a job? In 1949, '54, '63 with the fur-coat business, and now. Time to find another dump. Were cops as a species dumb and lazy? Yes. But occasionally a cop came along who was merely a half-wit as opposed to a full-fledged dummy, and if the half-wit had initiative and got a notion to check out old cases it might be a problem.

The ex-wife of one of Church's buddies owned the icehouse, the final asset of a once prosperous dynasty. The guy had something on her—a marriage collects a variety of leverage over time—and he in turn owed Church for something. When the three thieves got to Newark, Gus had already snapped the trailer's lock and pulled out one of the TVs. But it wasn't a TV. No one knew what the fuck it was. The gizmo inside the cardboard box was made of black-and-white plastic, a four-inch square rising out of a rectangular base a foot and a half wide. Were you supposed to step on it? The shape reminded Pepper of those shoe buffers in hotels. Two other, smaller plastic squares trailed brown cords.

Church tilted the box into the light. "Magnavox Odyssey."

Here the criminals competed over who could sound more per-
plexed.

"Tennis," Gus said.

"There's a TV on the box but there's no TV inside," Church said.

"Says that's the *master control module.* Those things are the
player controls. 'Fits any brand TV black-and-white or color.' "

"Table tennis," Burt mumbled.

"And hockey."

The pressing issue was how much they'd get for the devices, if
anything. They stashed the boxes in the basement and the Ala-
bamans departed to dispose of the eighteen-wheeler. A police
siren emerged from the silence and retreated. Church cursed.
He said he should have stuck to Baltimore, his usual hunting
grounds. It was a disaster whenever he got it in his head to branch
out. "This is Frederico's all over again." Pepper was unacquainted
with the caper in question, but what crook did not recognize
regret over a setup gone wrong.

Back to the city. Once in the El Camino, Church said he had to
make a stop on Clinton Ave—the man did not elaborate. Money
or a woman, what else could it be. Pepper made him take a circu-
itous and nonsensical route to avoid Hillside as he was not in the
mood to have something stirred up. Newark the Fucker, Newark
the Pest, Newark the Thing with a Hundred Snake Faces—his
hometown had streets and corners that sucker-punched from the
fog of yesterday. The old ghosts were groggy and slow, but they
remembered your weak spots.

Church pulled up in front of a white-turned-gray clapboard
house on Avon. Pepper used to play baseball with a kid who lived
around the corner, Jimmy Temple. Stepped on a mine in France
three days before he was due to ship home—so long, Shortstop.
Church produced a brown bag from beneath his seat and walked
into the dark house. The door was unlocked. He ran out a minute later, no bag, chased by a big hollering broad, her house slippers slapping echoes on the concrete until the El Camino made
it around the corner. Pepper didn't ask. Church didn't say. Five

minutes later the man busted out in laughter and didn't stop for miles.

It took three weeks for Church to find a buyer in the Bronx, a Lithuanian with tendrils in home electronics. The offer: a measly few grand. The machines retailed for eighty bucks, but they weren't exactly flying off the shelves. They did a deal for the game consoles. A week later Pepper was in Donegal's and got word that Dootsie Bell had "expired" in prison, brain cancer. Misery is a money pit. The widow, the kids, no burial insurance meant no scratch for the funeral—Pepper gave the wife a bunch of cash for expenses. Dootsie had dumped Pepper at Harlem Hospital once instead of leaving him to bleed out by the side of the road. The bill had to come due eventually. Come November cash was tight and then Zippo came along.

\* \* \*

With Lucinda Cole's disappearance, the production was stuck on the rocks. It was her movie after all. Nefertiti was in every scene, save when they cut to the criminal mastermind's yacht sanctum to have him explain his methods (sparking the race war) and motivation (post–race war domination). They'd shot those scenes the first week, as the actor playing the Baron—white guy—needed to split for a dinner-theater gig, *Who's Afraid of Virginia Woolf?* on a transatlantic cruise, Miami to Le Havre. "Had to cut an hour but the heart of the play is the heart of the play." Once they gave up on the scene at the CCNY entrance ("We'll go with a straight exterior shot without her"), the crew moved to the Anthropology Building for the classroom scenes and hoped she'd show up.

Pepper's last visit to a college campus was the time he and T.T. ripped off that Stony Brook lab, years ago. (Never did find out what was in that barrel but still remembered his relief that it did not explode when it fell off the dolly and bounced down the fire stairs.) He lingered before the flyers and posters in the hallways—working with the film kids made him curious about what made the young set tick. Everybody's research when you're crooked, another variable in a setup down the line. Closed-circuit cameras, electronic eyes, people: same shit. Notices for the requisite protests and marches and candlelight vigils decorated bulletin boards and office doors. Posters for midnight movies like *Plan 9 from Outer Space* and *Freaks*. Those odd creatures had slithered past Pepper's TV at obscure hours; getting rubes to pay money to see them was a nice con. Sign-up sheets for rap sessions, consciousness-raising groups. Even though Carney had explained it one Easter dinner, Pepper found his very literal interpretation of "consciousness raising" hard to shake. What do you do with it once you get it up there? Sometimes that was the whole problem with life: Chumps abounded with a mentality stuck this high when yours was that high.

Pete the Grip and the rest set up in the classroom in case Lucinda appeared. Zippo had worked some angles with CCNY for the use of a warren of tiny-windowed offices across the hall. *Nefertiti*'s crew settled in like student protesters who'd taken over the premises to protest the bomb or the war or Whitey in general. Obeying a homing instinct, Pepper installed himself at the messiest desk in the room. He flipped through a textbook on primate behavior. Inside, a spread of glossy pictures featured monkeys wearing metal caps attached to electrodes.

Just after six P.M., Lola called him over. The production assistant had been fuming and fussing all day, sniping into her Windsor walkie-talkie and sighing dramatically. For the last few minutes she had been whispering into the phone, eyes darting, reminding Pepper of a stoolie who suspects everybody knows he's ratted them out. She handed him the receiver.

It was Zippo, simultaneously frantic and spaced out—the man was a multitalent. Nobody knew where Lucinda Cole was. She was staying at the Hotel McAlpin, where the production had put up some of the cast, courtesy of one of the film's backers, who got a business discount through his aluminum-siding business. His daughter was playing the sassy cocktail waitress in the nightclub scene. The hotel had called demanding compensation for the damages to her suite, which was a shambles. It looked like she'd had a party that got out of hand. No sign of Lucinda.

"Can you come downtown?" Zippo asked. He lived on Greene Street.

*Come downtown.* Like he was a beatnik or a donkey. "I ain't going downtown."

Zippo met him at the Whistle Stop on Fifth Ave. It was two doors up from 125th, announced by a blue neon outline of a tall gent tapping his foot. The Whistle Stop attracted an older clientele, locals alienated by the current temperament of the neighborhood bars and clubs. Around the corner, up the way, the new joints were loud and angry and ruled by a younger crowd that—in their brash clothes and militant anthems and anarchic fearlessness—rebuked a previous generation's mannered rebellions. The middle-aged men and women shrank when they passed so the youngsters wouldn't knock their drinks as they stormed the small dance floors. The old-timers shook their heads at the vulgar lyrics of the new funk. What kind of twisted mind committed such filth to vinyl? They beat it to the Whistle Stop to be among their kind. Friday and Saturday nights at the Whistle Stop, the Robert McCoy Trio performed two sets of drowsy, free-form jazz, a musical complement to the watered-down drinks that the bartender Lonnie served with amiable dedication.

Pepper had been there a few times with Hazel, and thus associated it with straight-world types. Zippo was dressed in mourning, all black. He greeted two patrons as he made his way to Pepper's perch at the bar, and it turned out he knew Lonnie. The director's personality had made Pepper forget he was from the neighborhood.

"I used to play chess with his cousin," Zippo said as the bartender mixed him a rum and Coke. His usual affect was distracted and aloof; not today. The disappearance of his star had grounded him.

"People come back or they don't," Pepper said. "It's up to them."

"I don't have the luxury of waiting."

"She's from here," Pepper said. He gestured vaguely at the bar, like she was about to walk out of the ladies room. What about her family?

Zippo explained that her mom was dead, her dad was long gone, and it didn't sound like there was anyone else. Her agent was worried. "He didn't go into it," Zippo said, "but he made it out like she'd had a rough time last summer, that she was pulling out of something. Drugs, booze, the wrong crowd—I don't know." The agent claimed to be hopping on a plane. "Said he was trying to reach her doctor to see what he says."

Head doctor, Pepper gathered. He told Zippo that he didn't see what any of this had to do with him.

"I'd like you to find her. Carney says you know what you're doing."

"If you think something has happened to her, you should go to the cops." Go to the cops like a square, like a normal person, which is what Zippo was. He was hesitant for some reason.

"They get involved, they'll feed the story to the newspapers. I don't need that kind of attention right now." Zippo looked over his shoulder. "I'm losing money every day. Maybe she'll show up tomorrow, maybe she's on a bender and will be back after the weekend. Maybe a lot of shit, but I got to get this movie in the can."

Pepper was getting paid whether they rolled the cameras or not; he had double-checked with Lola that afternoon. Zippo read his mind. "I'll pay you on top of what you're getting now," he said. "With a bonus if you find her."

A druggie having a relapse, there were uptown characters who might know who was supplying her. She was no Diahann Carroll but she was still a movie star of sorts and would kick up some gossip. He pictured this drug den he'd been in once, Mam Lacey's after she died. He'd barely talked to Lucinda Cole, but didn't like to think of her in one of those places. Those drugs get a hold of you, you can end up anywhere. On set, Pepper had found her eyes cold when viewed from an angle, but suddenly sympathetic and inquisitive when she met his gaze. No, he didn't like to think of her alone in one of those grim places.

"What kind of bonus?" Pepper said.

They did a deal for the missing person business and he told Lonnie that Zippo was picking up his tab. "Plus expenses"—isn't that how it went?

* * *

Downtown. A donkey after all. He took the 1 train to Christopher and headed east. Ten-thirty on a Wednesday night and the cold spell relenting, the Village streets were busy. Pepper was accustomed to the 125th Street version of these folks, the bummy clothes and insolent posture. He had difficulty wrapping his head around the white downtown version, particularly in the realm of facial hair. Hippie attire aside, black men generally kept their beards and mustaches fit and sharp, their Afros immaculate. These white kids walked around with stuff on their heads that— well, dead alley cats rotting behind garbage cans kept it more correct. The new shit was always upon you and you had to adjust, such was life, but the new shit came so fast these days, and it was so wily and unlikely, that he had a hard time keeping up.

He crossed Sixth Ave. The Twin Towers still startled him when they lurched into view, freed by this or that turn around a street corner. Looming over the city like two cops trying to figure out what they can bust you for.

The Sassy Crow was down MacDougal, on Minetta across from Café Wha? He remembered seeing the club's mascot on the sign when Hazel brought him down here to see that jazz combo last summer. The crow was coony—the black bird's big white eyes and cigar recalling some minstrel shit. He related as much to Hazel and she responded along the lines of "You know white people love that stuff." The sax-led combo had been playing next door at a tiny place called the Kaleidoscope Wheel. When Hazel suggested they stay for the second set, he did not hesitate. He never did refuse her a thing, did he? It was a nice night. He couldn't remember the name of the band, but A Bunch of Squirrels in a Burlap Sack Being Beaten by Hammers would not have been false advertising.

He descended the vertiginous steps to the basement club, into a physical reek of stale beer. Pepper disapproved of places with only one way in and out. Trapped smells, trapped people. The bouncer at the bottom of the stairs was a beefy crimson-faced white guy in a leather biker jacket, with a long beard cinched by multicolored rubber bands. In his work clothes (which were his always clothes), denim trousers and a brown canvas trucker jacket, Pepper didn't resemble the usual clientele. He gave his name as Zippo Flood, and the guy waved him in. Roscoe Pope's manager had put the director on the list.

The comedian had not been on set yet—they weren't doing his scenes until next Monday—but Pepper had already heard tales of the man's erratic behavior. Noise complaints from other guests at the Hotel McAlpin, an implication of midnight bongos, a transvestite hooker who beat the night manager with her high heels when asked to stop smoking cigars in the elevator. According to Zippo, Pope and Lucinda Cole had some sort of history out in Hollywood, and the hotel manager said that the night she disappeared, the staff had seen her with Roscoe. When Zippo called his room, Roscoe told him to go fuck himself. Hence Pepper's mission downtown.

He squeezed through the mob and pried open a spot along the wall through a familiar combo of physicality and glares. The room contained nine small round cocktail tables, all taken, and the crowd jostled in every free space. Pope currently had a hit record in *Memo from Dr. Goodpussy* and while he was in town he was trying out new material in a series of secret gigs, Zippo had said. The secret was out.

The opener was onstage, the Negro ventriloquist Leroi Banks and his li'l buddy Mr. Charles. Pepper had caught him on *Red Skelton* a few times. Mr. Charles's Afro had kept pace with the times and now possessed an audacious circumference. Banks had dressed him in jeans and a jean jacket over a red satin shirt with a yellow polka-dot ascot. The ventriloquist dressed square, as befitting a straight man, in dark slacks and a yellow argyle sweater. Cigarette smoke slow-danced in a cone under the stage lights.

Mr. Charles said, "Halfway to Vegas I get up to stretch, dig, and I start rapping to the stewardess. Asks me if I've ever heard of the 'Mile High Club.' " He had a deep voice, and his head swished back and forth, painted eyelids fluttering.

Leroi whistled. "Man, I hope you kept it discreet."

"I thought so—but when I got back to my seat, my old lady had my number."

"She called you out?"

"I had sawdust on my pants."

You never see a fat ventriloquist. Pepper was of the mind that this reflected the parasitic nature of the relationship, wherein the puppet leeches the life essence of the puppeteer. Which gave him an idea for a diet craze: the mass adoption of puppet side-kicks. Send the price of lumber through the roof. From time to time his mind turned to business ventures.

Pepper crossed his arms through the next routine, wherein man and puppet debated the finer points of romance, with the former endorsing the gentlemanly approach and the latter a more aggressive system. Vulgarities were expressed. "You a sap," Mr. Charles decided, "a stone-cold sap." If Pepper had a dummy that talked to him like that, he'd choke the motherfucker. Sitting on a man's lap.

Leroi Banks and his friend took a bow—Pepper got the sense the applause was more for the approach of the main attraction. There was a white couple seated at a table a few feet away, with an extra chair. The woman wore a dress with a bright floral pattern, and the man a slim black suit, with horn-rimmed glasses. He'd been writing things down in a pad—a critic for a newspaper or a G-man investigating an obscenity case. Pepper sat down and turned the chair away from the table. He nodded at the white couple, who traded nervous looks and moved their cocktails close. Look, his lower back was sore from the movie job. Usually he didn't work so many days in a row.

A wisecracking yippie type bounced onstage, the MC. He shared a few nasal cracks about mayor-elect Beame ("You have to admire a man who runs for captain of the *Titanic*") and introduced Roscoe Pope. Pope took two steps onstage, gasped at the crowd in mock horror, and pretended to retreat in fear. He adjusted the microphone stand. He was disheveled, in wrinkled green corduroy pants and black satin baseball jacket.

"Great to be back in New York," he said. "*The Big Apple.* Catch up with some friends. See my man Christian. He's a smooth cat, always a good time with Christian. But—why do parents name their kids after stuff that's about them? It's great that you have God in your life, you don't have to bring your kid into it. I like a lot of things. Should I name my kid *Eating Pussy*? 'Here's my son, Eating Pussy.' That's not right. Hang a sign on a child for some shit you like."

The audience laughed and Pope's face changed: They had passed his test. Now he could do as he pleased. It was like when you impress bystanders or hostages with the fact that you'll hurt them if they get in your way, Pepper thought—they grant permission. Pope pressed on, taunting a couple foolish enough to sit in the front row: "Your man eat your pussy? No?" Relishing the mischief. "These two going to be fighting all the way home now. *Why don't you ever eat the pussy, dear?*" He let them off the hook and struck up a bit about a black crime fighter named the Red Conk, who gains superpowers after applying radioactive hair straightener. He has various adventures until he gets lynched by Super Cracker for using his X-ray vision on a white lady. "Strung his ass up. That's why I don't mess with white women—when anybody's looking." Followed by an autopsy of *Gone with the Wind*. "This white bitch talking about, *Oh, no, they're going to burn my house down.* They should burn your house down, bitch, you're a slave master. I had a match, I'd burn it down myself."

He reached for the glass of water on the little stool beside him. "We get movies like that because they don't teach history right. In school? All sorts of shit you don't know. 'George Washington crossing the Delaware.' It's a famous moment in American history. They don't tell you he was crossing the river because he heard there were some slaves on sale. *Row, bitch—I got that Founding Father discount!*"

A white lady up front yelled "Preach!" and a hulking, potbellied man in hepcat sunglasses along the back wall guffawed in anticipation of every punch line. Knew all the routines. On that coke, probably. He was a fan, but also part of the gang, a generation that took for granted that a black man could talk like that and not get his ass shot. What kind of rooms did Pope play in the South—mixed places like this, or chitlin joints, or not at all? Pepper had heard the comedian was far-out, picturing one of those button-down Bill Cosby types, but a bit rougher. This was a new-type Negro before him, and a room full of people tuned in to his wild style. The *Nefertiti* film crew, the college kids, now this hip downtown assortment—he was up to his ears with this new breed and their new shit.

Like at this table with the white couple. The man jotted notes, but also laughed along with the room. He wasn't a Fed; he probably worked for *The Village Voice* or one of those underground rags where they teach you how to make your own bootleg bomb. (Pepper's opinion on this matter obeyed the Fried Chicken Principle: Why make it when you can buy it?) Pope must be on a government watch list or two. How many times did they arrest Lenny Bruce? For running his mouth. Treat a white man like that, what would they do to a black man?

Pope chuckled at something he said, like he, too, couldn't believe he hadn't been strung up yet. "A lot of folks in the 'hood don't like white people," he said. "Because of history. But how could you not dig them? They're everywhere. Like dirt. Can't hate dirt. You may not want it in your house, but it does good stuff. Plants and trees live in it. For instance."

Pope sipped his water. "White dude in the back is like, *I liked his comedy routine until he started getting racial.*" He snickered.

A pale, skinny chick in overalls and a bright green cardigan weaved her way through the bodies. She elbowed a man in the stomach or stepped on his foot and he barked at her. No, it was too packed for Pepper's taste. Fire breaks out, a crazy son of a bitch with a pistol or a switchblade, cops on the hunt—there was no easy escape if something popped up. Hazel had dragged him to these tiny places a few times, to see music or have a drink, and she made a point of making fun of his skittishness. "What'd you, rob a bank?" He'd grin. It was nice when someone got your number. Not that she knew what he did for a living, but she got a general handle on him pretty quickly. Probably why she split on him.

Roscoe Pope's body turned plastic—stout and militant, then wilting in cowardice, then staggering half in the bag—and his voice equally supple as he cycled through guises and characters. Preacher, white dude, ghetto dude, angry sister, the neighborhood wino, as if he were a transmitter hooked up to the private thoughts of a cramped subway car. Also Richard Nixon: *"Get that nigger Khrushchev on the phone!"* Despite Pepper's certitude that the man was a jerk, he admired the fearlessness. It was like what he felt about Zippo—the kid was tedious but it took guts to fight inside the white man's system. You had to believe in your invincibility. Be a superhero, like the Red Conk, like Nefertiti. The Red Conk got strung up. Pepper hadn't read the screenplay so he had to wait to find out what happens to Nefertiti.

"Saw in the paper that the oldest man in Africa died," Pope said. "Oldest man in Africa—he was a hundred and ten. Can you imagine? Killed himself. No, he did. Left a note saying, *God forgot me. God forgot me.* I know—that's heavy. I'd never kill myself. I like pussy too much. Cocaine's not bad either." He made a greedy snorting sound.

"Grim Reaper come knocking on my door when I'm fucking, I'd be like, *Come back in five minutes, I'm about to bust that nut.* Okay—one minute. Fine—thirty seconds. But suicide is always sad. Bible says it's a sin. Unless you're a hundred and ten. You make it to a hundred and ten you can do whatever you want. White people haven't killed you yet, you get a free pass. *Look, bitch, I've seen everything. I'm outta here.*"

Pepper crept as close as he could to the stage before the standing ovation retarded his progress. Then he muscled through to the backstage hallway. If he noticed the irritation and anger of those he jostled and pushed, there was no external indication. In the hallway, Pope dallied with two women who'd been sitting in the front row, his finger diddling the coin return of an old pay phone.

"Pope."

The comedian scanned Pepper up and down—the clothes, the lines in his face. He refrained from whatever crack he was going to make. "Yes, brother?" He winked at someone behind Pepper and made his fingers into pistols.

"I work for the film company," Pepper said. "*Secret Agent: Nefertiti—*"

"Man, I told that fool I don't know where that dizzy bitch is."

Pepper touched his arm, lightly.

Pope's eyebrows bent. He turned conciliatory. "Let me use the john," he said. "I'll be out in a minute. That okay with you?"

Pepper nodded and moved out of the corridor, toward the small steps that led to the stage. The room was clearing, buzzing as the audience traded impressions. *If white people haven't killed you yet, you can do what you want.* You didn't have to reach a hundred years to get to that place. In a world this low, dumb, and cruel, every day white people ain't killed you yet is a win. It was after midnight. He'd survived another gauntlet.

As for Lucinda Cole—had she made it through? Overdosed somewhere. Holed up in a drug den. In need of someone to drag her ass out before something permanent went down. "I'm coming," Pepper said aloud, he don't know why. It came out irritated and weary.

After five minutes, he realized he was wrong—there was a back entrance after all. He walked down the hallway. The ventriloquist poked his head out of his dressing room, disappointed to see Pepper and not whoever he was expecting.

"You just missed him," Banks said. The dressing room opposite was empty. The ventriloquist pointed to a stairwell lit by a red lightbulb. Up the steps it led to the back alley that the Sassy Crow shared with the tiny club next door.

Wring that little bastard's neck.

# FOUR

Pepper lived in a two-room apartment above the Martinez Funeral Home, corner of 143rd and Convent. The sound of the organ swam between the floorboards like a ghost. "The Day Thou Gavest, Lord, Is Ended," "All People That on Earth Do Dwell," etc. It wasn't too bad, living over the dead. It was like living on top of the subway, which he had also done for a time: Commuter or corpse, those below were just people in transit, en route to where they had to be. On occasion he sat by the window and ate egg sandwiches in the Egon recliner Carney got him a few years back and worked on his theory about which mourners are the last to leave the service.

The next morning found him up early, energized by revenge scenarios. A younger man would have stormed over to Roscoe Pope's hotel last night, manhandled security, and busted into the comedian's room. With age came pragmatism. These days a good night's sleep was more important than appeasing one's taste for payback. The sooner he hit the hay, the more rested he'd be for tomorrow's asskicking.

The Hotel McAlpin was in Herald Square, thick of it, a twenty-five-story red brick behemoth hunched on Broadway. Decent folks complained about Times Square these days, what with the pimps and hookers and pickpockets and general seedy weather. Pepper thought Herald Square was worse. He had arranged his life to avoid concentrated messes like Herald Square, places where the straight world gathered to conduct their day-to-day. He timed this visit so that he'd miss the morning rush hour and precede the lunch-hour discharge from the dour high-rises. Nine-thirty A.M.—also before the pilgrims from the boroughs and Long Island and Jersey hit the famous department stores, Macy's, Gimbels, Korvettes, and other shrines.

He had to admit it—the first time he saw Herald Square, years ago, before the war, he was impressed with the white man's skyscrapers, the white man's towering apartment buildings, the glass-walled restaurants, those big stores crammed with all the stuff he couldn't touch. A few miles uptown, Harlem was beginning its slide, in burned-out tenements full of ghosts and stores that never reopened, the schools without schoolbooks. Herald Square had caught up in the years since. It always catches up— the consequences of how you've chosen to live, and people all over the city were choosing poorly. The indifferent attitude toward sanitation now included midtown, where gross pyramids of trash ruled the street corners. Newsstand racks gloried over the details of last night's terrible crimes. EVERYTHING MUST GO and LAST CHANCE and 75% OFF signs were on the march up Eighth and Ninth Avenues, advancing on Herald Square in scattered forays. Pepper had never voted, but the current state of affairs was almost enough to get him to make some inquiries about the process.

He remembered Jackie Robinson used to keep an apartment at the McAlpin, so he assumed it wasn't as racist as some of the other luxury hotels. The facade was luxurious enough but inside it was a real beauty. The lobby was three stories tall, the biggest one he'd ever seen, made of marble and cream-colored limestone with gigantic columns and arches. The scale reminded him of Grand Central. They didn't make them like this anymore. Just as well. No need to make everyone feel more insignificant than they already are. At this hour, hotel security gave him a quick onceover—he didn't fit the profile of the purse snatchers and con men and perverts making the papers across the country, informing everyone that the Big Apple was off-limits, busted, and dangerous.

Before Pepper came downtown he checked with the "production office"—a room in Zippo's apartment—to see if Lucinda Cole had shown up. She had not. He got the room numbers from the young man who answered the phone, who had a yokel accent and a genial phone manner that the city had not beaten out of him yet. Cole and Pope were on the same floor. Convenient if she wanted to see Pope, not so convenient if their history was bad.

"Mr. Pope?" He heard Pope snap at someone behind the door of room 1412, and a female voice complain in return. The woman asked Pepper to wait while she put something on. Pope resumed his abuse.

Pepper recognized the woman from the Sassy Crow—she was the bucktoothed white girl with long, curly red hair who'd yelled out "Preach!" a few times during the show. She was wrapped in a sheet, booze vapor issuing from her skin.

Pepper pushed past her. Pope asked who the hell it was and when he saw Pepper emerge around the corner cursed out his companion for letting him in. He was half under the covers, his skinny arms and chest suggesting an exercise regimen that consisted of hoisting a coke spoon. "Who said you could come in here?" Pope demanded, putting up his fists.

The comedian didn't understand the situation, so Pepper slugged him. The girl gasped, like a white matron in a screwball comedy. "Get dressed," Pepper told her.

Pope was stupefied. He didn't speak.

The girl snatched up her clothes from the floor—scavenger hunt—and retreated to the bathroom, trailing the sheet on the dark carpet.

Pepper sat down in the burgundy leather armchair by the window. He glanced out at Broadway. Up the ave, in the middle of the street, a man swung a metal rake and menaced the trunk of a blue sedan. The honking reached the fourteenth floor in an irritated burst.

"You remember me?" Pepper said.

The comedian nodded and probed his jaw.

"I'm with the film production." He couldn't bring himself to say that Zippo sent him. The man was such a ridiculous character that it was degrading to admit being in his employ. *Film production* sounded like there were consequences, with an emanation of lawyers and money men and insurance underwriters.

"What's your name again?"

"Pepper."

"Why they call you Pepper?"

"Nobody calls me anything," Pepper said. "You were the last person to see Lucinda Cole. What'd you get up to?"

"It was nothing—we go back. She was my lady for a while, so. We're on this movie together, it's natural we're going to hang out."

"I asked you what you got up to."

Pope told him that he ran into her at the bar downstairs and they had some drinks. It was his first night in the city—he came to town early to try out some new material and see some people. "I only saw her back, but the way she was standing at the bar, I knew it was her. It's just the way she holds herself, like royalty."

Pepper was of two minds—indulge the man's nostalgia and let him get comfortable, or push him and dominate. "Downstairs— then what?"

"Then nothing. It was last call and I knew she wasn't going to be giving it up, no matter what kind of rap I was laying down." He made a rueful chuckle. "I was trying, boy. But she was nervous and it was in her eyes—she was jonesing."

Pepper had been on *Secret Agent: Nefertiti* for a week and hadn't observed anything off. "Using? Back on it?"

"More of a pick-me-up, right? Get you through the night. She said she was heading up to 107th." That was the home of the dealer Quincy Black, he explained. You were in the entertainment biz, Quincy was a dependable and discreet connection. "I would've gone up with her, but I had a, uh, health scare last month. Fucked me up. I mean, I'll take a little refresher, but I'm on that macrobiotic shit now." Pope cocked his head. "You listening in? Get your ass out here."

The groupie stepped out of the bathroom. "You call me, Roscoe," she said.

It did not seem likely to Pepper that he was going to call her. Pope told her to beat it and delivered an epithet. She slunk away, giving Pepper the finger and sticking out her tongue on the way out.

Lucinda Cole. The next step was clear. Pepper said, "Get dressed."

"I'm not going anywhere."

"You're taking me to Quincy."

"It ain't even noon. That nigger ain't up."

"I know how to wake people up."

Pepper refrained from grabbing the man by the scruff and marching him all the way. Pope didn't see the world like other people but Pepper hoped that getting slugged in the face had set him right, like how you kick a vending machine or a stuck jukebox. The comedian behaved when the elevator doors opened and the car turned out to be full of fresh-faced tourists gearing up for their New York safari, and he didn't try anything when they hit the lobby, whose leather couches and club chairs had started to fill up. Guests meeting up before they headed out, suits from the surrounding office buildings rendezvousing with visiting clients.

The dark wood of the big reception desk resembled the hull of a ship, with the uniformed staff at their stations peering out into the sea of the lobby. The manager emerged from an office behind reception and Pope jerked a thumb at him. "His face, right?" he said.

"What?"

"He has a racist face—you see it."

It was true. His white hair was swept back in an elegant wave, like in a museum portrait, its color bringing out the pink in his wide face, which was knobby in lobe, chin, and cheek. The blue eyes signaled cool, barely suppressed rage. There was no doubt about it—his was a racist face, more Southern Cracker racist than New England Plymouth Rock racist. Pepper couldn't suppress his smile at the description.

They pushed through the revolving doors. The buildings on the square generated hostile eddies of wind, funneled by the concrete and glass. Pope said, "Sometimes you see someone and they just look racist, right? They can't help it. My money manager is this white guy, Spencer Tomlinson." An iceberg of slow-walking tourists floated toward them. Pepper and Pope separated and reunited on the other side. Pope continued: "At the end of our first meeting, right, I say how nice it was to meet him and he goes, 'Because of this' and he puts his finger on his nose. And I go, what do you mean? He says, 'That's okay, I know I was born with a racist face.' "

Pope checked to make sure Pepper was chuckling before he rammed him, knocking him into an old white lady carrying A&S shopping bags. Pepper and the lady were on the sidewalk, and then he was up and in pursuit. Always plenty of bystanders to help an old white lady to her feet. Old black ladies, you're on your own. The comedian was halfway across Thirty-fourth Street, heading uptown. Pepper zigzagged around the Checker cab—tourists in the jump seats gawking—and the Exeter Moving van. He didn't see any patrolmen but it was Herald Square so they were near. He caught up with Pope at the corner of Thirty-fifth and this time gripped him by the neck with one hand and bent the man's arm up into the small of his back. He twisted him around and head-butted him in the nose.

Pope cursed, eyes watering. "How am I supposed to make this movie with my face all swole up, nigger?"

Pope had a couple of days to ice his nose before he hit the cameras. Pepper told him that Angela the makeup girl was pretty good. Last Monday she took ten years off the guy playing the police chief, some magical brown blend of hers.

Pepper had a headache the rest of the day and from then on

remembered this morning as his retirement from headbutting. It was a young man's game.

\* \* \*

The Times Square station abounded with escape routes; Pepper kept a hand on his quarry's arm. People in Times Square these days kept their eyes to themselves—if they hadn't learned firsthand that the game had changed, surely the daily reports from the nightly news and newspapers and their cowed circle kept them appraised. At any moment your day might lurch into tragedy—Juilliard student shoved onto the tracks, mother of four stabbed for six dollars and a pastrami on rye. Rats hopped on the tracks fighting over discarded pizza crusts and knishes. Teenagers threw food down there to see them fight, Roman emperors overseeing the games.

On the downtown track a 2 train pulled in, its metal skin writhing with bright, multicolored symbols. A few years ago the cars were covered in grime and soot, as if the darkness of the tunnels had rubbed off. Now miscreants descended upon the cars at night in the train yards of the IRT and the Flushing Line, the terminuses of 239th Street and Coney Island, hopping chain-link to attack their canvases, loaded with shoplifted aerosol paint cans. The clack-clack of the metal ball inside that agitated the paint while they contemplated their next avenue of assault. Names, deadbeat slogans, boasts, and invective exploded on the train cars in balloon letters and sharp-angled glyphs, rainbow dispatches for the people on platforms and the bystanders on the street who saw them zipping through the air on the elevated tracks.

People complained of course, but Pepper didn't care if some kid wrote his name on the side of a subway car, or the wall of a tenement, or a dry-cleaning van when its driver wasn't looking. The city was covered in names, on plazas and parks and bridges, and most belonged to crooks. Whoever Remsen and Schermerhorn were, they didn't get their names on street signs for being decent men, that's for damn sure. The world didn't work that way.

The Transit Authority maintenance crews beat back the graffiti, hosing it off so there'd be room for the next day's messages and handles, but the names of the crooked city fathers—the slavers, money pimps, and fat cats—would never be washed away. They were indelible.

Pepper had no beef with the graffiti kids. Let them roam.

The uptown 1 pulled in before the 2. The conductor in the lead car said, "Let 'em off, let 'em off." The hordes shuffled. Make a cross section of Times Square, ant farm–style, and you'd see a collection of mobs—the ones huddled on the platforms below waiting for the train car doors to open, and the ones on the sidewalks above waiting for DONT WALK to become WALK. At their respective signals, both groups surged forward.

There were no seats. Pepper stood between Pope and the door. The comedian nodded, resigned after the escape attempt. Pepper had seen it before in men he'd beaten over the years, the satisfaction with a token attempt to reverse the situation. It didn't matter if it worked as long as you could tell the fellows or yourself that you tried something.

Pope said, "Talked to Hal Ashby last week at a party. He's doing a movie about the circus. Writing a part for me—the ringmaster. Black ringmaster of a white circus—ain't that a gas? And I'm in New York City doing this crummy picture."

Pepper nodded. Fiftieth Street. He'd been chased into this station once and lost them when he jumped into the tunnel. They only follow half the time if you beat it for the tracks, he'd learned.

"This guy Zippo? I don't think he's all there. I think that nigger's got a screw loose, you hear me?"

"I agree."

Pope's expression turned overcast. "This thing with Lucy. You think she's okay?"

"How would I know?"

"She never missed a day of work, even when she was snorting one day into the next. I thought I was bad, shit—I used to call her the Hoover, the way she vacuumed that shit up! But she always showed up to the set. 'We don't get second chances,' she used to tell me when I was fucking around, sleeping in. You need people like that in your life—tell you to get your ass out of bed, right?"

Pepper thought of Hazel naturally, but was not going to signal inclusion in Pope's fraternity. But he did miss her. He didn't mind it when she told him his business, didn't mind a lot of things about her.

Pope sighed. "Quincy is cool, but he has these guys who handle his business sometimes, I heard some bad things. You think one of them did something to her? She goes up there late at night and—"

"I don't know."

"We should have taken a taxi if the movie is paying for it. I'm famous, bitch." He delivered *famous* with a quiver, as if unable to hold on to the notion. He met Lucinda Cole three years ago, he said, at the house of a Los Angeles player. Pepper had never heard of the guy, but Pope kept repeating his name, the way low-level hoods invoke neighborhood gangsters and bosses, like everyone is supposed to know who they are and regard them with the same fear and reverence: Don Cornelius, Don Cornelius. *Don*—was he in the mob? Pepper gathered the man was in the music industry. He'd ask John or May who he was, next time he saw them.

Don Cornelius held a July Fourth cookout and Roscoe Pope saw Lucinda enter the patio from the walkway along the side of the house. "You know how it is, you recognize someone from the movies and then you see them in person and it knocks you out? It was like that but times ten."

Pepper had seen Martin Balsam coming out of Trader Vic's once, back in the old Savoy Hilton, so he understood.

"Everybody had a thing for Lucy from *Miss Pretty's Promise*—she was fine. Finer in person—but you know, you're working on this movie. A Black Athena."

"Nefertiti."

"Black Athena. I don't know how I got it up to rap to her. I was all"—he mouthed gibberish—"but that was the start. She'd heard of me—not seen my act but heard stories of my partying, that Vegas stuff. She listened to me. You let me talk, I'm going to get you."

Pepper tuned him out. The ghost station caught his attention, as it always did, that fleeting apparition beyond the windows. Look at a subway map and downtown all the stops are close together: Rector, Wall, Cortlandt. Only a few blocks apart. White people were lazy back then—lazier—and didn't want to walk too far. Then they got smart—too many stops slow things down. Back in '59, they closed the Ninety-first Street station, so the 1 went from Eighty-sixth to Ninety-sixth. It made sense. Pepper didn't remember activists marching up Broadway with SAVE OUR NINETY-FIRST STREET STATION! signs and handing out pamphlets like they do these days over every little thing.

But it had been one of his stations. Dolly had lived on Eighty-ninth when they were together, so he'd split from her pad, snag a coffee at Metro Donut, and hop on the 1 at Ninety-first. Ninety-first was a door into Dolly's law-abiding world—and how he got back into his own crooked one. He liked getting on at Ninety-first because it meant he was returning to where he belonged. Sometimes when he hung out with Carney and Elizabeth and the kids, Pepper thought about how he had chosen to live, and where. He thought about all his passed-over stations.

When they buried Ninety-first it was like they buried those days too, the good parts and otherwise. No going back. The platform remained even if the street entrance was covered by concrete. Walking on the sidewalk above, he forgot it existed. In the tunnel he sped through it and some rides—not every time—he stared into that harbor carved into the rock. What's been happening in there, among the advertisements for discontinued products and posters of forgotten motion pictures and Broadway flops? Punks sneak in to paint graffiti over what other guys threw up last week, layer over layer, like the buildings above—put it up, knock it down, another takes its place. But what's been happening that can't be captured in the five seconds when his train shudders through? As a crook he knew that everybody gets up to something when nobody's looking.

The ghost station remained. They passed it. One day when he had time he'd walk down the tunnel from Ninety-sixth and visit. Up close, see it for real, what it's been up to lately.

"I told her to fire her manager," Pope said. "She was doing this TV shit, *Dragnet* and *Adam-12,* glamorizing the pigs. Man, she was Sister Josephine from *Miss Pretty's Promise*—you don't put her up for chump shit like that! It's a modern-day plantation out there. I got these white directors sucking my dick right now because I'm hot. Got to make a splash while I can. But when they stop giving a shit, I still have my jokes. What does Lucy have, except what they decide to give her? Ten years after *Miss Pretty* and they got her playing nurses." He stopped to glower at a white man in a tan overcoat who disapproved of his colorful language. "When we were together, she still thought that big role was just around the corner. You come from the ghetto like she did, you have to believe that. The way out. That's why I felt bad when I saw her at the hotel. She didn't have that fire anymore. She looked beaten."

This young white guy with long wavy hair and a hippie beard was eavesdropping, his smile growing more and more broad as the rhythms of speech and turns of language proved that yes, the famous comedian walked among them. Was in fact standing over him. "Roscoe?"

"What?"

"What are you doing taking the subway, Roscoe?"

"This big nigger done kidnapped my ass, what you think I'm doing on the subway, motherfucker?"

The white guy looked up at Pepper. Pepper nodded.

Pope stepped forward and turned his body. "Buy your record, they think they own you," he said. He stared out into the indifferent void of the tunnel.

# FIVE

There were a hundred ways to announce that you were crooked and a hundred ways to un-announce it. You can peacock it up like a pimp, hang your shingle in polyester plumage. Push the latest high on a street corner, signaling customers with a furtive yet defiant air. You can un-announce like a banker, tucked into a double-breasted suit, installed behind a desk with your name on a plaque. Establish a front: Outfit a bodega or stationery store to hide the dice game out back. Or a furniture store. This was Quincy Black's method, catering to his clientele behind the facade of a renovated Harlem brownstone.

Many of the brownstones and townhouses uptown bore the metropolitan weather in chipped stoops, networks of stains and fissures, the marks of rascally vandalism. Hooligans' names carved into scuffed wooden doors, half-jimmied locks with cranky tumblers. Quincy Black's townhouse on 107th between Broadway and Riverside stuck out in its ramshackle row. With its precisely restored exterior, new double-leaf mahogany doors and matching shutters, number 316 aspired to detach and crab-walk over to a nicer block. In better weather the window boxes likely exploded with colorful arrangements, in contrast to the Thunderbird bottles and cigarette butts decorating the stoops next door. The brass fixtures gleamed. When Pepper pressed the doorbell, it sang proud and deep.

They waited. Pepper had ordered Pope to call the peddler from a pay phone outside the 110th Street station. Quincy Black was home. Now that there was no wriggling free, the comedian had grown excited about this unexpected expedition. He said, "I'm from Kansas, Jim. This is a trip. I knew big-time Hollywood movies had guys like you—fixers—but a low-budget job like this? Sheee-it."

Pepper clocked the tall Spanish man on the corner in the black overcoat. Earmuffs, cigarette. Was he looking at them? The man continued up Broadway, out of sight.

"You ever been to California?" Pope said.

"No."

"Where you from? The city?"

"Newark."

"Then you know what time it is. Quincy grew up in the Bronx, but then he went out to LA to live with his aunt. Her old man was in Nat King Cole's band, played on the TV show. Remember that shit? First black man with his own show. You know they shut that down quick." Quincy maintained that Hollywood was his finishing school, Pope said. Taught him how to run a game, not get played himself. Back in New York, he struck up with Notch Walker. "He won't, like, spell it out, but his shit comes from Notch. Good stuff, too." Pope mimed swirling a wineglass under his nose—"King of the World with a slight paranoid undertone."

107th Street. As far as Pepper recalled he had never committed a crime on 107th Street. No rush. He tried to remember the name of that peddler he set up that one time back in '61. The guy had his crew dealing on the corner of 103rd, stash house on 105th: Biz Dixon. Why had Pepper been tailing him? Right, another offbeat Carney deal, like this movie job. Digging up dirt on that big Harlem banker from Carver Federal, with the drug peddler as a side play. Never did get a handle on why Carney had been after them—after he slugged Carney in the face for getting him mixed up in it, Pepper had moved on to the next job. The furniture salesman will get you into trouble, like his old man. At least his wife was nice, and the two kids.

Quincy Black opened the door, decked out in brown corduroy trousers and a white silk shirt embroidered with tiger heads. He was younger than Pepper had imagined, slim and long-limbed, with plucked eyebrows and a pencil mustache. He gushed. "Roscoe! You look great! Congratulations."

Pope smiled. "For what?"

"For all of it, brother! All of it!" Pepper and Pope stepped into the vestibule. Quincy gave Pepper a once-over.

"I'm Pepper."

"Good to meet you, brother." Quincy pointed to the low bamboo rack by the foot of the stairwell. "They go there."

Pope was acquainted with the house rules and bent down to take off his sneakers. He signaled for Pepper to join him.

Yet Pepper did not remove his shoes.

He was thinking about the patches of light on the polished banisters, the freshly vacuumed hallway runner—staff. How many people did Quincy employ to keep up the place and where were they now?

Quincy regarded Pepper's black brogues and said, "Thanks, brother," as if Pepper had heeded his request. Which he hadn't. Quincy added, "In Oriental cultures it's part of the arrangement between host and guest."

Yet Pepper did not remove his shoes.

A large man emerged from the back of the townhouse, tiny-headed and round-bellied like a ten pin, lumbering from the kitchen. He wiped his left hand on his yellow apron and peered down the hall at them, taking the measure of the situation. His other hand held a butcher knife. Cartoon salt-and-pepper shakers cavorted across the body of the apron.

Yet Pepper did not remove his shoes.

It was not Pepper's intention to be difficult. It was a matter of personal principle: socks were holy. To straights and squares, the criminal world was defined by chaotic forces: the violent and the unruly, the reprehensible and the forbidden. But Pepper governed his own little corner through iron rules and logic, and if asked to explain his system (don't work with dopeheads, never knock over a bank on a Tuesday), he could do so (though no one ever asked). His disproportionate affection for socks, however, was idiosyncratic and belonged to the realm of the unsayable, like the formulae of love or the final name of God.

His appreciation took root in the freezing Newark mornings of his childhood. Cotton swaddled around his feet, no matter how threadbare, allowed him to face the mirthless cold. In the Pacific theater during the war he came to respect and revere fresh, dry pairs as a ward against trench foot, parasites, and myriad fungal depredations. The first thing he did when he got back to the Green Valley Motor Lodge after the botched McCarran job was to peel off his blood-soaked footwear; he didn't feel human again until he put on a new pair of cotton-poly socks. People were often disappointing; a fine pair of socks, seldom so. They were not to be displayed casually, at a stranger's demand. He slept in them, only took them off to bathe or to make love, although on two occasions they had been cut off by emergency room personnel while he lay unconscious. At this moment he was not making love, and the highlight of his day so far had been a long hot shower. No, he could not stoop or bend in the front hallway of Quincy Black's townhouse. It was impossible.

Quincy put his hands on his hips. "Ros, what's up with your friend?"

Pope frowned and wilted.

Quincy sucked his teeth. "I got white carpet." He addressed the man with the butcher knife. "Pickles—welcome this nigger to the house."

Roscoe Pope in his time working dingy clubs and jukes in the great Midwest had witnessed all manner of impromptu and messy violence—rotgut-fueled knife fights, cruel psychopaths terrorizing prey, bloody back-alley retribution. He was hard to impress. After the fight in the parlor hall of 316 West 107th Street, he resolved never to sass Pepper again. Foreboding imagery aside, Pickles probably just wanted to make some intimidating noises—scare the man a little—and get back to whatever he was doing in the kitchen. He liked to bake, Pope knew. He started to warn the bodyguard to chill out, but the event was over too quickly.

Pickles ripped off the apron and tossed it to the parquet floor. He advanced, holding the butcher knife before him as a knight charged with his lance. Pepper moved swiftly, like a mean gust between skyscrapers, nabbing the man's wrist and checking him against the stairwell. Three family pictures jumped off their nails and fell down the stairs at the impact. Pickles heaved himself free and rammed Pepper into the opposite wall of the hallway. Pepper stayed the knife with his left hand, and smashed the bodyguard's Adam's apple with his right. He lifted his foot—here time slowed down for the eyewitnesses to apprehend what was about to transpire—and pulverized Pickles's naked, defenseless foot with his big, black shoe. The knife fell silently onto the tight fibers of the runner.

Pickles's screams withered to a croak. Dispatched with the nonchalance of a man crumpling up sandwich paper and tossing it in the trash. Pepper kicked the butcher knife down the hall and hoisted Pickles to his feet. He marched him into the adjacent parlor and shoved the limping man to the curved, coffee-colored leather sofa. The gigantic sofa dwarfed the bodyguard and reminded Pepper of the ventriloquist's puppet the previous night. Tiny man, dangling legs. The two armchairs were mammoth and sumptuous, and the paintings on the walls covered by expensive scribbles. Pepper was rarely in rooms like this when their owners were home.

A rug of perfect white covered the majority of the floor. One imagined it stained easily.

Pepper nodded to Quincy, to indicate that his host join his employee on the couch. Without being told, Pope leaned against the fireplace where Pepper could keep an eye on him. From the painting above the mantel, an old black man in plantation master clothes scowled at the proceedings.

Pepper grabbed Pickles's lapels and pulled him forward. He

asked Quincy how many people were in the house, slapping Pickles for emphasis without taking his eyes off Quincy's face.

"Just us," Quincy said.

Pickles croaked again.

Pepper told him to spit it out.

"The Armand bank-truck job."

Pepper shook his head. In ignorance. In reproach that a man would refer to a job—any job—in mixed company.

"Shaved head? White sunglasses?" Pickles said. "That was my thing."

The Armand Armored Truck Company—sure. Pepper recalled their earlier meeting. He'd been invited to join the crew but declined the rip-off for many reasons. They had met in Put Put Lewis's house out in Corona to go over the setup. Put Put had converted his basement into a rec room, with a mirrored wet bar, leopard-skin stools, and two black-velvet paintings of naked women on horseback. Kept offering cocktails to justify summoning them there but no one was in the mood for anything more complicated than Canadian Club rocks. Reasons for passing: The wheelman talked too slow, like he was from the South or missing gears upstairs. Pepper liked a fast-talking wheelman, for consistency, the complete package. Then there was Put Put. Put Put was a known type, a man who appeared at your elbow and waited to weasel into your conversation with tales of jobs gone wrong, shit-eating grin like it was the highlight of his day. To be so lacking in self-respect as to advertise one's bad luck and incompetence.

Finally, Pickles. Pepper caught him picking his nose, under the harsh interrogation-room track lighting of the rec room. Hard to put faith in a man's subtlety and discretion when he can't pick his nose right. In retrospect maybe that's why they called him Pickles.

"Remember me?" Pickles asked. His eyes watered.

Pepper said, yeah.

Quincy huffed in disgust. "Pickles. Pepper. Pope—what is this, some kind of fucked-up convention?"

Pope said, "Man, you don't want to mess with this dude."

"Bring some motherfucker in to rob my ass and tell me to calm down."

Pepper exhaled loudly. "I'm here about Lucinda Cole. She was here two nights ago."

"So what?" Quincy said. "She forgot her purse?"

Pepper scratched his jaw. His host got two free wisecracks in return for him not taking off his shoes, but the next one meant a pop in the mouth. "Tell me about it," Pepper said.

He hadn't seen the actress in two years, Quincy told him. "She tried to clean her ass up, and we're always the first to get dropped. Until they get a hankering again." He was a fan of her work, and of her as a person. She was always polite and comported herself well, "not like a lot of the heads who come through here." The actress was lucky he was home when she called; he and Pickles were supposed to see that killer snake movie *Sssssss* at the Maharaja Theater on 145th, but the times in the newspaper were wrong "as motherfucking usual."

Now assured that he was not being robbed, and merely had to violate customer privacy, Quincy adopted a relaxed tone. "She looked good, but she always does," he said, crook to crook. "She never showed her habit, you know? Didn't want any powder, just something to help her sleep. Complained the movie was running her ragged. People go on about how tired and run ragged they are, then ask for something to turn the volume down more."

In response to Pepper's question, he added that she left around midnight. "Hooked her up with some Valium. In and out, didn't want to stay and chat."

"Valium."

"Practically raining Valium out there these days. Corporate pharmaceutical profit strategy is the same as ghetto strategy: Flood the streets, get them hooked."

Quincy began to expound on how the Nazis basically invented

the modern-day tranquilizer industry by forcing the drug company Roche to relocate their Jewish scientists to the United States, but Pepper raised his hand: *Stop*. He turned to Pickles. "What's he leaving out?"

"That's it," Pickles said. He rubbed his sore foot in gentle circles. "You know, sometimes people want to get to their goodies lickety-split."

"Too true," Pope said, wistfully.

"Chink Montague looking for my ass, I'd be scarce, too." Quincy laughed.

Pepper's headache piped up: Still here. He told him to spill it.

"She was running out the door and I asked her if it was good to be home," Quincy said. "She grew up around here, uptown. Said it was good to be back, except for all the familiar faces."

"Like Chink?"

"I didn't bring him up—she did." He flopped his shoulders. "He used to go with her when she was starting out. Bought her clothes, helped her 'get discovered.' She said she was mostly laying low downtown, but that night she was shooting in some shoe store uptown, the phone rings and it's him on the phone."

Pepper pictured the movie setup at Carney's place. Lola had taken over Marie's office. "What'd he say?"

"I don't know man, ask Columbo." Pepper stiffened and Quincy eliminated the sarcasm from his tone. "Didn't say. But she came here so he must have got her riled up."

Pepper withdrew four steps. He checked on the defeated Pickles, whose slouch and pout signaled that he was unlikely to cold-cock him on the way out.

Pope said, "We done?"

Pepper nodded.

"Mind if I stay and catch up with my man Quincy?"

Pepper gave him a look. "Macrobiotic."

The comedian chuckled and rubbed his palms together. "It's hard out here in the Big Apple—man needs every boost he can get."

Pope had brought a violent man into the drug peddler's house and made him rat out a customer, but from Quincy's expression he bore no grudge. Another reason Pepper had never worked retail: It required a forgiving nature.

Pickles sat up. He said, "Hey, man."

Pepper stopped in the doorway.

"Why didn't you take off your damn shoes?"

"Hole," he said. "In my sock."

# SIX

They were tearing up the street outside the Martinez Funeral Home again, exposing the layers beneath the black asphalt. The jackhammers did not stop, the racket went on for hours, and it was as if the noise from out of the hole was that of the machine of the city and you could now hear the true operation of the metropolis. The noisy industry of valves and pistons, the great gears grinding against each other, the clack and snap and bang. Maybe after midnight in the hours of crime and sleeplessness you may hear it, too, if you listen closely: a distant whir or rumble.

When he woke it was dark and quiet. After his visit to 107th Street, Pepper had returned to the McAlpin to check out Lucinda Cole's room. It had been trashed; he wanted to see what he could find in the mess. The hotel hadn't cleaned up—probably waiting on the insurance company. Get the film company to pay, then your insurance: double-dip. What Pepper saw was not the aftermath of a party, as described. A vase had detonated against the full-length mirror on the door, shattering them both. The floor lamp had been ripped from the wall and bent in half—the shaft was too thick to snap completely. This was rage.

By the time Pepper got back uptown, his headache had evolved into an insistent, malevolent throb. Ideally a headbutt demolished the victim's soft tissue—the nose was the most popular target—but he'd caught the plane of Pope's forehead and knocked something loose inside his own thick noggin. He swallowed a bunch of aspirin, staggered into bed, and when he opened his eyes the street work was done and it was night.

He cut across 143rd and down Amsterdam to meet Zippo. His time on *Secret Agent: Nefertiti* made him think the massive lights on the south side of 140th Street were part of a film. A different sort of production was underway. The red, white, and blue banner strung from the eaves of the five-story buildings read HOMES 4 HARLEM. Ribbon-cutting ceremony on a new city housing development that wasn't supposed to look like public housing, as if using orange brick instead of red would confuse people.

David Dinkins jabbered at the podium. He was one of Charlie Rangel's and Percy Sutton's cronies, probably bucking for a city hall job now that Beame was in charge. Pepper's distaste for Dinkins owed to the man's naïve opinions on "the crime problem." Crime isn't a scourge, people are. Crime is just how folks talk to each other sometimes.

The sidewalk civilians were good, law-abiding types, churchy-looking men and women in their fifties and sixties. A few young moms thrown in. He assumed they were mothers—what else could motivate them to stand in the cold but the possibility that their loved ones might get it better than they had it?

Dinkins wrapped it up and gave the mic to a man he introduced as former district attorney Alexander Oakes. Pretty boy. Pepper had seen him on the news a few times, applauding the white man beside him at appropriate moments. He'd ditched his dark pinstripe suit in favor of a man-of-the-people work coat with the H4H logo stitched into the breast.

"And I'd like to thank Jake's and the Amsterdam Gardens for providing the food tonight," Oakes said. "I asked good Mr. King if he'd made enough cobbler for all the people we expect and he said, 'You'll see.' There are going to be a lot of disappointed faces, that's all I'm going to say, brother. You know black people can eat some cobbler." Oakes smiled and the crowd chuckled.

The prim line of buildings had gone up in a blink. Pepper remembered the row of abandoned tenements, half of them sootened and hollowed by fires, the burned-out buildings like black gaps in a rickety smile. Then the empty lot, with its indecent glimpse of the city's innards. Now this five-story housing, nothing fancy, but respectable and—if they hadn't cut corners and had kept the construction grift within a reasonable range— a decent place for people to live.

"Before we head into the community room for the first time and you see what a wonderful job they did, I want to get serious for a moment." Oakes waited for the ambulance and its siren to pass. "Some people say Harlem's on its way out. The whole city is going down the tubes. Can't get a decent wage, landlords got us in a vise grip, and city hall's an empty suit." The crowd murmured, surveying their private complaints. "Drugs on every corner, kids growing up with the wrong kind of role models. It doesn't have to be this way," Oakes said, "unless we let it. It starts here. On these streets, in places like this. You used to walk past this block all the time, past the buildings that used to stand here, and be reminded about how bad they let things get. These houses, and the others like them, will finally provide a safe place for working New Yorkers to raise a family." Hokey enough for multiple amens even if they were only in it for the cobbler.

Slick motherfucker. Pepper didn't trust him for dog catcher. If he wasn't running for something now, he would be soon.

\* \* \*

Pepper arrived at the chicken joint five minutes early. New Country Kitchen was packed, but Viola saw him squeeze through the doors and shooed away a young couple making for the last table by the window. She assured them something would open up momentarily. They were unconvinced.

Viola brought Pepper a lemonade. "You look like shit," she said.

The metronome *clop* of his headache was likely loud enough for others to hear. "Pays the rent."

Viola shrugged and returned to the kitchen, pausing to snap at the waitress to refill the napkin dispensers on the unsteady tables. The new girl was a meek little creature who shrank at Viola's voice. She wouldn't last long. They rarely did at New Country Kitchen.

From his spot in the window Pepper couldn't help but check out how Lady Betsy's fared across the street. The restaurant was half full, its patrons older than New Country's, regulars for decades no doubt. He caught a glimpse of Lady Betsy herself, hand on her hip, gabbing with customers. More stooped than in former days, and she had stopped dyeing her hair, which whorled like a white rose, but still in business.

Lady Betsy had owned that corner since before the war, an uptown chicken legend since the Great Depression. She presided over her operation with a blend of frank, backwoods wit and urban practicality, a pioneer in that particular New York City philosophical school. The paper place mats contained a biographical sketch adjacent to the menu, whose item updates and price increases Lady Betsy scratched in by hand, rather than waste cash on a new print run. According to the story, when Lady Betsy left her native Alabama to venture North, all she had was a bus ticket and a hatbox full of secret recipes. The red-and-white-striped hatbox remained on display in a glass case above the register like the jawbone of a saint.

In the midst of the daily Jim Crow tribulations and humiliations, Lady Betsy's family had assembled the instructions for an eternal feast. A refreshing scorpion spike of heat lay hidden in the collards, and the mac and cheese was a symphony of competing textures, but the chicken was divine, fried in the very skillet of heaven. The house dredge was no mere spicy dusting of cornmeal but a crispy concoction of buttermilk, flour, and dream stuff. To penetrate that wall of batter and gain the meat inside was to storm the keep of pleasure. Local politicians and famous songsmiths posed with the owner in photographs, amid framed citations and plaques from the spectrum of Harlem organizations—the big, the small, and the spurious. A tour bus used to make a special trip uptown and white people from all over the country—perhaps kin to the same white people who had persecuted Lady Betsy down South—poured out of the vehicle to partake, until an incident in which a neighborhood rummy exposed himself in an especially aggressive anatomical display. That put an end to the anthropology.

You had to get there early. In the old days, before the restaurant took over the palm reader next door and expanded the kitchen, Lady Betsy sold out of wings and thighs and drumsticks by nine P.M. So many people lined up you'd think Count Basie was playing inside. If Pepper was not mistaken, Carney's father was the first person to take him there—Big Mike was a proponent of a proper meal before a robbery. Breaking a guy's leg or casing a warehouse didn't necessarily require nutritional prep, but a robbery called for a hearty sit-down, without fail. Pepper, reluctant to offer praise on anything or anybody, privately assessed that it was the best chicken he'd ever tasted.

Then Viola Lewis opened her joint across the street in 1965. She was a slim, dark-eyed lady of indeterminate age and overdetermined mystery. She hailed from a witchy backwater in Louisiana, showed up in New York City with a carpetbag of money—it was said she'd enchanted the heir of a colored beauty product dynasty with a handful of goofer dust—and set herself up on the corner of 138th and Amsterdam. The grand opening was less than spectacular. How could this upstart compete with Lady Betsy's precious morsels? Eventually curiosity, and the oddly alluring scent from the New Country Kitchen's exhaust pipe, won out. (Rumor had it an additive to the fumes charmed the nose.) The surprising verdict: They did a bird pretty good in there. Existential arguments over which establishment fried the best chicken became a barbershop staple. Each joint converted its disciples, but Harlem is a sentimental place and set in its ways, and when the white world can take away you and yours in an instant some folks hold on to the sure and the same. Lady Betsy's maintained the advantage.

Opening a chicken joint across from a fabled Harlem landmark was a provocation. "It's a free country," Viola told Pepper. "I don't see what the big deal is, really," she said, lying breezily. Her voice was low and husky and she cut her syllables with the precision of a butcher. "If her chicken is that good, it shouldn't matter if a dozen chicken joints open up on the block."

This conversation happened in Donegal's one foggy night in the summer of '68. Somehow Viola had materialized next to him at the bar without him noticing—witchy. Her black hair was woven into long Indian braids that lay across her white linen blouse like two serpents. He recognized her. He'd supped in New Country a few times when the line was too long across the street, but had remained loyal to Lady Betsy. More or less. "I hear you pull jobs," she said.

She acknowledged the facts of the case: She and her competitor were stalemated in their struggle for control over the mid-Harlem chicken trade. "I stand by my product and believe it to be superior to my competitor's. But this war must end—definitively, once and for all, kaput." To that end she wanted to retain Pepper's services for a heist. There was a rogue ingredient in Lady Betsy's chicken among the paprika and cayenne and garlic powder, an Element X, that Viola could not identify, try as she might. "Last night I woke up in a tremble, certain that it was pickle juice in the buttermilk brine. It was not." As long as this variable eluded her, the war continued.

In his decades uptown, Pepper had stayed out of Harlem's innumerable turf battles and gangster intrigues. He disdained the mainstream criminal class for its insipid codes, grubby designs, and the low-quality individual it attracted: Fuck 'em. Viola's contest with Lady Betsy was as urgent as any mob war, with casualties measured in customers lost instead of soldiers fallen. He was stirred by her proposal, in his heart and by a tug in his groin. Those eyes—he wondered later if her acquaintance with dark powers was more than a rumor. They did a deal for the chicken job, shook hands, and the restaurateur disappeared into the Broadway mist.

As far as setups went, it was straightforward. The only wrinkle was that his employer wanted no trace of the break-in. Pepper retained the services of the best uptown lock man available, Enoch Parker. Enoch owed Pepper for a botched job a couple of years back, when the getaway car refused to start and they had to hoof it from the warehouse, lugging chinchilla coats up Sixth Ave, looking like runaway bears. "That shit's a breeze," the safecracker announced once the parameters were explained: pick the lock to Lady Betsy's basement door and the one safeguarding the recipe without damaging them. Both were cheap combination deals. Viola had bribed or beguiled a former Lady Betsy's waitress who had reported that the sacred recipes were kept in a tiny metal box in the back office.

The night of the job, Viola sat in her darkened restaurant across the street, watching Pepper and Enoch's swift entrance into the basement through the sidewalk doors. To be sure her path to this moment had been complicated and strange. Sometimes she stepped back from her life and regarded it as if it were a painting in a black museum, populated by murky figures, its caption gibberish. She smoked French cigarettes as she waited and ruminated to herself in a forgotten tongue. The streets were empty. 2 A.M. The thieves were in and out in ten minutes.

"Any problems?" she asked, locking the door behind them.

The "small metal box" described by the disgruntled waitress had turned out to be a late-model Aitkens wall safe behind a painting of the Statue of Liberty, but Enoch had dispatched it with aplomb. "No," Pepper said.

Pepper and Enoch followed Viola into the back office. She flipped through the black binder of recipes after fried chicken lore, nodding here and there to register a random insight. "Two drops of white vinegar." "Steam the beans until ~~defeated~~ they are defeated." She found what she was looking for. Her mouth moved as she pored over the fried chicken recipe. She stopped. Looked up at Pepper and Enoch, and smiled. The crooks crept away and returned the binder to the wall safe.

Viola made her move two weeks later via a big Labor Day promotion: two-for-one family buckets and a complimentary side. By the next Friday, word came down—New Country Kitchen was on top, and there it remained. Whether Element X was a spice, an oil temperature, or an interval of brining or resting or cajoling, when added to her own formidable recipe, Viola surpassed her nemesis. Plus, Pepper couldn't help but notice, she changed her frying oil more frequently, you could taste it.

Pepper's take came out to free chicken for life, once a week. (Negotiated down from free chicken for life, period.) Big Mike would have crossed the street, too, given the simplicity of the question: Who did the better bird? He had been a practical man.

A memory sprang upon Pepper, as he sat with his forearms glued to the slightly tacky Formica table, of a time many years ago when he and Big Mike were wound up after a job. Payroll rip-off, Sunshine Bakery in Secaucus. The bars had closed but Big Mike said he had a bottle at his house. This was when he and his son, Ray, still lived at that place on 127th Street. Big Mike went to fetch glasses from the kitchen and started hollering and cursing. He stomped down the hallway and dragged his son out by the ear. They stood in the doorway to the kitchen. "Look at all this shit in the sink! What's your job?"

Young Carney was so skinny he was a walking twig. His father twisted and he buckled under the pain. "Keep the house clean," Ray said.

"Does this look clean? Clean it up!"

Middle of the week, the kid had to get up for school in two hours. Pepper was about his age when he first walloped his old man and put an end to scenes like this. Carney Jr. wasn't the type, and Carney Sr. wasn't the type to abide such a thing, but you have to put that feeling somewhere and Pepper figured he'd seen it leak out from time to time during Ray Carney's jobs and schemes: the cold thrust of the knife.

Big Mike set down the whiskey on the coffee table. Pepper drank it as fast as he could without getting his host into a lather, and split. He couldn't see him, but in the kitchen the kid was still scrubbing.

* * *

Zippo spotted him from outside. Pepper's head dipped imperceptibly in greeting. The director was shrouded in black again, black trousers and a shimmering blouse underneath a black overcoat. "Smells the same," he said. He sat down opposite. "I love this place. People talk about the chicken, but the coleslaw is bananas. Sometimes I grab a tub and that's all I eat for days."

Pepper waved over the young waitress, who kept looking over her shoulder as if her mistakes were under constant tally. Which they probably were. Pepper ordered six wings and potato salad. Zippo went for two side orders of slaw.

Zippo asked if he'd found anything. Pepper asked him how much Chink Montague was in for on the movie.

It was Pepper's mistake for not figuring out the Chink Montague piece earlier. He'd forgotten the gangster's relationship with the actress. It had been fourteen years since the Hotel Theresa job, when Miami Joe had put together a crew to knock over the safe-deposit boxes. The haul hadn't been as big as promised, which was not uncommon. More rare was the discovery that Chink Montague's girlfriend had been a victim of the robbery— a young aspiring actress named Lucinda Cole. Local girl plucked from the gutter and cleaned up by a powerful hood, one who didn't cotton to having his gift ripped off. Add Miami Joe's double-cross and the whole episode was best buried.

Except for the part where it brought Ray Carney back into Pepper's path after so many years, his buddy's son all grown up and in the game. When Carney hipped him to the security job on the film, he'd mentioned uptown businessmen going in for points. If legit types were signing on, why not some of the more crooked operators, laundering dirty money through the well-cooked books of a low-budget film? When he was younger, Zippo had done his time on small-time grifts, kiting checks and hawking blue movies. He knew how to reach the local players. Hitting up Chink Montague took balls, though.

Zippo hunched at the reference to the gangster, shoulders hiking up to his ears: Don't mention his name in here. "Silent partner, that's a sacred trust."

"So a lot?"

"You think he *took* her?"

"It's not a druggie thing. Her dealer says she hit him up for sleeping pills. That doesn't fit with the mess in her hotel room." When Pepper visited her hotel room, he'd expected the aftermath of a party—wine stains on the couch, cigarettes put out in the plants, some broken glass. But the damage wasn't from a good time. It was from a bad time.

"He wouldn't do that," Zippo said. "Kidnap her."

"Why? It's not ZIPPO?" Pepper didn't know if he was more disgusted by his employer's stupidity or his naïveté. Chink had run most of Harlem at one point. He'd ordered kidnappings, done worse, and he knows he gets away with it. "What'd you, pimp her out? Tell him if he comes on board you'll offer her up?"

Their food arrived. Pepper dug in. Zippo crossed his arms and pursed his lips, as if he spied a big curly hair sitting atop his slaw. "That's not me."

"You didn't know?"

"I knew they'd stepped out together, I didn't know he'd do something like this."

They were making a movie about dirty Harlem and then the real thing came up and bit them in the ass. "More than step out," Pepper said. "He set her up, bought her fancy clothes." Gave her a ruby necklace that got two men killed, one of them by Pepper's hand. *Gave her a present* made Pepper realize: Today was his birthday. "Something went down in that hotel room," Pepper said. "A few hours after the shoot at Carney's Furniture."

Zippo made sure no one eavesdropped. "Lola's in the office, says there's someone on the phone who wants to speak to me. I figure it's an overdue invoice. It's Chink. He wants to talk to

Lucinda. What am I supposed to do? I wasn't pimping—it was an investor on the phone wants to say hi to what he's investing in. A simple hello." The conversation was brief, Zippo told him. "Five minutes later we were rolling. If she was upset, you'd never know."

"I was there," Pepper said. Nefertiti did not show weakness. But what about the actress, away from the cameras.

"One time," Zippo said, "I had a client who asked me to take some pictures of this big-shot businessman." His voice had ditched the manic, bubbly quality. "Naughty pictures, you know, to get the man in trouble. And I'm good at what I do—I see things. Most guys, blackmail pics, you're lucky the thumb's not over the lens half the time. But I see things, I capture them, and on that job I captured who that man was, and it ruined him. I didn't like the way it felt. You cross to that side of the street, you take one step and another and then you never come back."

He paused to make sure Pepper followed his point. His companion's face remained blank. He pressed on. "I use the camera differently now. I love Lucinda—she's a beautiful soul. When this movie comes out people will discover a part of her they've never seen before. I don't even know if she knows it's there. I'd never serve her up like that." He nudged his food with the fork and finally took a bite.

The cashier shouted, "Family meal, four Cokes!"

It was stupid to hit up a monster like Chink Montague, period, but extra stupid when there was a woman in the mix. But people as a whole were pretty dim upstairs, and if you started dwelling on this or that person's dimness, ranking it and measuring just how dim this or that motherfucker was, before you realize it half the day is gone. In Pepper's experience.

They ate without speaking for a few minutes. Going to 107th Street had reminded him of when he tailed that drug dealer Biz Dixon, but it had been part of another job, surveillance of Wilfred Duke, the big Harlem banker. Former banker—that nigger was on the run with everybody's money. Never did find him. But Pepper had helped set him up. He didn't know who Zippo had taken blackmail pictures of, but some people, they've earned it. Guilt was a mug's game, with chump stakes. Best to lay off that action.

Zippo waved to an old lady picking up her takeout order. She clutched the bag of chicken like it was her purse and she was walking down a dark alley. "We used to live in the same building," Zippo said. "When I was little." He wiped his mouth. "It's weird when people know you for one thing, but that person ain't around anymore, you know?"

Pepper shook his head.

"Like, I'm from around here and they still remember me for the fire thing, when I'm all about cinema now."

"The fire thing."

"That's why they call me Zippo. I used to light fires."

"For insurance money."

"No, for myself."

"You torch shit for no reason?"

"No, because I had to."

"Had to."

"To express myself. To put what's inside me out there with everyone else."

Pepper decided he didn't understand the artistic temperament. "Next time, get in on an insurance play, make some money at the same time."

What did Pepper have inside? Years ago he'd gone with a woman who informed him that he was, in fact, empty. "It's like there's nobody home." Janet, with that apartment on Morningside and the fucking parakeet. Another ill-advised excursion to the land of the straight and narrow. Empty: At the time he had been insulted. He cut her off. The assessment stayed with him and in time its rightness sat more comfortably. Back in the war, busting his ass on the Ledo Road and ducking typhoons and typhus, he'd had plenty of time to listen to the Burmese workers expound on life. How to detach a leech from your balls, how their wives curried their chicken, their mumblings about down-home Buddha shit. He hadn't seen a leech since, but that down-home

Buddha shit continued to pop up, lit up in red neon like the facts of life. Take that bottle of Coke that Zippo was drinking. You pay a deposit on the bottle for the glass, like it's worth something. But it's the empty space inside, not the glass, that makes the bottle useful. Call him empty: He had put it to work.

Zippo frowned. "Chink did get weird about the movie, though," he said. "Kept asking about when we were going to start shooting, where. I thought maybe he wanted a cameo. You ever work for him? As a bodyguard or—"

"I don't take money from guys like that." Foot soldier for assholes? He'd already done that in World War II. No. A man has a hierarchy of crime, of what is morally acceptable and what is not, a crook manifesto, and those who subscribe to lesser codes are cockroaches. Are nothing. In Chink Montague's knife-wielding days, when he did his own enforcing, he'd slashed his bloody path to the top of Harlem's rackets. For the last twenty years or so he'd preserved his empire of bookmaking, narcotics, protection schemes, and prostitution, enduring like an incurable condition, outlasting aspiring up-and-comers, entering into an accommodation with the Italians, and keeping the right cops, judges, and politicians fed with envelopes. Notch Walker had muscled into Chink's old territory of Sugar Hill with his grand designs, but Chink had kept the young gangster's encroachments at bay. Most of them. He'd lost his Lenox Ave numbers operation and a couple of blocks of drug trade, but he hung on.

After the Theresa job, Chink had turned Harlem upside down to find out who'd stolen his girlfriend's necklace. Didn't want to lose face, but maybe it meant more to him than just a pretty gift for this month's girl. Maybe she meant more.

Zippo asked him what he was going to do.

Pepper and Chink Montague had been in the same room before—in the back lounge of Pearly Gates, and once the big man had dropped in to preen at Corky Bell's poker game when Pepper was working security—but he'd never had the pleasure. One evening Pepper walked down 125th to find the mobster handing out free Easter hams to whoever showed up—throwing a bone to those he preyed upon. His fellow crooks embarrassed themselves when they spoke of Chink with deference to his power or resignation at their powerlessness. The man was vermin. Why shame yourself by flattering a cockroach for being good at finding crumbs. No, they had not met, but that quirk of fate was about to end.

Fuck it. Time to meet the man.

# SEVEN

The *Daily News* reporter covering the Lenox Avenue fire jazzed up his account with tales of the address's colorful history. For number 347 had seen dirty business. It was built by the French Bros. during the Harlem building boom of the 1880s. Real estate is speculative because you don't know if customers will show. The vice business isn't speculative at all; the hungry show up day and night. For many years Lemuel Gold ran the place as a brothel, with discount days for cops and Tammany Hall swells, until they found him floating in the Gowanus Canal with a sash cord wrapped around his neck. *The Gowanus Canal*—such was the enormity of his killer's contempt. Once split into apartments, the townhouse became a one-building crime wave, a multistory felony with a moonshine operation in the basement, a small-time numbers bank on the parlor floor, whores on the second, whores on the third, and an occasional opium den on the fourth with a sweet view of the Hotel Theresa. New ownership in 1953 turned it legit and a more law-abiding parade marched through the premises: poets and bricklayers, polio cripples and future aldermen. On November 15, 1973, the tenant on the top-floor apartment was a woman who took in needlework to supplement her waitressing job, monograms and light tailoring. The textiles caught quickly when the cigarette dropped from her sleepy hand.

By the time Pepper arrived, the entire structure was engulfed. Flames geysered from windows—hell had sprung a leak. Policemen shooed the evacuees farther away and the firefighters expanded their perimeter. Four buildings down, the patrons of Earl's Satin exited the premises for a look. The squares lingering to gawk and the crooked splitting the scene in the face of police presence. The club hadn't shut its doors yet. He hoped Chink was still inside.

Pepper had called Donegal's, relayed his request, and called back ten minutes later for the skinny: Chink Montague liked the Thursday action at Earl's Satin, the club he'd stolen from Smiling Rick many years before, along with the man's other operations. Not many people remembered Smiling Rick. Pepper did, without fondness. He doubted that Rick's customers noticed the change in management, whether they played numbers or had a hankering for unlicensed booze or pussy. Ask the runners, waitresses, and working girls and they'd probably acknowledge that of the two bad men, Chink put more effort into being wretched.

The city specialized in accumulated miseries and women in trouble. Women in trouble wasn't Pepper's usual line of work, but here he was again, second time in as many years. At least he was getting paid this go-around.

His job for Marie had been a freebie. He'd always respected her, the way she conducted herself at Carney's Furniture, her kindnesses to the Harlem characters who passed through the door, some of them decent people and some of them rotten. She didn't ask questions when Pepper used the store as an answering machine; his messages got through and his business proceeded unimpeded. Too smart not to know about her boss's side action and cool enough to hold her tongue, even if she was a straight arrow.

For a brief time, her husband, Rodney, had pretended to decency. Carney hired a series of sweetly incompetent secretaries when Marie left to have her daughter, Bonnie, and all concerned were relieved when Rodney allowed her to start working again. He was having trouble finding a job, she told Carney. No one believed he tried very hard. She started wearing long sleeves on hot days and big sunglasses—Shiner Specials—to hide her black eyes, but it wasn't Pepper's business how she lived her life. Until she asked it to be.

One day last October, when Pepper left Carney's office after some business, Marie touched his arm and asked for a word. She had a hard time spitting it out. They walked around the block. It was one of those October days when the cold sneaks up on you like a pickpocket. She stopped him in front of an abandoned tenement and made her request.

"You want him gone, or *gone*?" Pepper asked.

She hesitated. "Gone," Marie said, preferring the less ominous intonation.

He said, suit yourself.

Pepper intercepted her husband in the pool room off Nostrand where he spent his days. Rodney was tall, with a mouth perpetually on the verge of a leer and a shiny, shaved head reminiscent of a doorknob. They talked. Pepper made it clear he was to refrain from contact with his wife, and that he was permanently banned from New York State—no, make that the tri-state area. Rodney was skeptical of Pepper's resolve and required a demonstration of his depth of purpose, but Rodney was not accustomed to people who hit back, and none of the pool-room men intervened. Far as he knew, Rodney hadn't resurfaced since that day.

Pepper made a half-hearted show of being offended when Marie offered to pay him. Neither of them mentioned the matter again, and he assumed Carney remained ignorant. It was between the crook and the secretary.

On this job the actress didn't even know his name. He was doing this for money. And what else? To retrieve someone who had gotten off at the wrong stop. It was best to stick to your stations, he had learned, where you belong. Otherwise you'll get mixed up with people you shouldn't. It was true for squares, and it was true for crooks.

Something collapsed inside the burning building with a crackling finality. The crowd shrank back, gasping. It looked like the tenements on either side were going to go next. The lights of the fire trucks zipped across the facades in red and white. A burly fireman worried the controls of the truck's pump panel, directing the aerial ladder toward 347 as his comrades scrambled to their places, attending to the hose lines and advancing on the building. Let's get on with it. Pepper walked a bow around the crowd and into Earl's Satin.

The layout hadn't changed. Standard bar arrangement in the front room, a smaller lounge area beyond it, followed by the backroom office. Deeper you went, the more crooked. The bartender was an old-school player—Pepper recognized the tired, sullen gaze. Bartending for a Chink Montague spot seasoned you good and mean, accelerating the city's natural processes.

"You see what's happening out there?" the bartender said. "We're closed."

Pepper said he was here to see Chink.

"I don't know who you're talking about."

Pepper reached up to pull the man over the bar but before he could lay a hand on him, he took a quick nap.

\* \* \*

Historically, Pepper was unable to admit when he had been rendered unconscious. Whether coming to in the trunk of a Chevy sedan speeding down the New Jersey Turnpike or underneath a cocktail table in an after-hours joint or slumped on a wooden chair in the back office of Earl's Satin, Pepper preferred to describe his brief absence from the world as "closing his eyes for a second," as if he were some geezer who'd fallen asleep during *All My Children* and not an outlaw who'd suffered a blow to the head in the line of duty.

One thing Pepper couldn't deny or ignore was his headache, which had assumed a new horrific magnitude. He envisioned his brain as a roulette wheel, the pain a lead ball that bounced heavily in and out of the grooves, round and round.

He knew he was in Earl's because they'd kept the old black-and-white sign when they upgraded to neon out front. It hung on hooks above the dry fish tank, a few feet away from the red metal door that led out back. Most men who stuck centerfolds on the walls of their office didn't go to the trouble of framing them. Chink, or whatever flunky worked there most of the time, had honored the *Playboy* spreads of Jennifer Jackson and Jean Bell, the first and second Afro American playmates, with smart brass frames. Pepper didn't recognize the third naked girl so enshrined. Black Firsts—First Black Heart Surgeon or First Black Governor or First Black Playmate—got the glory, Black Seconds dwelled in the light of a dimmer fame, and rare was the Black Third who received anything near the respect due their office. If Pepper made it out of there, perhaps there'd be time to check out her name and other virtues.

There were three other men in the room. The bartender slouched against the filing cabinets, his demeanor grown more surly in the interval. The other man, presumably, was the one who'd induced Pepper to close his eyes. They called him Delroy. Pepper recognized him from around. The scar was distinctive, a ragged crescent in his cheek like a second mouth. Both men aimed their pistols at Pepper. Pepper moved his hand slightly to see if he felt the weight of his own gun in his jacket pocket. He did not.

Chink Montague was stationed behind the big gray metal desk, one of those two-ton Panzer deals from the '40s. Pepper hadn't seen the man in a while. Empire had exacted its price: The gangster looked like a doped-up lion in a shitty zoo.

He had been fearsome. Chink Montague's father had been a famous knife sharpener on Lenox, pushing his cart up and down the avenue and hollering the words on the sign: GRINDING & SHARPENING BLADES SAWS SCISSORS SKATES. He had tutored his son in the philosophy and bite of the blade. No small part of Chink's legend coming up concerned his knife work. Lop this, snip that. Earlobes, nostrils, what have you. For many years word was he'd flayed Whitey Gibbs alive over the 125th Street numbers trade and tanned the skin for a wallet, but as the years passed it was more likely he'd merely saved some pieces in jars. That he'd never done a bid upstate, or at Alcatraz like Bumpy Johnson, testified to his survival skills. Still, his station had exacted a price, written in his posture as he drooped over the metal desk, his grayish complexion, and the dark grooves under his red-rimmed eyes. Like Lady Betsy's: a faded institution taking up space.

His men were blind to his diminished state, or pretended to be. They jumped at his voice. "How's it looking, Delroy?" Chink said.

"It's a big fire."

"Should we get our asses out of here?"

"We cool. For now."

"I got insurance out the ass. Maybe rebuild and put a hair salon in here."

"Make good money on a salon," the bartender offered.

"That's why I said it. White man ain't killed me yet, a nigger can go into the beauty business if he wants to."

Pepper squinted. Was this that Roscoe Pope routine?

Chink turned to him. "Fuck are you?"

"I work for Zippo." He realized he didn't know his employer's last name. "I'm looking for Lucinda Cole."

"So?"

"She's gone. You talked to her the night she disappeared."

"Did more than talk," Chink said. Out in the street, a cop barked into a bullhorn. Chink pursed his lips. "I'm here because I'm waiting for a phone call. See if a man did what he was supposed to do." He shook his head. "Better not have messed this up."

Pepper wondered how you got access to the basement, and whether it was feasible to keep someone on ice there given the bar action above. *Was she down there?* He wondered how fast the fire was spreading and how long before he had to make a move.

Chink turned his attention to the bartender. "When we're done with him, I want you to go out there and make sure all those motherfuckers pay their tabs. Running out on their bills because of a little fire."

The bartender chuckled. Delroy looked uncomfortable. He

had worked for the mobster for many years and knew there was a good chance he was serious.

"Go to their houses if you have to," the mobster said. "Think they can cheat Chink Montague."

Pepper sighed to get his attention. "The actress."

Chink said, "I don't know where Lucy is. I tried. Now I'm done."

"You call her up," Pepper said, "she disappears."

"I'm going to pay a visit to that Zippo," Chink said, "ask him why he's telling niggers my business. What'd you say your name was?"

"Pepper."

"Pepper?" Chink said. "I don't get why parents name their kids after some shit they like."

Pepper gathered the routine was on the comedian's new record. It was hard to picture the mobster walking down those narrow steps to the basement of the Sassy Crow.

Chink chewed things over. "I remember you. They were doing the movie at the furniture store and you were watching outside. Money I put in, they can afford a real security guard. What do you do usually? Pump gas?"

Delroy and the bartender laughed.

Pepper blinked.

His host's expression clouded as it sunk in that Pepper was not intimidated. Pepper had observed that strong personalities tended to get confused—then incensed—by his even keel. There was nothing he could do about it, even if he cared. Who you are is what you are.

"Pumping gas," Chink repeated, as if Pepper had missed the insult. His captive remained impassive. It was like looking into a sewer grate, into the dark and unknown, and it got on Chink's nerves. Who was this bitch? In the old days, a man in his position would be bawling, crying for his mama. They see the flash of Chink's steel and piss themselves. But Chink didn't pull out the blade much anymore. They'd see the shakes. Goddamn it, did everyone know he's lost it? They must smell it, he must reek of weakness. He glanced at the telephone. It did not ring. Guineas cutting deals with his competitors, cutting him out of new action, little bitches like Notch Walker nibbling at his domain, a block here, a block there. It was all upside down. It was like when Lucy talked about the big Hollywood types controlling her life—the Italians had the same hold on him after all these years. Jump. Dance. A fucking puppet. Like a wooden dummy sitting on the lap of some dago bastard. Chink had been watching from the pay phone on the other side of 125th Street when Zippo handed her the phone. What had he expected to see when she heard his voice? See her face light up, that's fucking what. Sweet Leanne. In that dumb movie costume but still her, from Maplewood, like the first night they met when she was out with her cousin in the big city, in the Black Rose, too sheltered to know the nightclub was not for good girls like her and so delighted when he sent over champagne. Leanne Wilkes? That's the name of a schoolteacher or a nurse. She said she wanted to be in movies. Let me tell you about business, he told her. Doesn't matter what line you're in, the movies, the street—you have to have a good name. Let me think. *Lucinda.* That's right. *Lucinda Cole.* Come a little closer and look in the mirror right there, you'll see it fits.

In the old days he would have said: Rub them all out, remove them from the earth. Lucy, Pepper, his useless flunkies kissing his ass all day. Drop their corpses in the Hudson. The fire and the cops outside, waiting for the man to call him about the thing, and now this chump in his face asking questions—he popped a gasket.

"She doesn't even exist!" he screamed. "Leanne Wilkes, that's her goddamn real name! You don't even know who you're looking for, you stupid fuck. *Leanne Wilkes.* What kind of name is that for a movie star, that country shit? Country, suburbs—same thing. She's from Maplewood, New Jersey. Can you beat that? We got those magazines to say she was from the ghetto and everybody believed it. First thing I told her, you got to know how to present your ass. I dressed her up fine. Took her around to people. Then I'm yesterday's news."

There was silence, then the sounds from the street returned, and a pounding from out front. Chink got a hold of himself. He blotted his brow with a green polka-dot handkerchief. Nodded permission for his men to check the noise. Delroy cracked the door to the lounge, careful to forbid a glimpse of the tableau in the office. "It's a cop," he said. Another cop, his voice more remote, commanded the bullhorn, calling for an evacuation.

"Check it out," Chink said.

The bartender and Delroy exchanged a look: Delroy's turn. The bartender's pistol had dipped, and now aimed at Pepper's shoulder instead of his face. An improvement in Pepper's estimation.

Delroy slipped out. Chink asked the bartender, "You got all their names?"

"Sorry?"

"The names of those motherfuckers out there ain't paid for their drinks?"

On occasion, even a longtime flunky is at a loss for how to deal with a capricious and sadistic boss and will struggle for the right response that will not get him killed. How serious was he? The request was ridiculous, yet within the realm of Chink's whim. Pepper took advantage of the man's sudden awareness of his mortality by vaulting from the chair. The bartender had dipped his gun forty-five degrees and Pepper figured he had an opening. He was correct. He rammed the bartender into the filing cabinets, where the two men struggled before tumbling to the floor. The bartender was skinny but strong, and grappled like one of those South Brooklyn motherfuckers, his thumbs creeping across Pepper's cheek after his eye sockets. Fucker. Pepper heard a desk drawer slide open—he only had a moment before Chink grabbed whatever he was reaching for. The bartender's gun went off. The bullet eliminated two of the bartender's toes. Pepper relieved him of the gun and shot him twice in the belly.

When he raised the pistol and pointed it at Chink, the gangster's hands were in the air. "I told this bitch to keep this shit orderly," the mobster said. "Can't find anything in here."

Pepper directed Chink away from the desk. Keeping an eye on the mobster and alert for Delroy's return, he rummaged after the weapon in that top drawer. Chink was right. It was a mess, and no way to conduct business. He discovered the .38 and slipped it into his jacket.

Chink glanced at the door to the lounge. Pepper pulled back to the center of the room to position himself for the endgame, whether it originated from Chink or the bodyguard.

"I made her," Chink said. "Her whole story."

Pepper never did figure out where the knife came from. A secret pocket, standard-issue in the man's suits since his prime knife-wielding days. If Chink hadn't been softened by his long reign—and his palpable melancholy—perhaps the knife might have penetrated Pepper's throat, for that's where he aimed it. By the time the gangster withdrew the blade from his jacket, Pepper had fired. The gangster had a tell—a widening of his bloodshot eyes. Good for warning his men he was serious, but a bad habit in other confrontations. The knife buzzed past Pepper's ear like a mosquito and Chink collapsed against the back wall. Gutshot. Sirens outside, plenty of noise to cover the sound—Pepper decided to shoot Chink Montague twice more.

Pistol smoke braided itself to the ceiling. Pepper's headache piped up again, that lead ball hopping on the wheel. Dizzy. He had to remind himself of who he was, where he was, and why he had come here. Pepper. His parents hadn't named him that because they liked pepper. The kids on the block used to call him that when he was little but he had forgotten why. Something he did one afternoon that stuck with people. It didn't matter. They were all dead probably.

The door opened. Pepper and Delroy trained their pistols on each other. Delroy had appeared more capable than the bartender—Pepper didn't have enough information to make a calculation about how this was going to go. "Is the woman here?" he said.

"There's nobody," Delroy answered. He looked at the two bodies. Lingered on his boss. "He dead?"

"See the holes?"

"Yeah."

Pepper shrugged.

"Was going to ask for a raise."

"Should have asked sooner."

The two men understood something about each other. Delroy let his gun hand fall. Pepper did not follow suit. Pepper said, "What's out there?" Meaning the red metal door in the back wall.

"You can reach the street."

Pepper made a gimme gesture and the bodyguard slid the gun across the rug. Pepper bent for it and swiftly beat it outside.

The wind drove the blaze up the block. When the telephone rang twenty minutes later, Delroy was gone, as were the tenants who lived above the bar. Come morning, five buildings had been converted to shells. There were three fatalities: the seamstress on the fourth floor of 347 Lenox and the two criminals in Earl's Satin. Contrary to the report from the fire department, Harlem's criminal community maintained that the fire was started by Notch Walker as cover for the assassination of his rival. Indeed, by the end of the week Mr. Walker had expanded his territory to become the king of the uptown rackets. As was his habit, Pepper kept his mouth shut when he heard such nonsense, and sipped his beer.

The *Daily News* reporter didn't think the woman's name was worth including in the piece. She mattered. She was Eunice Hooks, originally from Chestertown, Maryland, and she had come to New York City to improve her circumstances.

# EIGHT

It was like she was waiting for him when he showed up the next day. A small duffel bag and two framed photographs sat at the foot of the staircase. "Mommy—my ride is here," she said.

Mrs. Wilkes shouted from upstairs and appeared a minute later to say goodbye. She was skinny and spry, not too much older than Pepper. She noticed the photographs and smiled at her daughter. "You think you're taking those?" she said.

"My place could use a little something new," Lucinda said.

"Your father's going to have a fit," Mrs. Wilkes said. "None of my business, though." She had appraised her visitor and a dubious expression overtook her face. There was something fishy about him.

"He's from the movie company," Lucinda said. On set, her voice was deeper; she sounded childlike now. She wore blue jeans and a black cardigan underneath a red-and-white houndstooth coat. Pepper hadn't seen her without Nefertiti's prodigious Afro wig. Her hair was cut in a curly bob; it suited. She told her mother she'd call later that evening. Pepper moved to help her with her things and she brushed him off, covering the photographs so he couldn't see what they were. He popped the trunk and Lucinda gently laid the pictures inside, facedown. She scurried back to hug her mother in the doorway and Mrs. Wilkes stood there, watching and waving, until they pulled away.

Pepper had borrowed the car from Buford that morning. The Dodge Charger was midnight blue, with a black vinyl top. Buford's mother lived in Hempstead and the bartender drove out there a few times a week, chain-smoking with the windows up the entire way. Bent cigarette butts jutted from the ashtrays like dismal weeds. Pepper scowled when he got inside and took a whiff. Buford said, "No one's forcing you to borrow it."

According to the telephone operator, there were two Wilkeses listed in Maplewood. Pepper headed first to the home of Mr. Lamont Wilkes, as he had never met a white Lamont. The house was a handsome Tudor nestled in oak trees, with cozy window treatments and a lawn of stiff, frozen grass. He rang the doorbell and Lucinda opened the door like she was expecting him.

He drove toward Walton Road. "You grow up there?" Pepper asked.

"My whole life," she said. "She keeps my room the same."

It was a charming stretch of Maplewood, the kind of place where white people build snowmen after the first big winter storm and gave them ridiculous names. Pepper had been in Hilton, around Springfield Avenue before, but not this neighborhood. How mixed was it? He wondered how her family had got on when they first moved in. They didn't speak for a time. "Nice house," he said.

"Nice neighborhood. They keep the streets clean." She checked her face in the mirror behind the sun visor. "You're surprised," she said. "I had an old boyfriend who said it'd be good for my career if I said I grew up in the ghetto. You know what? They ate it up. I said I was from Harlem in my first interview for *Miss Pretty's Promise* and from then on I came from a broken home—my daddy wasn't around, the whole thing." She grinned. "You say *Harlem* and white people get ideas in their heads. I didn't see the point in correcting them, seeing how much they liked it. Not just white people—I had black folks coming up to me like, 'I used to see you dance at Shiney's back in the day,' mixing me up with other people. My friends I grew up with tease me and congratulate me for getting over."

*Poor girl makes good* was a more interesting story than *suburban girl makes good,* he supposed. Pepper had heard of passing for white before but passing for broke was a new one on him. *Getting over.* He'd always liked that expression. Crooks make a big score, grab that jackpot, and law-abiding black folks *get over,* find a way to outwit white people's rules. Stealing a little security or safety or success from a world that fought hard to keep that from you.

"I was heading back today anyway," she said. "Zippo freaking out?"

"He was concerned."

"So they sent you to rescue me? I don't need saving."

"Has anyone in your life saved you from anything?"

She looked at him. "No."

"Ever?"

"No."

"Then it sounds like you don't got to worry about it." He grunted. "But they got a lot of people standing around getting paid for nothing. Had me looking all over. Roscoe Pope. Quincy Black." He refrained from linking himself to the dead gangster.

"Them," she said. She sat up straight. "You know about Chink, then. Because Quincy'll gossip like an old woman."

He didn't say anything, which she took as a yes.

"I was a teenager," she said. "I didn't know who he was when he waved us over to his table. My cousin Baby, she whispered to me: *He's a bad man.* She ran with that street crowd, running uptown to hang out. It was the first time she took me up there. Then I started going with Chink and didn't need a tour guide anymore."

"Gangster's girl is usually chew 'em up and spit 'em out. You look all right."

"Better than all right." She cracked the window to cut the cigarette smell. "My parents had a fit when Baby told them about us," Lucinda said. "I'd told them I was seeing a boy from CCNY—that's where Daddy went. But they couldn't do anything about it. Afraid of what he might do more than what the neighbors might say." Chuckling. "Then it got worse! You should have seen them when I said I was moving to California—'No one ever comes back from California.' They'd have preferred I had ten babies with Chink than move out there."

After Burma, no one had to sell Pepper on leaving New Jersey. He'd never been out West. He saw how it might broaden a person. Then again, Pepper himself had visited ten of these United States—eleven if you count Connecticut—and he couldn't say they'd made a big impression. A cup of coffee costs the same all over and the person who serves it is miserable in the same way, so maybe when you think you're moving around you're marching in place. "I grew up in Newark," he said.

"Oh, yeah?"

Not too much traffic. The wheels bit into a pothole. It seemed like they just put in this roadway and it's already falling apart. *It used to be on So-and-so Street, before they put the highway in.* He knew some boys from Orange who'd had a garage on Essex. A good place to get some wheels, and one of the mechanics knew a coins guy. It had been around here, maybe at this very moment he was driving through where it used to be. The highway had bull-dozed on through, splitting Orange in half, erasing the garage, all those nice Victorians, the churches, a playground or two, the whole thing. But it was faster to midtown now, so it was worth it in Pepper's estimation. Save ten minutes, that adds up over time.

"I saw you in that movie," Pepper said. "You were good."

"Oh, yeah?"

"You were that single mom telling off the punks."

"I've done single mom on TV a bunch, but if it was a movie it was *Birdie's Way.*"

"They're playing a transistor radio on the stoop and you come out and yell at them."

"*Birdie's Way.* I moved out there for *Miss Pretty* and thought I'd made it. Got good notices, too. Did a lot of appearances when the song became a hit. Then a couple of years and all they gave me was stuff like *Birdie's Way.*"

"It was all right."

"They paid on time."

He realized he was irritated with her. She'd been sitting on the couch with her mother fetching her cocoa while he was running around like a donkey, headbutting trifling fools and getting his bell rung.

The Manhattan skyline emerged for two seconds, misty in the ghost fog, and then another bend in the highway snatched it away again.

"Back into it," Lucinda said.

"Next time don't take the job."

"And do what?"

"You hide out in New Jersey because of Chink?"

"Chink." She huffed through her nose. "When I left Quincy's, he was outside. He'd called earlier that night when I was on set and it got me upset. I needed something to mellow me out. I'd been clean since August. It was a hard summer." She checked his reaction. "Sitting in that big Cadillac. I thought about running. But I've seen him do shit to people. Bad shit. Mostly he didn't do business when I was around, but we'd be out at one of his hangouts and his face'd get mad and I know he spotted someone. He'd have the man brought over for a . . ." She searched for a euphemism and gave up. "He said, you teach someone a lesson in front of everybody, it stays with them." She laughed. "Which is a terrible thing to tell an actress! Because my mistakes are out there for everyone to see, and he's saying no one forgets. I got in the car."

Chink wanted a cut of her earnings for setting her up when she was starting out, Lucinda said. She *owed* him. But that was just venting. He still loved her, he told her. He was leaving Harlem to retire someplace nice, an island. "I told him he was already on an island and he said, *Somewhere sunny.*" Harlem wasn't the same, he said. It was getting worse. The whole city was, and it wore on him. When the film was over, they could go live somewhere nice, he was making moves to get his stuff in order. She sucked her teeth in disbelief. "Know why I dumped him?"

"Like your cousin said, he's a bad man." Present tense.

"That part I was okay with. Back then. Back then I didn't understand. I had to go because the only way for me to be me was to leave who I was behind. All of it—back East, my family. My man." Lucinda turned on the radio and jabbed the buttons. She settled on a doo-wop song that wove in and out of static. "I got the part in *Miss Pretty's Promise* and they called me out to California and Leanne Wilkes was not getting on that plane. In a way it was Chink's fault—he's the one who bought me clothes for auditions and paid for my classes in the Village. He knew people— Hollywood people who liked to slum it uptown. The whole time he was schooling me to leave."

"I don't know you," Pepper said.

"So?"

"You're telling me all this."

"I don't get the impression you have a lot of people to gossip about me with."

Which was mostly right. He liked to talk to Carney at Donegal's, drinking beer. Carney wasn't like those other mopes. There were some other people he didn't mind spending time with. She was mostly right.

They reached Weehawken and the corkscrew of lanes in advance of the tunnel. The toll booth attendant took his money without looking at him. He had a racist face, as Roscoe Pope put it, but made no indication that he noticed Pepper's skin. Maybe shit jobs were the true path to equality, so numbing and dull that there was no room left in the brain for bigotry.

"Remember when they got that woman toll collector?" he said. "People were pissed."

Lucinda nodded, staring ahead at the tunnel.

One time he drove through with Gus Hooks, that old thief. Came from Alabama so he had that Southern shit running through his head all the time. Gus handed the lady toll collector the coins and yelped. "I accidentally touched her hand," he said.

"They ain't going to lynch you," Pepper said.

Gus was unconvinced. "You don't know," he told him.

Lucinda jabbed at the radio buttons again. Dead signal in the tunnel. Under the river, halfway through. Pepper asked her if she wanted to go to the McAlpin.

"Are they on location today?"

"Past few days, they set up, get what they can, and wait for you."

"I'd like to work," she said.

He pulled over at the first pay phone on the other side and called the Grotto. "Uptown," he informed her on his return.

"Where else?"

The West Side Highway was a hard grind. Traffic either way. He assumed another section had collapsed, it happened all the time, dropping cars and trucks through the roadway onto unsuspecting people below. The newspaper said one family was suing the city.

" 'You'd be my princess—like Jackie O,' " Lucinda said. "That's what he told me in his car. Jackie O? What's that make him, JFK? JFK got his ass shot."

Chink was beyond worldly distractions like love lost. You can't go back and do it over. Pepper pulled jobs for a living. The alarm goes off, somebody ratted to the cops, a hothead starts shooting—that's how it went down and you can't go back. Hazel. Even for her, even the possibility of being with Hazel again wasn't enough to make him believe otherwise. Most you can do is look from afar. Grab a look from your car and watch them come out those doors and disappear up the street, but you can't invite them in. The alarm's gone off, delivered its loud and final report, and there's no going back to how it was before it went wrong.

Although there was that one time in Edison when the wire tipped the precinct and they still pulled it off, but it was just that one time and you can hardly steer by miracles. Right?

Lucinda spoke. "Driver's up front, me and Chink in the back. Talking. We got to my hotel and I said, See you around. What did he want? What was he going to do to me? Then to have it be just, *I need you, baby,* it was almost funny. He let me go. I made it inside, counting every step, but he didn't stop me."

He asked why she tore up her hotel room. The room wasn't messed up because she'd been partying with a bunch of druggies, and her ex-boyfriend hadn't busted up the joint in a rage. Why do you smash a mirror? Because you don't like what you see.

"They thought it was Chink? No. It was putting on that ridiculous wig every day. That's what it's riding on? My comeback? This fucking wig? Then seeing Chink and Ros—to see how you've lived your life. Like—dumb. I hadn't thought about what it would be like to see Roscoe. He used to get coked up, fueled up—then get mean."

A semitrailer honked, startling her. Pepper lifted an eyebrow— that dude better not have been honking at him.

"I couldn't hit them, so I hit the room," Lucinda said. "You ever do that?"

"Sure. But I hit them, too, later."

"I never do stuff like that," she said. "Then I looked at the mess I made and did what any sensible woman would do: popped a Valium and hopped in a taxi. Overpaid the driver to take me home in the middle of the night." Hopping in a taxi was the cure for most of life's problems, she said. And a little something to get you through the night was a close second.

She looked classy in her outfit today. And comfortable and not at all like Nefertiti. He thought of Zippo moaning about the old gang fixing him in place, as the person he was before. Lucinda or Leanne had successfully ditched her old world. Now she wanted it back. For a time.

"You know what?" she said. "Sometimes you just want to go home and see your family."

As with the rejuvenating powers of California, the sentiment was alien, but he allowed the possibility.

He snagged a parking spot across the street from the church. They were shooting inside the Canaan Baptist Church on 116th, a low brick building off Lenox. Nefertiti seeking guidance from the old reverend before the big finale. The church was the former home of Diego's Candy & Cigarettes, if Pepper was not mistaken, as that fried-fish place was two stores over. Diego had been a go-between for a Ukrainian scratcher out in Coney Island. Pepper had never needed his services but everybody vouched. Yeah, a fake passport was not in his future. He wasn't going anywhere.

"I told them you wanted to work," Pepper said.

"Flew all this way," she said.

Pete the Grip spotted them and waved his arms up and down like a fool. Lola waited for the plumbing van to pass and dashed across the street. Two Vikings retrieved Lucinda's things from the trunk, the actress hugging the pictures to her chest so no one could see.

A chubby teenage girl, her Afro tucked under a bright red applejack, bounded over the electrical cables and intercepted Lucinda in front of the glass doors to the church. Lucinda bent down to hear her better. She smiled and signed the autograph.

Pepper locked the Charger and joined the set. The job was over, time to go back to work. They'll put her in her Nefertiti costume and wig and big white boots and the continuity girl will make sure everything matches how it was on the day she left. What about his own continuity? He checked: His scars were still where they were supposed to be. He was the same. Harlem was the same. Chink had been wrong about that—Harlem was the same place it had always been. It's the people who come and go, and the buildings, but Harlem never budges.

The sound guy leaned against the church wall smoking a cigarette. Troy, the director of photography, hollered at him. They better have his stool somewhere, Pepper thought, or these hippies were going to have a goddamn problem. All that running around, to have a job where you can sit on your ass.

# NINE

*Secret Agent: Nefertiti* finished its North American run in Times Square on a double bill with *Invasion of the Bee Girls.* It had crisscrossed the country in various markets since January and ended up at the Royalton Playhouse. Zippo sat in the eighth row for the three-forty-five showing, five seats from the left. He questioned the pairing at first but after seeing the films back-to-back saw the case for it: the Insurgent Feminine. People were lining up to see *Jaws* around the corner but porn houses dominated this stretch of Forty-second and it turned out that this was also the last day for the Playhouse as a (more or less) mainstream venue. Tomorrow marked the U.S. premiere of *Swedish Breakfast,* a two-week engagement.

The popcorn was stale, the soda flat, the attendance poor, and Zippo vibrated with joy. He floated each time he saw his baby on the big screen. Even the white guy masturbating and intermittently barking in the third row and the boozer snoring it off in the back could not extinguish his delight. When he considered his oddball journey as an artist—as a human being—*Nefertiti*'s existence offered proof of an invisible, benevolent intelligence somewhere. His friend Freddie had called it the Big Whatever. As good a name as any.

The reviews—the few that ran—were mixed. "Surely Zippo Flood is out of step when *Claudine* offers a more nuanced depiction of inner-city life and even television is stepping up with gems such as Cicely Tyson's magisterial turn in *The Autobiography of Miss Jane Pittman.*" Dave Kehr of the *Chicago*

*Reader* complained that the climactic fight in the mannequin factory was "a murky mess, and what little you can make out is devoid of life." More than one critic puzzled over the repeated close-ups and lingering takes of fires.

Reviewers like to trap you in their idea of you, Zippo thought, like friends and family who can only see who you used to be. That's why they reference other artists and movies to describe you—they can't elude their own context. No one had a bad word for Lucinda Cole, who "transcends the genre with her deliberate grace." Also: "Like a true pro [she] never lets on that she's in a thorough turkey." Also: "reminds the viewer of her debut performance in *Miss Pretty's Promise* and makes you wonder why Hollywood can't figure out what to do with her." Zippo hadn't talked to Lucinda since the premiere. Last week Doris said she'd caught her on TV as a schoolteacher or a social worker or something on that show *Good Times.* He owed her a call.

Zippo instantly forgave Lucinda when she returned to the set. To be frank he respected her for dropping out—he'd disappeared himself more than a few times, but no one had noticed. The shoot finished a week later without incident. Then it was in Zippo's hands.

On the screen, Nefertiti said, "It's up to me, then," and something skittered over his feet. Given the carpet of Jujubes, Twizzlers, and mealy hot dogs, it wasn't a question of whether or not the Playhouse had a vermin problem but only of the scope and magnitude. He dug his knees into the seat in front of him and lifted his feet from the floor. Best not to think about it.

*It's up to me, then.* Zippo remembered choosing that take last fall. He had installed an editing bay in the windowless Grotto room where he kept his moth collection and cut off human contact to "hunker and bunker." He was not a fast cutter. ZIPPO could be neither rushed nor coaxed; ZIPPO arrived on its own schedule. When he finished his snips and mad configurations, eight months had passed. He could not account for the time, only the result. American International Pictures had acquired *Nefer-*

*titi* soon after they wrapped and grew eager—then threatening and litigious—to get their mitts on it. Thus Zippo learned a lesson about retaining counsel to review your contracts, respecting deadlines, and the sanctity of final-cut approval.

While he "convalesced" in Bimini, AIP cut twenty minutes, including "Crisis Sequence #1," a three-minute shot of stalled traffic—Zippo's argument that the dead vehicles "conveyed the emptied soul of modern life" won few converts. They added three minutes of chase to the two car chases, inserted a brief love scene (body double for Lucinda), and shot a new ending where Nefertiti survives instead of sacrificing herself for the valley people in the blast radius. The film now concluded with Nefertiti accepting her next assignment from the super-secret spy organization, though it had to wait until she ref'd the charity basketball game at the community center. "Duty calls—but so does the 'hood!"

Nefertiti's glorious sacrifice in the explosion was the whole point of the movie—to find life's meaning in fire and annihilation. Zippo had never found it anywhere else. Another artist might've despaired at this disfigurement. He didn't care. His version still existed, even if the public never got to see it. Like a forbidden thought, it was enough to screen it in his own head. With the actors and crew to accompany him in his dream, his pastimes were no longer solitary.

When he emerged from the editing room the world had moved on. Blaxploitation was dead. The audience wanted finely calibrated blockbusters like *The Exorcist* and *Jaws,* not shabby entertainments. Sober dramas about black life, not ghetto shenanigans. Nonetheless, by the time it finished its run in the South, *Secret Agent: Nefertiti* had made its money back, and no one foresaw the rapturous overseas reception. The French adored it in particular and hailed Zippo as a "true auteur, a kind of Negro Preminger." Zippo didn't see the comparison but dug the enthusiasm. That's where he was headed tomorrow—to Paris, for talks and interviews and a conference on "The Future of New Cinema." Or "The New Future of Cinema," he couldn't remember. Robert

Aldrich was supposed to show up for an award and maybe they'd talk about *Kiss Me Deadly,* you never know.

A gang of teenagers tumbled through the auditorium doors, claimed a section, and lit up some reefer. They were rude and boisterous, glorying over some earlier escapade. Even this interruption couldn't curdle Zippo's mood—anyway, the credits were rolling. What a crew he had assembled! Pepper—no last name. Zippo wondered if he'd seen the movie. Lola tried to track him down for the premiere, to no avail. The last time Zippo saw the man was when they wrapped and he asked to take his picture for his portfolio of the crew. "What do I need my picture taken for?" Pepper said. "I know what I look like." Zippo tucked him in the credits under Special Thanks, below the legit investors. The silent partners remained unsung. No one from the Chink Montague organization, or front companies, or estate ever came knocking about the gangster's profits. Like the toothbrush money, Zippo found a use for it.

FILMED ENTIRELY ON LOCATION IN HARLEM U.S.A.

Zippo exited the Royalton and blinked in the late-afternoon glare. Hard to believe it was still light out. The old biddy in the ticket booth was asleep. Across the street hung a big billboard for Roscoe Pope's new movie *Chimp Cop.* A cop with a chimp for a partner. Pope was already deep in mainstream crap by the time *Nefertiti* opened. It paid, Zippo supposed.

He turned uptown and hummed "Nefertiti Has Come (You Gonna Get It)," the closing theme. There was no talking Page out of the title even though it meant "The Beautiful Woman Has Come Has Come." Zippo smiled—the one thing AIP hadn't dared mess with was Gene Page's magnificent score. Zippo had required an echo of the funky melancholy of *Blacula,* so he hit up the man himself. Page was amenable. He was currently arranging for Barry White, whom he'd met when they worked on Bob & Earl's classic 1963 single "Harlem Shuffle." Doing more and more solo work on movies. Zippo showed him a rough cut in the Grotto when Page came to town for the release of *Can't Get Enough*. Page started scribbling notes during the first scene and didn't stop until the final explosion. "I got you, baby," he said. He delivered three weeks later. The strings were fucking bananas.

Page didn't make the premiere but most of the crew and the above-board investors showed up at the New Yorker Theatre. Zippo didn't like parties per se. He made an exception. He invited folks from the old days—people like his babysitter Pru and Miss Naughton, the social worker who'd helped him out when his life turned weird—and they cheered and hooted at the right moments. They seemed to like it, the movie, that fraction of him on view. If they liked that part, maybe they liked him, too. Everyone got good and loaded at the after party. Carney even showed up with the missus. He said they'd done a good job of making his office look like a real criminal hideout. Zippo was about to point out that they hadn't changed a thing when Carney added, "I'm proud of you, Zippo. You did good." Fatherly-like. His wife said it was past their bedtime and steered the furniture salesman to the door. Yes, it was a good night.

There was some kind of protest up ahead on Broadway—Save the Bomb, Ban the Earth, what have you—so Zippo veered west on Forty-sixth. One last errand before his flight. If he remembered correctly Ninth Ave in the Fifties had a bunch of old-school hardware stores and perhaps one of them stocked White Fox Turpentine. Costello Hardware & Paint used to sell it when he lived on 132nd uptown. Cans were hard to find but worth the search. It never failed to bring him back, the heat of a White Fox Turpentine fire on his face, and it was like he was a kid again, just starting to understand the shape of his sadness. Out of step even then, lost among the tall buildings.

# THE
# FINISHERS
1976

"When he walked the streets, he
superimposed his own perfect
city over the misbegotten one
before him, it was a city of ash
and cinder heaped hundreds
of feet high, emptied of people,
wonderfully dead and still."

# ONE

It was a glorious June morning. The sun was shining, the birds were singing, the ambulances were screaming, and the daylight falling on last night's crime scenes made the blood twinkle like dew in a green heaven. Summer in New York that bicentennial year was full of promise and menace in every sign and wonder, no matter how crummy or small. How Ray Carney's day ended up taking such a turn, he had no idea. To be surrounded by people who ate their pork ribs with a knife and fork.

Yes, the Dumas Club, at a fundraiser for Alexander Oakes, newly declared candidate in next year's race for Manhattan borough president. Never too early to turn on that money spigot.

Carney popped a deviled egg in his mouth. He plucked his shirt—it was getting warm in there with the windows closed to the street noise. Across 120th a chubby gentleman in a white mesh tank top washed his Cadillac and played salsa at an impertinent volume. So moved that he sang along, soaping. His buddy hunched on an aluminum beach chair on the pavement, slapping his thighs and smoking a cigarillo.

Twenty years ago the block had comported itself differently. Now plywood covered the windows of two burned-out brownstones opposite and a troupe of shabby men rotated through the stoops to sip Ripple from brown bags. *What's the word? Thunderbird!* Ambrose Clarke, the current Dumas Club secretary, regularly called the cops about the shooting gallery up the block, to no avail. To be ignored by the police as if he were some *ordinary Negro*—the humiliation. Elizabeth had hired a jazz combo called the Robert McCoy Trio for today's event, and their music smothered most of the car washer's hit parade. Oakes frowned when the car radio harassed them between jazz standards.

Jimmy, Carl, Hink—the old waiters and bartenders circulated, muttonchopped and deathless, murmuring "Of course, sir," and sharing a conspiratorial nod when you ordered your usual. Some of the plants had died and been replaced, and they had to dump the carpet when Clemson Montgomery had a stroke in the middle of the Founder's Night recital and splashed claret hither and yon, but other than that the room was unchanged. The leather club chairs where a generation of Harlem dignitaries had honed a hundred grubby schemes sat well polished and waiting. The same oil portraits of deceased members hung on the walls; no member of note had kicked the bucket lately, or no one big enough to dislodge the pantheon.

Carney twisted his Dumas club ring on his finger. He'd been scarce in recent years. He attended the mixers for prospective members to boost those without the usual bourgie pedigrees— first-generation college guys like him, the bootstrappers and self-made men. Occasionally he and Calvin Pierce had a drink. Pierce refused to meet anywhere else; once Carney split for home the lawyer prowled the premises on the intelligence-gathering missions that were the foundation of his work. Carney was settled and secure now, in every aspect of his businesses, and had less need for the Dumas contacts. He'd never had the stomach for all the glad-handing theater and self-congratulation, and now was too old to fake it. Sometimes he had a hard time remembering the whole fuss about joining, it was so remote.

Ten minutes in, the place was packed. A sightline opened. Elizabeth was across the room talking to Pat Miller, who introduced herself to everybody as Adam Clayton Powell Jr.'s "favorite cousin." Carney's wife raised her eyebrows: checking in. She knew him too well to fall for one of his practiced salesman

smiles—*It's the perfect accent piece* or *Think of it as an investment in joy*—so he mustered a simple *all is good* wink. Relieved,
Elizabeth returned her attention to Pat Miller and bobbed her
head at the woman's nonsense.

She'd been fussing over the arrangements for weeks, in charge
of corralling the engaged women of her circle, the advisory-
committee types and habitual board-sitters, while her father
Leland made sure the Dumas mainstays made an appearance,
checkbooks or IOUs in hand. Elizabeth and her father fundrais-
ing for the Oakes boy—one Strivers' Row family saluting another.
Leland had been ill last winter with a case of pneumonia that
got complicated, but tonight he looked better than he had in a
long time. The opportunity to toast Oakes—who would have been
his son-in-law if the world made any kind of sense, if Elizabeth
had any sense—had rejuvenated him. That or the Geritol. Carney heard his cackle and turned to see Leland with Abraham
Lanford, the son of Clement Lanford, the onetime Harlem fixer
and statesman. Reminiscing over a colorful grift or cherished
embezzlement in bygone days.

Fundraisers were one of the few occasions where women were
allowed in the club (not including the girlfriends and mistresses
smuggled in after hours by the few potentates with keys). Carney
was glad Elizabeth's friends had shown up—Candy Gates, out in
public for the first time since that "Casanova con man" ran off
with her life savings, and Elena Jackson, also out in public for
the first time since Bernard ran off with that exotic dancer from
Baby's Best. Some of the ladies from the travel agency were there,
identifiable by their puzzlement over some Dumas member's
eccentricity.

Calvin Pierce elbowed Carney. "So much for testing the waters."

Carney shrugged. Alexander Oakes wouldn't have announced
this early if his handlers hadn't worked out the angles. Carney's
gaze fell on the jazz band over by the parlor fireplace. The drummer nodded at him. Carney couldn't place him.

Pierce was unsteady. His cheeks were flushed. Carney pictured the lawyer's busy day: three-martini lunch, followed up by a pass-out nap on the DeMarco sofa in his office (ten percent discount from Carney's Furniture), then a subway ride up to the Dumas Club to start the next round. The lawyer had left Willis, Duncan & Evans last year to go solo. Signed the lease on a nice office suite in the Pan Am Building looking south, a change of view to mark his change in views, as he now represented the companies he formerly worked to destroy. He still shook them upside down to see what change fell out of their pockets, but he no longer divvied up with their victims, the survivors of the scaffolding collapse, the widow whose husband had expired after the surgeon forgot the forceps next to the spleen. The money was better. It usually was when you crossed the street, but the host of new demands left him exhausted, the ones Pierce owned up to and the others. Pierce had stopped bragging of sexual temptations resisted, which Carney interpreted as temptations indulged. Run you ragged, all those responsibilities.

"You reaching into your wallet for this guy?" Carney said.

"Got to pay to play. The Board of Estimate alone." Every Democratic hopeful in next year's races would demand tribute from the greater Dumas community. And get it. "You?"

"He's already got his hooks in." Carney nodded toward his wife and daughter, who were welcoming one of the old guard—Gideon Banks, from the telltale withered neck—into their conversation. The month before they had informed him that he lived with the founders of Women for Oakes. May designed the logo. Harlem needs this, Harlem needs that. "Isn't it time, you know, we had someone a little younger in charge?" she asked. Elizabeth had engineered a rescheduling of this affair so that May would be home from college. May was volunteering in Oakes's campaign office this summer, on top of her filing job at Seneca Travel & Tour. Carney had offered her a job at the furniture store, at more pay than her mother was offering—learn the ropes, get a feel—but she had passed.

"Oakes got you coming and going." Pierce laughed. "You see Ray Jones showed up?"

"Sends a message," Carney said. Jones was schooling some young campaign aides by the window, waving an unlit cigar like a conductor's baton. Time was, you had to get the nod from J. Raymond Jones if you wanted to be a judge, or borough president, or head up to Albany. Then Bobby Kennedy outmaneuvered him back in '67 and got Jones booted from his throne at the top of Tammany Hall. The former kingmaker still had juice, though. David Dinkins, Charlie Rangel, and Percy Sutton—the heirs to Jones's Carver Democratic Club—couldn't show their faces at this event for obvious reasons, but Jones's presence let people know that Alexander Oakes had the tacit approval of the Harlem clubhouse. Or hadn't earned their disapproval. Once Sutton officially announced that he was forgoing another term as borough president to go after Abe Beame, any endorsement of Oakes could be out in the open.

That spring Carney had made the switch from *Eyewitness News* to *NewsCenter 4*. There was a little black-and-white Panasonic in his office that he put on at five. The *Eyewitness News* theme was a classic, no question, but Chuck Scarborough's mix of empathy and gravitas proved a fine companion as the workday wound down. Which meant Carney had seen Sutton do his coy little dance about a bid for Gracie Mansion a few times. "I'm not now a candidate for mayor," he told the cameras as he departed the Harlem State Office Building, "but I certainly have the *capacity* to be mayor. If Abe Beame doesn't run, and the polls continue to show me doing as well as I am, I think I would make the run for mayor. In fact, I'm rather certain I would, and with a large body of support."

So: Sutton was going to throw his hat in the ring and waited for the most providential moment to announce. By announcing early, Oakes was well positioned. And if Sutton ultimately decided against a mayoral run, Oakes could step down and endorse the man's reelection, bank the exposure and money for his next campaign. His press conferences when he was at the DA's office, his Homes 4 Harlem promotion, this campaign bid—the Boy from Strivers' Row had mastered getting his name out there.

Was the trio playing "The Star-Spangled Banner"? This fucking bicentennial shit was driving Carney batty. It was inescapable, like a dome of red, white, and blue smog. He had to come up with a July Fourth sales ad by Friday and was stumped. He feared that any patriotic, flag-waving bullshit he included in his promo would come off as exactly that.

"Look who it is—Mr. Man," Pierce said.

John squeezed through and shook Pierce's hand. He socked Carney in the arm and said, "Hey, Daddy." They were almost the same height. John's cuffs stuck out of his jacket sleeves. Carney had bought him that jacket last winter.

He told John it was nice of him to come out and support his mother. John nodded and said, "You, too."

It had leaked out, his contempt. In general, Carney tried not to expose his kids to his private menagerie of animosities and disdain unless the target was remote ("This Joe Namath is a lot of hot air") or educational, providing a lesson about the disreputable types one encounters on life's journey ("That old man at the corner store tried to shortchange me again but you know I count my change"). Alexander Oakes might be a pretty boy sponging off the ill-gotten gains of his family, the emptiest of the city's empty suits, a mediocrity powered by greasy charm . . . he could go on . . . but the man was an old friend of their mother and if Carney was doing his job as a father May and John would arrive at their own appraisal in time.

Perhaps John had overheard last Thursday when Elizabeth discussed the hors d'oeuvres and Carney said, "How about a pig in a blanket?" It was entirely possible John had been in earshot. Or perhaps last night when Carney had asked his wife when to show up for *"the event,"* as if a third world dictator were throwing himself a parade and every citizen had to show up or face the firing squad. Maybe John had been within earshot when Elizabeth responded, "You've always been mad at people who had it easier than you. It's not his fault."

Carney: *Hmmm.*

"I know you think he's had it all handed to him," she said, "but the thing about Alex is that he's a hard worker."

"Of course."

"Do you want me not to do it?"

"I'd never tell you what to do."

"Yeah, Ray, but you'd let me know. You wouldn't say it but you'd let me know."

No, John couldn't have overheard because they'd been in bed with the door closed. Carney had turned over and said he was looking forward to tomorrow, might even iron a shirt.

Yes, his animosity had leaked out at some point. Carney drained his drink to the ice. To ground himself he tapped his jacket pocket, where he kept the envelope containing five grand for Andy Engine.

Since New Lincoln had let out for the summer, John had been working at this Baskin-Robbins down on Madison in the Eighties. Carney had offered John his old summer job at the store and was informed that the ice-cream shop had "more girls." When Carney was his age, he considered himself lucky to get any job, let alone two. Luck meant that when Big Mike took off for weeks, or months, chasing a setup or a woman, Carney was able to pay for groceries. And Ma Bell, and keep the lights on. He didn't wish that burden on his children. Scoop away, but—seeing his son in a blazer conjured an image of John smoking a pipe and snapping his fingers for scotch—stay away from places like this when you grow up.

Carney reached over to squeeze his son's arm, like he did when the boy was little. *These growing bones in there.* John asked if he could see *Midway* with J.J. at the Loews 86th. It was the voice he used to hit up Carney for an advance on his allowance.

"The Charlton Heston?"

"It's in Sensurround."

Carney nodded. "You can't hang out all night."

The boy promised not to. Then grinned.

Leland clinked a tall thin glass with a spoon. The band cut out. It was Carney's natural instinct to creep toward the door when people started speaking at events, to facilitate a quick getaway if necessary. He obeyed it.

Elizabeth wore a new, sheer white blouse with thin blue stripes that Carney had never seen before. She opened with an appreciation of how many people had shown up—"old friends, new faces." The politically engaged and those making their very first contribution to a candidate. May handed out Women for Oakes buttons to those in front as Elizabeth explained why they'd started the group. "Everybody feels it—we have to get our butts in gear! The city's falling apart. We have enough people hanging around *on the corner,* we need someone like Alex *in our corner.*" Carney had heard her practicing the speech that morning. He had often told her that she would've made a good furniture saleswoman if she had been so inclined, but there had never been much enthusiasm for a family business.

Leland took over the proceedings and remarked upon the great legacy of the Dumas Club, its storied contributions to Harlem's political life. Raised a glass to the elder Oakes, taken from them too soon. "Often I'd see the light on in his office—you remember what a night owl he was—and pop in for some of his wisdom over a glass of port. He never failed to right the ship." He pronounced upon the nature of time: "It seems like just yesterday I came downstairs—they must have been in kindergarten—and happened upon Alex and Lizzy playing doctor." A number of people in the room chuckled. Elizabeth gave a disdainful shake of her head. John frowned and checked his father's reaction.

"Now he's all grown up," Leland said, "a grown man with an impressive list of achievements, and eager to add to it—by fighting for all of us. Not just Harlem, not just uptown, but everyone from Wall Street to Washington Heights." He grew misty. "Since his father passed, I hope I've been there for him, and now he wants to be there for us, in city hall."

It was Oakes's moment. He stepped to the microphone and flapped his arms to tamp down the applause. He had retained his football player's frame when his cohort had softened into a lumpy middle age. Gray at the temples, dignifying him without undercutting his still-boyish face. The last few years, Oakes had sported a fashionable two-inch natural. He'd returned to his tight, wavy curls that harkened to an earlier age and which, it must be said, the girls and ladies adored. Oakes was fine-tuning his playboy image lately, informing the *Daily News* that he "hadn't met that special someone yet" and "anyway, the City of New York comes first these days."

Oakes smiled at someone across the room—wide maw, white-death chompers out—and Carney thought, Oh, he's going to win.

The room quieted. The car radio interjected, *"Toro mata rum-bambero y toro mata."*

The candidate cleared his throat. He opened with a list of thanks and Carney started going over next week's shipment from Sterling, rearranging the showroom in his head. Slide the Egon sectional over by the floor lamps, give up on this season's DeMarcos, they weren't doing any business. He rejoined the fundraiser when Oakes's tone shifted to signal the conclusion. "Mr. Sutton has not announced he's running for reelection. Who knows—he may have other ambitions. I'm concerned today with sharing my intentions—not anyone else's. If Mr. Sutton does decide to run again—well, Manhattan will be a better place for our conversations about what's next." Oakes had preachified his speech patterns. Carney pictured Leland or one of the Harlem power brokers sitting Oakes at a school desk and forcing him to study the sacred Powell sermons.

Oakes wrapped it up. The Robert McCoy Trio eased into a tranquilized version of "Take the 'A' Train" that was more like "Take the 'A' Train When a Trash Fire Has Disrupted Service Up and Down the Line," and the conversation resumed: assessments of the candidate's performance, his chances, was there more food coming out. Carney gave John five bucks for the movies and when he looked up Alexander Oakes was in his face.

"Ray!" He executed a he-man maneuver but Carney's hand had been mashed by all the best uptown bruisers over the years: It was a draw. "Glad you were able to step away from your store," Oakes said.

"I am the boss." What did he think, Carney was sweating over the books all night, guzzling Pepto-Bismol in an undershirt?

He nodded. "You've come a long way." The edge of his mouth curled.

"How's that?"

A campaign staffer tugged Oakes away and aimed him in the direction of Lyle Morrison, executive vice president of Freedom National Savings. Carney's drink was empty, the glass warm from sitting in his mitt. *Come a long way* from what?

He'd stayed longer than he needed to. His family was on the other side of the room, separated by people. Carney tried to catch Elizabeth's eye. Once again, the drummer winked at him. Right: Stan Hayes, three-card monte dealer and occasional second-story man. Three-card monte, drums, third-degree burglary— quick hands were an asset. They smiled at each other and Carney saluted. Two guys wearing their daylight masquerade. Well, they were not the only ones. The question of whether Stan was a thief who moonlit as a jazzman or a jazzman moonlighting as a thief was moot, as he was mediocre in both endeavors and Carney had his own midnight industry to worry about. He split.

\* \* \*

The city was being tested. It was always being tested and emerging on the other side in a newer, stronger version for having been laid low, but everyone forgot this from time to time and so they were quite distressed by the latest manifestation. Distressed by the crime wave, which was very alarming, and the empty city coffers, which caused such misery, and the general state of wrongness, which left few unscathed and most navigating personal labyrinths of despair. They had been prepared for the latest calamity by rehearsal disasters big and small, but it was hard to remember that in all the hustle and breathless rushing here and there.

Carney for his part was attuned to an improvement in consumer sentiment. Your basic glimmer. Furniture sales—sectionals in particular—were up over the same time last year, the showroom not so gloomy in the afternoons. There had been solid growth in scores and rip-offs over the last three quarters, with a lot of activity in the rare-gem sector, a leading indicator of market optimism. Take Andy Engine. He hadn't hit up Carney in two years and then strutted in yesterday with a sample case full of Afghan lapis that lay on the black velvet bed like holes punched through to a perfect blue universe. "Fell into my lap." Martin Green took them off Carney's hands and once Carney paid off the thief, there was time to grab a sub and be home to catch *Rhoda.*

On his way to meet Andy Engine, Carney returned to the site of the tragedy. He'd made a detour to see the building before the fundraiser. It tugged at him still, and he had time.

The city continued to burn, night after night. Not Fifth Avenue, but Harlem, Brooklyn, the South Bronx. 371 West 118th Street had been a four-story tenement presiding over the northeast corner of Morningside Ave. Behind its blackened exterior, fire had eaten its guts. At half past nine last Thursday night, a clock timer activated an incendiary device. The firebomb had been set in the rear apartment on the top floor to allow the fire to spread before it could be detected from the street, near an air shaft so that it was well fed. The room had been doused with gasoline. No one lived in 371. The landlord, Excelsior Metro Properties, cut the heat and power last winter to chase away the holdouts, then stripped the plumbing and electrics, anything salable.

At the time of the fire, the building was empty except for eleven-year-old Albert Ruiz, who was asleep in 2A. He and his friends had claimed the apartment as their "clubhouse." Like on *The Little Rascals,* but infested with roaches. The boys had been convening there since the weather warmed up. The junkies hadn't gotten a foothold, or the bums—there was no shortage of abandoned buildings, and the park across the street was inviting, judging from the sheds and lean-tos. Albert and his pals dragged in battered folding chairs, set up a milk crate for a card table. One boy raided his brother's *Penthouse* stash and started a lending library. On Thursday, Albert had arranged to meet his friend Pete at the clubhouse before they went to the movies: *Midway.* Pete got tied up playing duck and weave with his father, who'd been laid off two days before and had found his scapegoat. Albert fell asleep on the beanbag chair while waiting.

The firefighters said it looked as if he'd been trying to open the apartment door. It was stuck fast. Smoke got him. Five days later, he was out of the coma, attached to a machine that inflated his scored lungs. His mother, Mrs. Ruiz, stared at the ground when she told Carney what had happened.

Mrs. Ruiz and her three children—Albert had two younger sisters—had moved into the third floor above his store two years ago. She was short and thickset, harried but determined, her body tipped forward as if battling headwinds. Carney gave her the once-over when she first came to see the place but they had rarely interacted since; Marie handled that side of things now. Marie had informed Carney one day that she was "bored" and "unfulfilled" with her current store duties, which was convenient because managing the two buildings left him bored and unfulfilled. He started paying her to run the properties. You got a headache, you buy aspirin, and tenants were the mother of headaches.

On the first of the month Mrs. Ruiz crossed the showroom to drop her rent check on Marie's desk. Sometimes she paused before a DeMarco lounger or Egon credenza, a dreamy look overtaking her face as she arranged the piece in her living room upstairs.

The day after the fire, Carney was heading to Freedom National to make a deposit when he came upon Mrs. Ruiz struggling to open the residential door. He said, "Must be sticky." She gave him her key. It opened easily. He offered to help with the groceries even though she was the type to say no. She surprised him and when they arrived at her landing she said, "I told him I was making spaghetti and meatballs tonight but if he wanted some he had to wake up."

Carney tracked down the story in the *Post* that evening. The building had recently changed hands. The new owner, Excelsior, owned regiments of property uptown and in the South Bronx, and an alarming number of their buildings had been the victim of suspicious fires. The management company could not be reached for comment. The newspaper item concluded with "Last year there were a record 12,000 structural fires in the Bronx. One fire department official estimated that a third of them were set deliberately."

Carney told Marie the next day to keep tabs on Mrs. Ruiz and her son. "The store would like to help if it's possible." His idea of Albert was unformed; it was entirely possible the bowl haircut and chubby cheeks were produced by Carney's imagination to fill in the hospital scene.

A plane dragged black letters through the air: HAPPY BIRTHDAY AMERICA—200 YEARS OF LIBERTY AND INDEPENDENCE. Who paid for it? He couldn't tell, so he added: LOVE, BUCKWHEAT. The words zipped over the line of tenements, disappeared over the eaves of 371 West 118th. Cinder blocks sealed the front door and windows on the first floor. No more intruders until the wrecking ball came through. Case closed—certainly the cops were never going to investigate who put the boy in the hospital. If Oakes was serious about helping the city, he would've taken down the arson racket when he worked in the DA's office, instead of letting it get out of control. You pocket some fat envelopes working down there, Munson'd had plenty of stories.

Carney cut across Morningside Ave, into the park and toward the stairs that led up the ridge to Columbia's domain. The trees and scrabbly brush had mustered some green business, weeds drooped between the hexagonal paving stones, and the ancient rock dominated all with its craggy arrogance. Growing up he and his cousin Freddie had clambered and leapt from it in wild exuberance, detonated firecrackers and scraped their knees on its unforgiving planes, but he'd never known its name: Manhattan schist. Didn't exist anywhere else in the world, as John had explained it to him last spring. Morningside Park, one of the places where the bedrock foundation poked through, had been John's homework assignment for a unit on city landmarks.

"It's four hundred million years old!" John told him, poking the illustration in his library book. The result of two plates in the earth colliding under terrific, elemental pressure to heave up mountain ranges. The mountains were long gone but the unique rock remained, twinkling in the sunlight from embedded mica, holding the city aloft. High-rises—with their staggering tons of steel, concrete, and glass—can only stand where the schist is close enough to the surface to bear the weight. "Look at the skyline, Dad, there are skyscrapers on Wall Street and midtown, but not in Greenwich Village—the bedrock's too deep down." The spine of the city, keeping it all together. You can't see it except in magical spots where it will not be contained. Carney admired the dedication.

Since this uptown stretch of schist was too pricey and complicated to excavate, the neighborhood got a park out of it, and Columbia University claimed its royal perch over Harlem to the east, looking down on the peasantry below. Carney made a survey when he topped the staircase, like one of those long-dead city planners figuring out where to lay the grid.

These days Morningside Park was a no-man's-land separating the Ivy League kingdom from the residents on the other side. The park had always been dicey, but in the last ten years the muggings and assaults had ascended to myth: *Welcome to Fear City.* Last year Mayor Beame, staring down the city's impending bankruptcy, had threatened to lay off police and corrections officers, and the cops retaliated by handing out *Fear City* pamphlets to horrified tourists. When they warned visitors to "restrict your travel to daylight hours" and "remain in midtown areas," it was places like Morningside Park they drew their monstrous exaggerations from. The university warned its students to circumnavigate the park rather than take the stairs up the hill, and today Carney appreciated the advice. Bunch of money in his pocket, plus out of breath because he was out of shape. Why had he come this way? He never came this way. At the stone retaining wall, he returned his attention to the townhouse below and it clicked: He and the intersection had a history.

Opposite 371 was 370 West 118th Street, a five-story yellow brick building that had gone up a few years ago, affordable housing. He and Rusty had argued about it after Carney questioned the delivery address of a Sterling dinette. "There's no 3C in 370, I know the building. It's Front and Rear. Has to be 3F or 3R." The Sterling drivers—these crackers from Massapequa—always bitched over their Harlem deliveries and Carney wanted to forestall any complaints.

Rusty made the sad face he put on when Carney challenged his capabilities. "Ray, I double-checked it: 3C."

"I'm telling you."

Rusty crossed his arms. "Look for yourself." He and his wife, Beatrice, had been arguing lately, according to Marie. Carney figured this defiance echoed new household postures.

Back when Carney drove his father's truck he made the occasional delivery of a used sofa or bureau. He remembered the dingy marble steps of 370, the splintered black-and-white tile on the floor and the mismatched light fixtures. He had paid one of the neighborhood guys five bucks to help carry a quite pristine Collins-Hathaway couch up to the second floor. He'd forgotten the name of the customer but recalled the sunlight pulsing through the living room windows and the vista of the park. A year or two later, he had to chase the first-floor tenant around when the guy fell behind on his installment plan, Argent lounger. He was well acquainted with 370. On his way over he practiced his rant. "Make me get up from my chair and drag my ass down there . . ."

But the old tenement with the tight and tormenting stairwell was gone. This yellow-brick building had replaced eight town-houses, certainly big enough to have a 3C, even a 3M or N. Rusty produced a satisfied smirk when Carney returned. His pissy new orientation was regrettable. Beatrice had always been such a quiet little creature. Georgia peach. This place will help you find your voice if it doesn't break you first.

371, 370. The old city sat on one corner, opposite the new city. How did Carney used to put it: *Churn, baby, churn.* Atop the unchanging schist, the people replaced each other, the ethnic tribes from all over trading places in the tenements and town-houses, which in turn fell and were replaced by the next build-ings. The city will condemn 371 and the other three distressed properties down the line, raze them, and throw up new housing, like they were doing all over now. "Urban renewal": You have to clear the dead stuff before the fresh growth can prosper. Sure, shady landlords get their big payouts from the crooked insur-ance adjusters while the law looks the other way, and then the construction firms grease the palms of city officials for contracts, nice paychecks for everybody out of the misery, but people need places to live. Right? Mrs. Ruiz's boy is in the hospital, who knew if he was going to get out, but the clever men got paid. How fat were the envelopes when Oakes worked in the DA's office?

*Come a long way* from what, motherfucker?

There was no big, bright Homes 4 Harlem seal by 371's front door, so it belonged to a different community-improvement program. Carving up the blighted blocks, everybody getting a piece. Who got the bigger envelopes, prosecutors or community hustlers? Next fundraiser, he'd ask Oakes that very question. *Of course you've got the bid, for a little consideration.* Carney was starting to sound like his father, making everybody into a crook. He imagined Mrs. Ruiz's boy waking up alone in the dark apartment—Carney had been there, kicked out of sleep by a siren, or violence in the alley, or a rat skittering across his feet, overtaken by the sick awareness that no one was coming to help him.

He hadn't come a long way at all if the apartment on 127th remained so close; now instead of him living in it, it lived in him. What kind of man torches a building with people inside? Big Mike coming home those nights, stinking of kerosene and rot-gut. How many kids and mothers had he burned up, burned out? Carney knew the kind of man who did such things. They were never called to account.

Perhaps it was time.

# TWO

The next day he took his nephew Robert to Gimbels for some shirts. Ellen, the boy's mother, always rebuffed Carney when he tried to help out, so he told her the polo shirts were part of the Carney's Furniture uniform, and that as such, Carney was responsible for them. He had a side play to throw in two pairs of nice Levi's while they were in the boys department, and it came off without a hitch. The boy was a beanpole, like his father at that age, which made Carney smile. They took the 5 train up from Eighty-sixth and Robert kept reaching inside the Gimbels bag to touch the soft cotton shirts.

Robert was not a talker; he had inherited his mother's reserve. In general Carney preferred a silent companion, but he'd never broken through with the boy and in his eagerness for connection he made nonsense conversation. Like a lock man trying to spring a combination by spinning random numbers, no kind of lock man at all.

"Catch the Mets last night?"

"Mets? No."

The movement of the car shook the passengers. "Doing that basketball program again this summer?"

"Nah."

A poster for *Midway* flickered between girders in the 103rd Street station. "You ever see a movie with that Sensurround?" Carney said. "Where they shake the seats?"

"I saw *Earthquake*," Robert said.

"That was a good one."

Robert nodded. Carney left the kid alone. Big Mike used to call Carney out for being "so quiet," when he was just thinking his thoughts, so he let the kid be.

The first time Carney saw Robert was at his father's funeral. Freddie had a lot of friends Carney had never met—smooth-talking hoods and broke-ass alto sax players and Caucasian beatnik scam artists and socialist chicks from Garden City—so the thin, nervous-looking woman with the young boy did not stand out particularly. Ellen was Freddie's type, full-lipped with long black hair and black shadows under each eye, just like Janet Brown, whom Freddie had chased all through junior high, and daffy Penny Lewis, who had tolerated his cousin's mischief for a few months back in '52. The boy was two years old. He did not speak or fidget, he held his mother's hand and moved his head, chicken-like, taking it all in. Had his father's eyes even then, and Carney kicked himself later for not putting it together. He had not been himself in those days after Freddie died. They left early.

When the boy turned six, Ellen invited Aunt Millie to the party and she brought Carney along. Ellen had written to her the previous winter and laid it out, not asking for anything, just thought she'd like to know she was a grandmother. According to Ellen, she and Freddie had been together for a brief spell in '61. She never told him about their son.

"He's a nice boy, and she's trying," Aunt Millie said. Carney asked about a paternity test. She said, "For God's sake, look at him." Elizabeth berated him when she found out he hadn't brought a gift and that was the start of birthday toys and Christmas sweaters.

Ellen got married to a bus driver named Booker, an older man, a widower with two kids; the five of them lived over on Edgecombe next to the park. Booker treated Robert okay from all accounts, didn't hold anything against him. Booker made a good living, but there's nothing wrong with a new shirt or two from a close relative.

Aunt Millie had been trying to expand her grandmotherly duties for years. Ellen refused any overture that crossed her invisible line. Recently Carney discovered the same urge to reach out. With Robert growing more into his father's image, with the same jittery hand gestures and laugh—even though they had never met!—Carney found himself telling Freddie stories. Sharing his cousin's favorite movies, go-to sandwiches, the variety of mischief he'd conned Carney into. Robert pretended to be interested, affecting the familiar expression of a broke customer who'd drifted into a more expensive corner of the store and had to fake interest until he could make a getaway.

It had occurred to Carney a few weeks ago that Robert might need a summer job. A couple of hours a week, some local errands, fetching sandwiches, and organizing the files in the basement. He's looking for work next summer, or after school, the boy can say he has some retail experience under his belt. That's how it started, seeing his nephew without Aunt Millie around and not on a birthday. Discoveries, like the high-pitched laugh the boy let out when one of Larry's jokes vibrated on his frequency. Who knows? Maybe he'd start calling him Uncle Ray, instead of Ray.

No go, so far.

They separated at the subway exit. Robert walked up Lexington, turned, and raised the shopping bag in thanks. Carney gave him a thumbs-up. He called the store and told Rusty to lock up tonight. Plenty of time to check out the new furniture place on 135th to see what they had going on before he met Pepper.

An M100 bus rumbled east down 125th. The Anchor Bank advertisement on the side of the bus featured the Statue of Liberty, and the crosstown movement made her appear to run down the street, as if after a junkie who'd snatched her purse. The old broad was faster than she looked.

CELEBRATING 200 YEARS OF FREEDOM!
FROM YOUR BANK FOR THE NEXT 200
ANCHOR BANK OF NEW YORK

The city had escaped bankruptcy and sure ruin, Carney thought, but they didn't trust it, so they celebrated the old good news instead. Like by proxy. A bit overboard for his tastes. When the ad manager from the *Amsterdam News* had dropped by the furniture store to help with the July buy, he laid out his array of bicentennial images: Lady Liberty in various postures, the Betsy Ross flag with its thirteen stars, fireworks over the Capitol, fireworks over the NYC skyline. Riffs on Washington crossing the Delaware and signing the Declaration. Now they followed Carney everywhere. Whether hawking galoshes or retirement funds or dog shampoo, the same rah-rah images rushed to serve. On billboards all over town, Lady Liberty held a mustard-splattered Nathan's hot dog instead of her ledger, and Crazy Eddie's arranged the Founding Fathers around a document legislating "Insane Savings!"

There was the case of *The Spirit of '76,* the painting of the two drummers—one too young to enlist, the other too old—and the fife player leading the rebel soldiers across the battlefield. Carney had thought that the man was playing a flute, until John corrected him: "I learned about it in history class."

Classic painting, snapshot of the country's birth, etc. That spring Carney had encountered no fewer than three variations: One with the fife player sucking on a Dr Pepper; another where Loews movie theaters replaced the drums with big buckets of popcorn and had the drummers scooping deep; and one in which the three musicians marched down the middle of modern Fifth Avenue, oblivious to traffic, as part of the City of New York's "Look Both Ways" pedestrian safety campaign.

The whole thing was a big marketing push. Every other day there was a newspaper column huffing about "the American Experiment." As if the experiment hadn't finished and we didn't know the results. *What are you, Carney, some kind of Communist?* He had a few days to come up with something for the *News*. Free drink coasters for customers who can recite the Declaration of Independence while standing on one foot with their eyes closed.

200 YEARS BUT IT FEELS LIKE MORE—
ASK THE INDIANS
THIS JULY 4TH, SALUTE TRUTH, JUSTICE & 3-POSITION
ADJUSTABLE RECLINERS
AT CARNEY'S FURNITURE

Wait—"Truth, Justice, and the American Way" was the tagline of the Superman radio show, not some U.S. history thing. Mighty Whitey to the rescue. How about:

200 YEARS OF GETTING AWAY WITH IT

He liked the last one, and soon adopted it as a refrain.

\* \* \*

They talked fires.

"Your old man worked for a finisher named Wilbur Martin," Pepper said. A finisher put a building out of its misery, he said. The owner's at the end of his rope—taxes up to here, junkies taking over—so he sells the building to the finisher, who strips out the wiring, the plumbing, anything worth a buck, and then torches the joint for the jacked-up insurance policy. "You see Wilbur walking down the hallway, sizing the place up, you best be looking for another place to hang your hat. Big Mike put 'em to the torch when it was time to cash in."

"You smelled it on him." Big Mike had made grim jokes about splitting "like a roadrunner" once he lit the match—no timers, no alarm clocks for him. Carney had known that arson-for-hire was one of his father's sidelines but had never pictured how it went down. The people in the apartments next door, the sleeping children, the bedridden old man unable to rise from his bed. He was angry for a moment that Pepper had confirmed the truth he had avoided.

They were in Donegal's, curtain of twilight coming down and Broadway deciding who it was going to be tonight. Pepper and Carney sat at the bar, with a sparse carryover crowd from happy hour behind them. As in the Dumas Club, the decor had not changed much in the last fifteen years. Busted neon stayed busted, wobbly tables got wobblier. The Dumas men continued to prosper; achievements here were measured differently, like the death of the only other person who knows what you did that night, or your kid doesn't hang up when you call after all these years.

The bar was sleepy. In the old days the TV thundered when *Lucha Libre* was on, to the patrons' rabid endorsement. This evening's wrestling was a new program, featuring a league Carney had never heard of. Sound off, the matches a pantomime. Donegal's population had dwindled. Fewer boasts about jobs gone right and commiserations about jobs gone wrong. They were dying off, the old crooks and hustlers and flimflam artists, or upstate after an ill-advised scheme to cover medical bills or six months' back rent or new teeth. There had to be another version of Donegal's five blocks over or five blocks down that served half-bubbly drafts to a younger generation of thieves and hoods.

Their regular bartender, Buford, only worked Mondays and Tuesdays now, leaving anyone who used the bar for messages to the inconstant attentions of Toomey. Toomey's father was Italian, and he drew his Sicilian heritage into service as an excuse when called for fucking up everybody's messages. "I got my mind on other things, you know?" Meaning, ladies. Meaning, it's 1976, why don't you get an actual fucking answering machine, you cheap bastard?

On the TV, the wrestlers had migrated outside the ring to duel with folding chairs. "I haven't seen Mr. Fuji in a while," Toomey said.

"He still wrestles," Pepper said.

Pepper looked good. He was on his feet again, after having thrown his back out "carrying an unconscious body." If it had been anyone else, Carney would have asked for an elaboration, but he knew one was not forthcoming, plus it sounded like business as usual to be honest. The old crook was bedridden for six weeks. Carney had John run up chicken and puzzle magazines, missions from which his son returned bewildered. Uncle Pepper was a professor of esoteric disciplines.

Now he was back. If anything, Pepper seemed more formidable after his recovery. Always a deliberate creature, he moved and talked half a beat slower now, and it made him more dangerous, like a lion appreciating a pack of gazelles at a watering hole, mulling over the menu. All the time in the world.

Carney asked if he'd ever joined his father on a fire job.

Pepper never criticized Carney's father in front of him but didn't hold back a blink of disgust. "You do something, maybe you don't do something else." Pepper put a match to a motherfucker's house on occasion, but that was personal, not business. He glanced at Toomey. Toomey was tight, he wasn't going to run his yap to anybody, but he was less adept than Buford at pretending not to eavesdrop. "But it wasn't like it is now," Pepper resumed. "In the Bronx you have to sleep with your shoes on. People setting fires every night, and not just guys in it for the insurance."

Carney had heard about that—blowback from another dumb city policy. If you were on welfare and wanted to move from your vermin-infested, crumbling-down, city-owned apartment into another, you could qualify for a couple of grand for moving expenses and furniture—if your place burned down. Says it right there on big signs at the welfare office, like instructions. What was a striving soul to do? As with everything in the city, there were small-time plays and big-scale scams, and the savvy player knew which ones deserved your attention.

A redheaded walrus capered around the ring, surprisingly fleet-footed, bells drooping on his big jester's hat. "Who's that?" Pepper asked. The wrestler threw his hat into the crowd and beat his chest King Kong style.

"The Big Fink," Toomey said. "New guy out of somewhere."

Pepper kept his eyes on the match. "I don't have a handle on what you're asking me, Carney," he said.

Carney explained again about Mrs. Ruiz's son, and the hospital, and his rage that whoever torched the place was getting away with it. "I want you to find out who did it."

"Why?"

"For the kid."

Toomey sensed Pepper's gaze on him and resumed stacking the coasters.

"Just curious," Carney said.

"Nobody's just curious. People only say 'just curious' when they're the opposite of that. Doing legwork for cops again?" This was a reference to the first time Carney had retained Pepper's services, which had involved shadowing a drug dealer named Biz Dixon. It ended with Pepper giving Carney a black eye.

"I'm not going to the cops," Carney said. "It's for the kid. He lives upstairs. He deserves better."

"Everyone deserves better. This guy you mentioned—Oakes? You figure to nail him for it?"

"No, he used to work downtown and probably looked the other way when someone asked him, but I mentioned him because he's the type of person who would do something like this. Get this— Elizabeth and May are campaigning for him."

Pepper sighed. "And when I come up with the guy who did it?"

"I got it."

"Got what?"

"Let's start there."

Pepper finished his beer and Toomey poured him another. "How much?" Pepper said.

They did a deal for the Arson Job and caught the next match, a Terry Sanchez and Huck Jablonsky tag team against two pikers in gold spandex. Carney tried to figure out what differentiated a wrestling outfit from a ballerina outfit. Flummoxed.

John had called Carney into the living room two weeks ago when Muhammad Ali made a surprise appearance on *Championship Wrestling*. The setup was Gorilla Monsoon grappling with Baron Mikel Scicluna while Ali watched from the front row. Supposedly

Monsoon weighed four hundred pounds, but that had to be PR, for there was no way that black leotard could have contained such abundant majesty. The Baron went down and Ali, outraged at the shenanigans, ripped off his tie and shirt and climbed into the squared circle to taunt Monsoon. They danced around each other like sleepy bears, Ali tossing a few jabs, until Monsoon swooped in, snatched the heavyweight, and lifted him onto his shoulders for some airplane spins, round and round . . . It was all promo for the upcoming "The War of the Worlds," a money-grab match between the boxer and Japanese wrestler Antonio Inoki.

The question sat there: How does a big walking dink like Monsoon take out the Greatest?

"So he's in on it," John said. "It's all rigged?"

The boy was catching on.

"It's a show. They're all in on it." The wrestlers, the promoters, the audience, too. If the audience is in on it, too, is it rigged or merely the world as it is?

Carney finished his Budweiser. On the wrestling program it appeared as if the heels had replaced the ref with their own evil ref while the good guys were distracted.

It was customary when he and Pepper did a deal to move on to other matters of importance, such as a dissection of commonplace frustrations of city life. Disappointing mass transportation experiences, price hikes in everyday staples, the new vermin. Carney turned from the wrestling show and said, " 'You do something, maybe you don't do something else.' " But why do *that*?"

Pepper shrugged. "That's how it goes down sometimes."

"It's not right."

"No. But that's how it goes down sometimes."

The next afternoon they were eating lunch in Marie's office. It was Carney, Larry, Marie, and Robert, who'd gone out to Ricci's for sandwiches. Larry was reeling in his nephew with a tall tale that was about to swerve off-color, and Carney realized he hadn't thought about the boy in the hospital, or the fire, or the slight at the fundraiser all day. Getting it off his chest had been helpful.

Distracted by images of the boy waking in the dark apartment alone, he'd been seized by a kindred terror, but the feeling had receded. He had noticed that sometimes if he shared a fear or regret or a thing that gnawed at him—told Freddie, Elizabeth, and now Pepper—it relinquished some of its power, slunk back to where it came from. Disburdened him. Indeed, he might have forgotten about the job until whenever Pepper asked to get paid, had not that meeting in Donegal's initiated a series of events that neither man was able to contain, with lethal results.

# THREE

The most famous arsonist in New York City history was Isidore Steinareutzer, aka Izzy Stein, aka Isaac Chernick, aka "Itchia der Warcher," aka Izzy the Painter, after his habit of posing as a house painter when purchasing kerosene, one of his accelerants of choice. Izzy was the head of what the cops called the Arson Trust, a network of fraudsters responsible for hundreds of fires all over the city. Undercover fire marshals tailed Izzy the Painter for seven months, posing as hucksters, plumbers, gasmen, and Yiddish peddlers, before they arrested him in the summer of 1912.

When he came down from Sing Sing to testify at the Manhattan courthouse, the newspapers were aghast at his "Startling Revelations of Incendiarism." The Trust, Izzy said, consisted of the "mechanics" who lit the blazes, insurance agents who wrote the inflated policies, public adjusters who wrote off small fire damage as a total loss, police lookouts, tipped-off firemen who quickly arrived on the scene, and nobodies who provided alibis for a price—"the cogs in the wheel of the big conspiracy." Izzy himself specialized in Jewish Harlem, but he ran firebug gangs across Manhattan, Brooklyn, and Queens. Ratted them all out and still got twenty-four years. Landlords hit up Izzy for his services, but so did tenants—rent a room, throw in some junk furniture, and then cash in the pumped-up claim. He carried benzine in a whiskey flask, sprinkled it on bedding and clothes, and then beat it outside to the street to catch the show. Izzy liked the money, he confessed on the stand, but also "liked to watch the fire engines."

But now it was 1976, and the city had cut back on most services, including larger-than-life crooks, to say nothing of legendary incendiarists. It was hard to generalize about criminals, Pepper had learned. He'd worked with shaky, pencil-necked dudes who went stone-cold when they kneeled before a safe, and bloodthirsty hit men who were thoroughly henpecked. But every firebug he'd met—save Big Mike, who was a generalist—had been furtive and squirrely both on and off the job. The profession attracted nutjobs. The type of guys Pepper sought were single-room-occupancy men, hot-plate men, shitty tippers who never passed a pay phone without checking for errant dimes, and they dreamed of fire.

Pepper took a run at the finisher first. The *New York Post* article named the shady owners: Excelsior Metro. Right there in the phone book. They rented an office above a TV repair shop on Broadway and 135th, the same space Sammy Johnson used to operate out of before the lawyer got put away for extortion. Sammy had bankrolled a few jobs Pepper had been involved with, fronting the setup money for a cut. Ghostly black-and-gold paint on the windowsill spelled out I'LL SEE THEM IN COURT on the half-moon window.

Pepper went on stakeout for a couple of hours—the bench in the Broadway median had a sad elm for shade—before he went up and picked the lock for a look-see. The two rooms were a front. Blank walls, rolled-up carpet, the desk drawers and rusty file cabinets empty except for mouse droppings and misspelled travel brochures, probably from the tenant between Sammy and Excelsior Metro. Some addresses were made for crime. Crooked lawyer, fly-by-night travel agency, slumlord HQ—it was like how certain soil was good for producing wine because of the minerals, or so he'd read. Suite 2 of 3341 Broadway produced a rich grift vintage.

The owner of the repair shop waved bills in Pepper's face when he asked about the neighbors upstairs: "You tell them I got their mail!"

Pepper moved on to the men with the matches. It wasn't like the firebugs were all hanging out at some firebug club, talking combustion rates and airflow. He started with an old acquaintance—Mose Hamilton, who'd torched a chunk of Harlem in his heyday. His last fire was in '59, when he lit up a building on 167th and killed four people. Two kids. It was Christmas, a quiet news day, so the papers milked it and the chief of police took an interest. After a sixteen-year bid upstate he found a gig sweeping up at a pool room on Seventh Ave, Manny's.

Manny's was a mile and a half from Martinez Funeral Home. After being laid up for six weeks, Pepper relished a good walk. He hadn't popped pain pills in days, and after a lifetime of wearing the same style of black Keats shoes, had finally bought a pair of canvas sneakers. For years his various partners had suggested lighter footwear as a practical matter. They were miraculously comfortable. Pepper had reached an age where an "I told you so" was met with a thank you, as opposed to a punch in the nose, his preferred response since youth.

In his convalescence he sat by the window as mourners gathered and dispersed below, and took in the tokens of the stirring spring: hookers switching to lighter, more breathable fabrics; second-story men dawdling before fire escapes, considering their chances; the latest, worse generation of pigeons. They slapped up bicentennial shit everywhere, as if every day in Harlem started with the Pledge of Allegiance and a salute to Plymouth Rock. It said in the paper that on July Fourth a hundred old-timey ships were to parade through New York Harbor—who cares about some candy-ass ships? Then Memorial Day it got hot, like someone hit a switch: Summer in New York City, here the fuck we go again.

He had missed two jobs while laid up, which turned out to be a lucky break. The jewelry-store heist in Brooklyn Heights got real bloody, and the pigs pinched the entire crew at the Astoria warehouse rip-off—silent alarm. His injury was his guardian angel looking out for him. Church Wiley had reached out about a job; they were going to meet up next Monday. This looney arson gig for Carney was a way to get back in shape. White man ain't killed you yet, a little exercise won't either.

When Pepper caught up with Mose, he was in the back of Manny's, leaning against the Wurlitzer and drinking a Yoo-hoo. The jukebox was broken—a junkie had stolen the turntable—and the fluorescent tubes overhead blinked out WHAT A DUMP in Morse code. 11 A.M. at Manny's. The midnight shift of hustlers and die-hard idlers was sleeping it off, and the daytime crew had yet to punch in. Mose nodded at the bartender, who sized up Pepper and decided he had no problem if the codger grabbed a five-minute break. Mose wiped a funky rag over the small table by the john and they sat.

Prison had shrunk Mose, his neck and wrists bobbing in collar and cuffs, but he still maintained one of the city's great goatees, something you might find adorning the chin of an old midtown locksmith. Pepper asked about it. Some guys had heroin smuggled into the joint, or reefer; Mose's connection kept him in tubes of Dick Hyde's Beard and Mustache Oil.

He didn't want to revisit the whole fire thing. "I'm out, Pep," Mose said. "Look at me." He touched a singed spot behind his ear where the hair didn't grow, to remind himself.

"There are firebugs who do it for kicks because they're sick in the head, your basic pyromaniac. Handsy priest fucked them up, mommy slapped them around when they were little, whatever—they got a screw loose." He tendered the example of Fuzzy Pete, who'd lived in a flophouse down the street from Mose when he was a kid. His contribution to the genre? The "Fuzzy Bomb": a cigarette and a matchbook, wrapped in cotton from a mattress, all secured by a rubber band. Cigarette burns down, ignites the matches—there you go. This was no insurance play—Fuzzy targeted his former teachers and social workers. Like many a firebug, he liked to watch the show. "That's how they finally got him,"

Mose said. "Smoking a cigarette across the street while his old principal's apartment went up. He'd knocked him out and left him on the kitchen floor before he splashed gasoline around and lit the fuse."

But Pepper wasn't looking for a nutcase. Mose said, "After the psychos, you have what you might call freelancers. A gentleman needs a fire for a onetime thing, he offers a work-for-hire gig. That's what I did—freelance jobs. My name came up if you asked around. You know me, Pepper—I'm steady."

Pepper grunted. They had worked together a few times, nothing worth mentioning.

"I liked the planning," Mose said. "The setup—it wasn't too far from pulling a big robbery job, juggling all that shit. Don't look at me like that. How many times you been pulling a heist and it goes down the toilet because of the other guys? Torch job, I don't have to rely on nobody but me."

Pepper was skeptical of the comparison, and expressed it using off-color language. "I'm not looking for a one-off operation. This guy is in a crew."

"Yes. Could be any number of people." A large man in a Hawaiian shirt entered the pool room. Mose paused. The customer went up to the bar and ordered a rum and Coke: harmless. "These arson gangs today," Mose said, "in Brooklyn, the Bronx, all over uptown, they got the whole racket down, better than how we did it in the old days. They have regular guys they use. Young guys. Everybody I used to know is in the can or dead." He said he'd ask around. One or two names popped into his head, give him time to pin down the details. "What's it to you?"

"A boy got hurt in the fire. I know his father." The lie popped into Pepper's head, he didn't know why. Carney had never told him the boy's name. "Little Remmy."

"Little Remmy?"

Pepper nodded.

Mose sighed. "You never want to hurt someone."

One of Mose's victims in that Christmas fire had been a newborn, Pepper recalled. Mose said in the old days, a lot of the fires were set up by tenants. They set them in the afternoon, when the guy—or gal, 'cause women got in on the action, too—was at work, and had an alibi. "Now it's night work, and you never know who—"

"And you, Mose? You done with fires?"

Mose gestured at the pool room. The lights ticked overhead. "If I go to jail who's going to mop up the vomit?"

Pepper asked him what he was drinking. Mose looked at his empty Yoo-hoo and asked for a seven and seven.

The drink arrived. Mose stopped Pepper as he headed for the door. "What happened to that girl you used to step out with? Schoolteacher?"

Shit, that was a long time ago. No need to think about that. Pepper said Mose had him mixed up with someone else.

* * *

After Mose, his misfit census began in earnest. He got the names of firebugs who turned out to be in prison, out West, in the ground, retired. People directed him toward young wild-eyed men of the pyro school and slow-talking geezers who fantasized what he'd look like covered in gasoline. Some men had been victims of their own fires, their skin an inventory of evil works. He pressed them or employed "polite persuasion." He got nowhere.

Take Wilmer Byrd. Mose had left his name at Donegal's. Byrd worked for two finishers—a Ukrainian who owned a fleet of limousines and had a taste for dilapidated Harlem townhouses, and an Italian guy whose destroyed Bronx properties, when plotted on a map, looked like a worm's route through an apple. Byrd used the same kind of firebomb as the one on the 118th job and the same top-floor rear apartment placement. The firebug had made it known he was looking for work.

Byrd lived in a flophouse on Ninety-third off Amsterdam and in the afternoons hung around the Off Track Betting parlor a few blocks over on Broadway. Pepper beat it down there at eleven, before the first race at Aqueduct. He buzzed a series of apartments and mumbled into the intercom when someone answered. They let him in. Most of the hallway lights were shattered, thin wire filaments poking from broken glass. Usually, the radio or TV was blared out from apartments when you walked through a dead-end joint like this, but Byrd's building was eerily quiet. *Last stop, everybody off.*

The firebug lived on the third floor. "Exterminator," Pepper said.

"Exterminator," Byrd repeated. Such a fanciful notion. The door opened an inch and Pepper pounced.

The walls of Byrd's apartment were grimed, adorned with peeling wallpaper that sagged like waning bouquets, but the place was classily furnished, from the dark green Oriental rug to the tasseled lampshades to the polished dark wood of the end tables. Fucking doilies abounding. It was the neatest flophouse room Pepper had ever seen. "Huh," he said, impressed.

Byrd cringed in anticipation of impending violence. He had a pigeon's physicality, a fine-boned vulnerability. "I have the money," he said.

Pepper frowned. Gamblers. He explained he wanted the line on the fire last week, 118th Street.

"I don't mess with fires," Byrd said.

Byrd knew how to take a punch. *Punch,* singular. He was soon forthcoming.

Sure, he did fires for people, Byrd conceded. Different parties. But he wasn't uptown that day. That was the day of Victor Wilson's funeral out in Jersey. The wake went on past midnight—Victor's brother worked at one of the Newark breweries. Did he know him?

Pepper did. The man had been utterly useless in life but had found a small amount of utility in death by providing Byrd with an alibi. He'd verify. Pepper asked him what he knew about the fire, who were the players these days.

"Who are you?"

Pepper said he worked for the insurance company. "I hate insurance fraud," he declared. "Everything about it."

Byrd gave him leads that turned out to be worthless. Pepper ran around Harlem like a donkey. A lot of these guys had straight jobs, something on paper for their parole officer, and he had to interrupt them at work. Straight jobs in all kinds of places. He'd never stepped inside a bridal store before—the punk in question knew firebombs and sewing machines, versatile—and couldn't remember the last time he'd been in a bowling alley. Pepper chased the guy down Lane Seven, that fucker blubbering and clomping on the wood the whole way. No one came off well that afternoon.

By Friday, Pepper decided he was ditching this gig once he hooked up with Church Wiley, whether he nabbed the guy or not. He finds the firebug—then what? The next stage of whatever Carney had planned, like that time he had Pepper tail the banker and the drug dealer. At Donegal's, Carney had kept bringing up this Oakes character he disliked. What was their beef about? An idea occurred to Pepper, immediately shaming him—Elizabeth had been nothing but decent with him all these years. On the one hand Carney thought Oakes was shady enough, and on the other too cowardly to get his hands dirty. As if part of Pepper's job was to prove Oakes didn't do it, to demonstrate that the guy was too stupid or chickenshit. Like a reverse detective.

Perhaps his was not a temperament suited to this kind of assignment, with the finessing and the gently plying and such. His encounter with Leon Drake, for instance. A running buddy at Nathaniel Barber gave Pepper the name of a guy who in turn led him to the man. "That nigger's flammable."

Although Pepper was not aware of it, Leon Drake shared a characteristic with Izzy the Painter in his well-defined hunting grounds. Izzy had worked a swath between Ninety-sixth and 106th on the East Side, a teeming immigrant outpost with its own language and God. At the time of his arrest, the firebug had been on these shores for ten years, long enough to study the hostile world beyond his streets. America called them across the water and then chewed them up. Survival meant manipulating flaws and outwitting the system. You'll let me insure four bucks of furniture for three thousand dollars, sight unseen? *Done.* Whether the new arrivals were crooked or straight, whether the idea was a rationalization or a hope, they believed that if they made it through, their children faced less dire calculations.

Leon Drake, too, grew up under an antagonistic order but never summoned much interest in striving upward on its terms. His aspirations lay in ash. There were strivers next door, across the street, Harlem was full of strivers but Leon was not one of them. The arsonist had a supernatural acquaintance with his home turf. He knew it all, it was the crucible of his personality—every storefront, which sidewalk grates clanged underfoot, the alleys, fire escapes, the getaway exits through basement doors and their distance from the street, which tenements hit max occupancy and which townhouses had rotted through, the proximity of the fire hydrants and fireboxes. He knew every crack and corner, and the more he understood, the more he hated. 116th to 125th between Morningside Ave and Park! Leon despised every inch, from the grimmest of the grim subbasements to the tips of the bent television antennas piercing the sky. When he walked the streets, he superimposed his own perfect city over the misbegotten one before him, it was a city of ash and cinder heaped hundreds of feet high, emptied of people, wonderfully dead and still. Such was his antipathy that if his employers stopped paying him tomorrow, he'd torch 'em for free—a building here, a building there, slow torture.

The man was not running for head of the block association, in other words.

Word had it Leon put two buildings on the south side of 118th to the match, diagonal from 371, where Carney's tenant was injured. He worked at Cooper's Fish on 125th. At lunch and supper their line went up the block. Every five years Pepper gave their fish sandwiches another chance and each time he got sick. No one else complained. Cooper's was also a fishmonger, with rows of porgies, snapper, and flounder on ice that slowly melted and dribbled pink water into white buckets. Winter days the reek bordered on unholy and come summer descended into full blasphemy, despite the exertions of three gigantic standing fans.

Leon worked the fryer. Sweat-sheened, twitchy, and beady-eyed, he did little to rebut a negative firebug stereotype. Pepper had been informed of the man's frequent cigarette breaks, when Leon padded out two doors down to smoke and stink of fry oil. His target soon stepped outside.

It was two on a Friday afternoon, just after the lunch rush, the sidewalks of 125th a furious stream. Sometimes it was prudent to brace a man when there was no one around and other times it was nice to slug him in front of witnesses to underscore the desperation of the man's position—an entire Apollo's worth of people could be watching and no one would help. Pepper and Leon hadn't even gotten into it and already men and women were clearing a spot, just picking up on vibes, alerted to impromptu mayhem by their city survival systems.

"Leon!" The cook tried to place Pepper. He immediately apprehended the nature of this encounter. There was no hiding Pepper's personality, which was December when the days got shorter and shorter: cold and relentless. Inevitable. He didn't like Christmas trees, or babies, or owing anybody anything. Any smile that broke out on his face was a mutiny swiftly put down. He was not there to present you with an oversized check from the sweepstakes company or a dinner invitation from Raquel Welch. Pepper was an emissary from the ugly side of things, to remind you how close it was.

Leon didn't wait for Pepper to speak. He ripped off his hairnet and snarled.

Pepper blinked. Toe-to-toe with a fry cook on the One-Two-Five. Thanks, Carney. The firebug emitted a stench of hot oil and sweat, and Pepper was momentarily back in Newark, a little boy watching his stinking father return from a shift in the hotel kitchen. With the smell in Leon's corner, it was two against one.

Leon charged. Pepper gave in to his fate, took one on the chin. The arsonists he'd met this week had not been fighters. Starting with an intimation of violence set the stage for a quick confession. Not here. Leon knew how to fight. They danced around. Passersby formed a doughnut. How many tussles did 125th see every day, how much blood? He got a few licks in. Leon dove for a Coke bottle in the gutter. Pepper did not approve and brought his sneaker down on the firebug's head. His old black shoes would've been more useful, he noted.

The crowd whooped. An old man threw a carrot into the ring. Muffin crumbs flew from a church lady's yap: "Show him! Show him!" Rooting for him or for Leon?

Pepper's back held up, that was the main thing. Nary a twinge.

"The fuck do you want, anyway?" Leon said.

Pepper stared down the crowd. They got the hint. He helped Leon to his feet and they withdrew under the green canopy of Triple-A Travel. Pepper told him what he was after.

Leon rubbed his tongue over his bloodstained teeth, spat a red glob on the sidewalk. He squinted. "Come to my place of work asking about some fire somebody did?"

"No one told you to raise a fist."

"I lose my job, there will be hell to pay, I promise you that," Leon said.

He asked Pepper to repeat the particulars. Leon told Pepper that he was in the Tombs last Thursday night. Picked up for a scuffle in Happy's. "Not that it's any of your damn business."

Pepper believed him—a call to Happy's later that afternoon confirmed matters—and once again he doubted his fit for this assignment. Sometimes Pepper beat the wrong man, and the man happened to wear a hairpiece. If this man was black, he picked up the man's knocked-off hairpiece and returned it in a form of reluctant apology. He was cold, but not without feeling. He had developed a little ceremony at this point, like when the military presents the American flag to the family of a dead soldier: thusly. Pepper felt a quiver in his back as he bent to retrieve the hairnet from the pavement and put it in Leon's greasy hands.

* * *

Somebody named Joe left a message at the bar. They gave a time and an address. Buford would have demanded more information, but Toomey was filling in, and when it came to saloon answering services these days you got what you paid for. Pepper moseyed over.

He'd been wrong about Mose, that they'd never worked anything big together. On his way to the meet he remembered the alarm-company deal back in '52. People still talked about it, like Don Larsen in Game 5 or seeing Jackie Robinson on TV for the first time. Old-timers, anyway.

The brains behind the Bulldog Security Co. job was a young man named Uncle Rich. Uncle Rich's brief career in Harlem crime had been outlandish, flashy, and memorable. If Donegal's had a Hall of Fame that consisted of more than initials scratched into the wall above the urinal, surely Uncle Rich's portrait would have been up there next to greats like Grady Cooper, Vic Thurman, and the Count. In his youth he got sent up the river for stealing a bundle of *New York Times*es from a midtown newsstand. Ten-year bid. On the inside he commenced his studies—analyzing the big scores and botched break-ins, the spectacular heists and life-ruining debacles, interviewing madmen and broken masterminds alike—and emerged into the free world as the architect of visionary capers.

It couldn't last and it didn't, but before he got taken out Uncle Rich brought Big Mike and Pepper in on schemes. That first job had its origins in the postwar alarm-company boom. Everybody was getting their establishments good and wired—doors, windows, vaults. Any serious business maintained a dedicated line to one of the big security companies. "We're in an arms race," Uncle Rich told Pepper and Big Mike. They were in the basement of Saint Andrew AME Church over on 147th. The church rented out space, and the crook was interviewing prospective crews in fifteen-minute slots.

"Johnny Law comes up with an advancement," Uncle Rich said, "we figure out the countermeasure, and the game continues." He removed his specs and rubbed them with a handkerchief. Everything about him was precise: his movements, his diction, how long he maintained eye contact. As if he had timed it out and rehearsed it all before you knew you were going to meet. "I got to thinking," Uncle Rich said, "what if instead of deactivating the alarm system, you deactivated the alarm company?"

Bulldog's representatives wore down shoe leather poaching clients from the Big Three: Argo, Top Lad, Valiant. Bulldog was out of Chicago, where they'd sewn up an exclusive contract with Ma Bell; like mobsters expanding their territory, they were moving in on established players. The sign-up deals for switching were pretty generous, and they gave you a nice sticker to put in the window to identify you as a client. And a target. "That's how I got the idea—it says, they all use the same key for the front door." Gideon Gem & Diamond on Broadway defected, and Fabrizio, and a few other uptown jewelry outlets that maintained a substantial overnight inventory.

Bulldog's New York headquarters was on Ninety-fifth and First Ave. Uncle Rich had a finger, a phone-company lineman who'd helped set up their main switchboard. The company's web extended uptown and down through the telephone cables. Trip one of those wires, Bulldog dispatched a team and rang you up. Next call after that was the cops if you didn't have the code word for the account. If the switchboard itself—and the men who manned it—was removed from play, what treasure awaited an enterprising burglar before the heat came down?

Uncle Rich knew, and felt no need to elaborate on that or how he was going to engineer such a feat. Bulldog HQ was his end. Pepper and Big Mike's concern was the target he'd chosen for them: Fabrizio's on 125th. Once Uncle Rich neutralized the security company's magic box, they'd get the signal and take it down. In and out. "Can you handle that?"

Big Mike said, "Shit." Pepper shrugged.

At nine P.M. on the first Monday in August, Pepper and Big Mike entered 24 East 125th and walked up to the second floor, the home of Liberia Insurance. From afar, their worn gray uniforms and black cases identified them as workmen; up close one made out the Rogers Plumbing patches on their backs. They bypassed the insurance firm and accessed the roof at the top of the stairwell. They traversed three rooftops, and set up on the black tar beach over 18 East 125th. The doorknob to 18's stairwell had been punched out two days prior. They waited for the signal.

Three months later Liberia Insurance vanished, along with tens of thousands of dollars in premiums. This was unrelated to the Bulldog job, but indicative of the slippery nature of Harlem at that time: Here today, gone tomorrow with your money.

Out on the tar and looking down 125th Street. Pepper thought about the heat, and how it pushed folks into funky behavior. Pent up all day, sweating out, then a trigger sets you off. The '43 riots had been August events, and the rooftops had been full of men and boys throwing bottles and bricks and bits of ripped-off mortar down at the cops. Giving them the Blitz.

But Pepper was on the roof for business, not pleasure. He said, "Pull this setup downtown, you make a killing."

"Yeah," Big Mike said. Meaning, this was a waste of a good scheme, as Harlem's jewelry vendors didn't carry the same volume of high-quality stones as a Madison or Lexington joint like Spears Winthrop or Edgeworth Jewels.

"But," Pepper added, which was all he had to say to communicate that working downtown had its own complications. Dispatching three—four? they didn't know how many places Uncle Rich was hitting tonight—black crews below the Ninety-sixth Street Mason-Dixon Line increased the possibility of police interference.

"Though," Big Mike said, to indicate that Bulldog's response to a Harlem client was not the same they'd give to a downtown client. Anytime racism helped the rip-off logistics, it was like God was giving His blessing.

"Sure," Pepper said. As in, tonight's setup was tonight's setup and they'd take what they could get.

On the street below, someone walked down Lenox singing along to a transistor radio.

Pepper asked Big Mike how his kid was doing.

He said, "He minds himself."

At eleven-thirty, Pepper and Mike directed their attention across the street to the northwest corner of Madison. The human traffic had quieted once the liquor store turned off its lights and rolled down the security gate. Then eleven-forty-five—time. A minute passed. Pepper imagined the chorus of cussing going on in his partner's head. A skinny man in a white T-shirt turned the corner—it wasn't him. Two minutes late. Pepper inhaled. Then he appeared—Mose. At the corner he lit a cigarette, tossed the match into the gutter, and kept walking. Pepper and Mike hit the stairs.

The third floor was the home of Jackpot Printing, which produced the pink numerology sheets for Big Top Lottery twice a week. PISCES! PLAY 280 FOR HOT RETURNS!! BIRTHDAY BOYS AND GIRLS ARE ADVISED TO HIT 478. Closed Monday. Below Jackpot was the showroom and office of Fabrizio's, an Italian holdout. They'd sold overpriced wedding and engagement rings to a generation of Harlem Negroes, for some the first in a lifetime of special-occasion purchases at the store. The Italian jewelers stayed put when many of their competitors relocated downtown after the neighborhood "changed over." Fabrizio's had paid protection to the Lombardi brothers for many years, but the deterioration of that crime family's fortunes made for uncertain status. Retaining electronic protection was a smart investment.

It was a silent alarm. Pepper and Big Mike had to trust Uncle

Rich and his downtown team had done their bit. They'd know toot sweet if things had gone south.

Big Mike took out the three locks on the front door—more loudly than Pepper liked—and they were inside. They looked at each other. Nothing happened, and nothing was supposed to happen. During the daytime, the jeweler's was splendidly lit, charging the gemstones and jewelry in the display cases. How many scores of young, broke Romeos had been snared by that glittering array and been impelled to payment plans? At the end of the day Fabrizio's salesmen transferred the velvet racks to the wide Aitkens lockboxes beneath. Pepper and Big Mike knew their way around this model Aitkens, which had been designed to delay access until security or the law arrived. Tonight that was not going to happen.

Eleven minutes later, they had emptied the front room's wares. In the office there was a big safe with the really nice stuff, but Uncle Rich had tempered his ambitions. It remained to be seen if the other crews stuck to his outline once they were inside their targets. Pepper and Big Mike nodded at each other, tested the heft of their black cases, and entered the stairwell, almost colliding into the man coming down from the printing office.

Per his own protocols, Pepper had staked out the building himself the last two Monday nights. There had been no activity above the first floor. The man shouldn't have been there. He was a chunky man in his late thirties, in a nice black suit and a bright red tie. Forgot something in the office and returned after a night out. He realized what he'd stumbled into. Big Mike commenced to strike him in the face with the butt of his flashlight. The third blow sent the man to the landing, the fourth sprayed a fan of blood on the wall, and the fifth terminated his movement.

Big Mike didn't have to do it. They would've been gone before the man got to a phone. But Mike Carney was like that. Five minutes here, five minutes there, and the encounter never occurs. It wasn't Mike's fault. Wasn't the printer's fault. That's just how it went down that night. Thousand other nights it comes out different. Like the kid in the building that got torched. Thousand other times he's nowhere to be seen, but that day he is.

After that night, Big Mike's dented flashlight blinked out sometimes, and he'd look at Pepper and shrug.

The two thieves rendezvoused with Uncle Rich at seven A.M. in a parlor-floor apartment on 139th off Broadway. Uncle Rich declined to brag about how it had gone on his end, rare modesty in their profession. "It's the wires," he said. "You control the wires, you control the game." Big Mike told him about the witness. Uncle Rich nodded and returned to the Fabrizio haul, holding a diamond brooch up to the table lamp. Once the fence came through, he'd pay them off.

They'd work together one more time. Six months later, Uncle Rich hired Brooklyn boys for muscle at a meet. Day of, the men rubbed out everybody who showed up and made off with the cash and the goods, but that was Brooklyn for you. Uncle Rich got his face blown off. Some of the Donegal's crowd held that he'd faked his death—"How do you know it was him?"—and split to Mexico, but Pepper had little time for crook gossip.

The Bulldog had been a real job, not like chasing down some damn firebug. Pepper checked the address Toomey gave him. 104th Street this far east was a gauntlet of dreary, final-lap tenements and junkie beachheads. He'd made good time—it wasn't dark yet. Number 159 was in the middle of the block.

No, they didn't make them like the Bulldog job anymore. It was an entirely different game nowadays, he thought, as the baseball bat clopped him at the base of the skull. They hit him two more times before he went down, and hit him again.

# FOUR

It was 6:27 P.M. when Toomey delivered the ambush message to Pepper. At that moment Carney and Martin Green were at the Subway Inn in midtown drinking beer. Martin remarked upon the narrowness of Lexington Avenue sidewalks.

Carney said, "It's true."

"Rush hour, all those delivery trucks, you have to take a number for the right of way."

"If you're an avenue, act like an avenue. Not a side street."

"Fuckin' A."

Two drinks in, Green's Brooklyn accent broke the surface. He had mentioned Sheepshead Bay over the years. Carney didn't know much about the neighborhood except that it was toward the end of the subway line, where the city ran out. Every borough had those spots where the tracks stopped and then you were stuck. Not Staten Island, he corrected. Staten Island had moved in next door one day and hung around. It didn't quite fit in with the rest of the block, no one knew what to do with it, but there it was—leaning over the chain-link fence during the cookout, giving unsolicited advice about weed killer, and mooching another beer.

This was Carney's first visit to the Subway Inn. According to the framed article next to the register, Marilyn Monroe and Joe DiMaggio had a favorite booth back in the day, but it was difficult to imagine that the famous still frequented the place. Red neon glinted on the aluminum frames of the chairs, the bottle regiments at the bartender's back, and the glass curving over the jukebox's guts. A few women in light summer blouses and pencil skirts sloshed gin and vodka in thick glasses, jackets off in the heat, but today's happy hour had attracted a mostly male clientele. Carney knew hustlers when he saw them, and the bar was two-deep with white-collar hustlers, pink-faced and shouting over the black music from the Wurlitzer—good old Motown, not "that disco stuff"—scheming after the big score that would deliver them to middle management. Raised in segregated hives on the Island and in Jersey—and yes, Staten Island—they congregated here and un-noosed neckties, rolled up sleeves, the daily dread descending upon them without office chores to distract them. After a couple of drinks and confessions they'd disappear home down a side pocket or corner pocket but now they ricocheted against the walls, the bar, and one another, clacking and clacking.

Carney and Green met at the gem broker's apartment in the East Eighties for business, but once a year the man invited Carney out for a drink. He was pleasant company. The last few years had seen him grow more conventional, ditching the Aztec amulets and red-lensed sunglasses in favor of bespoke blazers and khaki slacks. Martin had even started referring to a girlfriend, Ally, who sold fancy paper at an *ooh la la* stationery store on Madison. "She keeps me grounded," he said. "How is your Elizabeth?"

"Keeping busy." Seneca was still booking a lot of summer travel, and the campaign took more of her time. This week was an exception for Carney; the nights when he ducked out for a drink, or to meet a crook under cover of ducking out for a drink, were more rare. Elizabeth was now the one who went out evenings, meeting friends or working for Oakes. Last evening she and May had passed out buttons and caps outside the 135th Station and collected signatures. The replacement pens were coming in next week, after the first run spelled the candidate's name as "Oates."

"I don't know who Oakes is, but he can't be worse than these jokers we have now," Green said. He looked over his shoulder.

The jukebox cranked out "Jailhouse Rock" and a bunch of drunks sang along, butchering Elvis's moves. No one heard Green when he leaned in and said, "I have an idea I'd like to share."

He had a Swedish colleague who was interested in a very specific precious stone, he said. Quantities of it. The stone in question was elusive at the moment in most markets, but the Swede had identified three American sources. The Americans were not inclined to sell. The Swede was drawing together plans to intercept—

"Intercept?" Carney said.

"His word. He wishes to execute a plan to intercept the stones and he asked me to help facilitate that. I thought of you."

"That's not what I do." He finished his beer.

"Of course not. It's straying for me, too. You know people that no one else knows. They might be the right people."

"That's not up my alley."

Green smiled. "I had to ask. Some people get an itch and a notion to branch out."

Carney said he appreciated the invitation and got up for a glass of club soda. They stayed at the Subway Inn for another ten minutes. Green was heading to Maxwell's Plum to meet a German contact who'd read about the place in a magazine. "He thinks he's going to do coke in the bathroom with Bianca Jagger." Carney was off to catch up with Pierce at the club. The lawyer wanted some advice.

They shook hands outside. The express was right there, but before he went underground Carney couldn't help but notice the dead lights above Bloomingdale's loading dock across the street. He wondered if someone was coming back in the wee hours for unauthorized shopping. Negligible foot traffic after midnight. Perhaps the lights had merely reached the end of their life. It was not a crime to recognize opportunities.

These East Side stations—so far underground in places. Something to do with the schist, maybe, the rock determining where the subway lines can run. All that stuff you can't see that shapes how you live every day, and you know nothing about it. He waited on the platform next to an ad of revolutionaries lobbing crates of tea into Boston Harbor: KEEP THE LIPTON, DUMP THE REST.

*A very precious stone.* Carney broke down his meeting with Green on the train uptown. Green declined to specify what his colleague was after. Emeralds, a specific family of diamond? There had been something in the papers about a big robbery in France last week, some famous emeralds in the haul.

It didn't matter. Carney had no interest in the front end. Thieves removed an item from the straight world and converted it to stolen merchandise. Whereupon the fence helped transform the stones and gold coins and necklaces into legit goods again. Fences versus finishers. What did a finisher do? They took something from the straight world—a four-story tenement, a three-story row house—and delivered it into the dark side through fraud, arson, injury, death. The wrecking ball came, took the structure down to the crater, and the developer returned the site to the straight world again. On the voyage between the legit and the not-legit there were plenty of opportunities for enterprising individuals to wet their beaks. Like the subway, the trip depended on where you hopped on.

Carney was going to stick to what he knew. Solid and dependable. Like rock. Green had always been careful in his work with Carney. If he was changing his business, exposing himself to new dangers, perhaps it was time for Carney to find a new contact.

\* \* \*

As men set upon Pepper with baseball bats, Carney was humming "Afternoon Delight" and bopping up the stairs to the Dumas Club. The time was 7:55. The after-work crowd in the parlor was clearing out for Friday-night engagements with wives or mistresses. The older men, the stray Montys and Rutherfords, nestled in their favorite club chairs and sofa spots, emptying small dishes of mixed nuts and tumblers of peaty scotch. Carney discovered Pierce in his favorite chair by the window, reading the Real Estate section of the *Times*. Pierce beckoned the waiter.

Pierce needed to work out a problem. "Remember that lady I was telling you about—works in my office?" Carney remembered something about his partner's secretary—they were messing around, she had a fiancé in Boise, what if his partner got wind of it? In the meantime, this CPA had moved into the suite across the hall, and there was a young woman at reception he'd been chatting up. "Am I crazy?"

"Man, what do I know about that?" Carney said. Pierce didn't want advice, he wanted to bray.

Pierce opened his mouth but the fire engine's wail stepped on his lines. Ambulance sirens and fire-truck sirens sang all day, but since the torching of 371 Carney pictured what they were rushing toward, what unfolding misfortune awaited.

" 'Where's the fire?' " Pierce said, chuckling.

"You've heard of finishers?" Carney said.

The lawyer waved his hand. "Don't believe everything you read in the papers," he said. Deliberately set fires only accounted for a tiny fraction of the problem, he told Carney, less than ten percent. The real reason was the deteriorating city itself.

Before the current fiscal crisis and all the cutbacks, Pierce said, there were decades of urban renewal projects that obliterated communities and industrial zones in the name of progress. "Ramming the highways through, bulldozing so-called slums, but they were places people lived—black, white, Puerto Rican. Knock down the factories and warehouses, and you wipe out people's livelihoods, too. The white people take advantage of those new highways out to the suburbs and flee the city into homes subsidized by federal mortgage programs. Mortgages that black people won't get. And the blacks and Puerto Ricans are squeezed into smaller and smaller ghettos that were once thriving neighborhoods. But now those good blue-collar jobs are gone. Can't buy a house because the lenders have designated the neighborhood as high-risk—the redlining actually creates the conditions it's warning against. Unemployment, overcrowded tenements, and you get overwhelmed social services. It's started—the breakdown."

"What does that have to do with the fires?" Carney liked his idea of bad men skulking about with their cans of gas—sociology, or whatever this was, seemed like a cop-out.

"It's not arson—it's years of shitty urban planning biting us in the ass. You see it in Harlem," Pierce said, "not two blocks from where we're sitting. One system fails and then the next. The slumlord takes over a building, doesn't keep it up. Boiler busted, no heat. Cheap space heater overloads the old wiring—that's a fire. Junkies and winos move into an empty apartment, get loaded and drop a match—that's a fire. Teenagers fucking around in an abandoned building. The building next door goes up, too, and now the whole block is getting sick. One after another. RAND looked at the numbers." An uptick in fires, they found, was preceded by a spike in public-school enrollment. Chased out of one neighborhood by slum clearance and fires, their next stop becomes the new overcrowded crisis zone. Counting down to the next collapse. "It's a chain reaction. There's arson, yes, but it's just a small part."

Carney had heard of the RAND Corporation. On *60 Minutes,* something about the Soviet Union. Nuclear war? Pierce explained it came out of World War II—engineers, physicists, and military planners who started a think tank after the Axis surrendered. "They had to find something to do with themselves, right? They call themselves 'systems analysts' but they're just the usual gang of egghead white guys who want to run shit. The U.S. government is their main client, and they're plugged in everywhere. Nuke scenarios against the Russians, how to fuck over Castro. In Vietnam, they analyzed Viet Cong attacks and troop patterns and told the army where to drop the bombs and send soldiers. All done by computer. Mayor Lindsay—you remember—he's walking around Harlem in '68 during the riots, looking at Detroit and Watts and getting the willies and he's like, what if we took all this

American know-how that can send a rocket to the moon and use it to solve the problems of the urban city? He makes some calls and that's how we get the New York City–RAND Institute, studying the police department, fire department, health, housing. All paid for by your tax dollars."

"How'd you get so up on all this?"

"How do you think? I sued their asses." He toasted: to billable hours. "I'm an expert on this shit now. RAND moves in, the city gives them carte blanche, they wheel in their charts and big mainframes and start looking at the city the way they looked at fallout patterns and the NVA. What to do about the fires, they're asking each other."

"Didn't they close down fire stations?" Carney asked. He caught the protests on *Eyewitness News*. Part cutbacks, part "efficiency." They did all these studies on how to fix the fire department, and ended up closing station houses in the very neighborhoods most afflicted by the runaway fires. Which led to more fires and more destroyed blocks.

"Rich neighborhood," Pierce said, "they hear the city wants to shut down the firehouse down the block, next day they're on the phone nipping that in the bud. South Bronx doesn't have that kind of juice. We got hired by community organizations to stop the closures.

"I sued them three times. First two times, the judge dismissed the cases once the city trotted out those RAND studies. Numbers can't be racist, right? But the data can be dumb or wrong, though, and if you feed shit into the computer, it gives you shit right back. The whiz kids got their heads up in the clouds so they can't see street-level shit—like traffic. What if the reasons two firehouses have different response times isn't bad performance but traffic? Some neighborhoods got it, some don't. On Park Avenue, the hydrants work. A mile up in East Harlem, the pipes are still disconnected from unfinished road work from ten years ago. You can't see it from the clouds. Wrong assumptions, they add up, and everything gets worse."

He took a sip of his whiskey. Sitting before Carney was the Pierce that he hadn't seen for years, the civil rights crusader, Black David standing up to the White Goliaths. Pierce shared the closing arguments he'd rehearsed but never got a chance to deliver. "Third time I sued them," Pierce said, "I was working for Uptown Gardens. Run by Kwame Miller, this Black Panther who continued with the grassroots stuff after the big split in the party a couple of years ago." Pierce named some good works—a school-lunch initiative, a sports program. "Solid stuff."

One day Uptown Gardens finds an envelope on their doorstep—whistleblower from inside the institute. "Remember Daniel Ells-berg? He's the RAND guy who slipped the Pentagon Papers to *The New York Times*. It was like that. It was all in there—their own internal study on urban policy over the last thirty years, all the shit I was just talking about. The system is broken. The firehouse closures were going to make it worse. They buried the report, and went ahead."

From Pierce's tone, the story wasn't going to end with justice served. "They get to Miller," Carney said. "Some hush money?"

Pierce lit another cigarette. The ashtray was a huge crystal knob on top of a pedestal, a solid piece of ash disposal. "We had it in black-and-white. Moynihan's 'benign neglect.' In '68, Lindsay's planning commission says it outright—if East Harlem and Brownsville burn up, think of how much money we can save on slum clearance before we redevelop it. Cheaper to let it burn and they can rebuild. We had them dead to rights on the race angle." He glanced around to see if implicated parties were enjoying a Friday-evening drink. "But then we get a call. Uptown Gardens has dropped the suit. Mr. Kwame Miller moves to fucking Bimini, and a couple of weeks later the city terminates the RAND contract. Not saying it's all connected but—yes, that shit is definitely connected."

Carney made his hands into fists as Pierce talked. He was getting angry but didn't know what set him off. Pierce wasn't describing anything new. Was it the kid? You see things from up in the clouds and you miss how it plays out in the street. What puts the Ruiz boy in the hospital—the fire, or everything that made the building empty in the first place?

"That's how the city works," Pierce said. "Look at Oakes—last time we were here we were opening our checkbooks for him. But when he was a prosecutor, I didn't see him taking down these slumlords and crooked insurance agents. Arson case hits the DA's office, that's the last you're going to hear about it. City buys up that dead property, or seizes it outright through eminent domain, and sells it to a developer for cheap, or an organization like Homes 4 Harlem assumes control—there's a lot of money in 'urban renewal.' "

"The borough president, he gets a say in who gets those redevelopment contracts?"

"Officially, no. The borough president is your voice in city hall, ha ha. In practice, he's a member of the Board of Estimate, along with the other BPs and the mayor and the comptroller, and it's the actual smoke-filled room of guys carving up the city, just like in the old days. Boss Tweed shit. Occasionally you hear rumblings from the Feds about suing to break up the Board of Estimate on constitutional grounds, but until then it's the Wild West."

Carl the waiter cleared his throat and asked if they wanted another round. Pierce ordered another scotch and Carney a club soda.

"Let's just say the borough president has a big bucket and a big ladle and he's doling out whatever to whomever he wants. For some consideration . . . A lot of our fellow members are banking on Oakes getting in there. They probably already owe him for looking the other way when he was a prosecutor, and he's the type of man who keeps track. You saw Ellis Gray at the fundraiser, licking his chops. You don't think Sable Construction wants in on those low-income housing contracts? Dave Parks? Newsome? There are a bunch of guys waiting on an Oakes regime. That second generation of Dumas gentlemen." He raised a glass to the portraits on the wall. "Their daddies did it, now it's their turn."

"Envelopes moving around," Carney said. Self-perpetuating graft, like the self-perpetuating fires. Once it gets going, it doesn't stop. "And what about you?" he said. "Now that you're hanging your own shingle?"

"I do work for the city. I'm happy to represent all different kinds of clients." He grinned. "When it comes to politics, I write checks same as everybody else. Like you."

Carney shrugged. "I didn't have much of a choice."

Pierce stubbed out his cigarette. "Who does?"

* * *

Carney arrived home at ten minutes past ten o'clock. Trouble was making good time to his front steps. He beat it by twenty minutes.

Dark windows. He still said "Hello?" as he stepped into the hallway. The echoes made him glum. He'd gotten used to not having May around the house, and now John was out more often, working at Baskin-Robbins or off with his friends. Elizabeth was scarce more nights. She said she'd be late tonight, but the specifics escaped him. It was only him in the house these days, more and more, like on 127th, after his mother passed and his father gave himself to the streets. He couldn't place her in the apartment anymore, her face a dark blur. Carney flicked on lights as he moved through the rooms, as if he'd discover his family on the couch or chairs, waiting for him.

The kids had left a note on the kitchen table—Daryl Clarke was having a party up the street. Next to it was a phone message John had taken: "Marie called. She says 'Albert is off the ventilator.'"

Wonderful news. Should he send a card? Flowers? He'd ask Marie on Monday, maybe even walk up to the apartment himself to see if there was anything he could do.

Elizabeth came home—she closed the front door in her signature fashion, firm and final, to shut out anything gaining on her. He hollered from the kitchen.

"How was your day?" She saw John's note. "Daryl Clarke's house?"

"Aren't they away?" Carney said. James and Baby Clarke had aggressively talked up their West African vacation for months. They had booked it through a Seneca rival, Motherland Tours. Whether Baby was sticking her thumb in Elizabeth's eye was up for debate.

Elizabeth was unconcerned about what the kids might be up to. "Sometimes you have to let them think they're getting away with something." She asked after Pierce, and he said the lawyer had droned on about the responsibilities of running his own shop. Carney didn't mention the omissions in her candidate's campaign literature regarding graft and extortion.

Elizabeth's eyes shined: tipsy. She wore a blue-and-green summer dress that she'd put in the back of the closet because it had grown tight. It fit again. Was she growing her hair out again? It was the longest it had been since her mother passed.

"Janet and I went for a drink at the Whistle Stop after the meeting," Elizabeth said.

Right. Janet was another member of Women for Oakes. She had recently moved from Texas after a divorce and had an active social life, Carney was coming to understand.

"It's a nice place. They don't play the music loud."

That last part came out as a kind of lament. The campaign was more than helping out a childhood friend, he saw now. It gave her purpose as Seneca receded from her life. She'd gone to work for Dale at Black Star soon after college and made the travel agency into the thriving operation it was today. Dale was in no hurry to retire, and when he did, he'd never put a woman in the top position. Even if Elizabeth basically ran the joint. She'd finally realized that fact last year—that it wasn't hers, and never would be. It was Dale Baker's, and then whichever one of his sister's idiot kids from the Miami office he handed the keys to.

When Carney knocked Oakes, and the campaign, he was

knocking her hopes for herself. Oakes was crooked, but Elizabeth didn't know that. She believed what she set down in the Women for Oakes pamphlets: that change was coming.

Elizabeth read Marie's message. "Ventilator?"

"Isn't it great? The boy's doing okay."

"Who?"

"The boy upstairs from the store." He ran it down but her face remained blank. Was it possible he hadn't mentioned it? "The main thing is that he's getting better."

"I didn't realize you knew him."

"Of course I know him. Arnold is my tenant."

"Albert."

"Albert, Arnold—that's not the point."

The front door rattled in its frame. The doorbell rang for a blink, as if it had shorted.

There had been some break-ins on their street, taking advantage of the back alley. Elizabeth looked at the skillet on its peg by the stove. One time they thought they heard an intruder and Elizabeth had armed herself with the cast-iron skillet as they roamed the house after the source of the noise. They never did figure out what it was. "They have keys," Carney said. The kids wouldn't forget their keys at the same time. "I got it," Carney said.

It wasn't a druggie or a wino. He recognized the windbreaker through the window in the door. The door fell inward under Pepper's weight. His face was swollen, slick with sweat and blood, and he collapsed on the floor of the vestibule before Carney could catch him.

# FIVE

Professional bruisers recognize the distinctive thump generated by a baseball bat striking human muscle or fat. It's not a squishy, soft-tissue sound, or a pulverize-fingers sound. It is substantial, meaty and authoritative. That Friday evening on 104th Street, Pepper reckoned that it was better to produce that sound as the slugger and not the sluggee, offering up one's thighs, small of back, or skull as a drum. He'd been distracted by his annoyance at Carney's assignment and his nostalgia for more daring jobs, and they got to him. Okay: Get back in it.

There were three men, one to oversee and two to clobber. Pepper drew himself from the concrete. The next blow smacked his lower back and his knees buckled. Like he was struck by lightning—but the lightning kept going. He writhed on the pavement. The man in charge yelled instructions. They carried Pepper into the backseat of a red Cadillac DeVille. The car pulled out.

The boss barked from the passenger seat, one hood drove, and the other recited his favorite threats and dug the muzzle of a revolver into Pepper's cheek. Pepper relaxed his body and slumped on the vinyl seat, staring into the floorboard. It helped with the pain. The man with the gun reeked of bad cologne that had evaporated into crappier cologne. Pepper wheezed in and out as he attempted to regain mastery over his body.

"... uptown." Pepper recognized the voice. Vicious, rumbly. From where? He had been on a job. Not with this man; he had been warned to keep an eye on him. Security. Security for one of Corky Bell's poker games. Not lately—before Corky kicked the bucket. Loudmouth bitch, taunting better players: Reece something. Enforcer and top lieutenant to Notch Walker. What the hell was his problem? Get out of the car and figure it out later.

The driver cursed and beat the horn three times. There was traffic. Friday evening—people dressed up and walking slow to show off their fancy clothes, taxis to dinner and movies, yokels driving into the city for a night out. They didn't put one in the back of Pepper's head, so they wanted information or a different location to torture or kill him for some reason to be determined later. The car stopped short. Reece said, "Watch the fuck out!"

Pepper was bent in a slump behind the driver. The gun eased off his cheek. Pepper shifted his weight toward the door and Bad Cologne said, "Don't fucking move!" and bonked him on the head. The light changed—the Cadillac lurched forward.

"Some goddamn cops," the driver said.

"Chill," Reece said.

Bad Cologne moved the gun from Pepper's face and fixed his posture to look less hinky. "Speed up a little," Reece said.

The three of them looking around, trying to play cool, Pepper figured. Gun, hood, door.

He reared back and slammed his shoulder into Bad Cologne, pinning him. Pepper got a grip on Bad Cologne's gun hand. They grappled in the backseat as Reece said, "Chill, chill!" The gun went off—floorboard. It was loud. The driver stepped on the gas. The motion knocked Pepper and Bad Cologne backward. Reece cursed. Bad Cologne's fingers loosened. Pepper gained control of the piece, fumbled with the lock, and rolled onto the pavement. The green moving van tailgating the sedan almost obliterated him. Motorists struck up a honking match, trying to out-noise one another. Pepper hobbled south down Third Ave, ducking. Was the Cadillac still headed uptown or had it stopped? A little girl eating ice cream stared at him, mouth smeared with vanilla, agape, as her mother recoiled in horror. Blood running down his face? Blood running down his face. He didn't see the police car. He crossed 119th, staggering and hopping. They'd have to follow him on foot, no way to reverse in this traffic. Them: boxed in. Him: dizzy and panting. At 118th, he veered west, opposite the flow of traffic, saw no one chasing him as he rounded the corner. Eight doors down, he stumbled into the cubby of shadow beneath the stoop of a boarded-up brownstone and shut his eyes.

The next time he opened them he was in Carney's living room. No—he'd gotten there under his own power somehow, which implied he had opened his eyes. Had he been run over by a green light's worth of vehicles on the way? He lifted his head—let it drop again.

Carney and Elizabeth whisper-argued in the hall.

"I don't know that he wants to go to a hospital."

"What? Look at him—he needs a hospital."

"He doesn't like doctors. You know he's a big baby underneath."

"I know what kind of man he is, Ray. Don't try that."

"He made it here—it's where he wants to be."

Pepper closed his eyes again. It was still dark when he next woke. Curled on his side. Bath towel under his head. A rubber bag of melted ice had slid off his face. He tried to move and it felt like his blood had turned to broken glass and shot around inside him. He counted to ten and shuffled into the kitchen, where the radio was on low. News station. Gas prices out of control.

Elizabeth was up reading a big hardcover book—*Centennial*. She observed his slow progress into the kitchen with pursed lips. The yellow paint job was new, he thought. She held her hand out, indicating the seat across from her at the breakfast table. She rose to aid him when he tottered, but he made it to the chair. The Felix the Cat clock over the sink said it was past three.

Bleary as he was, Pepper had no trouble discerning his host's sour mood.

"I got jumped," he said.

"Jumped! By what, a Mack truck?" She mumbled something.

"What?"

"I said you better not get blood all over my goddamn couch." She rose. "Let me get more ice for that pack."

She twisted the ice tray. They say these new plastic ones were better than the metal ones with the lever, but he wasn't buying it. Elizabeth refilled the ice bag and told him she was going to bed. His room was made upstairs if he wanted to sleep in. "Otherwise the kids are going to wake you. And they'll have questions about 'Mack trucks.'"

*His room.* He had only stayed there once, on Carney's birthday. It had been a swell evening. He'd been moved to make more of an effort to understand other people and it had made for a good time. At different points during dinner he took in the family's faces and puzzled at why he felt so comfortable. "What's this cake?" "Betty Crocker." The rain really started coming down, he was tired, and when Elizabeth told him she'd had the kids make up the bed upstairs, he didn't put up his usual fight. He had wondered what it'd be like to wake up in a house like that, see the light coming in. Uncle Pepper. Don't call him that, but he had a room upstairs with a thick, red oval rug, a pine bookcase full of Carney's business-school textbooks, a rocking chair, and a bed that only he slept in, as far as he knew.

Pepper hurt pretty bad when Carney came in the next morning. He had awakened multiple times, waiting for sunlight. Sunlight meant that the white man hadn't killed him yet.

Carney held up Bad Cologne's pistol. "I got it before Elizabeth saw it," he said.

Pepper reached over and tucked the gun under his pillow. "I'll tell you later" was all he felt like saying when Carney asked what happened. He recited a phone number and asked him to call his doctor.

Elizabeth checked in on him. She was less irritated than she'd been last night. "You sure you're okay?" She left eggs and bacon and a glass of Tropicana. John and May stopped in to say hi, skittish and worried. Like they were little kids again. Carney or Elizabeth had told them not to pry so they acted like this was a normal visit. He told them he'd be better in no time. They gently closed the door. Pepper turned to the wall. He thought, Reece Brown, Reece Brown.

Dr. Rostropovich knocked on the door to his room two hours later. No effete practitioner, he appeared to have attended medical school among mountain men and rowdies; his neck was a tree trunk and his hands were made for mangling, not healing. The doctor was not much of a talker. His idea of bedside manner was pretending he'd never seen you before. As far as Pepper knew, his practice consisted entirely of the jammed-up, gutshot, and otherwise fucked over. You crawl away from a rip-off, bleeding out on the gravel, Dr. Rostropovich was your guy. He probed where the bat had collided. He eavesdropped on Pepper's insides with a taped-up stethoscope. He sensed where Pepper had hurt his back without being told, and poked it with a cold metal instrument. The cut above Pepper's eyes had closed up, he observed. He left pills.

Carney came in soon after with chicken soup. He closed the door behind him and sat on the desk. "I told her you got into an argument in a bar and the guy's friends joined in."

"That's ridiculous, some dipshits taking me in a bar brawl. A salesman who can't even lie right."

"Where's that doctor from?"

"You call him up, he comes around."

"What did he say—do you have a concussion? Need X-rays?"

"I got to take it easy."

"That's his diagnosis?"

"He's not that kind of doctor."

"Not what kind of doctor?"

"Not the kind who believes in all that stuff. You call him, he comes." Pepper pointed to Dr. Rostropovich's glass jar of pills. "You got a glass of water?"

\* \* \*

Three days later Pepper and Carney were parked four doors down from Optimo on 107th, waiting for Dan Hickey to come out. The wind overnight had swept out the humidity and the clouds made the city seem like it was wrapped in a bum's dingy overcoat. Carney read *The New York Times* he'd draped over the steering wheel while Pepper tapped the outside of the passenger door, brow knit, considering different combinations of violence.

Pepper and Carney didn't have much to say to each other until the float came up the avenue. They heard the music first, a jumble of horns and drums. Reluctantly, they looked back to see. A small green rig tugged the parade float, which was decked out in red, white, and blue—the colors of the American flag, and also the Exxon oil company, sponsor of this roving display. The Exxon tiger mascot gyrated and strummed air guitar as two ladies in hot pants and rhinestone tank tops cavorted and waved to the passersby. A honeycomb of amplifiers perched on the tail of the float, inflicting a funk version of "The Star-Spangled Banner."

Nobody paid it much mind on those Harlem streets. There was too much to do.

"Fucking Doodle Dandy," Pepper said.

"What are they going to do once Fourth of July comes?" Carney said. "They have to stop at some point."

"In the war—"

"You were in a war? Who won?"

Pepper looked at him.

"Pepper's feeling better," Carney said. He folded the newspaper and nodded at the cigar store. "You going to recognize him?"

No, Pepper did not remember the faces of everyone whom he had beaten and who had beaten him—he had trouble retaining the faces of the dead—but his encounter on 104th was recent, and they hadn't scrambled his brains that much. He was stiff, but more than up to the task of retribution.

His recovery was a matter of will and its modern assistant,

pharmaceuticals. Dr. Rostropovich's pills had kicked in Saturday afternoon and smoothed out Pepper's wrinkles and kinks like a hot iron. Pepper shuffled to the rocking chair, to-ing and fro-ing, listening to the transistor radio. Iraqi soldiers on the Syrian border, Jimmy Carter nabbing endorsements. He "closed his eyes" a few times. A crochet throw materialized on his lap. It was soft. When Carney came up for the lowdown on how Pepper ended up on his doorstep, Pepper said, "You."

Pepper had enemies, but none that resourceful or in any position to act on their hatred on account of physical limitations (maimed) or mental weakness (scaredy). He'd been off the circuit, laid up with his bad back, so it wasn't a loose end on a job. He had, however, been rattling cages all over Harlem, knocking heads, knocking the heads of employees, which meant employers, and some of them might have manpower.

It took a minute for Carney to accept that the ambush was his fault. "I told Elizabeth what I assumed had happened—you were slapping someone around for looking at you funny, and ten of his buddies showed up." He apologized.

"You think you're Superman, Carney," Pepper said. "The Red Conk. You come up with a setup, and it has to work, because it's yours." His father was like that, Pepper said. The money drawer in the bank pops open like magic, the watchman sticks to his schedule because you need him to. "You wriggle out of shit enough times, you start to believe you're bulletproof. When you're not. It comes around. It catches up."

Pepper had taken some lumps for Carney. He'd be up on his feet soon. And when that happened, the least Carney could do was drive.

In the upstairs room, Pepper gathered what he knew about Reece Brown. Pepper worked security at Corky Bell's poker games plenty in the old days. Low hassle, good money. Hoods and crooks showed up to play with the locals and slumming white folks, but they respected the game. When Pepper had to manhandle someone, it was an angry player on tilt after a bunch of bad beats, not a stickup man. The muscle work for Corky dried up. Then one of his games got robbed—by a white cop no less. He renewed his interest in proper security, and reinstituted his New Year's games to send a message he wasn't running scared. Pepper was there, eating tongue sandwiches and glowering, at those final '73 and '74 games.

Reece attended both. His nose, chin, and ears came to a ratlike taper, with a hungry malevolence glinting in his eyes. He'd stolen the Black Panthers' style—black leather coat, turtleneck, and occasional beret—but his sneering mouth, full of gold, hipped you that he did not devote the majority of his energies to social activism. Reece wasn't a bad poker player in Pepper's estimation. An ungracious winner. Intimidating in the showdown, from the other players' expressions when they went heads-up. Corky had tipped Pepper as to who he was: Notch Walker's right-hand man. On call to remind those who trespass how power preserves itself: swiftly, bloodily. "If he acts funky, take it outside quick, is all I'm asking." Reece didn't cause any trouble and they'd had no interaction.

As he rocked in the rocking chair, in the hot room on Strivers' Row, Pepper remembered the weasel Reece brought with him. Confronted with a big bet, Reece leaned back in his chair and gossiped with his flunky, both smirking, to get in his opponent's head. He was medium height, compactly built, with big, red-brown curls on his head and jug ears. Both his profession and cologne were criminal. Dan Hickey was his name; Pepper inquired when the pair returned for the '74 game. The next time Pepper saw Hickey, he was hitting him with a baseball bat, the less powerful of the two sluggers in a post-beating assessment. A fact that suggested Hickey was the one they should brace first. Church Wiley and his job would have to wait.

In this era of Notch Walker's empire, its structure and routines were well documented. After the death of Chink Montague, Notch seized his nemesis's territory, consolidating the south Harlem rackets with his own Sugar Hill operation. A realignment of that size causes ripples: this night spot is taken over, that bar changes from a Montague hangout to one controlled by Walker goons, back-room business changes addresses. Those whose live-lihoods and survival were determined by the new geography of power—criminals—maintained maps of where it was safe to go and where it was not safe to go, where this Walker operative spent his nights and where another had acquired a controlling interest. Best keep track.

Civilians registered these transitions as routine phenomena; they were in fact local expressions of higher-level forces. *The bar across from Eddie's closed.* It was a Montague front made redundant in the new order. *That Italian restaurant we went to on your birthday has really gone downhill.* The plan is to strip it and torch it for insurance three months from now.

It was not lost on Pepper that Notch Walker was now king of the Harlem underworld because he had killed Chink Montague a few years back.

Dan Hickey spent most of his days at Optimo on 107th and Madison. As a mid-level operative in Notch Walker's operation, his habits were no secret. Carney ventured inside on reconnais-sance and was surprised to discover a stocked and functional tobacco and stationery store, not a jive, half-assed front. Hickey had a real cashier up front, and appeared to keep his illicit busi-ness confined to the back room.

He was Reece's bagman, rounding up protection money Mon-day afternoons. Pepper would nab him when he departed on his rounds. Until then he and Carney sat and watched in Buford's new Buick LeSabre. Pepper shook his head when Carney told him that May had borrowed the family car to go to Great Adventure in New Jersey. Elizabeth had promised that she and her friends could take the car to the amusement park weeks ago.

The Buick was a sweet ride. Chocolate with a beige hardtop, and a string of weird buttons on the instrument panel that did God knows what. Take your temperature, read your palm.

"Elizabeth still sore?" Pepper asked.

"I'd say she's glad you're doing better. That's the important thing." Carney tapped the steering wheel. "She knows all about my father and that you worked with him. I've never gone into detail and she's never made a big deal about it. Main thing is, she considers you family. She doesn't want anything bad to happen to you."

Pepper pointed. Hickey hit the street, strutting in red, white, and blue shorts and a lime-green guayabera. His red hair—and big ears—stuck out from under his straw porkpie hat. He was eating a pear, slowly, cheerfully savoring the fruit.

He didn't see Pepper coming. One rarely did. Pepper hooked his arm around Hickey's neck in a way that appeared friendly to bystanders, before Hickey's face collapsed as he registered who had him, and the .38 poking his rib cage. Pepper led him to Buford's car, cooing menace into those jug ears all the way. Hickey dropped the pear.

Carney drove them over to 132nd and Twelfth Ave. Their destination was a three-story building situated in misery between the elevated sections of Riverside Drive and the Henry Hudson Parkway. The two overpasses cursed this area, which hunkered in the shadow of one for part of the day, then the other as the sun traversed. Some warehouses limped along, loading bays opening and closing in last-gasp commerce; most were abandoned. At night the desolate stretch by the river was ceded to dark elements and dire business.

If he could help it, Pepper only came here during the daytime. Carney told him he'd only passed overhead in a car. Until today.

Pepper made out the faded letters on the brick: LIBERTY BISCUIT CO. It had been a long time since the premises had been associated with anything sweet. A high-end Spartan Inc. combination lock—out of place in this run-down patch—secured the metal gate covering the door to the factory offices, and once it was unlocked, the gate had to be thumped in two places before it unstuck and allowed access. The late Paul Miggs showed Pepper the trick when they divvied the Castle Island haul.

The usual urban scavengers had taken over and defiled the factory floor. A mountainous tangle of machinery had been heaved against one wall, preventing access to the managers' domain. Which meant the offices were musty but hadn't been broached by the druggies and vagrants. It was a good hideout. You could split a take there if you were a paranoid type or lamming it, and it served as a quiet place to beat information out of an individual.

The Liberty Biscuit Co. hoarded days of heat, and walking inside was like entering a giant, funky sneaker. Pepper stifled his smile at Carney's reaction. He explained the place wasn't his, he was borrowing it. "Though can you borrow from a dead man?" Hickey dragged his feet. Pepper smacked his head.

They set up in the former reception area. The coffee table featured a *Time* magazine moon shot extravaganza, and Sidney Poitier beamed from the cover of *Ebony*—it had been a long time since the orange leather couch had welcomed someone on biscuit-related business. A section of grimy burlap lay over the receptionist's desk, covered with rust-mottled tools—pincers, an assortment of hammers, serrated things with handles. A vise was clamped on a corner of the desk where a Rolodex should have been, and a shrine of crumpled Burger King bags rose between two dead plants. Old ad campaigns featuring the Liberty Biscuit Baby covered the wood paneling, enlisting the big, monstrous, blue-eyed infant as a material witness to what transpired in the room, and sometimes soaked into the dirty beige carpet.

A wood-grain nameplate on the floor in the corner read MS. LOON.

Pepper considered Ms. Loon's desk and chose a humble crowbar.

Hickey hadn't spoken since Pepper nabbed him. "Who's he?" he asked. Carney at that moment was wiping dust on his pants.

Pepper said, "My lawyer." He took off his windbreaker, folded it in half, and laid it on the coffee table. "You like a bat. I like a crowbar. Different strokes." It began.

Carney retreated to the doorway and crossed his arms. Winced. Flinched. Turned away.

Dan Hickey gave it up.

Leon Drake had called them last Thursday night, he said. Hickey wiped his bloody nose with his hand and leaned back on the leather couch. They met at Optimo. When he heard what Leon had to say, he rang Reece and had him come over. "Leon, he's pissed off," Hickey said. " 'I do good work for you, I'm not trying to get hassled at my day job over some fire years ago.' Reece tells him to slow down. Leon says this guy came to the fish store, trying to pin a fire on him. Why's this guy asking about 118th, we haven't done shit there in years. Leon doesn't know. None of us does. Next day, Reece is like, 'Bring this guy in, we'll ask him.' "

Carney perked up. "Leon does arson jobs for you, but not last week."

"He's cuckoo, one of these die-hard firebugs. I get a load of his face the first time it comes to pay him, I said, 'This man digs fires.' Piss him off and you wake up in a bed full of gasoline, you know?"

Pepper scratched his jaw. "You do the legwork—find the firebugs, fix it up tidy."

"It's a side thing. You work for Notch Walker, he keeps you busy. But sometimes you need extra money."

"Sure," Pepper said. He glanced at Carney. Carney knew about sidelines.

"Like 118th. We took care of some tenements there a couple of years ago. Absentee landlord, city can't track him down. Building inspector goes in to check it out and he falls through the floor, that's how fucked up the place is. Someone wanted it burned out. We take care of it. City of New York seized the plot, flips it to this community group cashing in on all this urban renewal money— you know, help us clean up the ghetto and we'll write you a check. Look at the place now, you'd never know how fucked up it was. It looks pretty nice."

"And last week?" Carney said.

"Wasn't us."

" 'Us.' I get you're in the arranging business, but who are you arranging it for?"

"Oh," Hickey said. "I don't know."

"Nah?" Pepper said.

Hickey shook his head.

Pepper tapped the crowbar on his thigh.

Hickey said, "A man named Alexander Oakes. He's connected. Development money from Albany, downtown. He tells us where to hit and, you know, things happen after that."

Carney overcame his shyness. He stepped into the room. "Hold on."

One thing Pepper had learned from working with the family over the years, you'd have an easier time grabbing a bone from a junkyard dog than getting a Carney man to let go of a grudge.

# SIX

Carney got up that morning with a plan to head to the office, finish the summer ad buy, take Robert to McDonald's for lunch, and spend the rest of the afternoon going over the books. Drop in on Mrs. Ruiz— can't forget that. He didn't know he'd be leaving with Pepper. Payback had healed the old crook—planning, anticipation, execution, and basking in his bloody ingenuity afterward. When her mother passed, Elizabeth got a copy of that book *On Death and Dying,* which identified the Five Stages of Grief. When Pepper was laid low, the Four Stages of Putting Your Foot Up Somebody's Ass provided similar comfort.

The old crook had recovered overnight. Pepper had stayed in his room all weekend, sleeping most of the time. The kids brought soup and sandwiches upstairs and they played checkers. They tried to teach him that board game Risk but it didn't take. "I never heard of half these goddamn countries." Monday morning Pepper came down the stairs, creaky but resolute. If Elizabeth hadn't left for work, she would've marched him back upstairs. Carney sized him up. Pepper scowled back.

Hours later they were in a disused baked-goods factory in one of those parts of the island that seem on the verge of falling into the sea. There were whole stretches of the city where it pretended to be sane and civilized, Carney thought, and places where that pretense broke down, and the biscuit factory resided in one such place. In a zone of harsh static between radio stations playing zippy tunes. He'd never had the pleasure of walking around there before, but it was a day of novel experiences. Pepper had introduced Carney to half an alphabet of felonies over the years, Class A felonies, Class B, F. *Kidnapping* was a new one.

Inside the factory, Dan Hickey's mention of Oakes stirred Carney from his state of mortified unease. He asked how Hickey got mixed up with him.

Reece got pinched on an extortion charge back in '72, Hickey told them. Facing a lot of time. His lawyer comes in for a meeting one afternoon and says that a small fee will bury the charges. Reece didn't get the name of his guardian angel until months later. Oakes walked into Ted's 127 Bar, a Walker hangout on Eighth, and introduced himself. There was a tenement on Convent he wanted removed. That was the start. "Sometimes it was an insurance play and Reece got a cut. Sometimes there was Albany money that'd show up years later once construction started, and after a while Reece asked for a cut on that back end instead of up front." As a prosecutor, Oakes took money from landlords and shady insurance guys to look the other way on the arson jobs, but when he left city hall he got on that redevelopment gravy train, and that's when he hit the jackpot. " 'Antipoverty funds.' It sure was anti our poverty!"

"What else?" Carney said.

Hickey interpreted his interest as a sign he might avoid further punishment and became an avid raconteur. "He used to brag," Hickey said. "That's why we had to talk to him a few times, he runs his fucking mouth too much." One night they were in his office on 135th waiting for Reece to show up. "He's on the phone, acting all hard. He gets off and started going on about how this guy thought he had something on him, insurance adjuster trying to juice him. Oakes is like, 'You're the one who's got to watch out.' " He tells Hickey how he goes to his safe, pulls out his ledger, and starts reading off dates. " 'April 2nd, 1973. Ring any bells? May 15th. Ring any fucking bells? You do insurance—I know about insurance, too.' That shut him up, he says."

Hickey didn't know if Oakes's performance was showing off or a message to not fuck with him. "I was going to warn him not to get in Reece's face with that shit, but that ain't my job." He paused. He looked at Pepper. "It was Oakes who told—*recommended*—that Reece pick you up. See what your angle was."

Carney snorted. Pierce had said, "He's the type of man who keeps track."

Pepper said, "What's your boss's boss think about all this?"

Hickey was tentative. "Most things, Notch don't care as long as you give him a taste."

"Is he getting a taste of this action?"

"No."

Carney caught Pepper scanning the room, as if to confirm that it was a room without windows, and that there was no one to hear. "Don't," Carney said.

"What?" Then Pepper got it—Carney knew his tells at this point.

He didn't want Pepper to snuff the guy for beating him with a baseball bat. The blood spilled here, the blood to come, was his fault. Reece and Hickey had nothing to do with putting the kid in the hospital—they ambushed Pepper because they thought he was nosing around old business across the street. Carney had flipped a switch. A machine turned on and it was making a lot of noise but he didn't know what it did or made or when it was going to finish what it was doing. "You do this, maybe you don't do that," Carney said.

Pepper cracked his neck. He told Hickey they were going to put him on ice for a couple of days. For his own good. "When we catch up with Reece he's going to know it was you that snitched. We wouldn't want you warning him, making him mad at you."

The bagman considered his surroundings, the stains and remnants of brutalities, and looked forlorn.

"You hit me here?" Pepper asked, indicating the lump over his eye.

Hickey's face made the truth plain.

Pepper gave him tit for tat.

\* \* \*

Enoch Parker waited for them on the corner of Broadway and 118th. He got in the backseat of the Buick. "I had to tell my wife I came into Mets tickets. If she knew I was doing this . . ." That explained the Tom Seaver jersey. The safecracker was tall, with a long face and wide, alert eyes behind his black horn-rimmed glasses. His fingers were slender and delicate, an evolutionary advantage for a safecracker. Enoch's canvas Ringling Bros. bag sagged on its straps—heavy gear inside.

Pepper introduced Carney. "He's the wheelman."

"So I see," Enoch said. They headed north.

According to Pepper, Enoch had retired from safecracking and now taught chemistry at Carver High School. "Some of those kids really have a knack for the sciences." They'd pulled jobs together back when. In the spring of 1970, Enoch had a close shave after going twelve rounds with a mattress-factory safe and swore off the life. When Pepper let him.

"Whenever you need something, you say I owe you."

"You do," Pepper said.

"Doesn't mean it's fair to lord it over everybody." It was an act. The tremble in his voice said he was excited to join this excursion. Carney imagined it helped that the safecracker didn't know what they'd been up to that afternoon.

"This yours, Pepper?" Enoch asked. Hickey's porkpie hat had fallen to the floor in the backseat.

"No."

"It didn't look like you."

Once they handcuffed Hickey to the radiator, Pepper had informed Carney that he wanted to go after Oakes's records. "See what this slick motherfucker's been up to." They were in the Buick, departing the domain of the elevated highways and their shifting planes of gloom. Carney was busy consigning the biscuit-factory episode to the category of tall tale or dream. Would Pepper have killed Hickey? Did Carney really walk into the office next to reception and pluck handcuffs from the cardboard box marked "Candles"—and what was in those other boxes? When the hideout's planners bought the bucket at the hardware store did they say, "Excuse me, I'm looking for a hostage toilet, about yea big?"

Carney asked him, "You get the records and then what? The Feds?"

It was Pepper's turn to withhold the larger plan. If there was one.

"Blackmail?" Carney offered.

Pepper adopted a thoughtful expression. He told Carney to pull over at that pay phone and he called Enoch.

Enoch leaned into the front seat and put on 1010 WINS. "I want to hear the weather," he said. "Hey, Pepper, when's the last time we—"

"That fried-chicken thing," Pepper said.

"That was something."

The office of Oakes for Borough President was on Seventh Ave, two doors in from 135th. The bottom floor of a four-story townhouse, it sat between Brights Laundry and Hotline Records & Tapes. Red, white, and blue bunting bowed over the front window. The laundromat was still open but devoid of patrons except for an old biddy doing a crossword on the bench by the dryers.

Carney parked across the street. There was more action than he liked, a bodega over yonder, red and yellow lights blinking, and a takeout Chinese joint with a bedraggled GRAND OPENING sign. Not too close to campaign headquarters, but places that attracted foot traffic.

Enoch piped up when he got a load of the big poster of Oakes's smiling face in the window. "Wait, this is that dude on TV?" he said. "He's running for mayor."

"Borough president."

"Same shit," Enoch said. "You'd think he'd have a bigger office."

A prowl car cruised the intersection ahead. Pepper got out and stared at the cops as they moved down 135th, which Carney realized was the right move if you wanted to "act naturally."

Enoch grabbed his bag. "He ain't coming back?"

Carney shook his head. Elizabeth had told him that the Women for Oakes gang was meeting the candidate at a midtown fundraiser, liberal white-lady group. It was ten o'clock, and the event was likely breaking up, but he didn't count on Oakes returning tonight.

Enoch picked the front-door lock so swiftly he might have used a key. He and Pepper slipped fluidly inside. Carney lost the men in the darkness. Light from the street guided them. He was sure they were in the back office by now.

Oakes wouldn't be back—too much dirty work to do around town. From Hickey's stories, he was turning the city's routine corruption into a fat, legendary score. A real jackpot. He didn't think the boy had it in him.

Pierce's inside dope on the fire epidemic was news to Carney, but his explanation of the borough president's powers was no surprise: Of course it works like that. There are always secret rackets underway that you know nothing about, even as they run your life. One racket brought mayhem, like the scams and rip-offs steering the city into decline, and another invisible racket held everything up so things didn't completely go to hell, like schist. They battled each other, they took turns at the wheel—bottom line, the world was a mess.

What was Carney going to tell Elizabeth about his day with Pepper? He'd stolen a moment earlier to call home and tell John he'd be out, but their weekend guest's behavior required more explanation. He gets beat up, is laid up, then he's out of bed and out all day with her husband. She knew Pepper was shady; he was Big Mike's running buddy. She'd never said anything. It was harder to keep your tongue still when "whatever he's into" is dropped on your doorstep. Elizabeth will poke at Carney, for sure. Like this gem from Saturday night:

"What do you *do* at that bar you guys go to?"

"Drink beer."

"Yeah?"

"Watch a game."

"Hmm." Insinuating. Not insinuating.

A trio of young ladies made their way up Seventh on the way to a night spot. They stalled before the campaign office, laughing over a joke, grabbing on to one another for support. Carney shrank in the front seat until they resumed and rounded the corner.

If Oakes suffered a misfortune and Pepper's name came up, that was harder to manage. For all of Carney's resentments, the campaign was important to Elizabeth, and so was Oakes. He put on a good show; she believed in her friend and the better city he promised. Oakes hadn't been involved with the fire that hurt Albert, but he'd engineered plenty of others, and a host of other crooked stuff. It's how he was taught. Carney thought of the portraits on the walls of the club, that crooked old crew of Dumas Founding Fathers who grabbed all they could and then tutored their sons. The sons put their daddies' faces on canvas and hung them in the club to remind themselves, the way white men slapped the names of their own master crooks onto street signs. Of course Dale was going to hand off Seneca to his nephews after Elizabeth's hard work—there's a code of how to keep running things, and they stick to it.

How will she react if she discovers Pepper is involved? She gets on to Pepper, she's on to Carney. No explanation would suffice.

It was too late. He was in too deep.

He was here tonight because a boy he didn't know was caught in a fire, and a spark had caught Carney's sleeve. To avenge—who? The boy? To punish bad men? Which ones—there were too many to count. The city was burning. It was burning not because of sick men with matches and cans of gas but because the city itself was sick, waiting for fire, begging for it. Every night you heard the sirens. Pierce blamed years of misguided policy, but Carney rejected that narrow diagnosis. From what he understood about human beings, today's messes and cruelties were the latest version of the old ones. Same flaws, different face. All of it passed down.

It was in Carney, too. In his words and deeds, in a thousand tiny moments, his father had provided lessons in how to be in the world, and Carney had taken notes without knowing it. Or he knew it but didn't accept it. His father was a crook and he was a crook. When Mike Carney died, Ray Carney inherited his old Ford truck. It got around decently and helped with deliveries and pickups those early years with the store. More significant—his father had stashed thirty grand in the spare tire. His bank, containing one big score or what he put away over time from hijackings, heists, muscle work, stickups, and the occasional torch job. Carney had used the cash to open the store.

Fire money. Carney built his business on his smarts, his industry, his refusal to fail. Fire money was in there, too.

Pepper opened the passenger door, startling him. He carried a big black garbage bag.

Enoch got in the back. "Wheelman's supposed to keep the car running."

"That was quick," Carney said.

"Enoch does his job," Pepper said. Carney and Enoch appreciated this as Pepper's highest compliment.

They were on Broadway headed downtown when Carney asked about the bag. Did Pepper swipe the petty cash on his way out? There was more than a ledger in there.

"When I figure it out I'll let you know," Pepper said.

Enoch chuckled.

What was he doing? Carney pulled over on 122nd next to a fire hydrant and got out. Left the keys in the ignition.

He lived in the other direction.

* * *

The next morning was a Tuesday, but Carney was going to pretend that it was a normal Monday and that Pepper's latest tour of his dark world hadn't happened. He fell asleep enumerating the things he'd accomplish at the office and woke up eager and committed. Carney had initiated a series of events, but the old crook had assumed responsibility, is the way he saw it. The impulse—to hold someone accountable for once in this miserable city—had been laudable. It was time to step away. The boy was on the mend. Yesterday Carney had been an accomplice. Today he was a salesman of fine furniture and home decorations, a card-carrying member of the 125th Street Business Association, and this year's sponsor of the Convent All-Stars, a Little League team of negligible ability and less distinction. He was going to act like it.

A rich blue sky had moved in after the evicted clouds. Rusty had already opened the store when Carney arrived. He heard Carney and waved and tucked in his shirt. Rusty offered to close more often and was usually the first one in lately. Trying to avoid the family, Carney gathered. Beatrice hadn't visited the store in a long time, kids neither. He'd read an article about white churches hosting weekend trips where battling couples work things out with a priest, get shit off their chests and whatnot. Was that a white-church thing and not a black-church thing? He and Rusty were overdue for a meal at any rate. Maybe that new seafood place on Broadway.

Marie popped her head into his office as he sat down to review the ad material from the *Amsterdam News*. "You get what you needed done?" she asked. He nodded. Carney hadn't explained yesterday's absence apart from a cryptic "I have some stuff on my plate."

In the old days, Marie wouldn't have referred to such an irregularity. She never commented on the odd things she encountered in a typical day at Carney's Furniture, whether it was a cryptic message from Pepper about a hijacking or a wild-eyed visitor clutching a leather satchel and declaring, "I got to talk to the Big Man about something." Or Detective Munson's weekly envelope pickup.

Marie had blossomed since Rodney left her. "Some ladies,

their husband runs out on them, they give up," as Larry unfortunately put it one day. Her vivacious turn made Carney realize how much of her good cheer all those years had been an act; the real thing, the real Marie, was twice as compelling. He loved to look up from some horror on his desk to catch a customer's face after she squared them away—"No problem, sometimes the bank makes a mistake, it happened to me last week"—and see their gratitude that someone in their wretched day took the time to be kind. Marie ran the store's day-to-day and shepherded the rentals with dedication, but at six on the dot she was out the door to get home to Bonnie. She was dating an industrial plumber named Dennis she'd met during her church's toy drive. They played in a bowling league apparently; Carney tuned out when she talked about it.

Carney said, "All taken care of."

Marie said, "Good."

Weekday mornings were slow. An orchestra tuning up, hitting stray notes, getting some blood in the joints. Rusty attended to the few customers. Carney arranged the ad templates on his desk so they resembled panes, scenes in a stained-glass window. Lady Liberty summoning immigrants hither. The Founding Fathers huddling around the Declaration like it was a Tijuana Bible. The musician trio from *The Spirit of '76* slogging through bullets and blood. It shouldn't be this difficult—he had twenty years of slogans and sales come-ons to repurpose—but he found it impossible to play along like everyone else. To pretend that what they meant by freedom was the same thing he meant. As ever, he didn't fit the templates.

Two hundred years. A hunk of rock had more history.

Robert showed up five minutes early. The boy was always a few minutes early, which Carney took as a sign of fine character. That, and his interest in sales. One slow day last week Larry was bitching about "rainy-day commissions" and Robert asked how commissions work. Carney launched into the philosophy of revenue sharing, salary-commission compensation arrangements,

288 | COLSON WHITEHEAD

the ramifications of the court case *Martini Shoes v. Carson*. The boy yawned only once.

With his new red polo shirt tucked into his Levi's, the boy looked like a Junior Sales Associate. Robert told him that yesterday Marie had started him on the files downstairs. Should he continue? Carney said, "Sure," and opened the trapdoor to the basement.

"I like it because it's cool down there," the boy said. He descended the wooden steps.

Marie knocked on Carney's open door. She asked if he got her message about the boy upstairs. "You want to send that card you've been talking about?"

He was about to say "Yes," when the first firebomb exploded.

# SEVEN

The glass shattered on the birch Egon coffee table and the wick ignited the burst of gasoline. Last week Carney had rearranged the showroom, swapping out the DeMarco leather sofa—less inviting in summer months—so that the new Egon sectional, upholstered in a dark mustard cotton-acrylic blend, stood in complement to the low, squat coffee table. It had been an elegant display. The cotton blend went up like that, as did the Modern Arabia rug beneath it, and the thick True America curtains on the wall, which Rusty had forced Carney to install "to make a real living room scene." The flames poured up the drapes and the wall and spilled along the ceiling like a backward waterfall.

The second Molotov cocktail landed on the opposite side of the sales floor in Dining Room, exploding in the center of Sterling's expandable dining-room table, the anchor piece of their 1976 Glamorous Living line, and splashing flames throughout that section and into Recliners. The four recliners—real beauties, a solid representation of the kind of options out there, whether you were new to the market or looking to upgrade—ignited speedily.

The man who threw the firebombs watched the progress of his blaze, his body rigid. He wore thin leather gloves and a white ski mask that showcased his pink, wet mouth. The driver of the red Cadillac was similarly masked, but not as much of an aficionado: He honked. The arsonist shuddered, kicked out of his dream, and returned to the car. The red Cadillac sped away.

A gob of flaming liquid landed on the jeans of the sole customer in the store, a General Electric appliance repairman named Bill Worth. He did not panic. He grabbed a pink throw pillow and bashed out the flames.

Rusty snatched the fire extinguisher by Dining Room, where it had been dusted but otherwise untouched for fifteen years, and attacked the second fire. The fire was already outside the scope of civilians to remedy. Rusty was in the front of the store, on the other side of the flames. Sterling's patented polyurethane core, while providing a model of space-age comfort, also produced acrid clouds of smoke upon ignition. The smoke rose to the ceiling, pooled, poured forth in black waves. Soon the path between the two fires would be impassable.

No, no. The scene froze in Carney's vision—then he snapped on. Robert was downstairs. He yelled after his nephew and unlocked the Morningside door. Had Marie gone out on an errand earlier? He shouted after Marie—she stood in the door of his office. She'd already called the fire department. Robert was out of the basement now. Carney told Marie to warn Walt, the owner of the bar next door—sometimes he was in this early, opening up—and to take Robert with her. He said he was going to get everybody out from upstairs.

He grabbed the keys to the apartments and ran out to Morningside and around to the front door. Rusty yelled, "Oh, Lord! Oh, Lordy!" as he trained the extinguisher on the new Sterling ottoman. The gap between the two fires no longer existed—the showroom was cut in half. Rusty saw Carney and yelled something unintelligible and ottoman-related.

Carney grabbed Rusty's arm. "They're coming," Carney said, "Marie called." The salesman retreated from the flames. A gust of heat washed over them. He put the keys to 381 into Rusty's hand. "I got the other one." They split up.

The entrance to the 383 apartments was on Morningside. He hadn't used this key ring in a long time. He cursed. By now passersby were starting to stall, what was happening, what was happening. He screamed at them to call the fire department. He got the door open. He remembered 2R and 2F before the tenants moved in, and he was shocked—crazy thought—at how much was going on over his head that he knew nothing about. Harold had a fish tank. Carney bent over his desk all day, tracing tributaries of cash flow in his head, and there were fish in a tank above him, swimming, black ones with long spokey fins, orange-and-white guys with big round eyes. No one was home. Third floor, either. He pounded on the doors, gained access, searched the rooms. Mrs. Ruiz kept their place tidy. The furniture was modest, a hodge-podge of styles. He'd give her a break on a Sterling, except how could he show it to her when it was going up in flames, the entire showroom and the collections, his store? Albert shared a bed-room with his two younger sisters. The girls slept in a bunk bed and Albert had a twin made up in *Star Trek* sheets. The girls' beds were unmade. Albert's had not been slept in.

Phil in 3F didn't answer. The keys didn't work. He pounded on the door and ran outside.

Rusty said he'd gotten everybody out of 381. Mr. Stevens had been passed out, he told Carney later, but the racket and commo-tion made him think he was in Pearl Harbor again, and he was out on the sidewalk in his drawers in seconds.

Carney ran inside through the Morningside door, ducking below the black smoke. He'd cut through the wall years ago to make a side door for his fencing business; now it was the only way to reach the office. The blaze had overtaken the showroom and advanced to the threshold of his office with a crackle and a whoosh. He opened the safe, swept some key documents into the wastepaper basket, and the cash, and since his filing cabinet was too heavy to move he settled for the top drawer containing records for '74 and '75. When he emerged, basket balanced on the file drawer, a fireman pushed him away and forbade another sortie.

The first ladder to arrive was parked across Morningside out-side the church. Another engine pulled up at the intersection of 125th. Firemen hustled on the sidewalk, clearing the scene and advancing on his store, taking measure of the blaze. Carney gestured to the third floor—he couldn't get into the apartment on the third floor, there might be someone in there. The sirens had been going for minutes but he didn't hear them until he saw the black braid of smoke wend its way into the sky and the front windows shattered. Then the sirens filled his skull.

\* \* \*

The fire department talked to him first. A white fire marshal led him around the corner, where Carney would not be distracted by seeing his livelihood go up in flames. "You saw the man throw them into the store?" He had one of those lazy-mouth Long Island accents.

"No. Maybe Rusty did."

"You want to put that down?"

Carney was hugging the file drawer to his chest, his chin holding the wastepaper basket in place. He set it on the sidewalk.

"And who is this Rusty?" the marshal asked.

Once the fire was out, the cops wanted their turn. Historically, Carney avoided walking by the 28th Precinct, as his father had taught him. "Cops snatch you for some shit you didn't do, 'cause you're the first nigger they see." It was Munson's old station house. Perhaps the cop asking the questions had taken Munson's desk. The cop was white-haired, with a drinker's complexion and the bigot's stunted imagination. He was surprised Carney was the landlord, and wanted to know how long he'd owned the buildings. The insurance policy—was it new? "How was business? Economy like it is—tough—we see a lot of people getting desperate."

"Why don't you ask if I know who did it?"

"Do you?"

"No."

The cop looked at the file drawer and the wastepaper basket perched atop it. Carney was sitting with it between his legs, his knees locked around it.

Carney was dazed. The basement. He hadn't thought of what

shape the basement was in. All that water from the hoses if the fire didn't destroy it first. Floor models in good condition that he'd intended to put on sale at the end of the summer. Business records going back to when he opened the store. The console radios in the musty corner, RCA jobs he never got around to junk or dump at a swap meet. His store.

The cop said, "You say you saw this man throw two firebombs into your store?"

"I saw him throw the second one."

"What'd he look like?"

"I don't know."

He returned to the store. Above the broken shopwindow, above the dark hole where the showroom had been, smoke had painted his CARNEY'S FURNITURE sign black. Sooty streaks washed up the red-brick facades of 383 and 381. Fire crews had smashed the apartment windows, to rescue people who might be inside, or to shoot water through, he didn't know. One fire truck remained. The fire department had blocked off the corner.

Rusty gave Carney a desperate hug, careful not to dislodge the file drawer and the basket. "Yeah, boss," Rusty said. He had stepped up in Carney's absence. Marie had gone home to be with Bonnie; she was rattled, and when the events sank in she started weeping. Robert had called his mother and she took him home. It'd be a couple of days before the fire department let anyone in the building. The inspectors had to poke around, make sure the buildings were sound.

Everybody was safe. Time slowed down. Mrs. Garcia from the bakery up the street embraced him. He barely knew her. "I'm so sorry," she said, eyes red. Yes—a shopkeeper understood the loss the way normal people couldn't. You run your own business, you understand what it is to build it, and to lose it. She tried to stick a bag of muffins in his hand. His hands were full.

Rusty took the muffins and pointed up Morningside.

Elizabeth waited up the ave, sitting on the back steps of St. Joseph's. Ironically, the church had its front door on 125th, and a Morningside entrance as well, just like the store. The second entrance had been bricked up—perhaps the preachers had their own nighttime sideline at some point—but three steps remained. Elizabeth saw him and wiped her eyes with her handkerchief and waited for him to come to her.

It didn't hit him until he sat on the steps. He set down his office salvage. Down the street he saw his store from that new angle, and it was as if the building belonged to someone else. The fire someone else's tragedy, the misfortune of a stranger he had no connection to. In the instant that the store existed outside of him, an alien object, he felt it: run over by this express of grief that left him mangled in the dark. He had worked so hard—no one knew how difficult it had been. There had been no one, no witnesses, until the hard part was done. *You've come a long way.* Working hour upon hour, enduring those waves of setbacks and reversals, sweating and suffering under the eyes of that cruel and dispassionate boss: The City. It had been him against the City for so long, tussling, until he and it finally came to an arrangement: You don't fuck with me, and I won't fuck with you. His own Declaration of Independence. Or so he thought. The City had reneged. The City had taken his store to add to its heap of spent tenements, burned-out townhouses, craters, and rubble-strewn lots. Another broken address on an island full of them.

They sobbed together, Carney and Elizabeth, for as long as the street let them get away with it, entwined.

"Rusty said everybody was safe," she said.

"Yeah," Carney said.

May and John had come when he was at the precinct. She told them they'd see him at home. He thanked her.

"He threw Molotov cocktails?"

"He did."

"Because of your other business."

"Yes." It had never occurred to him to come clean. She said it, asked him straight-out, and there he was saying, Yes.

"You sell stuff that falls off a truck sometimes," she said. "The rugs. I know that. That's how people do it. Daddy always used to brag about getting a deal on stuff that fell off a truck. But this isn't that, is it?"

Carney asked her how she knew about the rugs and she said she'd known for years. Back at their first apartment, he was on the phone talking to someone about "hot rugs" and she was on the couch. He thought she was asleep, but she was not.

Rugs. He didn't remember the conversation but no matter. Elizabeth thought his rugs were hot: fine. Some had been, in the old days, before he stepped up his fencing sideline. He used to sell appliances that Freddie had ripped off—she knew those were hot, Freddie being Freddie. Uptown rules—rules get bent in the name of survival. She was okay with that. When he had to duck out suddenly at nine P.M. to deal with a shady character, she let it pass. It wasn't a woman, because he knew she would've castrated him in his sleep if he messed around. She assumed his hot merchandise was harmless, small-time stuff because her husband wasn't built for anything heavy. For all her insight into him—which he cherished, which he was grateful for—the nature and scope of his criminal operation escaped her. The part of his character that made it possible was too foreign.

Rugs, then. "Maybe it's the rugs," Carney said. "I don't know what happened. Harlem today—"

"People don't do that. Just walk into a place and do that." She took his hands. "Are you being safe? Are you keeping us safe?"

No. If they knew where he worked, they knew where he lived. It had been a long time since bad men threatened to steal his life from him, take Elizabeth and the kids from him. They'd taken his store today. If they'd wanted to go after him the other way, they would have. His family was safe tonight. Tomorrow?

Carney said, "It's okay. Yes, some of the stuff in my store has fallen off a truck. You're right, that's how it works up here. Sometimes the guys who pick it up when it falls off a truck are not the most upstanding members, but this is—I don't know what this is."

"You all could have been killed," she said. "Robert." The kids. May and John weren't working there this summer but they could have.

"There are quicker ways if you want—" He squeezed her hand. "They weren't trying to hurt me."

"They? So it is somebody you know."

He shook his head.

"Somebody who knows Pepper?"

"I don't know. But we're safe now."

* * *

At his urging, Elizabeth took a cab back to Strivers' Row with the things he'd saved from the fire. Carney told Rusty he had to split downtown to deal with the insurance company—could he stick around in case something came up?

He turned the pay phone on 125th and Broadway into his temporary office. Had they hit Pepper, too? He lived over that funeral home. There was no answer at Pepper's, but the funeral home picked up after the operator put him through, which meant it was not a pile of ash. Carney tried Donegal's. Buford was on tonight, thank God. Pepper had run out, Buford said, but if you called, you were supposed to come uptown. "I don't know—sounds heavy," he said. It was worrisome that the bartender had departed from his standard indifference.

The walk uptown was a numb march. Every few blocks he slumped to the benches of the Broadway median, exhausted. He wanted to run back to the store, knock past the barricade and into the showroom. His office. What if the buildings are beyond saving? The fire inspector will deliver his report. Pepper was right. He'd come to think of himself as impervious. The apartment on 127th Street, the madness of Harlem, the white world and its quick, mean hands—he'd had to grow a concrete skin for a concrete city. Not concrete, something harder, like schist. But the fires had been drawing near. Every siren since the city started falling to pieces had been a countdown to the siren that was coming for him. Maybe the fires had been coming since his father first struck a match and threw it into a pool of kerosene on some unlucky tenement floor. It catches up with you.

Instead of going inside when he got to Donegal's, he split for a bench to collect himself. The fire at the store leeched his energy. Some asshole kept honking. Carney turned to curse at the guy and saw Pepper in the Buick.

"Tough break," Pepper said when Carney slid into the passenger seat. He'd been buying insoles for his tennis shoes and the drugstore clerks were talking about a fire down the street. "I got a feeling."

Carney didn't speak.

"Tough break," Pepper said again, clearing his throat. Gruff sympathy.

Carney's mind went somewhere.

Pepper said, "You're in shock."

"Yeah."

He told him that Reece had called the bar. Reece wanted to meet. Both of them. "He said next time, it won't be your store."

Carney made his hands into fists on his lap. "How'd they put me with you?"

"All types of hustlers and losers in there," Pepper said. Meaning Donegal's. "Reece asks after me, I've been getting messages at the bar. Anybody hangs out there, they know we associate."

And when Oakes hears Carney's name, he knows it's no coincidence.

"He wants what I took from the safe, and he wants us to bring it to that club of yours."

"What?"

Pepper shrugged. "Tonight after hours." The old crook started up the Buick. He had an idea to check in on their guest at the biscuit company, see if he had any insight as to what they were walking into. "You bring him food?"

"Who?"

"The guy."

"Before or after my store burned down?"

"Slipped my mind, too. Thought maybe you got it."

"I did not."

Pepper rubbed his jaw wearily. He pulled over and ducked into a bodega. He returned with a paper bag full of candy bars and pork rinds.

Carney felt bad that neither he nor Pepper had remembered to leave the lights on at the biscuit factory. At the scrape of the security gate, Hickey yelped for help. The bagman was weeping when they entered the reception room. "I heard things moving," he said. Snot ran down over his lips. If the bagman had any complaints about the menu, he did not share them.

Pepper told Hickey if he was helpful, he'd be out tomorrow.

This struck Hickey as a reasonable proposition. "That was Leon," he said, in regards to the firebombing. Reece had used him for a similar play last winter on one of the Puerto Rican crews, pool-hall surprise. "Like I said, Leon likes his work. Broad daylight, middle of 125th Street—that's like psycho pyro Christmas."

Carney said, "Who's going to be at the club?"

Pepper said to him, "You're waking up."

"Reece likes that joint, acting like he's some upper-crust nigger. Which is why Oakes takes him there." Reece grew up in the Frederick Douglass Houses on Amsterdam, Hickey said. His position in Notch Walker's organization elevated him to neighborhood swell: "I'm the biggest thing to come out of that place." Until a dude he grew up with, Lawrence Hilton-Jacobs, got cast in *Cooley High* and *Welcome Back, Kotter,* with his face on magazines and lunch boxes. Took him down a peg. "I hate that goddamn *Kotter.* Everywhere I look I see him."

The Dumas Club subscribed to *BusinessWeek* and *Black Enterprise,* Carney thought. Reece was not likely to be reminded of his friend's success inside its walls.

"Late night when it's closed, they talk business," Hickey said. "Smoke those Cuban cigars." They brought Hickey along once, to show off. "Nice place."

"Yes it is," Carney said. "I asked, who'll be there."

It will be Reece, Oakes, and one of Reece's boys. Clarence or Bollinger, his muscle. Not much going on upstairs, but loyal and sadistic, qualities not to be underestimated. Hickey said, "Notch doesn't know about this side business with Oakes, so Reece has to keep it close."

"What would Notch do if he got wind of it?"

"He would not be happy," Hickey said. "Everything above 110th Street, that's his, way he sees it. Gotta cut him in. And he ain't getting his cut of the fire business."

Carney gathered that initiative and independence were not management qualities Notch Walker valued. He knew Notch. The gangster sent a flunky by the store two or three times a year with stones and Carney liquidated them, usually through Green. High-quality stuff. Would Notch interpret someone messing with a lieutenant like Reece as messing with him, too? Punish everyone for bucking his authority, including those who exposed it—sure. Carney's arrangement with Notch wouldn't save him. There's always another fence.

Notch—and the Black Liberation Army general Malik Jamal— had taken care of Munson. Carney had set up the detective. Was there a way to put the mobster in play again? He'd never told Pepper about that night—it had been too nightmarish to dwell on. He'd gotten lucky. Judging from today, his luck had run out.

Pepper mentioned to Hickey that they'd broken into Oakes's safe last night, and that's why Reece wanted the meet.

"You niggers are crazy."

Pepper stiffened, insulted. "That just hit you?"

"You don't get it," Hickey said. "These are heavy dudes—city hall, big money."

"I get it," Carney said. The more he sat with it, the more Oakes's opportunities multiplied. It was like Oakes had opened a shoe store that got big and branched out and expanded until it was a department store. He was the Gimbels of Graft at this point. First Floor, Arson Payoffs, get off on Three for Redirected Development Funds. In the DA's office he got envelopes from landlords and firebugs, plus a cut from the padded insurance payout, which he parleyed into brokering fires, since he knew all the players. At Homes 4 Harlem he lined his pockets with urban renewal money, handing out construction and management contracts while continuing the arson-brokering piece from his prosecutor days. As borough president, he could aim that firehouse of Albany money where he liked, but also have the juice to plot where new housing goes in the future, which run-down lots and tracts will be fancy new developments years from now, whether ravaged by arson or accidental fires or bad luck. Shell company picks up the fucked-up property, loads up on insurance, and after the fire the city buys out the lot to redevelop. That's a lot of envelopes if you got your hand out at every step.

If you know what the future holds, what it will look like, you can buy it cheap today. What was the motto of Van Wyck Realty? *Building the Future.* Van Wyck bought up property next to hotspots-to-be, like Lincoln Center and the World Trade. Men in city hall determined where those projects happened before the Van Wycks even got wind. If Oakes was doing half this shit, he was raking it in. Top Floor, get out here for Crazy Power Broker Schemes and Home Appliances, careful on the way out.

Hickey said, "You're not going to tell Reece I said anything?"

Carney looked at Pepper: Time to go. Pepper nodded. When they got to the door to the street, Carney said, "See you tomorrow," and turned off the light. Hickey screamed in the darkness.

It occurred to Carney that if things went sideways and they didn't come back, Hickey was in for a rough time. If things went sideways, they all were.

# EIGHT

320 West 120th Street, the home of the Dumas Club, was built in 1898 by Mortimer Bacall, a German immigrant who made his fortune in patent medicines. His most popular tonic was advertised under many names, the most well known of which was Dr. Abraham's Pills, which purported to cure "city ailments" caused by urban living, the "noxious air," "insalubrious plumbing," and "excessive proximity of one's neighbors." The modern city was a new animal requiring new remedies. Bacall possessed the dexterity to invent both the infirmity and the cure.

Bacall was struck by a Lexington Avenue streetcar in 1911. The townhouse remained empty until it was bought fourteen years later by a trio of distinguished Harlemites: Dr. William T. Frye, physician; Clement Lanford, the famous lawyer and uptown political boss; and Al Gibson, of the Gibson Funeral Home. They had traveled separate paths to a place of prominence, distinction, and influence—time to start a club to mark who was of their rank and who was not. They purchased the property jointly and sold it to the Dumas Corporation a few years later.

The oversized Queen Anne townhouse was forty feet wide and a story taller than the surrounding homes. Against those more modest brownstones, it became a neighborhood landmark. They didn't make them like that anymore, with gables and green-shingled turrets, the curved windows and broad stoops. The days of such flamboyant design were long past. The days of more relaxed fire codes as well. The tiny basement windows were a nightmare if firefighters needed to ventilate a blaze, and the dumbwaiters, window shafts, and rear servant stairs provided an all-too-convenient thoroughfare for a blaze. An intense fire in the cockloft might destroy the roof supports and cause the top floors to collapse. No, it would never meet code today.

It was nonetheless an impressive building from the outside and a site of local fascination. Kids called it "the Mansion," on account of its scale and the parade of nattily attired Negro gentlemen strutting in and out of its grand doors. Ray Carney had been one of the neighborhood kids in awe of the place. Who were these men? Their suits were amazing, exquisitely tailored, sober but not without flair, unlike the cheap getups of his father and his crooked circle, garish, redolent of last week's whiskey and brawls. He needed to know what kind of men they were, and what happened inside. All these years later, after Carney did learn who they were, the texture and grain of their character, and had joined their number, he occasionally took a step back, when the mists of animosity parted temporarily, and appreciated what that generation had accomplished and what it meant to carve out a space for themselves in America. No, they didn't make them like that anymore.

Pepper parked the Buick on 121st off Manhattan Ave. Quarter past midnight. Last call at the Club on Tuesday nights was ten, the waiters started fussing and straightening up around dawdling guests at ten-forty-five and come eleven-thirty it was lights out and front doors locked. Carney heard the Legend of the Keys soon after he joined, the holy keys to the Dumas Club in the possession of the inner circle. One might bring a woman there after hours, or finalize a scheme to enrich one's bank accounts or prospects. Oakes's father had likely been so blessed, and the keys itemized in the man's will as an heirloom. If the old guard got wind of the late-night confabs between Democratic candidate Alexander Oakes and killer Reece Brown, they would've condemned them as a perversion of the club charter, but Carney saw them for what they were: Business as usual.

He asked Pepper where he stashed Oakes's files.

"That shit's still in the trunk."

"You didn't look at it?"

"What for? I know what it is. Stuff he cares about that pisses him off that he don't got it. I hadn't got around to figuring out how to use it."

"You didn't look at any of it?"

"These guys, it's all the same shit."

*Shit*: The names of prominent lawyers, judges, prosecutors, the heads of insurance firms, various criminals, firebugs, politicians on the take, big-time developers handing out stacks of cash, community organizers pocketing Albany funds, and whoever else Oakes was entwined with.

He had a point. *Shit* fit.

Powerful men nonetheless. Carney's business was in the yellow pages, his house in the white: He was easy to find. "I'll take it in," he said. "It's me they got leverage on." Pepper didn't have a wife and kids to threaten. Carney had roped him into his mess. The fire that afternoon, whatever waited in the Dumas—it was Carney's punishment. Pepper could hop on a Greyhound and set himself up in Maryland—or was it Delaware?—where he knew some people. He didn't have to go inside.

"No, they got leverage on me," Pepper said. "They said next time it'll be your house. Your house? They're going to fuck with your house? I got a room in there."

"Okay, Pepper."

Out on the street, Pepper retrieved the black garbage bag from the trunk and slung it over his shoulder like a crooked Santa Claus. Carney chuckled. Pepper gave him an irritated look.

"Do you have a gun?" Carney asked.

In other words, What was the plan? "I have a .38 they'll take when we walk in," Pepper said. "I got it off Hickey so it's theirs anyway." Reece and Oakes had to find out what they knew about their business. Who else knows. Did they return everything they stole. "What are we going to do? Got to get in there and have a look-see."

Not an inspiring report. Before today, Carney would've had a hard time seeing Oakes getting his dainty, well-moisturized hands dirty—it was the Dumas Club, for Chrissakes—but they had torched his store that morning and the gangster's profession was, actually, killing and maiming. The money involved bent all forecasts. "Who's the Red Conk?" he asked. "Yesterday you called me that."

"That comedian, Roscoe Pope, when I was working on that movie. It was one of his comedy routines. A Negro with super-powers."

Carney stopped. "What happens in it?"

"What do you think happens? He's a Negro with superpowers— they take him out. He thinks they can't touch him, until they do. I thought Pope was talking about himself. Being famous, the news-papers go after him, or the cops. But nobody's out to get that guy. When Pope goes down, it's himself that will do it. He gets himself."

Two brownstones down, a man on the second floor stuck his head out the window: "Can you shut the fuck up down there?"

Carney tilted his head toward the corner, where the street-lights described the majestic silhouette of the Dumas Club.

\* \* \*

Given the circumstances, it was foolish for Carney to expect Carl to open the door for him as on any other day, but he did. "Get in," Reece Brown said. He quickly closed the door behind them. The drapes in every window permitted no light to escape. From the street, the club was closed for the night.

Pepper had told Carney that Reece favored a Black Panther getup, but in the June heat he'd ditched the black leather blazer and stood before them in the foyer in black slacks and white short-sleeve turtleneck. He wore dark sunglasses, so incongruous in the Dumas atmosphere that for a moment Carney forgot about the gun Reece pointed at him.

The gangster motioned for them to raise their hands. The black garbage bag swung from Pepper's right hand. Reece made a disapproving face at their choice of carrying case. He took the black garbage bag and patted them down, removing the .38 from Pepper's windbreaker pocket. "Oakes!" He waved them into the parlor.

Alexander Oakes was mixing a gin cocktail. The sleeves of his crisp white oxford shirt were rolled up and his red-and-navy-striped tie was tucked between buttons. Carney had never stepped behind the mahogany bar; the waiters snapped at members who got too close, in a kind of shtick. It was an entitled display, as if despite the guns Oakes was a little boy engaged in dumb mischief. Dumb, dangerous mischief that got his store burned down.

"Carney! This is the best part of the late shift, man," Oakes said. "You get to do what you want."

Reece directed them to stand by the big, overstuffed burgundy leather sofa. The Burlington was a battleship; Carney had spent many evenings on deck listening to Pierce as the lawyer opined and tapped his cigarette over the pedestal ashtray. Next to Carney, Pepper surveyed the joint, taking in the furnishings as if he'd parachuted into a museum gallery. His lips curled like he smelled a dead mouse rotting in the walls. The faces of the founding members stared down at the interloper. Pepper stared back.

"Where's Leon?" Oakes said.

"He had to take a piss," Reece said.

"Been a while."

Leon Drake walked into the parlor and closed the French doors behind him. Reece had opted for the firebug instead of another member of Notch Walker's crew, to keep the circle closed, Carney figured. His Maker had not equipped Leon with a bruiser's physique, but had bestowed upon him unsettling nutjob eyes, a mighty weapon in their own right.

"So this is what it looks like," Leon said. "I grew up down the street." He had a knapsack on his back, and tugged the straps like a little kid.

Reece kept an eye on Carney and Pepper as he deposited the garbage bag on the bar. "Check it for a piece."

Oakes patted the garbage bag with an expression of exasperation at the man's excessive caution. He didn't feel anything suspicious. "Reece thought you'd be a hundred miles away by now, Carney, but I told him you'd show. Neutral territory. Safe." He sipped his drink. "How do you two know each other?"

Casual, like they'd run into each other at a cookout in the alley behind their houses, and Carney had been too slow to execute a getaway. "Family friend," Carney said. He gestured at the portraits, the Gallery of Muttonchops. "You got these guys, I got him."

"What were you going to do with it," Oakes said. "Go to the newspapers? The Feds? Prosecutors—even ex-prosecutors—don't go to jail, we skate. That's the point."

"They don't get elected," Carney said.

Pepper scratched his jaw. He looked tired.

"Where's my man Hickey?" Reece said. "You fuck with him?"

"He told us where to find it," Pepper said.

"Like I said," Leon said. "Stool pigeon."

"Hickey," Oakes said. "I was pretty surprised when I got back to my office last night and saw someone had ripped me off. Hickey's missing, after he went after this Pepper guy with a baseball bat." He looked to Carney. "Reece got word you and this guy Pepper were tight, pulling all sorts of shit over the years. It couldn't be anyone else. But why?"

"Get the fuck back over there," Reece said. Pepper had taken two steps closer to him. Carney hadn't seen it happen. Pepper moved back next to Carney.

"I asked Pepper to look into a fire on 118th for my own reasons," Carney said. "That put him on Leon, who thought he was asking after some shit you pulled across the street years ago."

"That's fucked up," Reece said.

"I lost my job," Leon said. "I loved that place. My boss heard I was fighting outside, he tells me to get the fuck out. My goddamn job."

Oakes shushed him. The firebug's eyes turned to slits.

"Own reasons what?"

"There was a kid in the building when it got torched."

"What do you care about some kid?" Reece said.

"I don't," Carney said. "That's the thing."

Oakes chuckled. "I told you he was wild," he said. He turned to Carney. "That was a nice night last week. Elizabeth really pulled it off." He took a drink. Carney thought Oakes was about to make a smart remark, but refrained. "The club showed up—it felt good. You'd think they'd have put more of us into higher office. Judges, we've got judges coming out of our ass, we've got behind-the-scenes players. But city hall? Downtown? We're overdue."

He poured a whiskey and held it up to Reece. The gangster's features soured—he was busy holding down their guests. Reece Brown had never heard of the Dumas before Oakes invited him. When Oakes opened the door and he got a look at how fancy it was, Reece thought it was some kind of pervert club. Notch thought he had style, fixing up his office above the Right Note with that leopard-skin shit and marble and velvet—that wasn't classy, it was tacky. This place was classy, and each time Oakes brought him here for business Reece endured a violent recognition—he was going to have a place like this one day. Dignified, tasteful, and expensive, as befitting the biggest, baddest brother to ever battle his way out of the Frederick Douglass Houses. Fuck Lawrence Hilton-Jacobs, he was in Hollywood now so he didn't count. Reece was the genuine article.

Oakes set Reece's drink on the bar and raised his glass to his father's portrait. "I like to think he's rolling over in his grave, watching this. He was always bragging about the little shit he pulled, getting this guy to pay him off, that guy. The Gentleman Bandit. Piker. That whole generation. What I've pulled? What

I'm going to do? He had no fucking clue about how the game was going to change."

Carney played with his Dumas Club ring, twisting it nervously. He said, "This your new campaign message?"

Oakes smirked. "I know he's rolling over when we're letting niggers like you in here. I was serious when I said you'd come a long way—you made a face, but I was serious. You remember the first time Elizabeth brought you to a party—Stacey Miller's birthday party. With your arms sticking out of your coat sleeves and your socks showing. We had a laugh. But she liked you, we all saw that. You got that store started up. I didn't think it'd last, but you made a go of it." He toasted Carney. "Didn't look too good today, though. Those smoke and flames shooting out? It didn't look good at all, man."

Leon said, "I don't miss." He grinned.

"When the old guys like Leland blocked your membership, I felt bad," Oakes said. "I voted against you, like everyone else, but I felt bad. The whole time you were a fucking crook!" He gestured at Reece. "Working with his boss! It's amusing. Turns out the old men knew who you really were the whole time."

Carney pictured the banker Duke, living it up on an island with all the cash he embezzled from his fellow members. "We were on to each other," he said.

Pepper wore his disgusted face, with the angry squint. Carney found it comforting. Pepper said, "You tell Notch about this party tonight?"

"You worry about your own self," Reece said.

Carney scanned the room, as he knew Pepper was doing, taking stock. Oakes behind the bar, Reece with a gun, Leon fidgeting. It smelled like a candle had burned down. He didn't see any candles. He met Pepper's gaze for a clue to what the old crook had in mind. Pepper betrayed nothing. Which meant some shit was about to go down or he had no idea at all.

Reece coughed. He said, "Check the bag."

Oakes opened the black garbage bag and went through the contents, letting it rest on the mahogany bar. He nodded as he sifted through, checking off his inventory. Not removing anything but examining it under the plastic, as if it would wilt and shrivel in the light, like a vampire. Oakes looked surprised, and plucked out a small card. He slipped it in his wallet and continued his search. He said, "Elizabeth know you're a fucking crook?"

Carney said, "She know you're a crook?"

"It's all there?" Reece said.

"So far," Oakes said.

"You got my name on anything, I want it in my hand."

"You don't have to worry about it, Mr. Brown."

"Okay," Reece said. "Let's get on with it." He aimed at Pepper's head.

Carney said, "Hey."

"We agreed not in here," Oakes said.

Reece shot Oakes in the eye. The candidate tumbled back against the liquor bottles and brought down a cascade of whiskey and gin with him when he dropped to the floor.

The enforcer backed up, watching Pepper and Carney. He moved behind the bar, feeling around Oakes's body with his feet. He gathered the mouth of the black garbage bag and cinched it. "Ran his mouth too much. It was either now or later. Notch comes down on me, or the cops." He sniffed. "Who needs him, I got this?" He stopped. "Something burning?"

They all smelled it, the smoke from fires Leon set upstairs. He had wandered through the luxurious rooms on the third and fourth floors, the sitting room with the mounted heads of the animals Ambrose Hemmings killed on his African safari, the library and its stained-glass scene of Harlem in farmland days. It was nothing like he'd pictured when he was little, observing the smartly dressed men disappear inside, gazing up at the curved windows. It was so fancy, he noted bitterly, so beyond his imaginings as to prove the smallness of his experience, his poverty in every sphere. No matter. He took out his gasoline. The Dumas Club, although sophisticated and refined, was nothing special when he thought about it. No more or less abhorrent than any other building in his neighborhood, a mere container for his hatred. Leon wrote his name in gasoline and when he felt that click in the back of his mind, that little latch closing, he lit a match and joined the men in the parlor.

Reece cursed.

Leon said, "I said there'd be hell to pay if you fucked with my job. Fuck all y'all." He seemed to snap his fingers and the wick on his little bomb caught. He tossed it at Reece, who fired back at Leon, tagging the armchair behind him. The firebomb—a glass ball the size of a Christmas ornament—exploded against the bar, splashing fire.

Pepper jumped over the leather sofa, crouching between it and the fireplace. Carney followed suit. He had long admired the geometric pattern of the parlor room's parquet floor—it alluded to the Moorish, or Arabian, provided a glimpse into another culture. Now Carney got to examine the floor close-up, real close. It was ridiculous to die in here. They had to get to the door.

Reece yelled at Leon and fired. A bullet whistled through the couch between Carney and Pepper. Pepper nodded toward the big window onto 120th. The thick drapes covered it, but the drop wasn't far. They crawled toward it. One of Leon's firebombs detonated on the drapes. The heat pushed against Pepper's face.

He peeked over the top of the sofa. Reece fired at Leon two more times, but the firebug was hidden behind the club chairs and the baby grand at the back of the room. Reece spotted Carney and shot at him, missing. He noticed that the black garbage bag had caught fire and frantically smacked at the flames.

Pepper rose, emerging from his hiding spot like a grizzly rearing up on hind legs. He charged and swung. The pedestal ashtray captured Reece right under his jaw. If this had been a baseball game—that was Carney's first association, a powerful slugger at bat—Reece's head would've been out in the parking lot. As it was, it (Reece's head) incurred spectacular damage. The enforcer went down.

Leon flung open the parlor door. Black smoke made a roiling advance into the room. The firebug stood on the threshold and cackled. "I told you not to fuck with my job!" He pitched his next bomb at the painting of Clement Lanford, founding member. It exploded against Lanford's sober face and launched tendrils of liquid fire.

Leon ran out, laughing.

Carney grabbed Pepper by the arm. The old crook was looking down at Reece. Notch's lieutenant was not going to get up. Carney nodded at the black garbage bag. Perhaps there was something to salvage.

"Fuck this place," Pepper said. They left the burning bag and made for the door.

The grand staircase was ablaze—the floors above were an inferno. The right side of the hallway rippled with flames. Carney and Pepper ran to the front door, stooped on account of the dense black smoke.

Out on the corner, Carney said, "I have to call the fire department." The dark drapes twisted behind the glass on the top floors, burning, dropping from view to expose the conflagration inside. The bay windows blew out. Shards crashed and hopped on concrete.

"Why?" Pepper started up the street.

"It's on fire."

"So?"

Carney caught up and they trotted to the Buick.

"They'll be along," Pepper said. "We got to get to Donegal's anyway. See which of those motherfuckers ratted us out."

Carney was dead tired. "Right."

"They'll be along."

In the old days, a neighbor would've spotted the fire before it got out of control. Mr. Edwin Powell across the street, for example, had been a true night owl and noted busybody. He grew up in Alabama, fled north in the back of a pickup truck, bouncing with five cousins. In New York City a colored man could be a man, a human being. Eventually he found a job mopping up at the Department of Motor Vehicles and a room overlooking the stately Queen Anne across the street. Edwin admired the Dumas Club and the Negro achievement it represented. He would've noticed a fire straightaway, but he passed ten years ago, the final cousin, and the other apartments emptied one by one until the vagrants got a foot in. So many houses on that block, same story. The city was going down the toilet. In the old days, someone would have called in the blaze before it got too wild. In the old days, people looked out for each other in Harlem.

# NINE

Jimmy Gray from Sable Construction was supposed to come over that afternoon to inspect the buildings for the preliminary estimate of how much to gouge him. Carney was avoiding the premises, so he sent Robert with the keys to let Jimmy in. He was still paying the boy though the store had been destroyed, to teach him a lesson about commitment and follow-through, keeping one's word . . . he wasn't sure what the lesson was, but he liked giving the boy money and hoped he'd waste it on something stupid, like Freddie would have.

Carney was a few blocks away at the time of the appointment picking up his new ulcer medicine. He decided to check on the boy. Robert stood outside the store in his polo shirt and Levi's, playing with his Twist-O-Flex watchband. Plywood covered where the front window and doors had been. By the time the plywood saw its first sunrise, it had been completely covered in graffiti. No profanity or dicks or tits, so Carney let it be.

"Hey, Uncle Ray."

"Robert. He's inside?"

Not yet. Ellis Gray, Sable's founder, jerked you around over how long and how much, but he showed up on time. This was the first time Carney had dealt with the son, now that Ellis was handing over the business. Carney cut him slack. Jimmy had warned him it was a busy month, the city being where it was these days.

"I'll take the keys," Carney said. "When Mr. Gray comes, tell him I'm inside."

"You're going in?" Everyone knew he'd been staying away.

"I'll be inside."

He went around. There was time to get the mural up on the Morningside wall before the Fourth. One of May's friends from college was "a really gifted artist" and would love the chance to get his work out there, she said, but Carney didn't have it in him. It had come to Carney one night after the fire: His version of *The Spirit of '76*. They wanted bicentennial flavor, here goes. Drums, fife, same shell-shocked stubbornness, but the musicians are black. Beat down, skulls full of dead-end thoughts, they keep playing. Preserving the color palette of the original, city gray and smog brown, with a background of three-story tenements, bleak and dark-windowed and "the pigeons circling above like vultures." This is their march—folly, fortitude, and that brand of determination that comes from ignoring reality. Up on the wall for all of Harlem to see: This is what we sell in here.

Carney's *Spirit of '76*. When he told people about it, they looked at him like he was nuts. The pigeon thing, for one. Throw up a mural, and those kids are going to scribble graffiti over it. Carney realized he was going to spend a lot of time explaining his intentions, so he dropped it. Instead, two dumpsters from Bellucci Sanitation sat against the wall, half filled with debris from the fire and whatever Harlem decided to contribute during the course of the day—bent floor lamps, busted toasters, pink slippers. Given the state of things, it was only time before someone dumped a corpse in there, but so far he had been "blessed," as Elizabeth joked.

He pressed his forehead to the Morningside door. Held it there. The metal was hot. He didn't care that he looked like a nutjob. It was his door. He glanced up the ave where he and Elizabeth had sat. Weeping in public—his dad would've slapped him. Yes, he'd wept in public, and also kidnapped a man and watched two others get snuffed that day, so perhaps that "made up for it," balanced the manhood scales, what have you. He unlocked the door.

Carney had stayed away. The American Eagle inspection put

a stop to excursions into his ruined store. The white insurance man had been so calm as he rendered his assessment, so cool in his postmortem, that Carney had been thoroughly defeated. The buildings might be saved—"You're lucky they have good bones"— but it was going to be a brutal undertaking. *See there, where the ceiling looks like it's buckling? An engineer's going to have questions about that.*

When the insurance man departed that afternoon, Larry was outside. He'd quickly found himself another job, music studio in midtown, A&R Recording. "Experience? My whole life is experience," he told Carney. He'd come by to give Carney treasure rescued from the wreck—his diploma from Queens College and his picture of Lena Horne. Larry had found them on the office floor, scorched by fire, warped by water. Carney thanked him, and threw them in the trash on the way home. He'd write the school for a replacement and search for a new photo of Lena. Something more recent. She was older, now. He was too.

That had been a week and a half ago. Bellucci hauled away the burned recliners, charred residue of rugs, kindling dining-room pieces, the cindered sofa frames with springs poking out. Carney's scorched metal desk and the waterlogged artifacts in the basement. He spent most days knocked out at home on his trusted Argent sofa, that little modernist dinghy bearing him above the waves. Between shifts on the Argent, he dealt with the American Eagle adjusters ("You say he threw Molotov cocktails into your store?"), cops ("Sure you don't know who threw Molotov cocktails into your store?"), the fire squad ("This kind of pattern is consistent with Molotov cocktails"), and the other entities who appear when someone throws Molotov cocktails into your place of business. There are procedures.

Amid the inquiries, he found time to settle up with Pepper for two days of arsonist hunting and Dr. Rostropovich's bill. "Expenses." Carney reminded him to release Dan Hickey. "Right." He assumed Pepper did so. He didn't bring it up the next time they talked—no one likes a nag. By then, the police's interest had tapered off. In a long season of fires, the Carney's Furniture blaze was among the stranger, but not the strangest, and not the largest or most fatal. It was eclipsed that night by the Dumas fire, and the discovery that a Democratic candidate for borough president was one of the victims.

To their credit the police did eventually arrest the owners of Excelsior Metro for the fire at 371 West 118th. The papers identified the firebug as "known arsonist Gordon Bellmann, of Bensonhurst." Carney tried to imagine what the man looked like, without success.

They beat the rap.

\* \* \*

Carney attended Alexander Oakes's funeral, though Elizabeth said he was off the hook. It was the least he could do, as one who was with him at the end. He liked going to funerals that were bigger than the one he'd have one day. They reaffirmed his modest lifestyle.

Elizabeth was torn up by her friend's murder. A city that was the stage for such twisted and inexplicable crimes needed men like Oakes, men of courage and commitment. "They'll never catch his killer," she said. "Who was that other body they found? Your store. People get away with these things, and we're just supposed to take it and go on with our lives."

"It's a terrible situation," Carney said. They were driving home from Evergreens Cemetery. The boxes of campaign pens to replace the first batch that had been misprinted had arrived at Strivers' Row that morning. What was she supposed to do with them? What was she supposed to do, go into work tomorrow and smile for Dale Baker like a good little girl and pretend everything was normal? Letting off steam after the funeral.

"Do you know how many women run travel agencies this size?" she said. "Black women? None—unless they've started it themselves."

"Maybe you should do that."

"What?"

"Start your own thing."

"My own company."

"I have some money put away. Think about it."

She was silent then as Riverside Drive scrolled past. They'd revisit this topic soon. He didn't have that much money put away but he knew where to get some. What else was an ongoing criminal enterprise complicated by periodic violence for, but to make your wife happy?

On that matter, Carney promised Elizabeth he was out of the secondhand rug business. She was right; it was dangerous. He'd have to take care in the future so she didn't worry.

"We'll probably never know why that psycho torched the store," he told her.

"Hmm."

\* \* \*

Carney stepped into his ravaged office. The walls were charred and scored, girders exposed like bone. The smoke and sooty water generated a rank atmosphere. The only thing left in the room was the safe. His Hermann Bros. safe looked unscathed, but the heat had warped the door shut. Time for a new one. How did Moskowitz put it? *A man should have a safe big enough to hold his secrets. Bigger, even, so you have room to grow.* The technology had come a long way since he was in the market. He looked forward to the hunt.

The light switch in the showroom didn't work. There were no lights. Sunlight snuck between the seams of plywood. He didn't want a good look anyway. It was terrible. Christ, what was the point? He rebuilds. They knock it down again. Last time he was here, strips of the ceiling hung down, burned insulation peeled from the walls. The sanitation crew had ripped all that away, exposing the blackened drywall, studs, and beams. It looked like it had been abandoned to the elements for decades.

As he stood in his devastated showroom, the daily calamities of

125th Street, the honking and profanity and screams, fell away. Hot day but he got the chills. Right: The last time the room had been this empty was the day he signed the lease, and half of it was still the bakery next door. He hadn't knocked through the wall yet. How had he gotten by with so little space! He had prospered and so had the showroom. If he had to do it over, he'd put in stairs to the basement and turn it into a second showroom. For lighting and rugs. Keep the furniture upstairs, but flip Dining and Recliners. It had been bugging him—to have the customer hit Living Room first, with some dandy Sterlings arranged there up front, then Recliners before they got to the other collections.

It was nice, that day he signed the lease and got the keys and it was his.

Good bones. Good bones holding everything up, like the ancient rock beneath Manhattan. Why had he stayed away? This was his kingdom. The thing to do would be to take over the second floor and expand upstairs. That way he could enlarge his office, Marie's. They'd outgrown those spaces, no question. It was unlivable up there now. He had to call Marie about the tenants' intentions—who was staying, who was already gone. The third floor wanted to stick around, he knew, except for Mrs. Ruiz. She and her kids had gone to stay with family in Washington Heights and were not returning. Did Marie say that Albert was out of the hospital? She might have. He should send a card.

No, it wouldn't hurt to ask Jimmy Gray about expanding the store upstairs. Logistics. The cost. Insurance wasn't going to cover it. It'd be expensive. He needed money. He had some. He'd need more. He had ideas. Martin Green, other stuff. With the store out of commission he had to bring money in. Keep his mind occupied. He had some ideas. The City tried to break him. It didn't work. He was genuine Manhattan schist and that don't break easy.

The Dumas Club was not as lucky as the furniture store on the corner of 125th and Morningside. The June fire reduced it to a lonesome shell and consumed the two buildings next door. They were condemned, and eventually the three lots were purchased by a Virginia-based developer with tri-state ambitions. The residential building that went up years later didn't fit with the rest of the block, the bright orange bricks were a bit too loud, its character overall dull and bereft of style. The city had recovered, they had survived, the future was here, and it looked like crap. The neighbors complained. It wasn't what had been there before, the people said, we liked the way it used to be. They always said that when the old city disappeared and something new took its place.